NFI: NEW FRONTIERS, INCORPORATED

BOOK TWO, THE NEW FRONTIERS SERIES

JACK L KNAPP

NFI: NEW FRONTIERS, INC

BOOK TWO, THE NEW FRONTIERS SERIES

By Jack L Knapp

NFI: New Frontiers, Inc.
Book Two, The New Frontiers Series

Copyright © 2016 by Jack L Knapp
Cover by Blair Howard

❀ Created with Vellum

DEDICATION

For Blair Howard

Critic, Confidant, Friend

PROLOGUE

The Sneyd-Tesla impeller was invented by Morton "Morty" Sneyd and his grandson Chuck, who based their work on an idea found in a Nikola Tesla journal. The device was subsequently sold to a company run by investor and CEO T. French "Frenchy" Fuqua. The company, known as New Frontiers, Incorporated (NFI), provided the money to develop Morty's invention.

A group of industrialists realizes the device is a threat to their business model. Led by Sol Goldman, they attempt to prevent NFI from developing the impeller drive. Some of their efforts involve financial pressure, but some are more direct; Sol hires a criminal and orders him to stop NFI any way he can. The man rapes Lina, Frenchy's daughter, in order to send a message, then later attempts to burn the factory. Chuck, a former Marine, responds by killing the arsonists.

Governments also become involved. The US Government's DARPA wants to buy the drive system, Russians attempt to steal it. Despite their worst efforts, development continues; a tramp ship and an airplane are modified to use the impeller system, and a first-generation spaceship, *SS Farside*, is built.

Regulatory agencies, spurred by Congressional pressure, move in and shut down NFI's factory. While this is underway, Russian agents attempt to seize the ship by a coup de main.

The crippled *Farside* escapes, taking with it most of NFI's portable assets, including a supply of completed impellers. A huge cavern on Morty's ranch provides concealment where the necessary repairs are completed.

Factories in Mexico build frames for the lifters that DARPA wants. Chuck's team of engineers and mechanics install the impellers; to preserve the drive's secret, NFI field engineers operate and maintain the lifters for the duration of the contract. The income from this contract finances further development.

The shut-down by the US Government forces NFI to diversify its operations. A Finnish company now produces completed hulls for new ships, bare units that are spaceworthy, but without the impeller drive system. The hulls are then shipped to Iceland for final preparation and installation of the flight control computers and impellers. Some flights are launched from Iceland, others from Finland. A lot of money is involved, and other nations hope NFI will base future operations there. Larger nations such as Russia, China, and the US remain a threat; the company avoids their airspace.

Frenchy hopes that distributing the company's operations around the world will avoid further trouble. He's willing to purchase components from the world's major nations, but refuses to base ships within their borders. A Chinese company produces components for NFI's automated orbital refueling stations, US companies assemble them. The refueling stations are shipped to Germany for final preparation and NFI spaceships launch them into orbit. The first three refueling stations are now operational, and more are planned.

NFI also establishes branch offices in each country that has significant economic ties to the company; the company's official headquarters is now located in Switzerland. The headquarters is an administrative and communications center as well as the official headquarters, which reduces taxes as well as preventing regulators from acquiring the drive system or shutting down the company. Most operations are done elsewhere.

SS Gypsy, one of the new ships, is now ready to haul spent nuclear fuel into space. The company intends to finance future growth in this way.

Japan, the first country to contract with NFI, vitrifies the active nuclear material by mixing it with silica, then fusing it into glass. The process is costly, but necessary for safe handling. The first cargo is ready, and the Japanese will provide ground handling equipment and personnel to help load it. *Gypsy* will transport the vitrified nuclear waste beyond Lunar orbit and launch it toward the sun, where it will eventually be destroyed.

The *MV Tesla* is no longer under the physical control of NFI. It's quietly hauling cargo around the Atlantic, hoping not to be noticed while accumulating user data.

Such is the situation as our story opens.

1

T. French Fuqua, CEO of New Frontiers, Incorporated, washed his hands, then studied himself in the full-length mirror. Today he'd worn a charcoal three-piece suit to the office. The coat was hanging in the closet, allowing Frenchy to examine his appearance. Vest over white shirt, striped tie, medium-weight wool trousers, European styling. His hair had turned silvery-gray, and there was a pronounced widow's peak in front, harbinger of eventual baldness. No surprise; his father had been almost totally bald by age sixty. Frenchy sighed; he was pushing sixty himself, and the job's stress had changed him. He was a man of medium height, no longer slender, and his new wrinkles reflected the stress of his job...had he gained another couple of pounds? Frenchy resolved to cut back on food and find more time for exercise.

But time was always in short supply. Too many of the world's powerful insisted on speaking directly to NFI's boss. The office reflected his status, deep pile carpet, original paintings by local artists, comfortable overstuffed chairs arranged to encourage informal conversation, an oversized antique desk and office chair.

The receptionist and secretary in the outer office subtly emphasized the importance of the company.

Occasionally he found himself wondering what impulse had caused him to speak to Morty Sneyd. He hadn't needed the money; his net worth at the time had been north of a billion dollars, but something about Morty's story had piqued his interest. Perhaps it was the challenge, a chance to show up Sol Goldman. Maybe it had been the lure of the gamble, of the enormous payoff if he succeeded. Or maybe it was the chance to prove that he was as much a businessman as any of the others he knew. Well, he'd done that, in spades!

The impulse had cost him. His fortune had begun to melt away, his investments tied up in one struggling company. He'd set up an annuity for his daughter Lina, enough to care for her and the children she would likely bear, but he'd risked everything else.

Frenchy had come perilously close to bankruptcy. American financial institutions had refused to extend the company credit. Then had come the fortuitous event that turned things around; DARPA was interested in Morty's discovery. Money trickled in, and soon he'd found that Asian and European banks were more willing than American banks had been. An initial visit to Deutsche Bank had led to a demonstration, where the bank representative had flown in the modified impeller-powered airplane. DB had cautiously agreed to a loan, and other lenders had followed. The video showing operating lifters had captured their interest, and revealing that NFI had an operating spacecraft was the icing on the cake. Banks would have preferred direct participation, but they had settled for loaning NFI the funds the company needed to expand.

Frenchy sat down behind the desk, then picked up one of the seemingly-endless reports from the waiting stack. The antique desk was huge, but even so, it was always cluttered. He needed to delegate more, that was clear; if only he could find able, trustworthy people!

Adelheid Laaksonen, Frenchy's executive secretary, interrupted his musings with a call. She was a trim woman of a certain age, gray haired, but with fewer wrinkles than Frenchy. Perhaps it was the Finnish lifestyle. People exercised more, so comparatively few residents of Rovaniemi were overweight. They also enjoyed an efficient government, a successful economy, and a social safety net. Adelheid's few wrinkles were at the corner of her eyes, indicating she smiled often.

"Frenchy, Chuck's on Skype for you. You've got half an hour before your next appointment. Do you have time to talk to him?"

"Sure, put him on."

Frenchy tapped the icon and brought Chuck up on the screen. The problem with having a son-in-law for a business partner was that Frenchy never knew why he was calling. "How's Lina? Not bad news, is it?"

"No, other than the fact that we don't see nearly enough of you, it's actually good news. We completed the DARPA contract and they've released the rest of our money. They're impressed with the lifters! I don't think they ever really believed they worked the way we said, so they insisted on testing them to destruction, planned crashes, water landings, the works. The last was one of the big cargo lifters, the 'flying trucks'. They insisted on flying it under remote control, and they wanted to take it high enough to clear buildings."

"What happened?"

"Sideslip, the same thing that killed Mel. The instruments sent false data and the flight computer couldn't recover in time. This crash was worse than the one that wrecked the Bedstead. We had to torch the frame to get the impellers off. We recovered the impellers from all the crashed units, by the way. That last flight also exceeded our recommended max load, and that's probably what caused the sideslip. If the cargo isn't perfectly balanced, you're going to get problems as you approach max gross. Control gets mushy, and whatever the computer tries to do just makes the problem worse. Anyway, the contract's finished. I'm sure they still want lifters, so what do you want to do? Offer to sell, or try to hang on to our monopoly? Do we know how long the banks will wait?"

"They're being patient. I showed them the Japanese contract and that convinced them. They'd really like to underwrite an IPO, but I have no intention of converting to a public stock company. The bridge loans will keep us going. We'll be completely out of debt in a year, maybe less. From then on, everything will be self-funded."

"Frenchy, we owe them, in a sense. They kept us going, and it cost them. Congress cut their budget."

"Yes, and no. They wanted to see what our lifters could do, we needed the money and their political influence. It didn't matter in the end, we still got shut down, so I think I'm done with the US government. If you don't want to see DARPA left out in the cold, suggest this: impellers are better, but there's another way. Tell DARPA that using fans instead of impellers will also work. If the fans are powerful enough, the lifters won't even need skirts to contain the ground pressure effect."

Chuck nodded. "I'll do that, Frenchy. By the way, we're going to want lifters in space, something like a modified version of the California King with an enclosed cockpit. Think of it as a space-to-space shuttle for shifting cargo. Eventually, our ships will be larger. There's a real chance they'll be too large to land on Earth, so we'll need a method of transferring payloads in space. That's where the space transporters come in. It would be worth it to park a few on each ship, then use them the same way that seagoing ships use small boats. We'll definitely need them on the moon."

"That's on my mind, putting a base on the moon. I want to get started as soon as we can afford it. Right now, most of our income will go toward servicing our debts and buying more ships. You're probably right about owing the Defense Department; if they needed lifters bad enough, I suppose we could hand over the ones we were using in space."

"Frenchy, sooner or later, they'll invent their own impellers. Think Manhattan Project, except this time they'll be after the impeller drive. It's only a matter of putting enough people to work on it, now that they know it's possible. At some point, I think we should offer to sell completed systems, lifters, converted airplanes, and spacecraft. The ships, the flight control system, we will have spent time and money on research and working out the bugs, so I think they'd be happy to buy from us. We could easily underbid any of the aerospace companies, because we've *already* invested the money. They would have to include research and development costs, which means we could underbid them and still recover our R&D investment."

Frenchy nodded. "That's always the threat, isn't it? Knowing it's possible, that's most of the battle right there. Given enough incentive, they'll look until they find it. By incentive I mean financial, of course. If governments are willing to invest instead of leasing or buying our technology, they'll figure out how the impeller drive works."

He looked down at his desk for a moment. "It just points up what we always knew, Chuck, we have to make money while we can. By reinvesting everything into the company, we've bought time to protect ourselves. NFI is in so many nations now, we're so diversified, that we *can't* be shut down. It's the same with money, some of our accounts are in dollars, but the rest is in rubles, yuan, pounds, and euros. No nation, not even an alliance, can freeze all of our bank accounts. We've got the solid head start we wanted. Even with government backing, I don't see anyone catching up in less than ten years. By then, while they're taking the first trips to space, we'll have orbital refueling stations, maybe even a base on the moon. That's the ladder to space, Chuck, to Mars, the asteroids, the giant moons. Maybe even to terraforming Venus. If that succeeds, *when* it succeeds, we'll own our own planet." Frenchy's tone was emphatic.

"Frenchy, forcing us to shut down our plant scared you, didn't it?"

"Damned right! I had to really scramble to get the lifters for the DARPA contract. I was lucky to get the frames on credit. The Mexicans knew who I was, so they were willing to take a chance. And we already had the other components stored at...ah, Aladdinsville." Aladdinsville was the conversational name for the huge cavern on Chuck's ranch.

"I know what you mean. Anyway, *Farside* is as good as new. What say I make a few of those Japanese cargo flights?"

Frenchy was silent, thinking. "No, I've got *Gypsy* for that. We'll have *Wanderer* operational within the month and more coming after that. The Finns promise to deliver a new hull every couple of months, as long as the money keeps coming. The current contract is for eighteen ships and it's open-ended, so we can add more if we need them. The income from the Japanese fuel rod transfers is enough to pay for them and start paying down the loans. The contract is expensive, but the Japanese can't afford to cancel it. That meltdown scared them.

"As for NFI, the impeller assembly line is working too. We're buying components from around the world, then assembling them in our own shops. I keep a very close eye on those. We're still in debt, but I think we're finally over the hump. I've got enough ships to transport the canisters as fast as the Japanese can convert fuel rods, which takes them about two weeks. It takes the Finns two months to build a hull, another month for us to install the flight controls and impellers and take it on a shakedown cruise. Three months, start to finish, to produce a completed ship of the *Farside* class. Thirteen weeks, about, and unless the Japanese screw up, we can count on making at least six canister flights during that time. Bottom line, I don't need *Farside* right now, the only holdup is Japan. I'd rather keep you to back up flights."

Frenchy continued, "We haven't flown enough hours to work out all the bugs, and picking up the cargoes on time is critical. It's an assembly line, but only so long as all the parts work together. If *Gypsy* is not available, *Farside* will take her place. She's the flexibility built into the system. Later on, I'll use *Farside* and one of the ships that's in the pipeline to service the French contract.

"Tell you what, Chuck, go ahead and give your bird a shakedown cruise. You need to make sure the repairs are holding. After that, keep her available until she's needed. What say I meet you at Aladdinsville in a few days? It will take me a while to finish negotiating with the French, then I'm scheduled to talk to Germany. They're considering a similar contract. When I'm done, I'll give you a call." Chuck nodded.

"Lina OK?"

"Doing well, Frenchy. No more space flights for her, maybe not for the next few years. Two babies will nail her feet to the ground. I can't tell if she's happy at the prospect of twins. She probably regrets missing the early flights."

"Well, it won't be long, and I'm sure she'll love the motherhood experience. I'm not sure about being a grandfather."

"Morty did it, though not with twins. You can too, grampa."

"She's due in twelve weeks, right?"

"Right, everything's going well. She'll be all right, Frenchy."

"That's good, just keep me advised. But I need to get back to work, Chuck. I'll call you when I get back to the states."

The connection ended and Frenchy sighed. Two visitors had arrived at the office while he was talking to Chuck. The parade never slowed!

"VACATION'S OVER, gang. I'm taking *Farside* out for a shakedown cruise. There's no reason to keep her here, so we won't be coming back. Will, you want left seat?"

"You take it, Chuck. What have you got in mind?"

"Fly to orbit, then tank up at one of the refueling stations. We should do a trial run."

"I doubt there'll be any problems. The fill tubes are flexible and independently steerable from the control panel, so all you need to do is take your time joining up. The radio beacon and docking lights will help."

"You're probably right, but until we try we can't be absolutely sure. The stations are easy to reach, the whole thing should be almost foolproof. We don't have fools flying our ships, but I'll be happier if we give it a try. We could take some of the maintenance people with us. *Farside* will be based in Iceland or Finland from now on."

"Tell me about the bases."

"They're absolutely necessary, not just for hangar space between flights but for maintenance. We're still working out the schedule, but so far, we expect to replace door and hatch seals every hundred hours. The rubber compound dries out and begins to flake, so the only way to prevent leaks is to replace them before they fail. Each hatch has an inner seal and an outer seal, but even so, after a hundred flight hours we start losing atmosphere. The leaks are slow, but we can't afford to have them get larger."

Will nodded.

"We're following a modified version of what airlines do, inspect after every flight, do preventive maintenance according to a set schedule, and every two years do a complete teardown and rebuild. Space flight is even more demanding than atmospheric flight, so proactive is better than reactive. The impellers are reliable, but even so there's no reason to take chances. We intend to replace them every six months. Old impellers go into the shop for teardown and detailed inspection. Any worn parts will be replaced. We expect bearings to fail, so they'll be replaced during every inspection whether they need it or not. Rebuilt impellers are as good as new, so they'll go into the maintenance pipeline. The batteries get similar treatment, except that we send them back to the manufacturer for inspection and recertification. Anyway, that means we need shops, which means bases."

Two men decided to fly with Chuck and Will, the others begged off. They helped load the rubber water bladder, so the task was soon finished. The pool that had filled the bottom of the cavern's sinkhole was almost empty; the water had been filtered and used as raw material for the orbital refueling stations. The immense photovoltaic wings provided the needed power; electrolysis split the water molecules, and the hydrogen and oxygen were compressed and stored until needed.

"Board in fifteen minutes, suits on. You can leave your helmets racked."

"I'll keep my fishbowl on, Chuck. One of us should be fully suited until we reach orbit. I'll take it off when we get there. If something's going to break, it will have done it by then," Will said.

"Good idea. I'll warm up the fuel cells and start checkout while you get suited up." Chuck kept his pressure suit in a locker at the back of the crew cabin. He would change while waiting for the fuel cells to come online.

THE CAVERN HAD BEEN FORMED by the same chemistry that produced the nearby Carlsbad Caverns. Seeping water dissolved the limestone, leaving an underground void that extended for miles. Part of the roof had then collapsed, leaving a giant sinkhole; similar events had formed the nearby Bottomless Lakes State Park. Chuck fulfilled a childhood dream by rappelling down the sinkhole's sides, then briefly exploring the cave. He noticed that there were few stalactites and stalagmites, meaning this cavern was probably younger than the Carlsbad Caverns when the roof collapsed.

There had been changes. The cavern now had an electrical system, using power drawn from the photovoltaic plant near the old ranch house. The California King, the company's sole remaining lifter after Mel's crash, had simplified the task of converting the cave into a workshop and factory. Lights had been installed, the cavern floor leveled. Metal buildings were erected on the new foundation, including a bunkhouse and a storage building that currently held NFI's stock of completed impellers. The new factory and shop were sufficient to maintain *Farside*, as well as manufacture new impellers.

Half an hour later, hatches sealed and indicator lights glowing green, Chuck lifted *Farside* to a low hover. Easing the ship ahead until he reached the sinkhole, he added power as soon as he cleared the cavern's roof. The ship rose, elevator-like, to the surface.

"Radar on." Chuck gave the command as soon as the nose cleared the surface. Will pushed the buttons, then monitored the display as the unit came online. Continuing his slow rise, Chuck slowly revolved the ship while watching the display. The only return came from the distant mountains.

The flight control computers seamlessly translated his commands; when the ship's up-angle reached sixty degrees, Chuck fed in power and the big craft climbed rapidly.

"We'll stay subsonic through angels 60," he explained. "It takes a little longer to reach the stratosphere, but we don't want to spook the neighbors. There's no reason to make people curious. They might decide to take a look at the cave, and we don't want that to happen."

"Agreed." Will reported the indications from his instruments. "Your course is east, speed 500 knots, now passing through 36,000 feet. Fuel cell output is nominal, impellers at 43% of max thrust, hakuna matata."

"Say *what*?"

"No worries, Chuck. What are they teaching you guys in school now?"

"Not that!"

"Impellers are at 75%," Will reported. "Cabin pressure remains nominal. Five minutes from orbit, prepare for weightlessness."

The two crewmen responded with "Got it" and "I understand". Chuck smiled. No standard pilot's jargon for them!

"I show us on course, ready to enter orbit. Reduce power...now," continued Will.

"Impellers at 5%, Will, maintaining altitude. Refueling station coming up in thirty minutes. I'm using the impellers to keep us down in a lower orbit, meaning we're overtaking the station. I intend to engage the docking program as soon as the station is in sight. I'll refuel first, then top off the station's water supply."

* * *

FORTY-SIX MINUTES LATER, Chuck disengaged the transfer probes.

"Any comments, Will?"

"Nope, that went so slick it's scary."

"I show us at 100% fuel," Chuck said thoughtfully. "You know, we've got enough to orbit the moon and return."

"You sure, Chuck?"

"Why not? How about you guys, want a sightseeing tour?"

"Sure," followed by, "The *moon*?"

There's always a doubter, thought Chuck. He rotated the ship and lifted the nose, gradually adding power. Acceleration pushed him into the seat as the impellers spun up. On course, he gradually reduced the thrust, holding it at one gee acceleration. He glanced at Will and got a nod of encouragement.

"You'll need to watch your fuel consumption. You should also file a report through the communications satellite. Old pilots and bold pilots, you know how that goes. I vote for letting our guys at Aladdinsville know where we're going. Maybe Frenchy can send a rescue party if we need one. You're just doing a loop around, right?"

"Right, no landing. I'll call in the report, you take the stick."

"I've got the controls."

The moon's image grew larger. The ship's velocity continued to increase; the cratered disk filled the screen, then became too large for the display. Chuck tweaked *Farside's* course, watching the image slide away to starboard. "One loop, maybe two, then we head for the barn."

"You're doing a slingshot?" asked Will.

"Right, that way we'll hold our speed for the return. I've got fuel for several orbits, but I don't want to cut it too fine."

"Watch your acceleration, then. You might want to dial it back now, otherwise your slingshot will send us where we're not ready to go."

"Go around in free fall, you think?"

"That's what the Apollos did, but then they didn't have impellers or enough fuel to do anything else. You'll have to fly the approach manually, there's no program in the computer."

"I'll fix that before we try this again. Dialing power back, prepare for microgravity."

The moon was visible through the side viewports. Will adjusted the starboard wing camera and let it pan across the surface.

"Altitude, Chuck?"

"I'm watching it, Will. We're not in orbit, I'm using the impellers to hold this altitude, meaning we'll spiral in during the second half of the loop. I'll boost speed as we come around and that should sling-shot us for home. I'll file a follow-up report as soon as we're on our way."

"Agreed." Will aimed the port camera and the camera on the vertical stabilizer toward the surface, then pushed the record button. "I think we'll get some good photos. They'll help when it's time to pick a base location."

"We'll have to do a walkabout."

"Sure, but the photo record is where it starts. You don't want to set your base in a crater."

"I'm not sure about that," said Chuck. "One of the earlier surveys reported water ice in those craters. If it *did* come from comet strikes, the ice might still be there, under the craters. Some of them, anyway."

"You think? Maybe so, but we'll need some kind of digging machine. Moon gravity is too light, the Apollo guys just bounced around; even chipping rocks, they came off the ground. We'll need a backhoe, maybe a dozer. You know those spent fuel rods we'll be hauling?" said Will.

"Right, first for the Japanese, then the French, probably the Germans too. Eventually, maybe even the USA. We'll have customers."

"The first cargoes won't be usable; the nuclear fuel will be distributed through glass in the canister, so they won't produce enough heat. But the ones still in the cooling pools, well...we should be ashamed to charge people. We *want* those spent fuel rods. I would even haul them free."

"You're going to dump them on the moon? Will, we'll catch hell from the UN, and the rest of the nuclear-capable nations won't like it either; they might cancel our contracts. Sure, we save on fuel costs, as opposed to launching from beyond the moon's gravity well, but..."

"Not going to dump them at all. You know they're hot, right?"

"Sure, they put them in pools to contain the radioactivity."

"That's not what I mean. I mean they're 'spent' only because they no longer have enough power to operate the generating plants efficiently. But they're still hot when they're pulled from the reactors, literally hot. The water keeps them cool."

"Okay, but we don't have water to spare. You're suggesting we might find some, but that's a maybe and right now, we don't have any."

"Nope. No water. What we *do* have on the moon is room, all the room we want."

"So... Will, you're going somewhere with this. What are you talking about?"

"I want to bring up a trencher, maybe a backhoe, battery powered, track mounted. The batteries will add weight to the machine, and on the moon we need all the weight we can get. Other than that, it will be like any other ditch-digger. I'm thinking we should dig trenches, then lay in pipes and connect them end to end. Once the plumbing is finished, cover the pipes with a thin layer of crushed rock or dust but don't completely fill the trenches. There's plenty of dust available. Lay the fuel rods on top of the fill material, then add another layer of rock so the heat stays in the trenches. Circulate a fluid through the pipes, collect the heat, and use it to generate electricity."

"Will that work?"

"Sure it will. Even if it doesn't work, we're no worse off; we just launch the fuel rods toward the sun like we planned. But I'm sure this will work. We'll need to pump the fluid through a heat exchanger, that will have to be inside a shelter, then transfer the heat to a second loop to generate power. The second loop circulates a hot fluid through Stirling-Cycle engines hooked to generators. Some of the electricity will drive the pumps to circulate the fluids, but the rest is free power for Moonbase. I figure the spent rods will stay hot for five, maybe even ten years, and by then we'll be ready to replace the oldest ones. Once the system starts, it will run continuously. Electricity will be available all the time, not just when the sun's up. After we build the system, it's all free. That's why I say we should consider paying for the spent rods."

"No way, if they're willing to pay us, let them. Those rods are a negative asset on the ground, they're only worth something after we deliver them on the moon. We're the only ones who can do that safely, so we charge for the service.

"Why don't we set up a meeting with Frenchy? He's got a conference in Germany later this week, but he'll be home after that. I like the idea, but Frenchy's the boss, so let's see what he thinks."

2

C huck parked *Farside* outside Reykjavik in an empty NFI hangar. He switched off main power, then locked the board.

After the Russian hijack attempt, a number of security enhancements had been made; in addition to titanium rods around the high-security lock, smaller titanium pins fitted loosely into holes around the cylinder. These were free to rotate, preventing removal of the cylinder by sawing. A cutting torch would have no better luck; the switches and wiring would melt first, effectively breaking the link between the flight control system and the rest of the ship.

Will and Chuck then went their separate ways; Will caught a flight to Finland, where he would meet Wolfgang Albrecht. *Gypsy* waited there, ready to make the first commercial flight to space. Wolfgang would command and Will would serve as copilot; he would also evaluate Wolfgang's performance, deciding whether he was ready to command *Gypsy*. Two mechanics completed the crew complement.

Will and Wolfgang had agreed on a rough flight plan. Wolfgang would fly *Gypsy* to orbit, top off her tanks, then land near Fukushima to pick up a canister of vitrified high-level nuclear waste. Japanese workers would load the canister and *Gypsy's* crewmen would secure it in the cargo bay. Pausing in orbit long enough to top off his tanks, Wolfgang would boost *Gypsy's* speed to escape velocity, then launch the container on its long trip to the sun. Detailed planning would take place after they got the latest weather briefing.

Chuck caught a ride into Reykjavik and ate supper, then checked into the company's leased hotel suite. He placed a call to Lina before settling in for the night. Chuck missed his wife, and a phone call was better than nothing.

There was another reason for making the call; Chuck wanted her to relocate to Australia. She would be safer there, but she had friends in New Mexico and Texas. Could she adjust to living in a strange country? And how would emigrating affect the as-yet-unborn twins? Lina was hesitant, still unwilling to decide when they ended the call.

Chuck found Frenchy at the company's Reykjavik office the following morning. He spent the first half hour explaining Will's idea for using the 'depleted' fuel rods, then mentioned the difficulties involved in transporting the cargo.

"We need a second-generation ship. *Farside* or *Gypsy* won't do, not without major modifications. We'd do better refitting them with extra fuel and oxygen tanks. In-flight refueling would be more efficient than stopping at one of the orbital stations."

"An interesting idea," said Frenchy. "But we can talk about it later. Why a second-generation ship, Chuck?"

"*Farside*-class ships can't haul unconverted fuel rods. If they're melted together with silica, we can transport them, but we can't use them. We need a way to carry unprotected rods, straight from the cooling pool. That means a different kind of cargo bay, one with shielding to protect the crew and a way to hold the rods. That means a larger bay that has enough room for the shields. More fuel rods means more mass, so we'll need stiffer walls around the cargo bay, adding to the weight. More mass also means more fuel cells and additional impellers. The new ships will also need insulation between the fuel rods to keep them from interacting with each other. If the rods get close to each other, there's enough active nuclear material to speed up the reactions, increasing the heat and radioactivity. They might even melt down. The Japanese can help you design the unit. It's to their advantage if we can haul more rods each trip. Transport would go faster if we didn't have to wait for them to vitrify the material. Even if we kept the cost of a single flight the same, we wouldn't need as many trips. We'll still send them off to the sun, but only after we've got as much use out of them as possible."

"It sounds feasible. Let me run it through engineering and I'll get back to you. What's next on your agenda?"

"I need a copilot, and so will Wolfgang. Will's off to Lapland right now, flying right seat on *Gypsy*, but we can't afford to keep using him as a check pilot. Will should be in charge of flight operations."

"I'll find copilots. Martha probably has several ready by now. You'll be flying formation in *Farside*, right?"

"Right, I'll be off Wolfgang's wing until he passes the moon. From that point on, all he has to do is continue until he reaches escape velocity, then dump the canister. I'll have time to finish the aerial surveys before he's back inside Luna's orbit."

Chuck switched topics. "I figure we'll need a large, flat area, at least a thousand acres. The fuel-rod trenches will need a lot of room, and the rest of the base has to be far enough away that there's no increase in radiation. If I see anything like that, I'll get detailed photos."

"Sounds good. But if anything goes wrong with one of the transport ships, you're *Gypsy's* backup and *Grasshopper* is yours if *Farside* isn't available. I'll look into Will's scheme, see what our civil engineers think. Too bad you can't haul even one bare fuel rod in the current cargo bays."

"It might be possible with enough shielding, but only one. Unconverted rods are heavy to start with, and they're shipped dirtside in water-jacketed bottles. The flasks weigh around fifty tons."

"You're right, that's too much mass. I'll get you your second-generation ships. Where do you want to base them?"

"Rovaniemi. It's right on the Arctic circle, cold in the winter but no colder than space, and the factory that's building our new ships is only ten kilometers away. We can deal with the cold. It's pleasant in the summer and the Finns are friendly people. Another advantage, the area is almost deserted. There's a wilderness south of our lease, and the Finns are serious about keeping it wild. I doubt we'll see any unexpected visitors."

"It's beautiful up there, that's for sure. I like the place, and not just because they have heavy industry. They make cell phones, they've got a weapons industry, they even build cruise ships. They're serious about their health too, although they're mad."

"Mad?"

"Yeah. I haven't tried it, but they work up a good sweat in the sauna, then jump out and run around in the snow while whacking each other with branches. Madness."

"Have you tried it, Frenchy?"

"Chuck, why don't you get me a list of people who are flight-qualified? I'll pick the best one and make him flight examiner."

"About that sauna, Frenchy..."

"On your way, Chuck."

* * *

"LET's look at your detailed flight plan, Wolfgang."

"I'll put it on the screen. I've got a hard copy, but it's just in case it's needed for backup."

"The screen's fine. Okay, on the first leg you're heading north over the pole?"

"Yes. I'm hauling a bladder of water to refill the tanks on Stations Two and Three. Station One can handle four or five more refuelings before the tank goes dry. I'll refill it on the next trip, or Chuck may get to it before then."

"What about here?" Will pointed to the landmass east of Finland.

"Right, I'll stay well clear of there. That's Russian airspace. I'll pass *here*, west of Russia and north of Sweden. In any case, we'll be well above the operational altitude of Russian antiaircraft batteries by the time I exit Finnish air space. I'll enter orbit *here*," pointing to the screen, "below and behind Station Three. I'll fill its tank, then slow down and catch Station Two on the next orbit. I'll transfer the rest of the water there and head south. I'll reenter atmosphere over the Pacific and approach Japan north of Tokyo. The landing beacon is *here*," pointing to a location to the east, "so I'll follow it to the landing site outside Fukushima. The course changes cost fuel and oxy, but they're necessary to avoid unnecessary chances. Anyway, we'll load the cargo at the vitrification plant, boost for space over the Pacific, and head out beyond the moon. *Farside* will already be in orbit, waiting to join up as soon as we clear atmosphere. Chuck's supposed to fly off our wing until we're about two thirds of the way into the trip. He'll head for the moon at that point. If there's a problem, we'll know about it long before we split up. We'll release the cargo as we approach the Lagrange limit, meaning regardless of our speed it's at escape velocity. From that point on, the sun's gravity takes over. The canister will approach the sun from above the plane of the ecliptic, vaporizing as it approaches solar north. There's not supposed to be any man-made craft up that way, and because it's above the plane of the ecliptic I don't expect asteroids or meteorites either. This first trip is the trailblazer, the rest of the transport flights will use our course data, so I was careful when I worked out the flight plan. Sound good to you?"

"What about weather?"

"Fukushima is partly cloudy, light winds from the south. The Pacific south of Japan is clear."

"I don't see any problem. The only real trouble point is here, north of the Gulf of Bothnia. You'll want to cross this zone *after* Russia passes off to the east. We'll notify Sweden and Norway, but they won't have a problem. They know we're flying empty or hauling water. No radioactive issues, in other words, plus they also want some of our business. Panit's due to open talks with Sweden next week, I'll have him mention it to them. But the Russians are different, we've had trouble with them, so make sure you don't overfly this area west of Murmansk."

"I won't. We've got about two hours before we can launch, so if you want to grab a bite to eat and a cup of coffee...?"

"Let's do it. Preflight *Gypsy* in, say, forty-five minutes, then we'll wait for the launch window to open. I'll file your flight plan with NFI headquarters in Switzerland."

* * *

WILL SAW nothing during the flight that concerned him. Wolfgang's control was flawless during the boost to altitude, and the flight computer docked at each station using the subroutine Chuck had pioneered. Refilling the water tanks took half an hour each. Topping off *Gypsy's* onboard hydrogen and oxygen tanks was also without incident. Wolfgang disconnected after the last refill, then slowed the ship, sinking to a lower orbit. They waited, impellers barely ticking over, as the Earth rotated beneath them. Wolfgang slowed the ship further, breaking orbit just as Japan appeared over the western horizon. The impellers slowed their descent and *Gypsy* passed easily through the upper atmosphere. Wolfgang turned the ship on its long axis, watching as Japan passed beneath them. A final correction put them on course for Fukushima. The big craft slowed as it approached the factory, hovering momentarily before settling onto its skids. The twin halves of the cargo hatch opened as *Gypsy* touched down.

An hour later, loading complete and canister secured, they began the takeoff checklist. Wolfgang dialed up the impellers but nothing happened for a moment. Finally, *Gypsy* sluggishly broke ground.

"Will, something's wrong! I'm at 94% power and I'm barely able to control her."

"The electrical system shows nominal, except that the impellers are drawing a lot of power. We're sucking more fuel too. The cargo has to be the problem, it's heavier than we specified. Damn! Did they do this deliberately? I'll have some Japanese ass if they did! You fly, I'm calling Switzerland. Wolfgang, bring your impellers to 100%, and if that doesn't give you control, prepare to jettison the canister. We're already feet wet, don't worry about what's underneath. We can take a final peek with the radar before we drop the canister."

"Is Frenchy in Switzerland, Will?"

"Doesn't matter, Wolfgang, they'll notify him wherever he is. I'll tell them what's going on. Do you want to abort?"

"Do I have a choice?"

"Yes. You're the commander, so command. I won't overrule you unless I think the ship is in danger. If you need to drop the canister, roll the ship belly up, open the cargo hatches, then unlock the clamps. Japan can fish it out of the ocean. Don't worry about *Gypsy*, she can fly upside down. The impellers are gimbal mounted."

"I'll try to continue the mission, Will. If you're okay with that, I mean."

"You're the commander, Wolfgang."

"Change of plan, Will." Wolfgang's tone was firm. "We'll tank at Station Two, it's closer to our current flight path. Notify Chuck. As soon as we've got full tanks, I'll head out. The trip back will take longer, but by using lunar gravity to slingshot us back, I can complete the mission. Shutting down the impellers should leave me with enough fuel to make turnaround for the moon after we launch the canister. Hang on, I'll run the numbers just to be sure..."

Numbers on the screen blinked rapidly, then stabilized. "Seven and a half hours, boosting at one quarter gee. We'll be short of the Lagrange limit, but the canister will be carrying enough velocity so that it will still head for the sun. You okay with that?"

"Do it," Will said.

"Tell Chuck to increase the standoff distance, I'd rather not have to worry about *Farside*. Also let him know I expect to slingshot around Luna, so he should plan for that. If possible, I advise he clear Luna before we arrive."

"I'll tell him."

The moon was behind the Earth when *Gypsy* reached the release point. Wolfgang punched the button, opening the cargo hatch's twin halves. "I won't use the cargo arm, Will; I've got a better idea. Your comment about dumping the cargo in the Pacific will work just as well in space."

Wolfgang gently rotated the ship around its lateral axis until the open hatch pointed toward the distant sun. The ship continued on course, 'flying' with the dorsal surface leading the way. "Unlocking cargo restraints now, Will. Prepare for negative acceleration, one half gee."

"Right, good move. The canister will separate and keep going."

"That's it. As soon as it's clear, I'll rotate the ship and head back. Fuel reserves should be enough. Planning to slingshot around the moon is just in case something else goes wrong. We'll pick up Chuck on the way and he can escort us back to Station Three. Otherwise, we might not have enough fuel to land."

The maneuver was completed without difficulty, and a minute later the canister sailed slowly away on its long trip to the sun.

"Call the repeater satellite, see if you can raise Chuck," said Will. "Let him know we're empty and on the way back. If he's where he's supposed to be, go ahead and use half-gee acceleration. I want to get home and chew some ass!"

"Copy, Will. Wait one...okay, Chuck's ready. Half a gee it is, Course changed toward the moon as it comes around, three point six hours to rendezvous. Start sharpening your teeth, Will."

3

Chuck refueled at Station Two, then headed back to complete the interrupted survey. He briefly considered landing to sample the surface texture, but realized he needed specialized help; the orbital survey would have to be enough, for now.

Eighteen orbits later, the survey completed, he increased power. *Farside* departed orbit and joined *Gypsy* on its way to distant Earth. The join-up was smooth and Chuck looked the ship over but saw no damage.

Chuck made a number of calls as he approached the atmosphere. His first call found Lina doing well. She wanted to discuss the proposed move to Australia, but Chuck explained it would be better to discuss it during his next trip home. His second call, to NFI's Swiss office, reported his return to Earth. A third call was less successful; Frenchy wasn't available, so the call was forwarded to his voicemail. Chuck left a message requesting a meeting with the company's civil engineering staff.

Will had his anger in check by the time *Gypsy* landed, but only just.

He called the company's Swiss office and dictated a report of the near-tragedy, then asked to speak to Martha Simms. She was the very competent American manager of the Swiss branch office, middle-aged, dark haired, slender, and unmarried.

"Call the Japanese company that prepared our cargo. I want a word with the person in charge," Will said.

"I'll see what I can do," replied Martha.

"If the Japanese try to stall, tell them I'm reconsidering whether to continue operating under the current contract. That cargo exceeded weight specs and it nearly caused us to crash. If it happens again, I'll jettison the cargo and let the Japanese deal with it."

"I'll keep that in mind, Will. Was there anything else?"

"Not right now. Tell them I'll meet with their representative as soon as he's available."

"Will you need maintenance or an overhaul on *Gypsy*? Were any of the components stressed beyond safe limits?"

"No. We launched the cargo as planned and made it home without incident, but we might not be that lucky next time. *Gypsy* is a good bird, she's got more power and better handling than I expected."

"That brings up another question. Are you ready to certify Wolfgang as a ship commander?"

"Absolutely. He'll need a copilot, but he's ready. You guys did a fine job of preparing him for command."

"Thank you, and I'll pass that on. That said, was there anything *else* you wanted to tell me?"

"No, Martha, that's everything. Thanks for your help."

* * *

CHUCK LANDED *Farside* at NFI's Base Reykjavik and turned the ship over to the maintenance staff. They would conduct a complete biennial inspection, with special attention paid to the repairs done in Aladdinsville, before preparing the ship for its next mission. For the moment, both *Farside* and *Gypsy* were idle.

The transmitter, which the Japanese had insisted on adding to the first canister, sent out a continuous telemetry signal. Satisfied, they paid NFI the agreed-upon fee.

The telemetry confirming that the Japanese container was on course for the sun. As a result, Germany, the US, and Russia were now ready to discuss similar arrangements. France had already signed on. As soon as ships were available, they would begin hauling French fuel rods. France had their own side-negotiations going; they were prepared to temporarily store rods from other countries until they could be disposed of. For a fee, of course!

Meanwhile, the Japanese were investigating the problem that Will had reported. They scheduled a meeting, and Frenchy decided he would also attend.

* * *

FRENCHY CAUGHT an early JAL flight and landed at Tokyo's Haneda Airport. Will, waiting at the baggage terminal, collected Frenchy's bag. The two took a shuttle bus to the hotel, checked Frenchy in, then headed downstairs to meet the Japanese delegation. Will explained what had happened during *Gypsy's* maiden voyage, and Frenchy agreed that the potential profits were simply not worth risking their ships. Something would have to be done, or the first Japanese cargo would also be their last.

Grim faced, they entered the conference room. The hotel had obligingly provided them with a certified translator; they would not have to rely on the language skills of the Japanese executives.

The men stood and bowed as Frenchy and Will entered. The two bowed politely in return, then greeted the men. Will got right to the point as soon as they were seated, still angry at what had almost happened. He was prepared to disregard protocol in order to leave no doubt that the Japanese company had behaved unacceptably.

"Which of you was in charge of preparing the shipment?"

"I regret to say that Mister Haruka will not be joining us. He was our representative to the company."

"Why is he not here, then? I specifically asked to speak directly to him."

"Mister Haruka..."

Frenchy cautioned Will as the man paused. "Keep your cool. Anger won't help."

"Frenchy, that guy damned near got us killed! I've got a right to be mad!"

"Get yourself under control, Will. I'll do the talking." Muttering, Will subsided.

"Sir, Mister Haruka has passed away. He cannot be here. We offer our apologies for the circumstances."

"What do you mean, passed away? He died?"

"Mister French, he understood his error. He could not live with the shame. He has passed on."

The silence lasted half a minute; the Japanese waited patiently, but neither Will nor Frenchy could think of anything to say. Finally Frenchy responded.

"I am sorry to hear that, but the problem remains. Does anyone know why the cargo canister was so overloaded?"

The Japanese man who had taken the lead looked at the others, who nodded back. He looked at his hands for a moment, gathering his thoughts. "I regret to say that we all share in Mister Haruka's shame. None of us expected Mister Haruka to act as he did."

"Why did he do that, Mister...?" asked Will?

"My name is Watanabe, Mister Crane. I am the chairman of this board. Our company has several branches. We collect the nuclear material, prepare it for shipment, and disburse funds to your company upon completion of a successful launch. My associates are members of this board, as was Mister Haruka. We speak for the parent corporation.

The man paused for a moment to make sure the two Americans understood.

"We negotiated with your company in good faith, but circumstances have changed. Mister French, we have been approached by officials from our government. We are still most interested in disposing of radioactive waste material and our government shares our concerns, but the government has other interests as well. How much do you know of Japan's affairs?"

"I've done considerable reading, of course, but I can't claim expertise."

Frenchy paused, deciding what he wanted to say.

"You're faced with a declining population. Births are not keeping up with deaths, and as a result the average age of your citizens is increasing. There's also the problem of uneasy relations with China and South Korea, plus a very high national debt. Your nuclear power plants are in trouble; part of this has to do with safe disposal of the spent fuel rods, but the issue is complicated because some of your people are hostile to *all* nuclear operations. It's understandable, of course; they don't want another Hiroshima, and the meltdown of the Fukushima reactors created difficulties. Japan experiences a number of significant natural events, earthquakes, typhoons, things like that, and there's no way of preventing them. Your government is moving toward greater militarism even as significant numbers of Japanese remain adamantly opposed to it. Japan imports more than she sells. This imbalance is draining money from your economy, creating pressure on the yen."

"Just so. Financing for our contract with you can still be arranged, but this has strategic implications. Our finance minister pointed out that you have offices in a number of nations, but almost all are in the West. I wonder if you might consider investing in Japan?"

"We did. The problem, Mister Watanabe, is that Japan's technical products are costly. As for establishing a base here, Japan has limited open space, which means land for a base would be costly compared with other locations. There's also the question of security. Your people have experienced violence recently."

"I see. I have little room to maneuver regarding costs. We still have the nuclear material issue, but our earlier efforts were here in Japan so the costs did not impact our foreign trade balance. By employing your company, we hoped to save money as well as reduce the environmental impact. This would do much to placate our citizens. The government has pointed out, however, that our national debt and balance of payments would be severely affected. Money transferred to you would have to be made up from domestic operations, which in turn would slow future development here in Japan. The projected sum is considerable."

Watanabe cleared his throat. "Such were the discussions we believe convinced Mister Haruka to act as he did. We believe he added the nuclear materials from an extra fuel rod to the mix that went into the canister. The uranium, plutonium, and byproducts from fission are much heavier than silica. His actions not only added weight, they made the canister more dangerous due to increased radioactivity. He endangered our people as well as yours.

"We can ensure this never happens again. In the meantime, the effect on our economy remains unresolved. We take an unusual step in explaining this matter in such detail, but we are in your debt due to the danger your employees experienced."

Watanabe's expression changed from apologetic to pleading. "Are there no unfilled needs that we can solve? We have excellent heavy industries as you know, we also are an island nation with access to the Pacific, surely there must be something?"

"To be honest, I can't think of anything. The only thing we don't have a source for at the moment is small space-capable fission power plants. We use fuel cells, and Japanese companies produce them, but your products offer no real advantage. They're no better than what we currently use. Fuel cells also won't work for the interplanetary ships we hope to build."

"May we have a moment to confer, Mister French? Perhaps something might be done."

The conference-within-a-conference lasted more than fifteen minutes. A great deal of low-voiced argument ensued; whatever the topic, there was no agreement among the men. Finally, Watanabe gained control. The rapid flow of Japanese caused the interpreter's eyes to widen; up to this point, he'd been quiet, bored with having nothing to do. Frenchy glanced at him, but the man said nothing. Whatever was going on, he did not want to tell the two Americans. They sipped water and waited.

"It is possible we may be able to help you. We have excellent scientists and engineers, and some are experts in designing nuclear units. Experimental work has been done on units similar to what you describe. It will take time, there's no certainty that our scientists will succeed, and the work will be costly. Can you guarantee purchase of such units if we can build them to your specifications?"

"I can. How many are you talking about?"

"How many do you need, Mister French?"

The negotiations continued for a few minutes more before both were satisfied with the arrangement.

"We have a final question, Mister French. Can you assist in financing the costs of development? Perhaps by transporting our fuel rods at a lower cost per unit?"

Frenchy glanced at Will, who nodded back.

"We can. We'll reduce the charges per shipment to half what you agreed to, the other half will be our contribution to the research effort. Let's say you match what we lose by reducing our fees, thus splitting the cost. We can offer something else; we will build ships that can carry unconverted fuel rods, reducing your costs even further. The new ships will have additional shielding around the cargo bay and between the fuel rods, so the fuel rods can be loaded directly from your storage pools and safely disposed of in space. I believe you already have equipment to handle fuel rods, so that should require no additional costs. But no more overloading, that has to be clear. My ship commanders will jettison the cargoes if it happens again."

Watanabe stood, then bowed assent. The others rose and bowed in turn.

Frenchy and Will shook hands with each of the men before leaving. Neither cracked a smile.

Until they were back in their hotel room. There the smiles turned into wide grins. "I wonder what kind of booze is available, Frenchy? I think we deserve to celebrate!"

* * *

CHUCK'S MEETING with the engineering staff did not go as expected.

"Here's the problem. You need machinery that can operate on the moon, in vacuum. You say you want an electrically-powered backhoe, but there are problems with that, starting with energy density. Batteries just aren't that efficient. They're also expensive, you've got to haul them a long way, and how would you recharge them? You want to use electricity from a power plant you haven't built yet. Not good engineering practice, Chuck. A critic might even call the idea dumb."

Chuck shook his head at the chuckles. "Okay, so how would you do it? Will's idea is a potential gold mine, it's just too good to give up. There must be some way, short of lines of men with shovels digging ditches on the moon."

"Why not use a diesel backhoe?"

"What, a diesel engine in space? Diesels breathe air, and the moon is pretty short of that!"

"Maybe, but let's explore the idea of no air. What part of the air does a diesel use?"

"Oxygen, of course, lots of oxygen. The more fuel you burn, the more oxygen the engine consumes."

"We already hydrolyze oxygen from water, that's how the refueling stations work. We could set up a station on Luna that would do the same thing. We can easily haul water to provide the raw material, that's what we do with the refueling stations, although we might not have to. There may be water on the moon, we just have to find it. It will be ice, of course, but melting it is easy. A pressurized container with a simple concentrating lens is more than hot enough when the sun is up. Maybe use a Fresnel lens, molded from the new transparent metal? If we can't find ice on Luna, we already have a base in Iceland, that gives us access to the North Atlantic. Think icebergs and the Titanic; icebergs are fresh water, so there would be no desalination problems. There's also Greenland, which would probably be willing to sell us ice from their icecap. That's fresh water ice, easy to mine, easy to transport. I've got a few ideas about that too. Have you considered a system of barges? They'd need their own power plants and impellers, but control could be exercised from a crew module in front. It wouldn't be remote control at all, just signals to operate the power and propulsion system on each barge. They could be joined in an extended line or clumped together in bunches, whatever looks best in practice. Each module would need to be self-sufficient except for control, but that could come from the flight computers in the crew module."

"Wow, I can see that working. How large were you thinking of?"

"A hundred tons, a hundred thousand tons, I don't think it would make a difference. Assembly of the barges would be a problem, but that's just cut and try engineering. Easy money."

"You don't think small, do you? Okay, eventually maybe we mine ice on the moon, but we can haul a lot of ice from Earth in the beginning, cheap. We land the ice on the moon, maybe leave it packaged in the transport barge. Now what?"

"We already have refueling stations. We upgrade that design to a larger one, maybe two or three of them, and park them on the moon near where you want to build your electrical plant. Feed them water from melted ice, you get oxygen and hydrogen by electrolysis. I think a diesel engine would work better, but we can look at a hydrogen-oxygen engine if we have to. But let's consider diesel. It wouldn't even have to be a four-stroke unit. A single-cycle power plant could work, since you're burning diesel with pure oxygen. Give me a minute to get this on paper."

Pencils came out and the yellow note pads were soon covered with drawings and formulae. "Two cylinder or four cylinder?" caused another intense discussion.

"What about weight? At one sixth Earth weight, you spud in your bucket and your backhoe lifts off the ground. What about that?"

"Yeah, but the materials are also one-sixth weight."

"Doesn't matter, it's extracting a bucket-load from the ground, whatever that's like. You have to rip the bucket through the dirt or whatever before you can lift it. Sometimes you only get half a bucket, maybe only a few scrapings if the ground is hard."

"Hmmm...could be a problem."

"Maybe make it heavier? How about powered augers, say one at each corner? They bore into the ground, so they could anchor the unit. Reverse them when you're ready to crawl forward."

"Okay, that's doable, but more weight on the machine would be simpler and you wouldn't need to waste time emplacing the augers. Tracks, you think?"

"Absolutely. How are you coming with that engine?"

"Got a first approximation. Four cylinders, because it might not be as efficient as I think, but here's the way it should work. No intake valves, just direct injection into each cylinder. Each stroke is a power stroke. Timing is important; the oxy has to be injected while the cylinder is halfway up in the reverse stroke. That's how you get the heating effect, from compression. Inject the diesel fuel when the piston nears the top of the cylinder, after the oxy is hot. Ignition takes place, the mix expands and pushes the cylinder down. No exhaust valves needed either. Near the bottom of the stroke, openings in the cylinder wall allow the gases to escape. Most of them will be cleared out because they're escaping into vacuum. Gases cool by expansion, so you channel the expanded exhaust gases past cooling fins molded into the engine block. It's like what happens using air cooling, but using exhaust gases instead of ambient air to cool the engine. No need to worry about pollution, nobody's breathing the exhaust, and it won't even need a muffler. The engine would be self-contained, modular, and much more powerful for its weight than any conventional diesel. It will probably need a heavy flywheel to smooth out the revolutions, though, which on Luna is not a disadvantage.

"I think we can do this. What do you think?"

"I think you guys are nuts, but I like it! If you can make this work, you'll have a nice bonus coming. Maybe a paid vacation in Finland! I know Frenchy likes the place; it may have something to do with the saunas."

"Saunas, you say? A whole month up there? It's next door to Sweden, and for that matter Denmark and Norway aren't far. And you did mention bonuses...?"

4

Alexander Zlotov, a deputy minister of Roscosmos State Corporation, was tired of the discussion. He had come up through the Russian Federal Space Agency, then transferred to Roscosmos when the RFSA had been dissolved. The name was different, but things hadn't changed much, if at all.

He dismissed his visitor and lit a cigarette. The military always wanted more than the RSC could deliver, but were never willing to pay for the development costs. Probably it wasn't the man's fault; no agency was truly flush, thanks to the worldwide petroleum glut. Low oil prices had forced a temporary change in the usual three-year fiscal plan. The new one-year plan might serve to ride out the downturn, but no one could predict what would happen when the spending caps were lifted. Most expected inflation to increase, but where it would stop no one knew. The president insisted on holding tight to the nation's gold and foreign currency reserves, meaning that the central bank was unable to support the sagging ruble. The conflict in Ukraine simmered, a military buildup in the Middle East was underway, and both sucked more money from an already-anemic budget.

The telephone's ring interrupted his musings. "Sir, I've been contacted by a Chinese official. He would like to meet with you on a matter that concerns both our nations. He would also like a representative of the United States and the European Union to be included. He suggests that he could speak to an American contact, a staff member in the office of one of their senators, and hopes that you might speak to someone in the EU."

"Curious. Why me? And why would he want to meet with all those people? Did he say when?"

"He hoped that you would suggest a date, but asked me to tell you that sooner would be better. He is concerned about an issue that affects space policy of both our nations."

"Did he say where he wants to do this? I'm not interested in going back to China. The place is too crowded, too polluted. Let them come here."

"Sir, that might not be possible. If the press found out..."

"I see what you mean. Well, not there, not here, and certainly not in the USA. No, this proposed meeting might not even be possible. Can't he send a message through the diplomatic pouch if he's concerned about security?'

"He said that a face-to-face meeting was necessary."

"You're remarkably well informed, Evgeny! What's going on here?"

"I've acted as a conduit before, minister. Your predecessor often used my contacts."

"Deputy minister, Evgeny. Why was I not told of this?"

"I believe it was in the briefing papers, sir. Our superiors know of my experience."

"You're saying I should have read that stack of boring documents, aren't you?"

"No sir. I would never suggest that."

"Well, no matter. Do we have a place where a low-level meeting might be conducted without being spied on?"

"Similar meetings have happened in Baku, sir."

"In Azerbaijan? Backward place! Why there?"

"It is quite isolated, sir. Very little of interest to the press goes on there. The Chinese official who contacted me, Chu Dien, has been there before."

"Meeting my predecessor, I suppose. It's not that far from Moscow, so transportation wouldn't be a problem. We've got enough left in the budget to cover the trip, I expect. I would only be gone a day or two, three at the most. What of the European? Do you have a suggestion?"

"I do. He's German, a man named Willi Kraenkel, but he works for the EU. Some sort of financial analyst, I believe."

"We do a lot of business with the EU, so we don't want to upset that. Neither of us would enjoy what might happen, Evgeny. With that caution, go ahead and see what you can arrange. I'll want at least a week's warning, preferably two. No surprises, Evgeny."

"I'll see to it, sir."

Deputy Minister Zlotov looked after him sourly. *Uppity clerk. Who did he know? More important, who was using him, and for what?*

* * *

CHUCK MET the chief engineer of NFI's spaceship design section in Rovaniemi. He was using Frenchy's office today; Frenchy was in Reykjavik and wasn't expected back for two days.

"Afternoon, Chuck. I was reading your proposal. That's quite a change you've got in mind, and that idea of hauling ice to the moon by linking barges together is intriguing. If we can make it work."

"I have confidence in you, Pete. So what do you think of the proposal."

"Not much, to be honest. Putting the hatch on the bottom, that's not difficult, but I'm curious why."

"It makes it easier to load and discharge cargo, Pete. We can also do without the two flight crewmen, reducing costs per flight. It also reduces the chance of the crew being exposed to radiation. We're not like other ships, we can hover, and the flight computers allow very precise control. What I'd like to do is package four fuel rods with insulation between them. The copilot would open the hatch, the pilot hovers over the package and descends until the copilot is able to engage the locks, then lift high enough to close the cargo hatches. I was thinking you could work with the Japanese to design the fuel rod pack, then have your guys make up a dummy so the crew has a chance to practice loading it. I wouldn't want to try the first hookup with a live cargo.

"There's another reason; there was a problem during the first flight. Will thought about dumping the cargo...it was heavier than outlined in the specifications, and had it been only a little heavier it could have crashed *Gypsy*...but Wolfgang was the pilot, and he wanted to keep going. He got away with it, but next time? Far better to dump the cargo than have it *and* the ship crash in the ocean. Or over land, for that matter."

"You're talking about a single-use ship to haul only one kind of cargo. Why even bother with a hatch? Suppose we make the cargo bay modular, so that when loaded it becomes part of the ship. We'd have to strengthen the dorsal frame and the two lateral frame members, but we'd save weight if we could eliminate the handling arm."

"Wouldn't that increase the expense, dumping a special-purpose container."

"It would, but how many would you really dump in space? I hear rumors that you plan on discharging cargo elsewhere."

"You know about that, do you?"

"Yeah, engineers talk, you should know that. That one-cycle diesel? They'll never get it to work."

"You a betting man, Pete? Some might think you could never get the new ship design to work. Not to mention a space train using modular barges."

"Point. I'll give you a hundred, Chuck. What odds?"

"Odds, Pete? Get serious!"

* * *

THE OLD RANCH house was lonely. Lina was on her way to Australia; she and her doctor had jointly decided that she should go now or wait until after the babies were born. The house seemed double empty without Lina.

Chuck opened a beer, then changed his mind. Pouring it down the sink, he put the bottle in the trash and grabbed his hat, then clipped the Sig-Sauer .380 to his belt; rattlesnakes had moved into the area, now that no one lived full-time at the ranch. Chuck followed the path leading to the small cemetery a quarter mile from the house. His grandparents were buried there, as were Mel's ashes. None of his relatives had wanted to make the decision, so Panit had made it for them and Chuck had seen to interring Mel's remains. Hopefully, this would be the last grave in the tiny hilltop cemetery.

Chuck pulled a couple of weeds, then looked beyond the graves. Was it really necessary to come here? Morty, Mary Ellen, and Mel lived on in his memories. This deserted hillock was no more than a place where bodies could be disposed of. But he couldn't make up his mind. What would Morty have thought of the idea? Would he have wanted Chuck to visit their graves?

Finally, still undecided, he headed back to the house. This time he drank a beer, then another, moodily waiting for the sun to go down. The silent house waited, empty, lonely.

It was past midnight before Chuck went inside.

* * *

FRENCHY GOT BACK to Rovaniemi late Friday and managed to catch Pete before he left for the weekend. "If you're not in too much of a hurry, I've got a bottle of Lagavulin that needs tasting."

The two sipped the scotch and Pete mentioned that Chuck had been there, but that he was now back in Texas.

"Pete, shouldn't Chuck be here? If he talked to you, wouldn't it make sense for him to be here too?"

"Why, Frenchy? Chuck's a pilot, he's not an engineer. You tell me what you want, I'll tell you if it's doable. Let's keep the working group small, okay?"

"Okay, then. I've got another ship for you to work on."

"One of the guys will do it, but probably not me. I'm pretty busy, working up Chuck's latest brainstorm. Or maybe Chuck's folly. Is this another cargo hauler?"

"Yes, and no. I want you to design a flying saucer."

"First question, why? What does the saucer shape have to do with hauling cargo to the moon?"

"Not to the moon, Pete. We're going interplanetary."

Pete shook his head. "Not with fuel cells, you're not. Okay, you could do it, but you'd be in free fall all the way. You can't carry enough fuel to boost that far, not at one gee or even a quarter of a gee, not and make it back. You thinking of hanging refueling stations out there in interplanetary space? You'll need bigger solar arrays as you get further away from the sun."

"No, this is different. Have you ever heard of SMR's, small modular reactors?"

"Sure, Los Alamos worked up a couple of designs, but they won't sell them. A number of private companies are working on this too, they got a lot of their design information from Los Alamos, but the last I heard no one had a working model."

"I may have another source, Pete. Keep it under your hat, okay?"

"Why not? I wouldn't want my guys to think I was crazier than I am. Design a ship around a power system that you don't have yet, that's reasonably crazy. I can gin up a few ideas, but how much weight does this saucer have to lift? How big are the reactors? Do you have performance specs, anything at all? Even how much power the SMRs are supposed to produce?"

"I'll let you know as soon as I have the specs, Pete. Get a few ideas down on paper so you won't have to waste time when the reactors are available. Maybe think of a one-reactor design and another that's big enough to need more than one. Morty always wanted three for reliability."

"Would the one-reactor version need to be saucer-shaped?"

"No, the saucer was Morty's idea. He wrote up a prospect sheet, back when I thought we could get reactors from Los Alamos."

"I'll find it if it's in the records. Thanks for the scotch, and I'll give you a call when I've got something worth talking about."

Pete nodded to Frenchy, then left the office. He was a good engineer and a better supervisor, a combination that was unfortunately rare. Maybe that was why he could afford to be prickly toward his nominal boss. Frenchy grinned after him, then left to put out a few fires of his own. It was amazing how many things went wrong when he was out of the office!

* * *

WOLFGANG ALBRECHT FOUND Will at his desk, working on the stack of papers that seemed never to shrink. Even in the age of computers, paper ruled.

"Got a minute, Will?"

"Sure, Wolfgang. Want a cup of coffee? I just made a fresh pot."

"Thank you, yes. I wish you'd try European coffees, Will. Yours are quite strong."

"Maybe I will. I can always stock a few pounds for when you visit. What's on your mind? Is there a problem with *Gypsy*?"

"I don't know. Maybe. Mikhail saw something strange, and I wanted to ask you about it."

"Strange?" Will asked, pouring himself a coffee. "Strange how?"

"Have you ever seen a faint glow around the nose of *Farside*?"

"No, never. I've only flown her a few times, so if it's not very strong I might have missed it. But Chuck would have seen it, and he hasn't said anything."

"The only time we noticed it was just before we dropped off that second Japanese shipment. Could it have something to do with radiation?"

"I don't know. I suppose we could find out. Feel like flying a water run to the stations and topping their tanks off? You could take a close look, see if you spot this mysterious glow when you're hauling something that's not radioactive." Will paused, thinking.

"If the glow is faint, you might have seen it because you were out beyond lunar orbit. It's pretty dark out there, you don't even get much reflection from the Earth since you're above the plane of the ecliptic. If something's going on with the ship, that would make it easier to see. There's a kind of glow, Cherenkov radiation it's called, in the pools where they cool the reactor rods. But that only happens when there's a lot of radiation. Your hair isn't falling out, is it?"

"Don't joke. I'm worried, I don't know what this is. It might even be my imagination."

"There's nothing radioactive about the impellers, and you said he saw the glow where the impellers are. The larger ones are aft by the wing roots, the smaller attitude control impellers are in the nose. It can't be the radar, that's not radioactive either, and you wouldn't see anything near the stern. Didn't some of the early Apollo and Gemini missions mention lights?"

"I don't remember, maybe it happened during the shuttle flights. I'd have to check. There's another possibility, but I'd have to run that through the engineering staff. They might have an idea."

"Is it dangerous? Do you think it's something that could endanger *Gypsy*?"

"I doubt it. You've made two long flights with no problems. Any computer glitches?"

"Nein... ah, no. They function as they're supposed to. The impellers too, even the cabin controls work as they should. Flying *Gypsy* is quite comfortable. But I don't understand this glow, and things I don't understand worry me."

"That's understandable, Wolfgang. Look, would you rather I flew the next mission? I'll see if Chuck's available to copilot."

"No, I think it better that he fly off our wing. Let him photograph the glow. Perhaps it is nothing. We might be imagining things. The cargo, it is dangerous. The Japanese admitted that the first cargo was more radioactive than it should have been. Would you like to fly the water replenishment mission?"

"I think I should. Just to be sure. If you don't mind?"

"Then I will fly as copilot. I can evaluate how well *you* function as commander this time!"

5

Lina reached for her phone as the agent announced that the aircraft was boarding. Frenchy answered on the second ring. She inched forward while carrying on the conversation.

"Dad, I'm off to Brisbane. I'm not sure..." Lina's voice was soft.

"I think Chuck's right, honey. The only thing keeping you safe is that the opposition isn't looking for you. You have to expect that sooner or later they'll find you. Think of the babies."

"I know. If I wasn't pregnant, I'd be with Chuck."

"You'd have a hard time keeping up, the way he gets around."

"Yeah, I noticed that," Lina said dryly. "They're about to take my ticket, so I have to go."

"First class, right?"

"Right, I need the room. The twins have a habit of kicking at the wrong time! Anyway, there was one more thing I wanted to ask. Did you finalize that sale?"

"I did. The power plant sold, and that means we're almost out of New

Mexico. The factory is closed and the ranch has only a caretaker crew. They'll watch the buildings, make sure vandals don't damage anything. I'm trying to sell the factory, but so far, no serious buyers. I don't know, I may decide to just keep the old ranch. Taxes are low, so it's not a drain on resources.

"But the power plant was sold, and I paid off the last of our debt with the cash. We also got a chunk of stock, which I decided to keep for the time being. We're a minority stockholder right now, but if more comes on the market, I'll see what I can do. Maybe gain enough for de-facto control?

"Speaking of stock, Sol's got a nasty shock coming if I ever gain control of his board of directors. I've quietly picked up a considerable number of shares, and as of now, I'll only need another five percent to call a meeting of the board and kick his sorry ass out."

"My, you do hold a grudge, don't you? I've got to go, dad, I'll call you when I'm settled."

"Enjoy Brisbane, Lina. Look around for property, but don't jump too soon. Make sure it's what you want."

"I will, dad. Bye."

Lina closed the connection and hurried down the long boarding tunnel, the last first-class passenger to board.

* * *

WILL UNLOCKED THE CONTROLS, then began the power-up checklist. Wolfgang watched, following his own checklist.

"Radios, Wolfgang?"

"Stand by. *Gypsy* to *Farside*, radio check."

"Five by five, Wolfgang, I'm picking you up through the satellite relay network. On station and waiting."

"Copy on station, Chuck. Checkout is almost finished, we'll launch in about two minutes. Say fuel status."

"Topped off, Wolfgang. I detoured by Station One while I was waiting."

"We won't need to refuel. Pete said that since we were off on a joyride, we might as well put auxiliary fuel and oxy tanks in the bay. Plenty of room since we're not carrying cargo, not even water. We decided it wasn't necessary. Will wants to boost at two gees, see how *Gypsy* handles with most of the weight aft."

"Copy two gees. We're in orbit, waiting."

"Roger. *Gypsy* out."

Will's takeoff bore little resemblance to his usual practice. As soon as *Gypsy's* nose approached vertical, he added power. The big ship responded, heading directly for orbit. *Farside* was now behind the Earth. Will intended to be in position by the time she came around again.

"*Farside, Gypsy*. Chuck, be prepared to break orbit and boost, I'm not slowing down. We'll go out past the satellite belt, get out where we can see what's going on. I'll have the cameras recording by the time you're in position. I'm picking you up on radar but I don't see anything unusual. Okay, I've got you visually, but I'm not picking up a glow."

"No glow, understood. Well, maybe it's only *Gypsy*. We're wearing electronic dosimeters and we've got film badges as backup. The Geiger counter is recording, sound is off. We'll find out how much radiation we picked up after we land."

"Copy dosimeters and Geiger counter, *Gypsy* same."

"Sounds good, Will. Okay, I've got you on visual, and you're definitely showing a blue glow. It's faint around the nose, but it seems to flow back along the fuselage until it reaches the aft impeller section. It's a lot brighter there. My impellers are spooling up, reverse thrust, speed is dropping, holding orbit with the impellers...rotating ship...okay, we're heading for you. Intercept course, estimate half an hour. Will...wait one...okay, I've got that same blue glow. Right now I'm at two and a half gee thrust and I can see the glow clearly. I'll see what I can get from the camera display. I'll also get a video record to compare with yours. Recommend we reduce thrust."

"Roger, Chuck, reducing thrust. Coming to one gee...okay, I'm at one gee. What do you see?"

"The glow is still there, Will. Check your Geiger counter output, if you would. If we're picking up radiation, our space careers just got cut permanently short."

"Roger. Wolfgang's checking now. Wait one." The radio emitted only the usual faint hiss of background noise.

"Chuck, Wolfgang's looking at the readout. We're getting *less* radiation, not more."

"Less radiation? That's a surprise. I'd say we've got the information we wanted, it's not just *Gypsy* and it has nothing to do with the cargo. Are you ready to head back?"

"Right, where to you want to land?

"I'll meet you in Finland. *Farside* out."

"*Gypsy* out."

Will changed course and headed down, passing through the upper atmosphere over the western Baltic Sea.

The radio clicked as the satellite tone opened the circuit. "*Gypsy, Farside*."

"*Gypsy* here. Problems, Chuck?"

"No. I asked Pete to meet us. He suggested Dolph would be more likely to know what's going on, so he's coming too. Dolph's the theoretician, but Pete will be the guy that has to design a fix if we need one. They should get there about as soon as we ground in Reykjavik."

"That's fast. They were lucky getting a flight."

"They didn't. *Grasshopper* is operational, she just finished her shakedown cruise."

"Wow, three ships in one place! Morty would have been proud. First time?"

"I think so. Diverting to Iceland at this time. Beware of *Grasshopper*, they'll be coming in and they may be a bit later than Pete said. I think they'll be down before we get there, but no use taking chances."

"I try not to, Chuck. *Gypsy* out."

"*Farside* out."

* * *

THE CAMERA RECORDINGS had just finished their second playback. The men were watching the monitor as playback began for the third time.

Pete was worried. "I don't like this. We don't know what's going on. I don't have any ideas at this point. That's why I brought Dolph, I wanted to hear what he had to say before I finalized any of the new designs."

Chuck and Will had brought their copilots to the meeting. Wolfgang doodled on a pad in front of him, Frodo watched as Dolph opened his laptop computer.

"What's that, Dolph? I don't recognize the model."

"It's new, first one off the production line. One of Intel's divisions produced it and the manager let me borrow it. I had to promise him a ride to space."

"Unusual?" asked Frodo.

"About as unusual as your name, Frodo. Frodo Baggett...your parents had a sense of humor! Anyway, this one has the new firmware. The CPU is part of the first quantum-based chipset."

"Fuck you, Dolph, I told you to knock off the jokes about my name! My mom was still woozy after the delivery and I think the old man was drunk. By the time she found out, the name was registered. She got even, though. He had a set of Tolkien first editions. She put the lot in the fireplace and burned them. The old man was fit to be tied!"

"I would have been, too. I'd probably have divorced her."

"He did. Anyway, you've got a new computer. Faster?"

"Oh, yes. It's the fastest laptop in existence and it has the computing power of a minicomp."

"You're not talking about a personal PC, right?"

"No, the workstation mini. It seems like all I have to do is hit the enter key and the answer is already there. Scary. Anyway, Will, I may have an idea. I looked at the Geiger counter's log. You had impellers on when you went through the Van Allen belts, but there was no increase in radiation. The only time radiation increased was while you were in zero gee, turning the ship to head for home. The only conclusion I see is that the blue glow acts like a radiation shield."

"I expected we'd need better shielding on the moon, but I thought the ship's hull provided enough protection for space flight."

"Yes, and no. The hull stops the particulate radiation, the alpha and beta particles, but that's all. There's some x-ray and gamma getting through. Pete, that's something for your guys to work on."

"I'll look into it, Dolph. But what is that glow?"

"Best I can figure, Pete, it's a thin plasma. I doubt there's much total heat involved, but there's more than enough electrical charge to capture or deflect charged particles. They're probably what's causing the glow. There appears to be two fields being generated by the impellers and they join together aft of the crew cabin. Chuck, you can answer this if you would. I'm told the impellers actually grip the fabric of space""

"In a sense, but Einstein might not agree. Grandpa told me about *his* theory, that space is filled with a matrix of interlocking gravitational and electromagnetic fields. He said the impellers try to push the fields, and since that's not possible, the impellers are forced to move by reaction. The matrix fills all of space, so it can't be moved, but objects can move through it. They become part of the matrix in the same way that solar wind particles or comets do."

Dolph paused, deciding how he wanted to phrase his response. "I don't know if he's right. I tried to model that mathematically using the laptop, but I didn't get anywhere. I trust the instruments, though. Your dosimeter and badges indicate lower levels of radiation, and the Geiger counter agrees. I think you'll be protected as long as the impellers are functioning, but you don't want to spend a lot of time in free fall."

"Simple solution to the free fall problem, Dolph," said Pete. "Better crew cabin insulation. I read an article in an engineering journal; the Chinese are experimenting with a plastic foam that they infuse with metals and metalloids. The atoms are scattered throughout the foam, so the process doesn't change the foam appreciably other than that most radiation is blocked. It doesn't last, though. It breaks down in a relatively short time, depending on how much radiation it's exposed to. If you use it in a ship, expect to replace the insulation panels every thousand hours or so. That's an estimate, based on what I expect to find in space. We could replace the insulation panels when we change the door seals.

"There's another option in addition to the foam. The plasma won't stop neutrons, but boron might. One of the boron isotopes absorbs neutrons. Depending on the numbers of linked atoms, you can get boron buckyballs, boron sheets, and that's not even considering oobleck. A layer of boron sheet or oobleck beneath the outer hull would work best. I'll see what I can find out."

"Oobleck? Pete, have you been drinking? Or are you pulling my leg?"

"No, it's real. Kids play with it. Depending on pressure, it flows like a liquid or freezes into a solid. I was thinking of a thin layer between the external hull and the layer of infused foam. I think it's possible to build self-sealing hulls; if the hull is punctured, the pressure would drop and the oobleck would flow to fill in the hole. As soon as it plugged the leak and pressure was restored, it would solidify. I'm still working on the idea, though. Anyway, there's a version of oobleck that uses boron. Chemically, it doesn't matter which isotope is involved, and boron stops neutrons."

"Be nice if it works. But what do you think of Dolph's explanation?"

"It's interesting. I don't know if he's right or not, but the important thing is that the plasma blocks radiation. The insulating panels would last longer, nearly indefinitely, in a low-radiation environment."

"Keep working on it, Pete. Your oobleck wouldn't work for a big hole, the fluid wouldn't have enough structural strength. Radiation on Luna is a slightly different problem, too; some of the time, the Earth is between Luna and the sun, so it acts as a shield. Luna itself blocks radiation about half the time. During the dark period, there should be less radiation. Still, the Apollo astronauts picked up some, half a RAD or so while they were on the moon. We'll need a solution before we can go there to stay. Mars will have its own radiation suite, though probably not as bad. Mars has a thin atmosphere, that helps, and it's a lot further away from the sun. That's the main source of radiation in the solar system, so the farther away you are the less radiation there is. It's an area function, radiation decreases by the square of the distance. Twice the distance from the sun, your radiation exposure drops to one fourth."

"Right," Chuck said dryly.

* * *

LINA TOOK the shuttle bus to the hotel and checked in. She looked around the lobby, realizing that it was much the same as any other hotel's lobby but with a few subtle differences. The clerk behind the counter had a pronounced accent. Lina finally understood, deep inside; she was in Australia. New Mexico, Texas, even the USA was a long way behind her. A faint lingering tension, there since the rape, vanished; it was recognizable only after it went away.

She would miss the old ranch house; she had wonderful memories of the first months after she and Chuck moved in. But Chuck's visits home had become irregular and brief, depending on how often he flew, and now Lina had the unborn twins to think of. A criminal had believed that Lina offered leverage he could use against Frenchy, so wouldn't another crook go after Frenchy's grandchildren? Could Frenchy resist if they kidnapped the babies and demanded the impeller drive in exchange for their lives?

Australia is safer, she thought, *but no place on Earth is truly safe.*

Criminals moved freely about, from nation to nation. She no longer had reason to fear the man with the white streak in his hair, thanks to Chuck, but there were uncounted others. No, even in Australia, she would have to protect herself and her babies. Lina resolved to rent, not buy, but only until she could build a place for her family that was easily defended. The house would feature an armored safe room, such that no one could break in without killing the inhabitants. Killing them would achieve nothing; their only value was as hostages. The thought gave her a pang, that her babies would be at risk. But the statistics didn't lie; even if Frenchy accepted the kidnappers' demands, most victims were killed, not released.

But where to build? Should it be here in Brisbane, or some other place? Was one place in Australia essentially the same as another?

She picked up a map of Brisbane and its suburbs as she left the lobby.

Building a place like she had in mind wouldn't be cheap, but cost really wasn't a consideration. NFI was earning money faster than she would have believed a year ago. The Japanese contract paid well, despite the payments being reduced to half the former amount, but cash was flowing in from other contracts. In addition to removing spent fuel rods, NFI would soon deliver the first components to orbit for Indian and Indonesian space stations, and France had contracted for a thousand launches with an option for more. The majority of the funds would be paid in installments after the cargoes were delivered to space, but the system was working. NFI also had contracts to service the new space stations, as well as transport Indian and Indonesian astronauts to and from the stations. The company still had problems, but money was no longer one of them.

How to start? Probably by finding out what local laws had to say about foreign property ownership.

Could she emigrate, become an Australian? Give up her American citizenship? What did that American passport really mean? What had the US government done for them, other than shut down their factory? What did she owe the country of her birth, now that it had effectively turned on her?

Well. Time enough for that tomorrow. If Australia didn't want her, Canada would. Or for that matter, Singapore. The daughter of the man who essentially owned NFI would not have to go begging.

6

Dolph's voice betrayed his excitement when he called Chuck.

"Chuck, we've detected the glow on Earth. Wolfgang's copilot spotted it because it was so dark out where he was. I'm guessing that the plasma field has been there since the beginning, just so faint that no one noticed it. But there's also another possibility; the atmosphere blocks most of the alpha and beta particles, so there was almost nothing to interact with the plasma. No glow, in other words."

"How did *you* detect it, Dolph?"

"We bolted an impeller to a beam that was inset into the floor of the lab. As soon as we spun up the impeller and turned out the lights, there it was. We didn't get a glow, only a few sparks, but I'd say the field makes a pretty good radiation detector!

"We also measured the plasma's effect on magnetic and electric fields, and both responded. Our results varied with the impeller output, more power generating a stronger response."

"But there was no radiation being generated by the impeller field itself?"

"None. The only problem, and I emphasize it's no more than a possibility, has to do with the radios and radar. Worst case, you'll have to mount the antennas forward of the nose impellers, outside the field. But they've been working so far, and we know they work through the Aurora Borealis and Aurora Australis on Earth, so I doubt it will be necessary."

"Tell your people good job, Dolph. The glow bothered me until you figured out what was happening, but now I'm more worried about radiation in space. What do we know?"

"Quite a lot, actually. There have been a number of rocket flights that measured the Van Allen Belts, for one thing. The glow we're seeing is like what we see on Earth, the aurora effect. Both are caused by solar ions interacting with a magnetic field.

"According to what I know of the impeller drive, it's creating an electromagnetic field that's simultaneously rotating and revolving. You're also generating high voltages, because the field generators are multiple secondary elements of a single Tesla primary coil. The plasma is likely being caused by the high potential.

"Conclusion, the field doesn't hurt you, it protects you. Two things come to mind right off; one, don't shut down the impellers unless you absolutely have to, and two, make better radiation protection part of all future ship designs. From now on, everyone who goes into space wears a dosimeter. Backup film badges wouldn't hurt, either."

"Thanks, Dolph, I'll get with you and Pete later. I was just thinking, rocket boosters are sprayed with foam insulation. Suppose we infuse the foam with metal and metalloid atoms? The insulation would still be lightweight, but now it would provide at least some protection while the impeller field was down. That should be enough for normal conditions, but maybe not from solar storms. I suspect they'd still be dangerous. Even on Earth, strong electromagnetic storms can knock out power lines as well as shut down communications. The good news is they don't happen by surprise; astronomers know when they're coming. Even coronal mass ejections are predictable, within limits. Solution, make space weather part of our checklists, just like airline pilots do. They get a weather briefing before every flight. If ships are already in space, maybe the impeller field will protect them. That won't help on the moon, though, meaning I'll have to rethink my ideas for a lunar habitat."

"Put it underground, Chuck, that's what NASA had in mind. The Apollo guys picked up some exposure on the surface, and it's cumulative. Even a small amount can add up to a lethal dose over time."

"Where are we going to house the people while they're building Moonbase, Dolph?"

"I'll come up with something. First idea, explosives. Blow a hole, dig out the rubble...easy to do in a sixth of a gee...then put an insulated cap over the top."

"Doable, I think. What kind of explosives?

"Probably shaped charges made of molded plastic explosive. What do you know about explosives?"

"Some. I used them in Iraq. Most of the time, we used blocks of TNT or C4. You just pinch off as much of the C4 as you need, mold it like putty, and stick a cap in. Hook up the clacker, bang. Nothing to it."

"A shaped charge directs some of the blast into a cone-shaped jet. It uses something called the Munroe Effect to contain the blast and focus it."

"Do I need to know about this? You build it, I'll blow it."

"It'll be done from orbit, Chuck. You can't predict where the ejecta will go. Keep that sixth of a gee gravitational field in mind. Expelled rocks go a long way, at least six times as far as you think they will. That's partly because of the low gravity, but also there's no atmosphere to slow anything down. The safest thing to do is set the charge, back way off, then watch it blow. You know this is going to create a dust cloud, don't you? Telescopes on Earth will see what you're doing."

"I doubt it. Moonbase will be on the side away from Earth."

"If that's what you want. Keep in mind that the far side collects more meteor hits."

"Most of those happened a long time ago, Dolph. If we put Moonbase on the Earthside, nosy neighbors will be watching. On the far side, we might get hit by a falling rock, but that's pretty unlikely."

"Your choice. That dust cloud will hang around a long time before it settles, so if anyone sends up a rocket, they'll see it."

"Unless they see the explosion when it happens, it's just dust. It could have been caused by a meteor strike."

"What about the ship? Are you going to conceal it?"

"No. I'll need it to install a commo link with the satellite system and probably to haul supplies. Waste of time I think, trying to hide it. If anyone is out there, they'll notice the movement. That need for a commo link means a repeater at the boundary between nearside and farside. I haven't selected the site for Moonbase yet, but so long as it has direct line of sight to the repeater, any communication would be sent on to the satellites. Not a problem, in other words."

"Do it this way, then. Set up your communications system first, because you'll need to be able to message Earth. Then use several shaped charges, big ones. Link them with detonating cord, fire the det cord from the middle so the shaped charges blow simultaneously. Depending on how that goes, figure on using secondary charges, maybe five to ten kilos of TNT each. Put the charges beneath the broken rock, and that will clean out the craters. Plastic explosives have high brisance, shattering effect, while TNT is a slow explosive that's better for kicking rocks out of holes. Wait a day or two after the first explosion to give the rocks time to fall back to the surface, any that are going to. If you wait long enough, it won't be a problem. Keep your people under shelter until they've got a fairly-clean hole to work in, and that should solve your radiation problem."

"You mentioned a large shaped charge, Dolph. How large?"

"That will be up to whoever you hire to blow the holes. Maybe a hundred kilos, I haven't worked it out yet."

"That's...two hundred and twenty five pounds!"

"About that, yes. You don't want to be living in a rabbit hole, do you?"

LINA SPENT the first two weeks getting acclimated to Brisbane. She found she liked the Australians, liked their relaxed attitude and upbeat philosophy. She considered buying or renting a car, but decided to wait; Australians drive on the left side, so she thought it might take more time to get comfortable with the traffic. The city was also strange. She knew nothing of roads and traffic patterns, other than that the city was laid out around Bramble and Moreton bays.

Having decided, Lina hired a car and driver. Traffic rules were also different; eventually, she would become familiar with the system, but for now she preferred a driver who could also serve as guide.

THE MAN WAS TALL, thin, and balding. He was also old enough to have grown a respectable set of wrinkles, most of them around his eyes and the sides of his mouth. Lina decided he smiled a lot, and more than likely spent a lot of time outdoors. He wore a battered brown hat, tipped back, and loose, comfortable clothing.

"G'day, luv. Front seat or back?"

"Front, for now. Do all Australians wear those hats, Mac?"

"You wear what you please, luv. I drive a lot of tourists, ya see, and they expect me to look like Croc Dundee, ay. The Akubra Snowy River helps me image."

Lina laughed delightedly. "So you dress up for the tourists, do you?"

"It doesn't hurt, luv. The hat's comfortable, now that I've bashed it around a bit, and the sun can be a bother this time of year. Rain, too. If yer a long-time banana bender, you expect rain this time of year, ay."

"Banana-bender, Mac?"

"Queenslander, luv. Lived here all my life. I wouldn't be happy anywhere else."

"You don't like other cities?"

"Brisbane is just right, I'm thinking. Not too hot, not too cold. Down south, they get more rain and 'tis a tad cooler, up north it gets bloody hot and muggy. Western Australia does too, and as for the outback, you can dry up and blow away out there. A man works up a good thirst and some think that a blessin', thems that like a cold tinny. But I make m' livin' drivin', and I can't afford problems with the booze bus, ay."

"You almost speak English," exclaimed Lina.

"Here, now, luv, that's no way to talk! I might say the same thing about you, y'know!"

Mac entered the stream of traffic, expertly negotiating lane changes. "We'll start with the city proper, north of the river. After lunch, you might like to see the South Bank. The Queensland Museum and the Sciencentre are worth a long look, and there's the Gallery of Modern Art if yer taste runs to that. We could schedule a trip to Mount Coot-tha, the Botanic Gardens are first-rate, ay."

"I'd rather see just one of the museums today, if you don't mind. If you're free tomorrow, I'd like to look at some of the nicer neighborhoods. I'm considering relocating."

"Are you, now? Well, Brisbane is top-notch, you can't do better. Got everything a body could want, and it's not like what yanks are used to at all. You need to watch for the snakes and such, spiders too, but yer neighbors hereabouts are likely to be friendly, ay. I hear they're as likely to shoot you in America as invite you over for a barbie."

"It's not like that, Mac. Oh, it happens, but..." Lina's face grew suddenly pale. She remembered that Chuck had been involved in a shootout.

"Is anything the matter, lass? I noticed you're preggers, do you need me to run by the doctor?"

"No, I'm all right. It was nothing. Perhaps it was something I ate."

"Aye, that can do it. Aussie brekkies can be a bit much until you get used to 'em. I'll slow down and pull over, you'll likely be right in a moment or so, ay."

* * *

TIM BENTSEN SWORE. Another film wasted; what could be the problem? The big telescope was focused off to the side, so it couldn't be reflected light from the moon. Could they have gotten a bad batch of film, or had light somehow leaked through the paper wrapping? Supposedly the chemically-treated paper was light-proof, but *something* was wrong. The image should have held stars; instead, a bluish haze covered most of the photo.

Tossing the ruined image atop the others he'd taken, he headed for the storeroom. There was usually a case of film somewhere about. If not, maybe one of the electronic cameras was available. They were usually booked up, but maybe he could wheedle a few minutes exposure time.

An hour later, Tim stared at the image. The blue haze was still there, but so was something else. A stubby winged shape, some sort of spacecraft, floated within the light. Could it be one of those NFI spaceships? But that was unlikely; any number of newspapers had run images, and none of them looked like this. Their ships carried dangerous cargoes to space and sent them on toward the sun; what would one of their ships be doing all the way over there? He scratched his chin, then went looking for the senior astronomer assigned to this shift. Maybe he would know something.

Putting down the hand lens, Franz Kehr, PhD, rubbed his eyes.

"It could be," he muttered. "I agree, NFI's ships shouldn't be there, but the only other choice is that this *isn't* one of theirs. It might be some sort of hush-hush military project, but that still leaves me wondering, because we usually get warning of a launch. Could this one have been orbiting the moon? I'm *certain* we'd know if there was a moon shot scheduled. It's common courtesy, and they're pretty reliable.

He scratched his chin reflectively, wishing that he hadn't given up his pipe. Tobacco could be a comfort at a time like this. "Maybe a Russian or a Chinese ship? But the Russians are still flying Soyuz capsules, and they look nothing like this. The Chinese don't even have that. Tentative conclusion, Tim, you just may have photographed the very first real unidentified flying object. Maybe even one from outer space."

"I don't believe it, Doctor Kehr. What are the odds?"

"If you'll pardon my saying so, Tim, astronomical. Pardon the pun, I mean. Still, Q.E.D.; The facts speak for themselves."

"My career is ruined! I'll always be the guy behind the tabloid articles, not the one who found an Earthlike planet around Alpha Centauri!"

"There's another solution, Tim. Say nothing."

"But shouldn't this be reported, Doctor Kehr?"

"It will be. I'll let it slip, but at the same time I'll deny that either of us had anything to do with it. You *could* take the credit, but as you say, the reaction might be unfortunate. You're still very new, very untried. Some will accuse you of faking the photo."

"You don't mind taking care of it?"

"I'll make a note in my journal, but I won't go public just yet. I'll deliberately leak it to one of the tabloids later on, perhaps in England. They're a feisty bunch, they'll publish anything. I'll just leave a note with the photo saying it was taken by an astronomer. That way, if any honor is to eventually come to someone, you can step forward. I'll corroborate the find, and the journal entry will prove our statements."

"Thank you, doctor. Thank you very much."

As it happened, Doctor Kehr posted a very short entry. 'Unusual object photographed', followed by the date and time. He could always mention Tim's name later on. On the other hand, if someone interpreted the find as happening during his, Kehr's shift, and perhaps concluded that he'd been the finder, well, that could always be cleared up with a few sentences. And hadn't he advised Tim regarding the find? Shouldn't an adviser receive some of the credit for risking his reputation?"

Yes, this was clearly the best way to deal with it. Doctor Kehr closed the journal and returned it to his desk. There were other images to capture, and precious little darkness remaining.

7

E vgeny knocked on the office door, then entered.

"Minister Zlotov, there has been a communication. Should I come back later?"

"No, let's have it now. Communication from whom?"

"It came from the American we met, Mister Pinchot Forberger. He works for one of their senators. He's a staff member I believe, which is how he came to the information."

"And what did Staffer Forberger have to say?"

"A spacecraft has been detected, Minister. One of their astronomers actually got a photo."

"Really? Where was this spacecraft?"

"Near the moon, minister. It may have come from the moon, or it may have come from interplanetary space."

"One of the NFI ships, you think?"

Evgeny was cautious when he replied. "I think so. It looks like the one General Stroganoff attempted to capture. But this one is surrounded by a blue glow, and there was no sign of that when we photographed the other ship. That picture was taken from orbit."

"Let me think." Deputy Minister Zlotov turned and looked moodily out of the window. Most of the snow was gone, the rest would melt in a few weeks. A few hardy flowers poked through the newly-thawed ground. Another ship? They were springing up like the flowers!

"Evgeny, where could this ship have come from? I shall be honest with you, we have nothing like this in development. I would know. How could the Americans discover something so unheard of?"

"I do not know, Minister. General Stroganoff believed they had discovered antigravity. Moreover, they appear to have a working model."

"Impossible. That's so far in advance of our knowledge that something else has to be going on."

"There was speculation some time ago that the American military was testing a hypersonic airplane, minister. A new kind of jet engine powered the craft, if the theoreticians were correct. At such speeds, the air blows out the jet flame, so conventional designs do not work. The jets they used generated intense heat, meaning that the exhaust showed a purplish tinge."

"Yes, I recall that. But the purple color was *only* in the exhaust. We know what caused that, it's new but not revolutionary. No, that can't be it, but perhaps that is where we will find the answer. Evgeny, where do the Americans hide their new developments while they test them? Where do their test flights originate from?"

Evgeny was hesitant. "Do you mean the facility in Nevada, Minister?"

"I do. What do they call that place, Evgeny?"

"I do not recall, Minister. Is it important?"

"I think so! What was the name of that film, the one that featured an extraterrestrial?"

"I believe it was called *Independence Day*, minister. But it was only a film. It revealed nothing new. The spaceship in the photo looks nothing like the giant craft in that movie. It also looks nothing like the one that flew away from General Stroganoff after his helicopter was shot down."

"Misdirection, Evgeny! Are the Americans wise enough to release a film so their people become accustomed to learning about strange creatures? Was the film an attempt to mislead us, make us believe we were seeing movie props instead of real, functioning, extraterrestrial spaceships? And where was the craft located, the one we saw in the satellite photos?"

"It was in one of their poorer regions, minister. I can find the answer."

"I remember it, Evgeny! It's why I am an important minister and you are just a clerk, I remember important things! The device was in New Mexico!"

"Of course, minister, I should have remembered that. But why is that significant?"

"What *else* is in New Mexico, Evgeny? Think, man!"

"Mister Robert Goddard conducted liquid rocket experiments there, and a man recently parachuted to earth from a balloon. Actually, the balloon only lifted the gondola to space. He jumped from that, not the balloon itself. The man was an adventurer, not even an American, Minister."

"No, no, Evgeny! The place is a hotbed of testing! Their rockets are fired from the proving ground and even the first atomic bomb was set off there! But there are persistent claims that a flying saucer landed during the Great Patriotic War, and the location is very near to where we photographed the spaceplane. They deny it, of course, but consider, Evgeny! What if they recovered an interplanetary craft intact? Or at least one that's undamaged enough that they could discover its means of propulsion! What would they do with it, Evgeny?"

"Send it to the White Sands Cosmodrome minister?"

"Perhaps they did, at least in the beginning. But then they moved it to Nevada, to this Area 51! The film was only a clever red herring, Evgeny! We must tell our Chinese friends of our discovery! Just think, Evgeny, you could become a colonel and I could become a full general!"

"If you say so, minister. Shall I telephone the others?"

"Not the American. He may not know the truth, or he may be concealing it, but in either case he's too close to their government. We must not let him know we've discovered their secret. Telephone the others, ask if a meeting at this time is convenient. Same location, I think. Set it up, Evgeny."

"Yes, minister." Evgeny shook his head as soon as he left the room. *Colonel, indeed. More likely, I'll wind up sharing a cell in Siberia with this lunatic!*

* * *

Frenchy, Chuck, and Will had lunch at a hotel in Switzerland. After the meal, Frenchy opened the discussion.

"We need to reorganize. Simply put, the job's gotten to be more than I can handle. Will, you've got the most experience with the new birds and you're familiar with the Japanese and French contracts. I want you to take over as general administrator for the contracts, the ones we have and the new ones coming up. You're the new Director of Flight Operations. The new *Insect*-class ships are yours as soon as they come off the assembly line. Pick your own people, but I'd suggest a separate manager for each contract. Chuck, you'll have the *Farside* class ships and you're in charge of the moon project. Don't tie yourself down, get a deputy or two to handle construction and planning. Will's area of responsibility will overlap yours, of course, but I don't see that as a problem. You've been working together all along. Financing for Moonbase will come from Will's contracts, and Will's ships will store rods on the moon, meaning his task is simplified. Hazardous waste will continue to be sent off to the sun. As for the orbiting manned satellites, the countries are still working on those. Chuck, you'll probably handle that. Your *Farside* class ships are better suited for the job.

"Income from our current contracts will pay for the new *Insect* class ships, but as soon as the last one is delivered it will free up additional money for Moonbase. Pete thinks we'll assemble our larger ships on the moon. That means Moonbase is our stepping-stone to outer space. From the moon, our first survey will be to Earth's Trojan points. There's at least one asteroid there, but we won't know whether it's valuable until we get there. Then it's on to Mars. We'll need a base, probably several, to exploit the main asteroid belt." Frenchy paused for a moment.

"There will be some money available immediately, Chuck, so you can get started on Moonbase right away. As for Mars, I expect building to go faster. Our people will use your techniques, the ones you develop while you're building Moonbase. We'll definitely need a larger budget, because I expect we're going to need several bases." Frenchy had leaned back in his chair. Now he sat upright.

"As for me, I'll remain CEO and chairman, as well as be in overall charge of groundside operations. Panit will handle acquisitions, Ben remains Comptroller, Martha is in charge of personnel, including recruiting and training. She will also continue as manager of the Swiss office, which will be expanded and remain our center for non-flight operations. She isn't interested in a pilot's license, so her responsibilities will continue to be ground-based." Frenchy paused to let his statements sink in.

"Questions or comments?" Frenchy sipped his coffee.

"Maybe. Who's in charge of research?" asked Chuck.

"I'll keep that, at least for now. Are you concerned about something?"

"I'm not sure. Dolph sent a follow-up about the blue field. He's detected waves, a sort of oscillation in the field. He also confirmed that the aft impellers control the shape of the field. The nose impellers are smaller, so the field they generate syncs with the field from the aft units, making it pear-shaped. It looks like a single field in the videos, but Dolph believes the joining is not perfect. The impellers generate separate fields, one at the front, one in the rear. They link together as soon as the impellers reach 17% output, and the more output there is the stronger the link becomes. Below that threshold, the field flickers. It's not strong enough to block ions, so the only thing protecting the crew is the cabin shielding. Some time back, we talked about transferring cargo and passengers while ships are under way. At this point, we don't know if it's possible. There's only one way to find out and that's to give it a try. Wolfgang and I will fly the first attempt."

Frenchy tapped his finger on the table. "Chuck, I'm not sure that's wise. Two of our most experienced commanders, including a director of the company and head of lunar operations? We can't afford to lose you."

"Frenchy, can I sit back and let someone else take all the chances? That's not the kind of leadership I learned in the Marines."

"Chuck, that was a long time ago. You're not a Marine now, you're about to be a father, you're the man I'm depending on to build our most-important facility. A lot of other people depend on you too. Generals don't lead from the front, because they're not expendable. It sounds harsh, but it's true. I don't want you flying that mission. If you think Wolfgang should fly it, I'll accept that, but put him in overall command. Let him know that it's up to him, and if he determines it's not feasible then it won't be done. We can always shut down the impellers long enough for transfers. For that matter, he could try it in the atmosphere, say over the Pacific. If something goes wrong, people would have a better chance of living through it if they had parachutes."

Chuck stared at Frenchy, then dropped his eyes.

"Frenchy, we're flying in space, all of the pilots. Everything we do out there is dangerous."

"Agreed, but some dangers should not be undertaken by corporate executives."

* * *

"AND ARE you well this morning, lass?"

"Well enough, I suppose. How do you fare, Mac?"

Mac chuckled. "Learning to speak the Queen's English, are you? I'm well, lass, very well indeed. And where are we off to this morning, ay?"

"I mentioned that we hoped to purchase property here. I'm interested in looking at the better neighborhoods. If I can find a suitable place, I may hire a builder."

"Let me think a bit. What of your husband, luv? When will he be joining you?"

"That's a bit up in the air for now. Oh, there's no problem, he'll be here, but...he flies." *True enough*, she thought. "His schedule takes him to different places around the world."

"Qantas, is it?"

"No, he's a... well, sort of a vice president of a different company. About that neighborhood?"

"We could look at Paddington, lass. It's just nearby to Mount Coot-tha, ay. Gone a bit pricy in recent years, but you might like it. You'll not like the hills, I'm thinking, not with you expecting, but we can still 'ave a look. Old Queenslander houses there, some new ones too. Got a fair number of Yanks living there nowadays, ay. But again, 'tis not cheap."

"How pricy, Mac?"

"A million and up, lass. There are banks to deal with the financials, and property changes hands often so they're prepared to loan on a purchase, ay. Can your husband's salary handle that?"

"If we find what we're looking for, yes."

"Well, then. I should have asked for more to drive you around, I'm thinking!"

Lina smiled as Mac chuckled. "And will you sit up front or in the back, luv?"

"The back, this time. I'll get a better view, being able to look out both sides."

"I'll just drive along Caxton Street, then. It will take us through Lower Paddington, along Given Terrace, then it changes to Latrobe Terrace and Upper Paddington. It's a pleasant place, is Paddington. The governor, of Queensland I mean, has his official residence there at Government House. I'm not sure whether he lives there, because it's been around a fair while, the old place. It was renovated a few years ago. It's open to the public twice a year, on Australia Day and Queensland Day. Government House Open Day, they call it, ay."

Minutes later, Mac pointed out a row of buildings. "That's Old Queenslander style, luv. It's passing, nowadays. People want new things, ay. Pity, that," said Mac.

"They're lovely! Very colorful, Mac. But I doubt they're for sale."

"Well, this being Paddington, you never know. But it's likely you're right. I'll just go on a bit further, ay. Maybe all the way out to the suburbs, maybe Burpengary."

Mac paused to allow a car to pull in ahead.

"Lots of shops, lots of restaurants. More sheilas than blokes in Paddington, I hear. Younger crowd, too. There are schools, parks, and of course Paddington's not so far from the city. The business district, I mean. Then there's Red Hill, a bit further on, and Petrie Terrace. Lots of hills, d' ye see, so terrace is a common name hereabouts. Separate villages they were, ay. Is this the sort of place you would be happy in?"

"I'm not sure yet. I don't want to make up my mind just yet. You were right, there are a lot of hills. It's all up and down, and when we're not climbing we're turning, so I'm leaning to one side or the other!"

"No help for it, luv. Would you like to go back to the city? Not so hilly there, if you're uncomfortable."

"Perhaps we should. I'm feeling somewhat queasy. I've never been bothered by car sickness, but that may be what's happening. I think I'd like to go back to the hotel. We can go out again this afternoon."

"Just as you say, luv. I'll take it slow, that may help, ay."

Mac turned on Enoggera Terrace road, and true to his word, drove as slowly as traffic permitted. A few minutes later he approached Route 31.

"I'll have you at your hotel in no time, luv. Are you feeling a bit better?"

"I'm not sure, Mac. But I'm glad we cut the tour short."

Mac turned toward downtown and increased speed, glancing in the rear view mirror. Something was clearly not right.

"Lass?"

"I'm sorry, Mac. I wasn't due...Mac, is there a hospital nearby?"

"Aye, there is. Just past the M3 Motorway we'll reach Saint Andrews, ay. Is it your time, luv?"

"I think so, Mac. I'm afraid the seat's a mess."

"Not to worry, lass. Let's get you checked in, they'll see you right in no time."

8

he looks tired, Frenchy thought. Lina was awake, but not speaking. She held Chuck's hand.

"How are you feeling, honey?" asked Frenchy.

Lina stirred. "Not too bad. They're discharging me today, but dad, I can't take my babies. The hospital wants to keep them a few more days to make sure they're healthy. I tried to tell them that the premature births had nothing to do with the babies, just a bumpy ride in a hired car, but they aren't listening."

"I'm not listening either, daughter. Let the experts do their job. They know more about premature babies than you do."

"That's what I said, Frenchy," said Chuck. "She didn't want to listen to me. Maybe you'll have better luck."

"I did some research during the flight; doctors believe that babies born as little as two weeks before full term are more likely to suffer from allergies, other problems too. Let the medical people do what they're supposed to, Lina. Time enough for you to be a full-time mother when the hospital says the babies can go home. Have you named them yet?" This was directed to Lina and Chuck.

"I thought of Charles and Charlotte, or maybe Charlene, but I decided I liked Robert and Roberta. So I made the choice," said Lina.

"I didn't get consulted, but I like Robert and Roberta too, now that I think of it. Bobby and Robbie, more than likely. The full names are more formal, but I don't want to raise our kids in a formal atmosphere."

"I agree. You're going to apply for Australian citizenship, Lina? What about you, Chuck?"

"Maybe. I haven't decided. To be honest, I may just explore something different. I was thinking of renouncing my American citizenship and becoming stateless. I expect more people will do that after we've got Moonbase up and running. I may be the first lunar citizen, or maybe the first Martian."

"I can think of a few advantages," agreed Frenchy. "But what about the children?"

"That's the only thing holding me back. It's possible they might have dual citizenship, Australian and American, but I haven't looked into it yet. I'm in no hurry. Some things I like about America, some things I don't, not the way things are now."

Chuck's face darkened. "Our factory is shut down, not because we did anything wrong but because politicians were bribed." He paused. "I wish I could see things changing, but it's the same old, same old. If NFI was still based in the US, we'd be under constant threat. We may not be done with them even now."

Frenchy's cell buzzed. He looked at the caller's ID in annoyance. "I told them not to forward my calls!"

"Frenchy here. Why are you calling?" His tone was abrupt. He listened, then interrupted briefly. "Is he going to be okay?"

Another pause. Frenchy now looked worried. "Keep me advised. See if Martha can take over, at least temporarily." Moments later Frenchy closed out the connection.

"Is something wrong?" asked Chuck.

"There's been a hijacking. Will's been taken to a hospital. He's unconscious."

Frenchy took a deep breath. "The hijackers tried to fly the ship on battery power and crashed it."

"How could they do that? The boards are locked."

"The phone call came from Will's deputy," said Frenchy. "He's a pilot, so he's familiar with the flight systems. He thinks the pumps never got switched on, so the fuel cells couldn't have worked. The hijackers would have had battery power, because that switch isn't locked; Wolfgang didn't want to chance of pilots being locked out, so the latest version only locks out the switches for the pumps. The computers have their own separate batteries, small ones, but that's enough for emergency control. The idea is that the crew would still be able to fly the bird while they work around a problem. Anyway, the hijackers got almost to Cherbourg before they crashed."

"As to flying one of our ships, we never tried to hide the control system when we flew the DARPA missions. We also flew people in the airplane, and after the Bedstead crashed the only things we managed to remove from the wreck were the impellers. The Department of Transportation got the rest." Frenchy shook his head. "I wish we'd thought ahead, but we didn't. I'm sure there are reports out there if anyone thought to look."

He continued, "Our people had no idea anything unusual was going on, so *Flea* landed and nobody was waiting to meet them. The crew locked the board and went in to scrounge a cup of coffee. Lucky for them; the hijackers might have killed or tortured one to force the other to fly the ship."

"So why didn't they grab the crew anyway?" asked Chuck.

"Maybe they weren't ready. They had just dumped Will, they would have figured the cops were out looking, and I imagine they were pretty excited at the time."

"Yeah," said Chuck. "I never thought of that. So they might have figured they could fly one of our birds, especially if they got anything from Will."

"That's what Will's deputy thinks, and I agree with him."

"What happened to Will?"

"He was already there for a scheduled meeting with the manager in charge of shipping low-level waste. Will wanted the French to adopt a standardized container, but they insist their container is good enough, it's our job to haul it. Anyway, a taxi dropped him off at the plant. He told his deputy he intended to pick up some stick time by catching a ride back with Flea. The deputy called the plant after he heard what happened, and they told him that half a dozen men approached the gate, knocked the guard cold, and grabbed Will. The plant's people called the police, but no one thought to notify us. The police never got there; it's a fairly rural area, they don't have many officers available, so they did the best they could. The few officers they had were put out to block the access roads, hoping to bag the kidnappers. It's a peninsula, so they were reasonably sure the road-blocks would work." Frenchy glanced at Lina to see how she was taking the news. She didn't appear to be upset, so he continued.

"That's not what happened. Most likely scenario, the kidnappers tried to beat information out of Will. He might have realized they didn't know about the lock and didn't tell them. Maybe they hit him too hard. Anyway, they dumped him, maybe thinking he was dead, then headed back to the plant to intercept whichever ship showed up. Will's deputy thinks that was their plan all along, grab the ship. They were watching the plant, Will showed up, so they snatched him. He was just a target of opportunity; they figured he would fly the ship or at least tell them what they needed to know. Most likely, one of the hijackers was a pilot, maybe all of them were." Frenchy paused to think.

"Anyway, the hatch was open so the hijackers just walked on board. That's when they found out that the board was locked. They had to know that the cops had been called, so they tried to fly the ship on battery and ended up crashing it. The hijackers may have died in the crash; our ships glide like bricks."

"Where did this happen?"

"South of Cherbourg-Octeville. The police are at the scene now, guarding the crash site. If the French government insists on holding *Flea*, we've got serious problems. The crew is still at the reprocessing plant, but they can't get to the crash site for two hours. Meantime, the French may decide to just look around, but they might also decide to grab the impellers."

"How did you get here?"

"*Cicada*. She was in port for a maintenance check, Lina went into labor, so I grabbed her."

"You stay with Lina, I'll take *Cicada*. She's at the airport, right?" Frenchy nodded. "I'll need *Farside* to control the site, and I'll use *Cicada* to recover the impellers."

"Be careful, Chuck. I'd rather not piss off the French if I don't have to. Where will you take the impellers?"

"Orbit first, probably the Moon after that. That's the safest place I can think of. I'll try not to make the French mad, but *Flea* is ours. They won't get the impellers if I get there in time."

"How long?"

"Two, maybe three hours. Flight time is less than an hour from Australia to Finland, it's a simple suborbital hop. I'll pile on the gees, meaning *Cicada* will need refueling as soon as I arrive. I'll pick up

Farside and head for the crash site, so *Cicada* will have to catch up. I'll call the base and have them prep *Farside*."

"Be careful, son. Call me when you get to France."

"I will. Take care of Lina, Frenchy. Baby, I love you, I'll get back as soon as I can."

Chuck reached for his cell phone as he hurried from the room.

"Jochen here."

"This is Chuck. Load the alpha wing pods on *Farside* and preflight her. I want to take off as soon as I get there."

"Jesus, Chuck, both of the pods? That's going to make the ship pretty heavy."

"I might need both. Anyway, it's better having both of them, otherwise I would have balance problems. I'll be there as soon as I can, maybe an hour and a half. Traffic problems are slowing me down."

"I'll tell Pete, Chuck. You need a crew, right?"

"Right, Frodo for copilot if he's available, two guys to service the pods. Load extra magazines in the cargo bay. Assemble a crew of mechanics too, they'll fly on *Cicada*."

"Don't worry about *Farside,* she'll be ready when you get here."

"Chuck out."

* * *

"Evgeny, Willi here. Is the Herr Minister available?"

"I shall see, Herr Kraenkel. Is it urgent?"

"It's important, but probably not urgent. If Minister Zlotov is not available, have him call me the moment he's free."

"Let me check. Can you hold?"

"Yes, but not long. I have other calls to make."

"Zlotov." The deputy minister's tone was sharp.

"Alexander, one of those items we discussed is...ah, potentially available. There has been a crash."

"In Germany?"

"No, but in the EU. It is possible that we might gain possession if we move immediately."

"Where is this...ah, device?"

"In France."

"Unfortunate. Do you have influence there?"

"Some, but influence is the word. I cannot exercise control. The French can be difficult, and they do not respect my authority. I am loath to even try; I prefer that the French not know of our interest. I do have a man, however."

"I understand. Is there anything I can do to help?"

"No, Herr Minister. I merely thought you would find this interesting."

"I do." Zlotov stopped for a moment. "Suppose the French were to gain possession of this item; it is their country, after all. It is possible we might exploit such a situation. I agree, we must move quickly. Gather as many men as you can, Herr Kraenkel. Make sure the man in charge can be depended on. Move as soon as there's an opening."

"Are we to use only our assets? What of our allies?"

"Think, Herr Kraenkel! Suppose we manage to acquire this machine ourselves? We are in a unique position at the moment; we are here, the others are not. Should we advise them of what has happened? Suppose they took the advantage?"

"I... see. Yes, I can find the men we need."

"Do so. And do not attempt to keep the item for yourself; my people have a very long reach. You would do well to remember that."

"I understand. But I called you, so *you* would do well not to forget. I also have assets, and their reach is as long as yours. It would take a word, no more than that, and your superiors would become very interested in your activities. They would...not approve."

"We understand each other." Zlotov broke the connection.

For the moment, Willi Kraenkel thought. *But only for now. Sooner or later, you will make a mistake.*

* * *

THE HATCH HAD stairs on the inside that unfolded as it opened; Pete was waiting when Chuck exited *Cicada*. He trotted toward the waiting *Farside*, now sporting a large pod under each wing.

"Status of *Farside*, Pete?"

"Ready, but be careful. The bird is going to be damned heavy."

"Both the same?"

"Yes. Rockets would have been lighter, so I thought about swapping an alpha for a Beta Pod, but I decided we don't need to rocket a friendly country."

"I agree, the two Alpha Pods should be enough. Loaded?"

"Yes, and I added reloads in the cargo bay, aft. If you need more than one reload, total two magazines per pod, you've got more of a problem than we can deal with. You're also at the thin edge of max gross weight. I couldn't have given you additional reloads if I wanted to, but I added two AIM-9 Sidewinders, one on each wing. They're not as heavy as the reload canisters, so you're still under max gross weight. Barely. The Sidewinders are mounted outboard of the pods."

"You think I'll need those?"

"No. You can always bring them back, they're expensive. But if you *do* need them, they're there. For that matter, the pods have limited trainability. You might be able to use them air-to-air in an emergency."

"Good job, Pete. Want to fly along?"

"Nope, I'm an engineer, not a warrior. You've got Frodo for copilot, plus a couple of men to handle the reloads. I scared up ten mechanics, they're boarding *Cicada* already. They've got individual tool kits and a few power tools. You hold off the bad guys, they'll recover the impellers. She's being refueled, ten minutes more I think. She'll be there almost as soon as you are."

"Right, then. Wish me luck."

Forty minutes later, Chuck approached the crash site. A dozen men stood near the wrecked ship. Six armored vehicles were parked off to the side.

"Frodo, you know anything about French tactical vehicles?"

"A little bit. Those look like older-model armored cars, probably the AMX-10Ps." Frodo typed rapidly on his keyboard and information scrolled across the screen. "Couple of versions, wheeled or tracked, light armor, crew of two, eight infantry troops and a commander. The tracked version we're looking at might be the earlier model, the description doesn't say. One cannon, 20mm, variable rate of fire. Command vehicles have a heavy machine gun, but I don't see it. Some carry the Eryx missile system, but that variant is relatively rare, according to this. Best guess, those are slicks, older model infantry carriers with only the 20mm cannon."

"So where are the troops?"

"Good question. They might be in the troop compartment, but that doesn't made sense. They may not have troops."

Chuck thought it over. "Okay, here's what we'll do. You take charge of the mechanics as soon as *Cicada's* down. I'll drop you right beside

Flea. Strip off the impellers, and if there's time, pull the computers too, but first priority is the impellers. We'll try to reclaim the hull, but I won't lose any sleep if that doesn't work out."

"I hope the French are in a reasonable mood," said Frodo.

"So do I. Cops I expected, but not armor or cannons. You mentioned the Eryx missile? What kind is it?"

"Wire-guided antitank bird, short range, obsolescent. Similar to the American TOW missile."

"I feel a little better now. When you mentioned missile...well, I don't want to dodge something like the Roland's missiles. *Farside'* doesn't have a lot of maneuverability. I can't turn with a fighter, and there's no way I could evade a missile."

"You keep them off our backs, Chuck, we'll pull the impellers."

"I'll come to a low hover, you bail as soon as it's safe. I'll watch from overhead, but don't panic if I have to move around. Keep the guys working."

"What about the explosives? There are a couple of cartons in the cargo bay marked C4."

"Pete didn't mention that! You think you'll need them?"

"I don't know. How about this, if we need the explosives, I'll radio you."

"Let's go with that. I'll let you know if the tracks get antsy."

"Good enough. Pop the hatch when you're ready for me to un-ass the bird."

"Will do. Good luck."

Frodo unlocked his straps and headed toward the back. The two crewmen came forward, and one slipped into the copilot's seat.

"You a rated copilot? Your name is Gulczynski, right?"

"Call me Gooney Bird, everybody does. They have trouble pronouncing my name. I've got some hours in the simulator, not yet rated, but I figure I'm better than nothing. Mister Jackson, people call him C. W., is just starting out. We've worked on the pods while we build up time in the simulators. We will handle the reloads if they're needed. The extra magazines have wheels and there's a machine that loads the rounds, but you'll have to set down. We cannot access the pods from inside, we must go out to the wings."

"Hopefully I won't need you. Call out the altitude for me, okay? I'm watching those armored vehicles."

"You fly, we'll help. I'll watch the altitude, C. W. will keep an eye on the armor for you."

"Call out the altitude."

"Five meters...descending through four meters...three meters.... two meters now, slowing."

"Copy, two meters to ground contact, slowing. I'll try for half a meter. While I hover, you monitor the radar and watch for unfriendly flying objects."

"How do I know if they are unfriendly?" Gooney Bird asked.

"If they're flying, they're not our friends."

"I understand. Frodo just left the hatch. *Flea* is a wreck, the frame is bent, the starboard wing is crushed. *Cicada* is landing now. Main hatch is opening, ten people are heading to *Flea*. Frodo is there now. You're at half a meter. The personnel hatch is still open, Chuck. Ready to button up?"

"No, leave the hatch open. Open the cargo hatch too. If they need access to the explosives, I'd rather be ready."

Gooney pushed a button on the copilot's station and waited.

"Hatch shows fully open."

"Going up now. Watch the radar. We won't get a great picture, too much ground clutter, but if anything is inbound we might see it."

"Understood. Okay, I show you at ten meters altitude."

"Ten meters...going up, I'm at twelve meters now. Assuming the optical altimeter is working."

"It works. Most of the time, anyway."

The two chuckled. "Gooney Bird, train the wingtip cameras. I want one on the armored vehicles, one on our mechanics."

"Roger, Chuck. I show movement...you've got half a dozen people heading for us. They look like French brass."

"Yeah, they do love fancy uniforms. That guy behind Fancy Hat has a loudhailer, so we should be able to hear him. You speak French?"

"No. You?"

"Half a dozen words. Okay, let's see what he thinks of this."

Farside rotated, slowly but smoothly, finally stopping with the nose slightly offset from the group.

"You don't want to face them, Chuck?"

"Let's be friends, okay? They wouldn't enjoy being in front of the radar."

"I had forgotten. Okay, they're stopping."

The man with the speaker handed it to the one Gooney Bird had identified as 'brass'. A rapid burst of loud French ensued, then the speaker lowered the amplifier, waiting expectantly.

"Gooney, do you have any idea what he wants?"

"Not a clue. Want to let me off too? I could see if anyone speaks English. Or Polish? I speak pretty good Polish, some German too."

"You want to go out there?"

"I think I have to, unless you've got an external speaker."

"Nope, something to look into for next time. Okay, stand in the door, I'll ease down to a low hover, you hop out. Any problems, I'll see what I can do."

Moments later, Gooney Bird walked up to the group and nodded. The uniformed people saluted, open hand visible beside their caps. Gesticulations and head shaking on both sides ensued. Finally, a look of distaste on his face, the officer began speaking. Gooney Bird listened attentively, then nodded. He half turned and gestured to *Farside*, hovering with the skids half a meter above the ground. Moments later Gooney Bird turned and walked back, reentering through the open hatch.

"He says the site is under the control of the Gendarmerie. I asked about the infantry vehicles, but he says they have their own chain of command. He did not call them, they just showed up. Maybe the French government is involved?"

"Lovely. Okay, go back and ask him what he means by them not being under his control. Stall."

"I will do this. There are other questions I can ask. How are the mechanics doing?"

"They've got a couple of impellers off already and they're loading them on *Cicada*. Looks like they didn't bother disconnecting cables, I see cut ends hanging down."

"Good, quick is better. Four men are working on that crushed impeller under the port wing. What of the infantry vehicles?"

"No engine smoke. I think they're diesel powered, most are nowadays. What about that turret? Was the gun facing this way before?"

"I do not remember."

"Well, it is now. Still want to go out there?"

"I must. Please don't shoot me. The gendarmes have pistols, but no long arms. Except for insisting on speaking French, the one in charge has been friendly enough. He seems a typical cop, unless we cross him."

"Go ahead, then. I'll be moving as soon as you're out of the hatch, I don't like those cannons pointing my way."

"I will stall as long as I can. I hope those mechanics work fast!"

Gooney Bird approached the group, this time holding out his hand. The group eddied around, each of the men coming forward to shake hands. The uniformed officers also saluted.

No question, the turrets of the infantry vehicles had shifted. The guns now pointed toward *Farside*. Chuck smiled and fed in power. *Farside* floated straight up, then moved to hover behind the tracked vehicles. Chuck couldn't use his pods from this position, but on the other hand the IFVs couldn't aim their cannons either. Standoff, but if they began moving, something would have to be done.

Below, the group with Gooney Bird had watched *Farside* in astonishment. Chuck moved the stick slightly, moving around behind the parked vehicles. Moments later, puffs of smoke announced engine start; whoever was in command of the armor had gotten nervous. The French officers suddenly turned and began running to their cars. Gooney Bird headed for *Cicada*.

He thinks on his feet, thought Chuck. *I'll keep my eye on him!*

Chuck lifted *Farside* until he was well above the vehicles. Below, the tracked vehicles began moving into a line, facing the crashed *Flea*. The mechanics had stopped working and were now crouched, peering around the edge of the fuselage and watching the slow advance of the armored vehicles.

Chuck glanced at the control between his seat and the empty copilot's. The vertical motorcycle-style control had five positions; the pointer was all the way to the left, the gun pods safed. Chuck selected 'Both' and twisted the control to the first position.

Turning *Farside* to point in front of the vehicles, he eased backward until his guns were trained on the open ground ten meters in front of the armored formation, a distance of about thirty feet. Pressing the button atop the pod controls, Chuck fired. Two GAU-8 Avenger Cannons, salvaged from a pair of crashed A-10 Warthogs, fired six rounds each and stopped, thin smoke drifting from the pods. Huge clouds of dust boiled in front of the armored vehicles, churned up a dozen 30mm high-explosive shells.

Would they accept the warning?

Chuck rotated the selectors to the second position. This time, the guns would fire twenty rounds each. The Avengers were now pointed at the rear decks of the armored vehicles. He waited, grim faced, thumb over the firing button.

9

"This waiting isn't doing either of us any good. Can we go see the twins, dad?"

"Sure, give the NICU a call and let them know we're on our way. They might not let me in, but I can watch through the window. Hang on, I've got a call...it's Chuck."

Frenchy listened, then a look of dismay crossed his features. "They did *what*? What are they doing now?" Finally, he responded. "Do what you have to do. You know the risks." Frenchy listened to the reply, then answered, "Lina's fine. We're about to visit the babies. I'm staying until everyone goes home. Not that we have a home yet, but I'll see about buying one while I'm here. If that's okay with you, I mean."

The conversation continued for another minute, then Frenchy put his phone away.

"Chuck sends his love. He's got his hands full at the moment. We don't want to offend the French, they can be touchy, but at the same time we don't want to hand them an impeller. There are French armored vehicles at the crash site. They're waiting, but Chuck has made it clear they won't get the ship without a fight. He armed the *Farside* before he picked her up, two pods with machine cannons, and he fired half a dozen shots into the ground to keep the armored vehicles back. There's a crew of mechanics removing the impellers and they're working as fast as they can. Chuck's covering them. For the moment, it's a standoff. He's hoping they don't want bloodshed any more than we do. But Chuck's fuel is getting low. He's going to land *Farside* and try to bluff them. His cannons are heavier than theirs but they've got more armor. They can take *Flea* if they decide it's worth the risk."

"Oh, dad, Chuck could be killed! What about *Cicada,* can't she help?"

"She's on the ground. The mechanics are loading impellers as fast as they can unbolt them. Frodo's in charge of stripping *Flea*. Chuck's current copilot is trying to keep a lid on things. I don't know if you've met him yet, name's Gulczynski. They call him Gooney Bird."

Lina chuckled, erasing the worry lines. "I'll bet he hates that name!"

"Probably, but he's a good man. Chuck is impressed."

"So what are you going to do, dad?"

"There's nothing I *can* do. We've only got two cannons, Chuck's got those, so I can't even send in reinforcements. We bought the weapons after that Russian hijack attempt. There are also rocket pods, he didn't mention those, but Chuck and Will are the only ones who know anything about them. As for finding another ship, they're either out in space or down for upgrades. Chuck's got the only two that are immediately available. The others are deadlined so Pete and his guys can install the spray-on insulation, and since it takes twenty-four hours to dry, the flight crews were turned loose."

"Chuck told me about that. Will it work?"

"We'll find out how good it is on the next series of flights."

"I wish I could be there. I'm worried sick," Lina said.

"He's more worried about you. We'll take care of the babies, Chuck can take care of himself."

* * *

CHUCK TOOK a deep breath and slowly expelled it. Circling, he brought *Farside* around until he was directly between the armored vehicles and the crashed *Flea*. The crew had resumed working on the remaining impellers. Two were using a cutoff saw to free up a badly-bent impeller attach point. Dust flew, but progress was slow.

Easing *Farside* to the ground, he reduced power to the fuel and oxidizer pumps. The impellers spooled down. Chuck reasoned that the drain on his battery reserve was worth it, but even so, if the batteries dropped to ten percent charge he'd have to bring the fuel cells online.

What would the armored vehicles do? Threatening *Flea* was one thing, but would they open fire on *Farside*?

Keying the radio, Chuck messaged Frodo; he had been helping the mechanics carry impellers and was breathing hard when he answered the radio.

"You may have noticed my problem, Frodo. I've got bigger guns, they've got armor and there are more of them. Hustle the guys along. Damage to the impellers is not a consideration. Get 'em off, get 'em loaded, let's get out of here."

"Working as fast as we can, Chuck. These guys deserve bonuses!"

"They'll get them. You may have to bring Gooney Bird out with you on *Cicada*. If things get hairy, I may not have time to wait for him. *Farside's* hull is mostly titanium, but those 20mm cannons will punch through if they're using armor-piercing ammunition."

"Understood. As soon as I can spare a man, I'll see what Gooney wants to do. What are the tracks doing?"

"Burning diesel. Engines are idling, cannons pointed at me, and if I pucker any harder I'll suck the cushioning right off the seat. But nobody's shooting yet, and one of the French cops went over just now and banged on the hull of the center track. No idea what he said. Just hurry; I don't want them to change their mind."

"You expecting company?"

"No, why?"

"I'm hearing jet noises off in the distance."

"Shit, shit...I can fight armor if I get off the ground, but if those are fighters, I'm hosed."

"They might be. Some kind of big plane with a couple of small escorts. Looks like a cargo plane, maybe a turboprop, the others... I can't tell, they might be helicopters. You have them on radar yet?"

"No, the radar is on standby. I didn't want to fry a cop by mistake. What are the planes doing?"

"Heading this way. There's no place for that big boy to land, but the helicopters could set down pretty much where they want to."

"Big helicopters or small ones? The French have assault helicopters."

"I can't tell. They're blocky looking things, all I can say is they have a single main rotor."

"Maybe they're cargo birds, coming for the impellers. They may try to pick them up here and load them on that big plane. Dammit, I'm looking down cannon barrels and even the cargo choppers might be armed! I've got a couple of Snakes outboard on the wings, but only two, and I don't want to start a shooting war with the French."

"Our guys are working on the last impeller right now. That crunched one gave us the most trouble, but we finally gave up on saving the wing and just chopped through it. That impeller's already loaded. One of the guys lost a finger; he got a little careless with the saw."

"Where is he now?"

"In *Cicada*, bandaging his stump. Tough guy."

"Okay, I see the helicopters. I'm restarting my fuel cells, so as soon as you get that last impeller, collect your guys and head for orbit. I'll join you there."

"Luck, Chuck. By the way, one of the tracks is revving his engine."

"Yeah, I see him. Chuck out."

The batteries showed slightly less than half charge, but Chuck decided the additional drain was worth the risk. The gauges flickered, the fuel cells coming on line as he brought the ship up using battery power. Moments later, all systems functioning, Chuck held *Farside* in a hover, 400 meters above the site.

The distant helicopters suddenly veered away; possibly one of the pilots had spotted the pods under *Farside's* wings, or maybe he'd seen the Sidewinders. Regardless, both had turned away and were now orbiting off to the west. Were they armed? If so, they could be up-sun in seconds.

Chuck suddenly realized he'd forgotten the radar. Swearing, he pushed the button. The radar display appeared in the center of the panel, two returns showing to the west, a third off to the southeast. *That's the cargo ship*, he thought.

"Chuck, we're done. Gooney is with us. We're spooling up now and... lifting. We're off the ground. We weren't able to get the computers. They took too long to remove, so one of the guys took a sledge-hammer to them."

"Got it, head for Station Two. I'll top off my tanks at one of the other stations and meet you there. I'll watch your six on the way up. Chuck out."

* * *

MARTHA CAUGHT A FLIGHT TO PARIS, then to Cherbourg-Maupertus airport, landing late in the afternoon. She finally found a taxi that would take her into Cherbourg, but by then it was late and she decided to wait until morning.

She ate an excellent dinner of oysters in a sauce served over pasta, followed by apple tart tatin. The wines did full justice to the meal. She felt pleasantly stuffed and slightly intoxicated when she returned to her hotel room.

Next morning, the hotel offered the usual rolls with butter plus an excellent assortment of jams and jellies; the region was noted for the quality of its fruits and vegetables. The coffee tasted good, so she had a second cup; Martha decided the area was worth another visit in the future. After checking out of the hotel, she took a taxi to the hospital and asked to see Will's doctor.

"Are you a relative, Madame?" the nurse asked.

"No, I'm a business associate. Our company wants to be sure Mister Crane is well taken care of."

"Of a certainty. I'll see if the doctor is available. Would Madame care to wait in the anteroom?"

"Is it possible to see Mister Crane?"

"I regret to say that he has not regained consciousness, Madame. The doctor may be able to tell you more."

Martha fidgeted, waiting. *How severe were his injuries? Could this small regional hospital provide the kind of care he needed?* She resolved to ask the doctor, who joined her moments later.

"We provide excellent care, Madame. For now, I suggest that waiting is our best option. Mister Crane may wake on his own. The radiographs were inconclusive. A mildly depressed fracture, a minor thing I assure you, is putting some slight pressure on the brain.

Surgery is not indicated at this time. Does Mister Crane have a personal physician?"

"Probably, but not in France. He was visiting the factory, a duty of our supervisory staff. He intended to confer with officials to ensure that we fulfill our part of the contract. Do you know what happened to him?"

"I have been in touch with the police, Madame. Mister Crane was assaulted near the entrance to the plant; there are guards, you understand, but they could do nothing. Mister Crane was abducted and beaten most savagely, there are bruises to the torso as well as injuries to his head. The police are conducting enquiries, but if they have information they have not chosen to share it with me. I am very sorry."

"He was abducted? I was not aware of this."

"Yes, Madame. He was released after about an hour, some distance from the facility at La Hague. Perhaps released is not the proper word; he was thrown out from a motorcar. He is quite fortunate to be alive. The park is used by lovers, you understand; they stroll among the trees and perhaps...well, I digress. Two young people saw the car, a dark van, but..." he shrugged, "there are many such. The couple telephoned the police and Mister Crane was brought here. We feared there might be other broken bones, but he is very fortunate. The posterior region of the skull sustained the most serious injury. We are monitoring his wounds closely. If swelling ensues, it may be necessary to transport him to a hospital specializing in such wounds. Relieving the pressure on the brain ensures the least amount of further injury. It is quite routine, I assure you."

"Can I see him? I've come quite a long way, I would not like to leave without assuring myself that everything possible is being done."

"Of course, Madame. The nurse will accompany you." The doctor's tone had grown frosty. He was obviously not accustomed to having his decisions questioned.

Will's eyes were closed, he was breathing slowly but easily. A cannula was taped in place, adding oxygen to aid his breathing. Tubes led into both arms, and machines blinked and beeped softly. "He has not been awake at all?"

"No, Madame. He was bleeding from the nose until late yesterday, and he has lost two teeth. We cleaned him up, of course. The bleeding has stopped, as you see, and the tubes bring glucose and a saline solution to maintain his systems."

"Yes," Martha said absently. Will's eyes were swollen, the surrounding tissue bruised and dark. A cut above his lip had been stitched closed, apparently part of the injuries to his face. A large bruise extended from the corner of his mouth to his hairline, just above the left ear.

"Here is my card; if decisions are needed you will call me?"

"Of course, Madame. Immediately."

Martha was reaching for her cell phone as she left the building.

10

Martha Simms was finally savoring her first cup of coffee, two hours into her workday. Mornings were always hectic, analyzing overnight reports, making decisions, scheduling conferences for follow-up. Much of her time was spent dealing with subordinates whose latest crisis could have been handled without her intervention. The burr from her telephone was doubly unwelcome. Martha sighed and accepted the call. A second cup would have to wait.

"Yes?"

"Madame, there's a message from Mister Crane's doctor. He's awake!"

"Oh, wonderful! Is he still on the line?"

"Yes, Madame. One second..."

"Martha Simms?"

"Yes. You are.. ?"

"I am André de Foucault, Mister Crane's physician. We spoke before, when you visited the hospital." The doctor had a pronounced accent.

"Of course. Forgive me, doctor, I should have remembered your name."

"Modesty compels, I am only one of the team who worked on Mister Crane. But I called to tell you the good news. He's awake!"

"Excellent, doctor! I was worried, the operation to relieve the pressure..."

"I believe it was successful, Madame. Mister Crane asked who we were and where he was, a most usual reaction. He seemed surprised, but we had only a short opportunity to speak. He sleeps now, a thing which is also not unusual. Patients with head injuries such as Mister Crane's often recover rapidly when they wake from the coma."

"Would I be permitted to speak to Mister Crane if I visited?"

"For a short time, depending on Mister Crane's response. I understand you're no longer in France?"

"No, I'm back at my office, in Switzerland. But I can be in Cherbourg-Octeville tomorrow morning, if that would fit into your schedule. Mister Crane's health is my first concern."

"Of course. I look forward to your visit with great anticipation, Madame."

Martha finished her coffee, now cool, and poured another cup. Frenchy would want to know; Martha sent him a text message. Consulting her calendar, she thought of what had to be done, what could be postponed, then rearranged her schedule. Her anxious secretary waited, hoping to gain her attention.

"That can wait, Marî. I require a private jet and a rental car, or if that is not available, a car with driver."

"Today? But that is not possible, Madame!"

"No, for tomorrow morning, early. I am flying to France, to Cherbourg-Maupertus Airport. I'll need the car when I arrive."

"Yes, Madame. Will you be returning tomorrow?"

"I expect so. The aircraft can wait. Instruct them to service it for a return flight and stand by."

"Of course. I'll see to it, Madame."

* * *

MARTHA TELEPHONED Frenchy as soon as the plane was in the air, returning to Zurich. She'd attempted to call him as the taxi carried her back to the airport, but had been unable to establish a connection.

"How is Will doing, Martha?"

"He's alert. The doctors expect a full recovery, at least physically. Mentally, I'm not sure. Going by what the doctor said, Will's memory may be a problem."

"He has amnesia? Martha, that's very bad news."

"Not total amnesia, more like holes in what he remembers. He knows who he is, he recognized me, but when I mentioned the hijacking he didn't remember anything at all."

"The hijacking took place after he was abducted, Martha. He wouldn't know about it."

"I know, but he also doesn't remember being abducted, and he has no idea of what happened to him. He was astonished when I told him the hospital was in France. He knows the doctor's name and the name of the hospital, they told him that, but he never made the connection. French names aren't uncommon in America, many doctors are immigrants, so he just assumed he was in New Mexico."

"That's not good. How long do the doctors think?"

"For a physical recovery, they estimate six weeks. There were deep bruises as well as the depressed fracture in the skull, plus there was the work done to relieve pressure on his brain. Mentally, they won't offer a guess. One of the nurses was more open, she said he might remember everything tomorrow or he might never remember some things."

"I guess it's time to make some decisions. Martha, can you handle the European operations, at least for now? It's a lot to dump on you, I intended to bring you along and allow you to work your way into the job, but I can't leave Lina and the babies. Chuck's...well, you know where he is."

"Yes. We hear from him daily, but he has his hands full. The French have taken *Flea* to a storage hangar. I understand they have also filed a protest with the American government. They tried to complain to the Swiss, but that went nowhere. The Swiss are business people, they like having us here."

"The French didn't like us before, they only did business with us because we were the only ones who could dispose of their radioactive material. They probably hate us now. Nothing to do about it, I suppose."

"Speaking of flight operations, that is one problem I can't deal with. I simply don't understand what the ships can do and what they can't."

"I'll talk to Chuck. He's supposed to come here, after he decides what to do with the salvaged units. He might have someone who could assist you."

"I've been meaning to talk to you about that. You've been very lucky so far. If you continue using the same locations and predictable flight times, you're inviting another hijacking attempt. You have enemies, they know where your facilities are, so count on it, they'll be back. Next time, they'll be better prepared. As for the last group of hijackers, Interpol has files on them. The French are holding the two survivors and the four bodies have been released to relatives. A Russian was in charge, but he was killed in the crash. The survivors are German. The others are a mixed bag, an American and a pair of Belgians."

"That doesn't sound right; gangs don't usually have members from different nations. Russian gangs, German gangs, that I can understand. The Mafia are Sicilian, or at least Italian. But no ethnic ties? Maybe this is a new development."

"Interpol doesn't think so. They suspect government involvement, perhaps an association of governments."

"Something to think about. Meantime, you hold the fort in Europe and I'll talk to Chuck about flight operations. He may have to do both jobs for now, or find someone to take over for Will. I can't do much while I'm here in Australia. I hate to do it to Chuck, Lina needs him too. But too many people depend on us. It's not just the money, we're finally in space and this time it's different. Private citizens are doing this, not just governments. Maybe, if we do it right, we can avoid the wars and the corruption, the constant political maneuvering for dominance."

"Good luck with *that*, Frenchy."

* * *

LINA DEVELOPED A MINOR FEVER, so her doctor readmitted her to the hospital. He thought it was something routine, but decided not to take chances. She responded to antibiotics, but remained hospitalized as a precaution.

The hospital room was cramped and dim; Lina's bed took up most of the space and a bewildering array of equipment stood here and there. Frenchy managed to acquire a chair and lamp which he'd placed in a corner as a makeshift office. He was working on a document when Chuck walked in, and a stack of others waited by the chair. Lina was sleeping.

Chuck walked quietly to Frenchy and held out his hand. Moments later, the handshake turned into an awkward hug; the noise caused Lina to stir. Chuck put his arms around her as she stood, the embrace turning to a long kiss. Neither of them noticed as Frenchy slipped quietly from the room.

The night was pleasant, the day's warmth chased away by a cool breeze off the bay. Frenchy admired the hospital's grounds, made visible by a system of lights mounted on meter-tall stands. His stroll soon turned to a brisk walk; he'd had very little time for exercise since arriving in Australia. An hour's walk would do him good.

Chuck had appropriated the only chair and moved it by Lina's bed when Frenchy returned. Chuck started to get up, but Frenchy gestured to keep his seat.

"Thanks for giving us some time, Frenchy."

"It's been an hour and a half, Chuck. I *do* need a few minutes of your time, but I decided it could wait."

"What now, Frenchy?"

"It's Will. Martha thinks he'll recover eventually, but he's lost memory. Whether he'll ever be able to fly again, only time will tell."

"Damn. Does he know?"

"Martha didn't say and I doubt she knows. She just said his memory has holes in it. Even a slight impairment will ground him, at least until he retrains. I want you to take over his job."

"Damn again. I was looking forward to building Moonbase. Is that on hold, or are you giving the job to someone else?"

"What about Wolfgang? Can he handle it?"

Chuck scratched his chin while he thought. "Probably. Let me talk to him before you decide. He keeps his cool, that much I know. Yeah, if he's got experts to handle the technical stuff, he could do it.

"What about you, Frenchy? When are you coming back? I can't fly missions and handle all the stuff Will was doing."

"We've got other people who can fly the ships, Chuck."

"I was afraid you were going to say that. What about Lina and the babies?"

"Lina will be going home tomorrow, but the doctors still won't give us an exact date when they'll release the babies. They mentioned low birth weight as an issue and said they wouldn't release them before they'd done a number of tests. They seem to know what they're doing."

"You're staying in Brisbane, then?"

"I am, at least for now. Later, I don't know. I handled the business decisions, but I'm no flyer, Will took care of that. You are."

"Yes, and I've also had business training, but you've got years of experience. Classwork is no substitute for that."

"I can do most of my work from here, and if you need assistance, I'll help. What say we take a walk? We can work out the details."

Chuck studied Frenchy's expression, but his poker face was still intact.

"Sure, I wouldn't mind stretching my legs."

Frenchy waited until after they'd left the building. "I didn't tell Lina, but there's a slight possibility the babies might have cerebral palsy. Boys are more at risk than girls. They're concerned about the premature birth, combined with them being twins. Both are risk factors. That's why the doctors are hesitant to let us take the babies home."

"I don't know much about cerebral palsy. Does it cause...well, mental problems? What about learning difficulties?"

"There's a risk, depending on a number of factors. Best thing to do, wait and see. It frequently involves some loss of mobility, meaning the child needs crutches or a walker, maybe even a wheelchair. The reason is that with CP, some areas of the brain didn't develop before birth. That said, many CP kids have normal or even above-average intelligence."

Chuck looked at the ground, eyes moist. "I hoped the kids might follow me into space at some point."

"That's natural, but you need to think your way through this. It may well be that your kids can live a normal life, even a better life, under reduced gravity. But let's not borrow trouble, okay? CP is only a possibility at this point."

"Lina needs me, Frenchy. How can I leave her? She'll never forgive me, I won't be able to forgive myself. What if I'm not here when the doctors find out for sure?" Two tears tracked down Chuck's face.

"Chuck, there's nothing you can do. You're right, Lina will need support, but what about our people?"

"I don't know. Give the job to Martha."

"She already ruled that out. She can't fly, and when I mentioned getting a pilot's license, she nearly panicked. Something's wrong there. Anyway, she just refused to consider it. No, Wolfgang can oversee Moonbase while it's being built, but he's not an owner. That's me, you, Lina, and Will. Lina can't, Will can't, it's you or me, and I can't fly. That leaves you."

"You already worked this out, didn't you?"

"Pretty much. Management's not rocket science, son. Yeah, you've got a wife and babies, but you've also got hundreds of thousands of people, two dozen ships with more still building, contracts...the stuff we're hauling is dangerous, and without our help, thousands of people, maybe millions, could be affected."

"You really know how to lay on a guilt trip, don't you? So who's in charge of this world-wide operation that's so important that I have to give up my personal life? You or me?"

"I hadn't really thought of it in those terms. But you're right. Neither one of us has a choice. I'll make it official. You're CEO, I'm chairman of the board and a consultant. How does that sound?"

"You really want me to answer that, Frenchy? Don't tempt me!"

The two walked silently into the building. Chuck stopped at the door to Lina's room. "I'll be back here once a week, at least. If I can't have that, fuck the whole thing."

"Agreed. I'll pick up some of the load until we can find someone else to help you."

"You explain this to Lina. I don't have the guts."

"I can do that. What about Moonbase?"

"I'll give Wolfgang a call. Poor bastard, he really loves flying. We're about to take his life away from him too."

11

T he office was large, airy, well lit, yet seemed confining. Chuck had become accustomed to seeing the moon and the distant unwinking stars through *Farside's* viewport.

And there were so many people! What did they do? Could he possibly manage the extended neo-empire called NFI? Who were his assistants? Could he work with them? Frenchy had, but Chuck wasn't Frenchy. His absence would be felt, as would Will's.

Well. There would be briefings, meetings, decisions to make. But first, he needed a replacement for himself, someone to take over the construction project on the moon. Chuck thought for a moment longer, then buzzed for his secretary.

"Adelheid, message Captain Albrecht. He was commander of *Gypsy*, but that may have changed."

"His new ship is *Gypsy Moth*, Chuck. What message shall I send?"

"Ask him to contact me the next time he's dirtside. After that, set up meetings with the department heads. I'll want a briefing from each of them, so have them set that up. I'll need one of the ships available...no, change that. I hate to take a ship off schedule, we don't have a replacement yet for *Flea*. What's our balance sheet look like? Can I afford a personal ship, maybe something smaller than *Farside*? Get with Pete, tell him I want a small ship, four impellers aft, two forward. He'll know what I mean. Let acquisitions know, they can negotiate with the factory. See how long it will take. This is second priority for the factory, replacing *Flea* comes first."

"Certainly, Chuck. I'll see to it. We need to discuss your personal schedule as soon as you have time."

"Add it to the list. Just don't schedule anything for the weekend. I'll be in Australia, leaving Friday around 6pm, arriving as soon as possible. I'll be back in Rovaniemi Sunday night, probably about 8pm local time."

"I understand. How's your wife doing?"

"She's home, but the babies are still in the hospital. She spends most of each day with them, as much as the hospital will allow. They sleep a lot."

"Babies do that, Chuck," Adelheid's tone was dry. "It's normal."

"Tell that to Lina! She worries."

"Any mother would. Maybe, if she had something else to occupy her time..."

"I don't know. I'll have to ask. Now that you mention it, I do have something she might be interested in."

"I'll be back in a few minutes. Would you like a coffee or a tea while I'm arranging your schedule?"

"Coffee, please. But don't you do it; send one of the clerks."

"I don't mind, Chuck. I'll get a cup for myself."

This too was new; there were so many demands on his time now that he *needed* a personal staff. Adelheid Laaksonen was his personal secretary and chief of staff. She had her own empire in a sense, the clerks, the communicators, the hundreds of unsung people who make an organization successful without ever being noticed. Chuck resolved to pay close attention to those he met and offer praise when it was deserved.

* * *

Captain Albrecht arrived at Chuck's office the following morning.

"Wolfgang, I was impressed with the way you dealt with that problem, the over-max-gross cargo."

"I was pretty impressed myself, after I had time to think!" chuckled Wolfgang.

"You like flying *Gypsy Moth*?"

"I do. She's got a lot more power, plus the fuel and oxidizer tanks hold more than twice as much as *Gypsy's*. She's a sweet bird."

"Ever get bored with flying, just the same old thing, haul a cargo past lunar orbit and send it off to the sun?"

"It's routine," Wolfgang's reply was suspicious. "But I love flying. There's nothing like watching the stars come to life as you leave the stratosphere, or watching the moon and Earth line up when you head back."

"I've got another job if you're willing to give it a try."

"Will it involve flying?"

"Some. I want you to take charge of building Moonbase. I'm stuck behind a desk now and I can't say I like it, but it's got to be done. It doesn't look like there's an alternative unless we hire from outside the company, and we can't do that. Are you willing to give Moonbase a try?"

"I don't know. I'll need to think about it. I've never done anything like that."

"You had never flown a spaceship either. There's a first time for everything. We need pilots, but more than that, we need executives. Most of all, we need people who can think under pressure. You've proved you can, and that's the indispensable quality a manager must have."

"You think I can do this?"

"I do. I wouldn't have asked you otherwise."

"I guess I can give it a try. But what if I don't like it? What if I can't handle the job?"

"We'll still need pilots, maybe a chief pilot. I don't know if Will can come back, for that matter whether he'll ever fly again. We're in a bind right now, and I need your help."

"Put like that, I don't have much of a choice, do I? Tell you what, I'll take a look at the job and let you know."

"Good enough. We're about ready to begin. We hired an engineer to blow holes, and the plan is to build habitats in the craters. The engineer's name is John Knox. Interesting man, he was an Army lieutenant until he lost his legs. We've got a lot in common, except I kept my leg. The shrapnel is finally out, but I still limp; scar tissue, according to the doctor. That's one of the reasons I liked being in space, there was less stress on my knee."

"I'll have a talk with John, see what I can do to help. What's he doing right now?"

"Getting the explosives ready. We're going to blow the craters to start with, then clean out any remaining rubble. He decided to use custom explosive packages because there's no commercial versions available."

"Really? I thought you could find almost any kind of explosives you might want."

"Not for what he has in mind. The entire base will be built underground. There's enough radiation on the surface to be dangerous over the long term. The ships are protected while the impellers are operating and we've also retrofitted them with infused-foam insulation, but people working out on the lunar surface won't have that. Some of our people are...well, as soon as they pick up more than half of the maximum recommended exposure, we'll have to find other jobs for them. They won't be able to work in space."

"I'll give him a call. I'll get with you after I look at what the job involves."

* * *

WOLFGANG MET John when he arrived at NFI's field in Iceland.

"John, what's in the boxes?" The two men watched as forklift operators approached *Gypsy Moth*'s open cargo bay.

"The pipes are scaffolding. The smaller boxes are rolls of detonating cord, the big ones are shaped charges."

"Those are shaped charges? They're *huge!*"

"They have to be. I had them custom molded, because I'm not sure what the regolith is like below the surface dust. We don't have the equipment to bore a test hole, so I decided to err on the side of too big."

"Regolith?"

"That's the broken rock structure beneath the surface. It's fairly thick in places, so I included it in my calculations. Then I added half again, just to be sure. It's not like there are neighbors to complain."

"Point taken. So how big are the shaped charges?"

"A thousand kilograms each." John's tone was nonchalant.

"You're loading four thousand kilograms of explosive on my ship?" whispered Wolfgang.

"More than that, actually. The detonating cord is also explosive, just different. It burns a lot faster. The shaped charges are octol, good for blowing big holes. There's a roll of time fuse too, but I'm not sure I'll be able to use it. I'll clip off three feet and do a test burn, then divide the time by three. That gives me the burning rate per foot. We're operating in vacuum, so I want to be absolutely certain that it won't change the burning rate. Or if it does, that the rate is consistent. I'll do half a dozen test burns, just to be sure."

"What about the shaped charges? Won't the vacuum change that too?"

"It might, but I don't consider it likely. I put that into my estimate too, it's why the charges are so big. Shaped charges work by using some of the high-pressure gases to squeeze the rest into a cone-shaped explosive jet. I'm using point eight meters as my standoff distance, that should be enough to allow the cone to form. The jet won't be focused as tightly as I would like, but it should shatter the rock for a considerable distance around the blast point as well as several yards underneath. Even if it doesn't have time to focus, it will still penetrate to a reasonable depth. I expect a lot of rubble left behind. Removing that...well, we'll have to see. Some of it will be blown out by the explosive jet, but not all. We don't have rock-moving equipment yet, so it might come down to hauling rocks out with the lifters."

"And how are you going to do that?"

"Slings and nets. Suspend them from the lifters, fly down into the cavity, have people pile on the broken rock, then bring it to the surface and dump it off to the side somewhere. I've already laid out where I want the power grid to go, but there's plenty of other places to dump the busted rock."

"Just like that?"

"Should work. If not, I'll just bring up more explosives and try again. Explosives are cheaper than manpower, you know."

* * *

FRENCHY HIRED an agent and spent several days looking at property near Brisbane. He found a house that was empty and paid for it with a check. The house was in good condition, recently painted. Frenchy hired a decorator, who consulted with Lina. She spent two weeks in the hotel after being released from the hospital, then moved in. Frenchy had a small suite of rooms in the main house, and there was a separate building for the staff who would make their lives easier.

A week later, Chuck took Lina to the hospital and joined her in a room set aside for them. A nurse brought the babies from the NICU; Chuck held Robbie while Bobby nursed.

"They've got that part down," mentioned Chuck.

"They're growing too. I think we'll be able to bring them home later this week."

"Great. That'll give you more time, not having to drive back and forth to visit the hospital."

Lina looked at him suspiciously. "More time? Babies take a lot of time, I'll have you know!"

"Well, sure. If you need more help, hire someone. The house is certainly big enough for an extra employee."

"It is. That man dad hired...he's some sort of mercenary. Or was."

"I wouldn't call him that, but Frenchy wants to make sure you and the kids are safe. Me too. Bert's a highly trained driver, knows any number of martial arts, so I doubt you'll run into anything he can't handle."

"We won't have trouble, Chuck, not here. Australia has problems, just not the same ones we dealt with in New Mexico. That's where dad went this morning, back to the US. He said something about settling affairs, whatever that means. He'll be back in a day or two."

"Back to New Mexico?"

"No, Hawaii. It's something to do with finance, and he needed access to brokers, but he didn't say exactly what."

"At least he waited until I got here. Anyway, now that you've got more time, I wondered if you might want to design the habitats for Moonbase?"

"But you're building underground, aren't you?"

"We are, but we won't be living in caves. What I had in mind is a kind of apartment in a box, a combination living area and survival capsule. The plan is that the engineers will blow holes in the surface. We clean out the rock, build foundations, and set up prefab habitats. We'll cap the holes with self-sealing domes. It's actually two domes, a smaller one that goes up first, a larger one over that, and a layer of chemical material between. We'll seal the dome to the lunar surface, but what if a seal fails? What if the domes spring a leak? Moonquakes happen, meteors can strike anyplace, so having sealable habitats adds a layer of safety. Tunnels with airlocks will link everything, but even those can fail. I want the Moonbase staff to have comfortable apartments, single or double depending, that can keep them alive in an emergency and that are similar to small efficiency apartments on Earth. We'll build the habitats dirtside, maybe contract with the same company that builds portable housing for military forces, haul them to Luna in one of the Insect-class ships, and set them in place. Add a layer of crushed rock or moondust thick enough to protect against radiation and the job's done. If we built the habitats on Luna, it would be difficult and expensive. There's no reason to spend money if we don't have to."

"What about utilities? They'll need electricity, water, waste disposal."

"Electricity won't be a problem. Ordinary sewage systems won't work, there's not enough gravity to ensure flow, so design in flash toilets. They use electric heat to combust the waste. Maybe we should just dry it electrically and recycle it, we'll soon have underground farms that can use the sludge. Grow lights are common, this will be the same kind of system. As for the waste, we'll need nutrients for the hydroculture system. Those are fish farms linked to hydroponic vegetable farms so they can reuse water. As for water, worst case, we haul it from Earth. I'm hoping we find deposits on Luna, maybe under the craters. We'll find out when we get there. Later on, we may decide it's cheaper to collect water from farther out, possibly from asteroids or comets, maybe from the rings of Saturn."

"Saturn? We're not even on the *moon* yet!"

"We will be. It's just a matter of time now. Some of our people like being on the moon, they may never go back to Earth. First Luna, then Mars, then on to the asteroids and the outer moons."

"I want to go out there, Chuck! Oh, not yet, but after the children are grown. I want to be part of it!"

"You will be, babe. I'll see to it. We'll go out there together."

12

Six weeks passed.

Long white strips of engineer's tape stretched across the moonscape, radiating out from a common center. Seen from above, the star configuration was obvious.

Wolfgang was nervous. The standoff supports for the shaped charges seemed spindly, but John had assured him they were strong enough, given the low gravity of Luna. Detonating cord lines led from each charge to a ring of det cord in the center. Two separate lines led to a smaller ring a kilometer away; the rings were a safety feature, ensuring that all the branch lines would fire. Two carefully-measured lengths of time fuse lay on the lunar surface, ready. A blasting cap was crimped to one end, a pull-ring igniter to the other. Attaching the blasting caps to the ring of detonating cord would complete the firing circuit.

"You know what you're doing, right?"

"I've done it before, Wolfgang. A few hundred times, actually, but who's counting?" John said.

"They let officers do that, John?"

"They insist on it, but I did a lot more of it while I was a staff sergeant. Trust me, you don't forget how it's done. I kept my hand in even after I got my commission. This is not my first big bang."

Wolfgang asked, "What was your biggest explosion?"

"I'm not sure," John said. "I took down a wrecked building one time, though none of the individual charges were very large. Still, there were quite a few of them, and they all went at once. Another time, the Taliban rigged a bomb as an IED, one of our duds. That was probably the biggest one. I was with EOD at the time, explosive ordnance disposal. We decided it was too dangerous to move the bomb. The officer in charge decided to blow it in place, and the Afghani contact agreed. I prepped the initiating charge and sent it in by robot, not that it would have made much difference. We were inside the blast radius. Sergeant Blowers controlled the 'bot, it placed the charge against the bomb and backed out, then we set it off remotely. The bomb went, leaving a big damned crater, and I can tell you it didn't do that neighborhood any favors either."

"Blowers?" Wolfgang chuckled. "A guy working with explosives named Blowers?"

"Yeah, that was his name. He was a Marine, the rest of us were Army. Good man."

"You were EOD?"

"Two complete tours, and two months of a third. I got my degree, BS in chemistry, between my first and second tour. I applied for a commission and started my third tour before it came through. Funny, in a way; all those years of blowing stuff up, I lost my legs to an IED while I was riding in a Hummvee. Convoy commander turned out to be more dangerous than EOD."

"Very bad news, John."

"Tell me about it. But the new legs work okay, some days I almost don't miss the real ones. Walking around up here is a lot easier."

"So what happens now?"

"You beat feet to the lifter and wait for me. I'll be along; I've got to clip the caps to the det cord ring, then pull the igniters. As soon as I do, Mister TNT is not your friend. I'll board the lifter and we get as far away as we can. I allowed five minutes to reach *Gypsy Moth*, you fly the lifter right into the cargo bay, then get us a long way from here."

"Surely the *Moth* is far enough away already!"

"Surely it's *not*. If we had time, I'd let this critter blow from way out in space. But thirty minutes probably gives us enough time to get far enough away. Probably. I had reliability problems when I tried longer test burns of the fuse, that's why I went with half an hour. We're going to need better explosives, stuff designed to work in space."

"What are you worried about, John?"

"Not worried, just cautious. That much explosive is going to shatter a hell of a lot of rock, and when the explosive jet bottoms out it will kick rocks out of the crater. Bottoms out isn't a good term, but I can't think of anything better; what happens is that the jet doesn't have enough energy left to break more rocks, but not enough doesn't mean *no* energy. Think lots of very hot gases, injected into a hole that's full of broken rubble. This is Luna, not Earth; low gravity and no appreciable atmosphere. Some of the ejected material will reach escape velocity, the rest will go a very long way. I don't think lunar gravity is strong enough to form a ring like Saturn's, but it could happen. If so, it will be a very faint ring, probably something like Jupiter's. Anyway, most of the rocks will fall back, but you don't want to be underneath even at a sixth of a gee."

"Why didn't you use an electrical timer, John? Set it for two hours so we could be a long way out in space?"

"Use an electric timer anywhere in the vicinity of an impeller powered ship? Nope, I'm not ready to suicide yet. Ready?"

"Yes. You're sure you want to walk that far? I could bring the lifter in closer."

"No, same reason. Even nonelectric blasting caps are sensitive, I don't even like using these tenth-of-a-watt radios. How far does that aurora effect extend anyway?"

"Not very far, that's why no one noticed it; that, and the low radiation at the bottom of the atmosphere. The lifters don't use the same impellers as *Gypsy Moth,* they're a lot smaller."

"Not very far is the key; let's err on the side of caution, okay? Head for the lifter, I want to pull the rings."

"John, I could do that. I've got ordinary legs."

"My charges, my privilege. Beat it."

* * *

THERE WAS NEVER ENOUGH TIME. Chuck agreed to meet the leaders of the Japanese consortium Friday afternoon, on his way to Australia. Who did what among the Japanese had never been established to his satisfaction, but it worked for the them. One man represented the government, a financier; another headed up a smaller consortium that sent the fuel rods to space in NFI ships, while a third was a nuclear engineer working with the company designing the small reactors. Three men appeared to have no discernible function. They obviously did something, they frequently took over the conversation, but Chuck had no idea what. Perhaps they represented other parts of the Japanese government.

Frodo landed Chuck's new ship at Haneda International Airport. Nominally copilot but usually pilot in command, Frodo would refuel *Lina*, then fly Chuck to Brisbane after the meeting.

A small electric cab was waiting to take him to the conference room. The Japanese representatives were already there. After greeting the men, he sipped his tea and waited.

"We believe our new reactor will meet your requirements. It uses thorium to generate heat, much the same as other reactors do. The heat drives a generator which is part of the unit. The startup costs were higher than expected, but since thorium is common compared to uranium, fuel costs will be less. We hope to be your sole supplier, producing the reactors, then replacing them periodically for maintenance. We will do all the necessary servicing here in Japan. There are costs involved, but they are internal and do not impact our balance of payments."

"Excellent! How many of the reactors do you have?"

"We have one at this time. It's completing reliability tests, but since the generator and other components are common to other systems, we do not expect problems. We will begin production within the month. Some will be for you, some for our domestic market as we begin replacing our older reactors. Our people will be happy to see the last one decommissioned, I believe. The remainder will go to other customers, most to the United States. Our priority is to provide reactors to our customers in Japan, but also serve your needs. You have underwritten half of the development costs, so other customers will have to wait."

"What are the Americans doing with small reactors?"

"Most will become part of a redesigned distribution grid, others will power military posts and similar remote locations. America is changing from a centralized system to one that is semi-distributed. Under the new plan, which as you might expect is facing considerable opposition from your Congress, the power grid will be transformed. Older generating plants will be phased out and replaced by smaller systems. These will consist of photovoltaic grids and wind generators for the most part, backed up by small, easily replaced, nuclear units. Some of the systems will have hydropower or geothermal power modules as well.

"It is not yet feasible to make each house self-powered, although most will have their own private PV unit. That's where the commercial system comes in; it supplements the private system, during the hours of darkness for example. One such commercial system would be enough to power a village, two systems could power a town. Cities will require more, but not larger, installations. The Americans expect to keep the nuclear components small, easy to replace, and therefore easy to service."

"Well, well! Scientists have been talking about this for some time, but nothing came of it."

"Nothing might have come of it even now, had the terrorists not succeeded in knocking out a large part of California's grid. The new modular system is being forced through by officials from that state."

"So when can I get my first three reactors, and how much is it going to cost me?"

"Six months, perhaps as little as three. Much depends on expanding our thorium production plant, but I can promise you three reactors in six months or less. About the cost, that's what we wanted to talk to you about. The rest of this could have been handled by telephone, but negotiations are sensitive, are they not?" The Japanese beamed at Chuck. The others were also smiling. Chuck shook his head ruefully; he still held a monopoly, the only craft capable of safely disposing of spent fuel rods, but the Japanese now had a monopoly of their own. And they had a reputation for being hard-nosed businessmen.

* * *

LINA STRAIGHTENED up and rubbed her back. Bending over the desk, necessary when changing the habitat design, stressed her. Anyway it was time to head for the hospital; the pediatrician had scheduled an appointment to discuss the results of her last visit.

He entered the small office shortly after she arrived and they exchanged greetings.

"Mrs. Sneyd, Robbie appears to be developing well. I have no real concerns at this point. We were concerned because the babies were born prematurely, but she's progressing normally. Bobby, however...have you noticed that he's not quite as active as Robbie is?"

"Robbie's trying to roll over, I think she'll manage it any day now. Bobby isn't that far along, but he nurses, he's happy and smiles at me..."

"Yes. His muscle tone isn't quite where I think it should be at this stage, and he hasn't yet demonstrated a preference for one hand over the other. It's not a problem, but I thought I should prepare you for the possibility. Twins, especially premature twins, occasionally develop cerebral palsy, CP. It happens to boys more often than girls when the twins are fraternal. Early detection and treatment are important. I emphasize that this is only a possibility at this point, but early intervention can help."

"Oh, God! Does that mean Bobby is retarded? Will he be crippled?" Tears formed in Lina's eyes.

The doctor wordlessly handed her a box of tissues. "Right now, it doesn't mean anything. Time will tell; he may catch up to Robbie, and even if the condition is present, the symptoms may be very mild. He responds well to you, that's a good sign. As for mental function, some babies appear to compensate, the child with cerebral palsy developing greater intelligence than his sibling.

"Not all babies progress at the same rate, although we expect them to reach development milestones at approximately the same time. This is true even for those who are premature, we adjust based on expected delivery date. The important thing at this point is that he's not keeping up with Robbie. While this is no more than an initial observation, I think it best I let you know. If, and I emphasize if, the condition is present, not all children have the same range of symptoms. At this point, I simply want to observe Bobby. Don't encourage him to go beyond his abilities; he'll know when it's time to roll over or sit up. If you keep a journal of their activities, that would help. I'd like to see both babies in another month. Of course, if there's a problem, call me immediately."

Lina wiped her eyes. "I'll make the appointment, doctor. Thank you."

"I'm sorry to be the bearer of bad news, Mrs. Sneyd. Love your babies equally. You'll be tempted to cuddle Bobby more, but Robbie needs you too. Take a few moments if you need to gain control. We can schedule around this room."

* * *

FRENCHY KNEW something was wrong as soon as Lina came in. Her eyes were red and swollen and she picked up the babies, cradling one in each arm.

"Is it Chuck, honey?"

"No, dad. He'll be here in another hour or so. It's Bobby. How do I tell Chuck?"

"What did the doctor say, Lina?"

"He thinks Bobby may have cerebral palsy. Oh, dad, my baby! He may be retarded!"

"And he may not. More commonly, there's a problem with muscle control. Bobby may need crutches or a wheelchair. So what? Most CP children grow up and live relatively normal lives. Anyway, as soon as Chuck's here, I have to leave. I'll be in Honolulu for the weekend."

"How do you know all this stuff?"

"Oh, no reason. I looked up premature births, and it happens fairly often with twins."

"Dad, have you met someone in Hawaii?"

"No, it's not that. I'm working on some financial matters, more personal than anything. The business is fine, Chuck's doing a great job. I'll be back on Sunday."

"Okay, dad. I don't say it often enough, but thanks. I'm glad you're here."

"I'm glad I can help. I'll consult a specialist while I'm in Honolulu. If Bobby has CP, he'll get the best care I can find."

Frenchy met Chuck as he walked in the house.

"Lina needs you. She just got notified that Bobby may have cerebral palsy."

Despite the shock, Chuck's eyes were shrewd. "You don't seem too upset, Frenchy. How long have you known?"

"The doctor mentioned it when he was three weeks old. That's why they kept them in ICU so long. Robbie progressed normally, Bobby was a little slower. I talked to the doctor two weeks ago; he was 90% positive by then. I decided not to tell Lina; there was no reason for her to worry, there was nothing anyone could do, and anyway the diagnosis isn't certain even now."

"I'll be in Honolulu for the weekend. I'll catch a flight and be back Sunday night."

"Why don't you take the *Lina*? I won't need her until you get back. I'll call the crew, they'll be expecting you."

"That would definitely speed things up. I'll be glad to, if you're sure. I may even continue on to New York. I figured Honolulu would have to do, because flying takes too much time."

"Go ahead. I'll spend the time with Lina and the babies."

13

J ohn Knox muttered "Fire in the hole" as he pulled the ring
on the first igniter, but only Wolfgang heard him. A spark
and tiny fizz of smoke, quickly whisked away by the vacuum,
showed that both fuses were burning.

Despite artificial legs and the restrictions of his space suit, John was soon at the lifter. Buckling himself into the rear seat took only moments, and by the time he'd finished, Wolfgang had the small craft heading for *Gypsy Moth*. Half an hour later, ship idling far above the lunar surface, they waited.

There was little to see at first. The flying rocks moved too fast and explosive-generated smoke vanished rapidly, so only a series of intense strobe-like flashes and an expanding shock ring confirmed that the shaped charges had blown. The site was immediately hidden by floating dust, roiling where the explosion had taken place, hanging above the surface further out.

"Okay, they all went. I counted the flashes. Wolfgang, my recommendation is to wait a day or two before inspecting the site, maybe even longer. You can't see much because of the dust and we don't know how long the rock-falls will last."

"I see what you mean," Wolfgang said thoughtfully. "That's something new, a fog of dust."

"Why don't we head back to Earth? There's nothing we can do, so why hang around out here in space? Once you've seen a few thousand moon craters, you've seen them all." John's comment drew chuckles from the men.

"Makes sense to me. Okay, I'll let Chuck know we're heading home. Iceland or Finland?"

"No preferences, but I want to talk to Chuck."

"Me too. What about you guys? Any ideas?"

The four crewmen seated in the rear of the cabin glanced at each other and shrugged. Finally one spoke up. "No real preferences. Good beer, fun people. Either one is all right."

"I'll ask Chuck where he wants to meet."

"Question for Mister Knox. Are we staying on the moon job?"

"Absolutely. You're still on the payroll, just take a day to unwind and check in tomorrow. I'll let you know when the next trip topside is scheduled."

"Thanks, Mister Knox.

"Chuck says Finland. He's bringing Pete along and wants to run a few ideas by us before he makes a decision."

LINA FRETTED. Chuck was gone and Frenchy hadn't returned from his last trip. She missed the warm feeling of support both had given her.

The new house was spacious, more luxurious than anywhere she'd previously lived. The staff was efficient and unobtrusive, available when she had something to say but otherwise going quietly about their jobs. They were also, in the Australian way, very informal. Maggie, the nanny she'd hired to help with the twins, was the one she saw most often. Calm, patient, efficient...was this the norm for those who worked for wealthy clients, or did it have something to do with the relationship between the aristocracy and their servants? Whatever it was, Lina decided she liked it, and Maggie was a treasure.

Bobby was progressing, if not as rapidly as Robbie. The doctor had refused to give a firm diagnosis, despite four monthly visits. Was it really CP, or simply the normal variation between babies? Despite herself, Lina hoped the doctor had been needlessly alarmist.

"Lina?" Doris, the housekeeper, waited inside the door of the nursery.

"Yes, Doris?"

"Your father has landed. He will be here shortly."

"Thank you, Doris. Ask him to see me when he arrives, if you please."

"I'll do that, Lina." Doris vanished as silently as she'd appeared. *What was Frenchy doing, all these visits to Honolulu and now New York,* wondered Lina. She intended to ask him; the trips had become a regular weekend occurrence.

She was sipping a morning cup of coffee on the terrace when Frenchy walked in.

"Morning, dad. How was your trip?"

"Better for me than the pilot. Trips don't take long when you're using the *Lina,* but he flew Chuck in, flew me to New York, flew Chuck back to Finland last night, then picked me up in New York this morning. I'm reasonably fresh, despite the jet lag, but he's drooping. Good thing the flight computers do most of the work."

Frenchy accepted a cup of coffee and a buttered roll, then continued. "I suppose we should change the name. It's not jet lag now, it's space lag. Same thing, but it's only going to get worse. I'll ask Chuck whether he's changed his mind about developing airplanes with impellers."

"He thinks the risk is too great, not to the passengers but to us. Sooner or later, someone will develop the impeller drive independently or they'll succeed in stealing one and reverse-engineering it. All those planes, all those pilots...the risk is too great."

"I won't second-guess him. Come to think on it, we've got another source we should be concerned about."

"If you're talking about the *Tesla*, Chuck hasn't forgotten. Sven Nelsen's her captain now, and Chuck believes that no one realizes she's different. She's been operating for three years now, why would anyone look twice at an old tramp freighter? Meanwhile, Sven is sending reports and he seemed happy with the way the impellers work, according to the last report. That's been a while now, but if things had changed, I think we'd have been informed."

"Yes, probably. That's good to hear, that the impellers are working well. I suppose there's no reason to fret, and again, Chuck's the CEO so it's his decision to make. How are the habitat designs coming along?"

"I've got a workable design and Chuck's happy with it. It's actually quite similar to designs done by several other manufacturers, so we won't even need a prototype. An Australian company is working up specs and so far, I'm satisfied. I can drop in and see how things are going as soon as they begin production."

"Here in Brisbane?"

"No, Sydney. But it's not so far as all that."

"I suppose. How are the twins?"

"Doing very well. Do you want to see them?"

"Yes. Bring them here, you think?"

"No, let's go to the nursery. They should be asleep by now."

* * *

CHUCK WAS LATE; a previous meeting had run longer than expected. Wolfgang noted the signs of stress, the new wrinkles and bags under his eyes. Chuck, still in his forties, looked like an old man. His hair was graying at the temples and beginning to thin. The job was clearly taking a toll.

"Sorry, let me get a cup of coffee and we can begin. John, good to see you; how did the shaped charges work?"

"They blew up, if that's what you mean. There's too much dust hanging around the site, so I decided to give the crew a break. I told them they're still assigned to the moon project and still on the payroll."

"Absolutely, we aren't laying people off. We're short of good people, we don't want to lose any. They're here?"

"Right, I gave them the day off. They'll call in tomorrow morning."

"Take them out for a few drinks, buy them a nice dinner on the company. How about you, Wolfgang?"

"I need to talk to you. Maybe it should be private, I don't know."

"If you think that's best, sure."

"I guess it's not important. Chuck, you remember I said I'd think about Moonbase?"

"Right, but I thought you were happy running the job."

"I'm not. I'm in over my head. I want to go back to flying, maybe run flight ops if that's still open. But I didn't understand half of what John was saying, and it's only going to get worse."

"Well, I'm disappointed, but if you're sure, then I'll find someone else."

"Maybe you won't have to look far. What about John here?"

"What about him? John, are you comfortable with having us talk about you like this?"

"Chuck, I've heard worse. If you're okay with it, I'm okay. I'll just fetch another pot of coffee, this one's empty, and you can say what you want while I'm gone. If that's all right with you."

"Sure, go ahead."

John left with the carafe. Wolfgang watched him go.

"Chuck, he's very competent. I talked to him on the way down, he's done a lot more than blow things up. He was an engineer officer, he commanded men and women, put up buildings and those instant-fort things they're using in the Middle East, he's good with people and is comfortable making decisions. Watching him made me realize my own limitations. He's the man for the job."

"Let me think about it for a moment."

The two waited in silence until John came in and warmed up their coffees.

"John, how would you feel about it, taking over the Moonbase job?"

"I'd like it. What about Wolfgang?"

"He wants to run flight ops. I'm inclined to give him the job, at least for now. We don't know what will happen with Will, and I'm sure we can find something suitable for him to do."

"He recommended me, did he? I guess I did good when I didn't blow us up!"

The three laughed, then Chuck said, "It's your job, then. Let my staff know what you need regarding people and supplies. Let Wolfgang know what flight support you'll need."

"I'll work something out on paper. I'll need more people, some of them explosives trained. I'll also need heavy vehicle operators. What happened to the idea of a heavy dirt-mover for the moon?"

"Almost done. The engineers built three of the engines before they got it right. The trials took longer than designing the engines and so far they've only been run in a vacuum chamber, but they work fine in there. The rest of the machine looks more like a tank than an earth-mover. It's a combination dozer and backhoe, and the backhoe attachment can be swapped out for a bucket. It's got big fuel tanks, oversized batteries, and a large generator to keep them charged. The batteries are not only for starting the engine, they're also needed to keep the fuel tanks warm. Otherwise, the diesel fuel would turn to petroleum jelly as soon as the sun went down. The tanks are insulated, but even so..." he shrugged.

"So how are we supposed to get it to the moon?" asked Wolfgang. "None of our ships are big enough,"

"In parts. The machine... we haven't decided whether it's a backdozer or a bullhoe... is being packed for shipment now. Lots of bolts and nuts and washers, including extra ones. You're bound to lose a few, working in gloves. Tools, too; there's a lot of redundancy. As for shipping it, we'll have it delivered and assembled in two or three weeks. John, you've got that long to find your operators."

"Shouldn't be a problem. So I've got authority to hire, fire, and run the job?"

"You do. See me if you have a problem."

"I'll do that. Thanks, Chuck."

* * *

CHUCK AND LINA each held one of the babies, who gurgled happily at the attention. Frenchy was home too; whatever he'd been doing was apparently ended. He sipped his coffee and glanced benignly as the couple played with the babies, then turned back to reading The Wall Street Journal. Finally, he laid the paper aside and said, "Say, Chuck, how about letting me have my grandson."

"Sure, Frenchy. I think he's due for a change, so you're just in time."

"Maybe I should hold Robbie."

"Too late; these two do things together! Come on, dad, I'll give you a hand." The two, carrying the babies, headed in for the nursery. Chuck poured a cup of coffee and picked up Frenchy's newspaper. He was still reading when they returned, ten minutes later.

"Frenchy, did you see this article?"

"Which one was that?"

"There's been a shakeup at your former company, the one where you were a director. Stock prices are way off and Sol's out. Apparently, he's not even getting the usual golden parachute; he was fired for mismanagement, and by the terms of his contract, he gets nothing. He's still got stock holdings, but considering what the shares are trading for now, they're not worth nearly as much as they were before."

"You don't say? Well, well...maybe Sol's misdeeds finally caught up with him! I can't say I'm sorry. I'll cut that article out and have it framed!"

Chuck shook his head and went back to reading.

It was only later that he realized Frenchy had never explicitly answered his question.

* * *

"Minister, were you expecting Mister Kraenkel?"

"I was not! You mean he's here?"

"Yes, Minister. Should I send him away?"

"No, let the fool in. I intend to put a flea in his ear! A wonderful opportunity gone, all due to his bungling!" Deputy Minister Zlotov conveniently forgot the previous discussion the two had had.

But there was no sign of Zlotov's anger when Kraenkel was shown into the office.

"Evgeny, bring tea! Mister Kraenkel, your visit saved me a telephone call, but are you sure this is wise? Someone may recognize you."

"I have other business here, so if I'm seen it won't cause comment. I wanted to talk to you about what went wrong in France."

"Yes, we should discuss that. But let me pour you a tea, surely it can wait that long? Would you like a splash of brandy? I have some, it comes from France. It's very good."

"A bit of brandy would go well, thank you. But about what happened in France, I have only a short time remaining. My flight leaves in two hours."

"Well, if you insist. Tell me of the fiasco."

"Not that, it was simply a matter of circumstances. I had only a few minutes, you remember, but I knew a man who would go as soon as I called. The Gendarmerie were there first, of course; by the time my man arrived, they had gone through the crashed vehicle and arrested two of the hijackers, the only survivors. They're still in custody, but they know very little so there's nothing they can say that will harm us. The other men were killed. One, I believe, worked directly for you."

"Yes. Convenient, wouldn't you say?" Zlotov's tone was mild, hiding the anger that seethed beneath the surface.

"I don't know what you mean. He was killed in the crash."

"Yes. But get on with your story, Mister Kraenkel."

"The police removed the survivors and ambulances took the dead away. The policeman in charge notified their crash response team, then waited for them to show up. They were on the way, but my men arrived first. The commandant of the Gendarmerie spoke to my man and may have recognized him; he tells me he became anxious after that, because if something happened, the authorities would realize he had a part in it. He discussed the situation with the other drivers after that, but they hadn't reached a decision when the spaceship arrived. Zlotov, it was heavily armed! It mounted some sort of aerial cannon and it actually fired warning shots in front of my men!"

Too bad it didn't butcher the lot of them, the incompetent fools! But none of this reached Zlotov's tone. "Fired on them? Really? And what did your man do then?"

"Nothing! He admits he was frightened, he and his men had cannons of their own of course, but he had no authorization to fire and no way of knowing what was happening elsewhere. The only thing he knew was that they'd been fired upon, and soon the two spaceships flew away. The policeman reported the incident to his superiors, but it appears nothing further will be done. My man reports they were lucky to get away without incident, although questions have been raised about his removing the armored vehicles without authorization."

"Ah, well. Perhaps there will be another opportunity. More tea, Mister Kraenkel?"

"No, thank you. There's no time, my car is waiting. Until next time, Herr Minister?"

The two shook hands and Kraenkel hurried out.

Zlotov sipped his tea and glanced out the window. *What to do?* Outside, the flowers were blooming. Spring had arrived in Moscow.

14

———

Six months had passed.

Chuck entered the office and found Wolfgang working at his desk. He stared at Chuck, then said, "*You* did this to me, you know. I could take a few days off between flights before, but now there's a stack of paper waiting as soon as I get back!"

"Quit whining, Wolfgang. You should see the stack on my desk each morning!"

"Yeah, yeah. What can I do for you, Chuck?" Wolfgang leaned back and rubbed his eyes.

"It's about that hijacking. If they'd managed to get the pumps online, they'd have probably gotten away scot-free. They wouldn't even have had to keep the ship, they just needed to set down long enough to unbolt an impeller and scram."

"You're right, but I don't see what else we can do. It's always a race between thieves and security systems."

"They worked around the lock, and in the process, wrecked a fifty-million-dollar ship. Maybe the next time they'll have someplace nearby.

"We can't have that. I'm considering a different system, one that no one can bypass. The flight computers are mounted forward of the control cabin, in the nose; they're close to the instruments, which reduces feedback delay, but a long way from the drive system. I know we're talking milliseconds, and even small amounts of time are important. But what we save in instrument response time, we lose in gimbal and impeller responsiveness. Suppose we put the flight computer in the aft section? Some of the instruments could also be moved aft, the rest can use a single-cable run from the nose to the computers. The control system would also feed into that cable, maybe two cables for redundancy. Maybe not even use wires at all; fiber-optic circuits are harder to tap into."

"Okay, you've got fiber-optic links from the cabin to the flight computer in the rear. Now what? How do you stop someone from accessing the computer?"

"Instead of a lock in the crew cabin, suppose we use biometric identification that feeds directly into the computer? Scan fingerprints, retinal patterns, the recognition systems are already in use, so the sensors are available. I'm thinking of setting up files on all captains and copilots, that's the easy part. The second part is more cumbersome, which is why I wanted to see what you thought. We already have a data link via the satellite systems, so what would you think of the captain identifying himself by biometrics, the scan travels to the computer by fiber-optic cable, then the data link sends the information to Switzerland. If the biometrics match that of the captain assigned to that flight, the Swiss office remotely unlocks the flight computer. If the data doesn't match, the computer locks the system down until a tech comes out and reboots it. Think about this; the hijackers got off the ground because they had access to the flight computer. Without that, they would never have stood a chance."

"I can see a couple of problems. One, you can't leave this circuit open, you'd have to make the authorization permanent, at least for that flight. I don't want to find myself flying a brick because I lost the link to the satellite system or the Swiss office. Once it's authorized, it has to stay authorized. I suppose it would be okay to have the ID system reset itself when the ship is powered down after landing."

"Agreed. That's easy enough to set up."

"Triple redundancy in flight computers. If they're going to control the ship, we can't take a chance on a computer deciding to lock out the crew in flight."

"That's already in the works. We're using two, we expand to three."

"Radio communication has to be separate from the flight computers. The computers can have their data link, but if there's a problem, I want to be able to call for help over a separate loop. That way, someone could fly a tech out to the ship if needed."

"Not a problem. Anything else?"

"It seems complicated, but I guess I can live with it. When do you intend to install this system?"

"I'd like to put it in one of the new ships first, but leave the current system in place for the time being. Test the new system thoroughly, see if it works the way it's supposed to, then make it part of the system as later ships come off the line. After that, retrofit the *Insect* class ships first, then the *Farside* class. The bigger birds are more exposed because they follow a schedule, that's how they got *Flea*. The schedule is set by the customer, so we don't have control over it. That's why we need a better system."

"Make absolutely sure it's working before you retrofit the older ships."

"Done. That's why I came to see you, but while I'm here, is there anything you need to talk about?"

"Other than the flood of paperwork?"

"There's nothing we can do about that. The contracting countries, the nations we overfly, the UN too, everyone insists on paperwork. I've got my share of it, we all do."

"I suppose. No, everything else is moving right along. Martha's finding people and running them through the simulator course. We do the final flight training here, of course. I'm being very selective."

"And so you should. Watch for anyone with unusual talent, there will be openings later on for different ships. Bigger ones."

"Different ships?"

"I'm on my way to meet with Pete and the engineering staff. Here's what I've got in mind..."

* * *

"A FLYING SAUCER?"

"Really, it makes sense. The saucers will be the first true interplanetary ship."

Pete looked around. Dolph was watching interestedly, others were doodling on pads before each place; engineers like having places to sketch out ideas or just to keep their hands busy. Two were sipping coffee or tea.

"Power system?"

"Three small modular nuclear reactors, SMRs. They're heavy, considering the small designs. Each has a footprint about the size of a Volkswagen bug and is expected to weigh nearly eight tons. It might be more."

"I'll need exact numbers. I can work up preliminary designs, but that's all they'll be, ideas on paper."

"Keep talking."

"Okay, if the SMRs weigh that much, you're going to need a lot of lift, so start with that. Simple math, 360 degrees around the circumference of the saucer, say we make it large enough to mount 360 impellers. The idea of using more small impellers is out."

"Lack of room?"

"That, and complications. Lots of control systems equals lots of chances for something to go wrong. Simpler is better. Since you're going interplanetary, make the impellers easy to service, so that means mounting them inside the skin. Begin with a deck height of two meters, about 7 feet. That means your impeller can be...let's see...call it six feet, rough answer one point eight meters long. Expand the housing...no, these won't need housings, they're internal. What about gimbals?"

"Simplified, I think, with limited range of travel. Maybe only a few degrees. I was thinking you could control the direction by applying more power or less, or reversing the voltages to switch impulse from forward to reverse. It could literally turn on a dime."

"That helps. But some degree of lateral motion would also help. Otherwise, you have to turn the ship in order to go where you want. Lateral thrust allows you to simply slip sideways. People claim UFOs can do that."

"Okay, but it would be better to mount the impellers about a meter inboard, not against the outer skin. Slightly closer to the center of the ship, so people could work around them."

"Doable. Better, in fact. Allow for five degrees of motion left or right too, that allows you to roll your ship around the longitudinal axis. Are three SMRs powerful enough to run that many impellers?"

"I don't have exact values yet. There are several types of SMRs, they put out anywhere from 50 kilowatts to 200 kilowatts. Each."

"That's plenty. Make bottom deck the reactor deck, because that's where most of the mass is. Second deck, impellers, let's make it the deck with the greatest diameter. Third deck, smaller, workshops and repair facilities. Storage, too; you're going to be out for months, maybe years, so you'll need lots of storage space. Fourth deck, personnel housing for the crew, sanitation system, laundry, gymnasiums, recreation room, you name it. Fifth deck, bridge and control stations. Communications, radars, engineering readouts and controls, plus things we haven't thought of yet. This deck would be the smallest. We'll probably need a hydroponics area, make that the fourth deck, move the personnel deck to fifth and the command deck to sixth. You're looking at a shape that's more like a toy top than a saucer. On the other hand, we might decide to make it a true saucer, one or two stacked decks, but really wide. You'd need a deck half a mile in diameter, maybe more. First impression, I don't know if we have materials that are light enough and rigid enough to build that. The spindle shape is simpler in terms of the materials that are available now. You're looking at one of the carbon isomers, sheets or nanotubes in matrix, maybe boron. Boron or carbon, they can be formed into sheets, buckyballs, nanotubes, maybe other shapes too."

"Is that a problem?"

"Maybe. I'll have to do some tests. Build it on Earth or build it on Luna?"

"Tell me about Luna."

"Low gravity, but doable. Even so, it would be better to build the parts on Earth and ship them to the moon for assembly. You can't build this ship from scratch if your workers are in space suits, not unless you want it to take years, so you're looking at building a factory first. Pressurize it so people can work in shirt sleeves. Put it on the surface to make launching easy. That means insulation, thermal and radiation. You'd need power systems for the building, electrical, maybe hydraulic and pneumatic, plus environmental control. That brings up a problem. How are you going to get a reactor weighing maybe ten tons to Luna? You'll need a ship that's big enough to lift the parts of your saucer. Are you set on a saucer shape as the first SMR design?"

"Well, no. Morty thought the saucer design was best because of the maneuverability advantage from using a large outer ring of impellers. Safer, too, because of the redundancy factor."

"Suppose we build an oversized ship similar to what we're already using, but with the SMR as the electrical plant. Mount bigger impellers at the ends of stub wings, use a cruciform arrangement this time. Big cargo hold forward of the power and propulsion section, as big as you want, but limited by the strength of the materials available. Maybe plan to load cargo while it's standing upright, you'd probably have to put supports at the ends of the wings to protect the wing and impellers. Another option would be to use the skid system we're already using with the *Farside* and *Insect* classes. I like the upright version better, because I think we'd gain some advantages in ship handling."

"How long to design a ship like this? Can we call it the *Cigar* class?"

"You're the boss, call it whatever you want. Are we looking at budget limits?"

"Within reason, no."

"That makes life *so* much easier! Design, couple of months. If I need more people...change that, I will need more people...I'll hire them. Same bunch of people as before, the Finns who built the other ships?"

"Any reason to change companies?"

"No. They have good quality control and they deliver on time. We could get it done cheaper, but not better."

"Better is good, so go with the Finns. Keep talking, Pete."

"My guys will design the hull and propulsion system, except for how strong the base is. If the SMR is larger or heavier, we'll switch in stronger frame members. Got to install a mounting system too, you can't have an eight or ten ton cargo flying around whenever you turn the ship. Weight distribution...could be a problem. All that weight in the back, not much up front. Some leverage, though...

"I pay you to solve problems, Pete."

"So you do. Okay, I'll get with the Finns. They've got good designers too, but we can't decide where the center of gravity will be until we know how much weight we're dealing with. Is Lina available to help with interior design?"

"No. She's busy with the babies. Being a mommy is a full time job."

"I thought that would be your answer, but I wanted to check. Okay, we'll get started."

* * *

FRENCHY STRETCHED out on the mat and allowed the baby to tug at his hair. Lina, holding Robbie, looked on fondly.

"You don't have a lot left up there, dad. If he pulls too much out, you'll look like an egg."

"It's not that bad, Lina! Besides, he's enjoying himself and he needs the exercise."

"He's not the only one enjoying himself, dad. You need to spend time with Robbie too."

"I do, I do! But a boy needs to have his grandpa around when he's growing up."

"Dad, that's a rubber ball you're holding, not a baseball, and he's far too small to be playing ball with you," Lina chided.

"He'll get there," said Frenchy. "Robbie too. I won't neglect her, but girls need mommy time more than they need grandpa time."

"They need both of us, Chuck too. He spends as much time playing with the kids as you do. If they're awake, daddy's in there with them."

Lina looked around. A sturdy low wall, easy to put up and take down, surrounded the wide mat. It allowed the children freedom to creep around on the mat, but kept them from leaving it. The exercise was obviously helping; Robbie was slightly ahead of the pediatrician's expectations, while Bobby was barely behind what was considered normal for a one-year-old.

"We think it's time to wean them. I'm not looking forward to it, but it has to be done." She stroked Robbie's head and smiled at her. Robbie smiled back, then stretched it to a wide grin.

"Have you noticed how attached the two are to each other? Even when I take one out to be changed, you can tell that the other is anxious. Maybe it will pass. They don't like strangers, but the doctor assures me that's normal. They've got the two of us, daddy, and their nanny. They warm up to the doctor too, but it always takes a while. He's good, though. He has both of them smiling and waving at him by the time the visit is over."

"I agree, he's a good man. He has a good reputation too. The babies seem to like him after they get over the shyness, and both of us like him too. Too bad he only works during the week. Maybe, if you asked, he would make a house visit next time Chuck is here?"

"It wouldn't hurt to ask. Anyway, it's time to feed these two and put them down for their naps. Out you go, Grandpa."

15

M
artha was waiting when *Lina* landed in Zurich. Will had joined Chuck on the trip, but seemed nervous while they were above the atmosphere. He looked through the transparent-metal ports at the unwinking stars and unconsciously shivered. The extra-atmospheric portion was short and he recovered during the descent, but remained quiet and seemed withdrawn afterwards. Chuck's attempts to start a conversation went nowhere, and finally he gave up. Will's condition occupied his thinking until they were off the ship.

"Are they here?" asked Chuck.

"They've been waiting. I ordered a light brunch as soon as I got your message. Good morning, Will; I'm glad to see you're looking better." Will nodded, but didn't speak.

"Couldn't be helped, Martha. The meeting went longer than expected, and I wasn't willing to shut it off to meet with these people. They consider themselves important, I don't."

"Chuck, don't antagonize them. They're either Senators or Representatives and they wield considerable clout in the US Congress."

"Let's get on with it, then." Chuck's tone was brusque. As far as he was concerned, the meeting was no more than a distraction designed to burnish the reputation of politicians.

"We'll take the shuttle car, Chuck. I booked them into the Zurich Marriott and reserved a conference room."

"What about that other matter, the school? I want to see how that's going."

"It's all laid on, Chuck. You're to meet with the Americans this morning, have lunch, then visit the school. One class is trying on the new space suits. It takes time for them to get used to the feeling. Another class is learning to assemble the sunshields. This is only a training version, of course, but it's the same except for the photovoltaic panels on top. They're only dummies, the LED's on the underside are powered by batteries."

"Sounds good. What about graduation rates, are they any better?"

"Unfortunately, they're not. Some people don't adapt well to the simulator, some never get accustomed to wearing the suit's under-layer. It's elastic, and if they have any circulation problems the suit emphasizes them. I don't know if there's anything to be done. We're at approximately 50% graduation rate, and the biggest influence on whether students pass or fail is simple physical condition; people who live in cities aren't very fit."

"What about hiring more outdoor peoples, farmers or whatever?"

"There aren't that many, and most of *them* have problems adapting to the technical base. Farmers aren't eager to go into space, even with what we're paying."

"Keep trying, Martha. We need more people who can work with their hands. Pilots we've got, it's construction guys and plumbers and electricians that we're hurting for. What about ex-military people? Are we getting any of those?"

"We are, but some have psychological problems. Chuck, I'm doing my best."

"I understand, Martha. Okay, I'll get off your case. Anyway, we're here. Politicians...what was it Lee said, 'I would rather die a thousand deaths'?"

"Lee who?"

Will held the door open, then silently followed them inside. The tables had been cleared, except for pots of tea and coffee. Chuck poured himself a cup and sipped appreciatively as Martha and Will found seats. He put the cup down and spoke.

"I'm Charles Sneyd, my friends call me Chuck. I'm CEO of New Frontiers, Incorporated. You've already met Martha, she's senior vice president in charge of our Swiss office. Will Crane is a major stockholder and has been our director of flight operations. He's currently on leave, recuperating from injuries, but I thought it important that he come along. I don't know your names."

The introductions went around, but Chuck stopped them twice to make notes. His face showed no expression. One of the names was Pinchot Forberger, introduced as a staff member to a Senator who'd canceled at the last minute. The name meant nothing to Chuck.

As soon as the introductions were done, he stood.

"This will only take a moment, then we can get on with the meeting. Senator Byington, Representative Chambers, will you come with me, please?"

The two stood and looked around, surprised at the attention.

"This way, please." Chuck accompanied them to the door. His voice remained low, but the people inside the room heard most of the conversation.

"You two can leave. Did you really think I wouldn't find out you were working for Sol Goldman, that you're the corrupt sons of bitches who got our plant shut down? My grandfather worked himself to death and you did everything you could to destroy his life's work! Get your sorry asses out of here before I lose my temper."

"Now see here, Sneyd! Do you know who you're talking to?"

"I know who and I know *what*. You're slime. Leave now, while you still can!" Chuck's voice had risen. Martha heard the anger and headed for the door, almost running.

"Will, help me! Chuck's lost control!"

Outside, Chuck's rant paused for a moment and Byington spoke up. "You arrogant ass! You can't talk to me that way!"

Will got there just in time, grabbing Chuck's arm as he drew back a clenched fist. He was barely able to restrain Chuck.

"Get out of here, quick! I've never seen him like this!" Martha urged.

The two men, ashen faced, backed away, then hurried down the corridor.

"Chuck, do you understand what just happened?"

"I... don't know. I guess I just lost it. I've been under a lot of pressure, and the sight of those smug bastards, realizing that they believed their position made them somehow immune... I just saw red. Really," he said wonderingly, "my view of them turned red, as if someone had put tinted glasses over my eyes. Maybe it was the blood vessels in my eyes, but I just couldn't stand it. Maybe I overreacted."

Fifteen minutes later, Will and Martha accompanied a red-faced Chuck into the conference room. "I'm sorry, just let me refill my coffee. I'm don't know what I can do to help the US Congress, but I'm sure you'll tell me, won't you?"

* * *

JOHN WAS WAITING ANXIOUSLY when *Goliath* landed. This ship, the second of the new *Giant* class, carried the main body of the construction machine. The operators had voted to call the device a bulldigger. John grinned and accepted the name, because the machine, after assembly, would have a rear-facing bulldozer blade and a backhoe in front. The backhoe attachment could be swapped out for a bucket-loader when needed, in the same manner as skid-steer machines. The bucket would be delivered with the second shipment, which also included the tracks and running gear. *Giant* would also bring the fuel storage tank and the protective dome, what the assembly crewmen called the 'tent'.

Farside was parked near the huge blast craters. A long power cable led from the ship to the site John had chosen for assembling the bulldigger. The fuel cells, assisted by the PV cells on the ship's fuselage, would provide electric power to the work crew until the fuel-rod system came online. For now, electricity was limited. The big machine, assembled, would dig the trenches; the next pair of flights would bring up pre-threaded lengths of pipe and connectors to join them together. A separate shipment would bring the pumps and Stirling-cycle engine generators to circulate the fluid and produce electricity. One thousand, one hundred thirty four fuel rods, unusable on Earth, waited; they had been deposited in a flat area a kilometer from the grid, separated far enough to prevent them interacting with each other. John expected delays, construction jobs almost always experienced delays of one kind or another, but he believed Moonbase would be ready for occupancy within a month.

"Let's go, we're wasting fuel! Get *Goliath* unloaded, *Giant* is just behind her. I want that tent in place before we quit for the day!"

The men boarded their assigned lifters and headed for the ship. Four lifters, each with eight impellers arranged similar to the original King, could never have lifted the heavy digger on Earth; on the moon, they had no problem at all. They hovered inside the open bay and waited while workers attached lifting chains. Despite the one-sixth gravity, mass remained, and inertia could be dangerous; the lifters took up the slack and lifted carefully, a coordinated dance that soon had the big machine out of the cargo bay. *Giant* moved in as *Goliath* departed, on her way back to Earth for another load.

The 'tent' wasn't a tent, despite the name. It was a huge dome made of engineered panels. Disassembled into its constituent carbon-fiber panels and packaged for shipping, the dome filled the rest of the cargo bay. The outside of the dome was covered with PV panels, while the underside held multiple LED units. The dome protected the men from solar radiation, the solar panels charged the batteries that provided power to the lights. Working beneath the domed cover, a second shift would begin assembling and prepping the bulldigger. Even after daylight vanished, the lights would remain on. During the long lunar night, a power cable from *Farside,* or later from the fuel-rod generating plant, would keep the lights on.

The men would work beneath the dome while the bulldigger operators dug the trenches. Sections of pipes would be joined together, forming the complicated system that would carry the working fluid beneath the fuel rods. Busy lifters carried assembled sections and laid them ready by the open trenches. Other men bolted pumps to supports and anchored them to the lunar surface, leaving only the final connections to be made after the pipe sections were joined in the trenches.

* * *

"WHAT ARE WE LOOKING AT HERE?" asked Chuck.

"The students are learning about the different versions of the space suits. They're currently wearing the inside absorbent layer, the one that wicks moisture away. They'll get the second layer tomorrow. The two layers make up the shipsuit. The third outer layer will be added next week, as soon as they're ready for pool training. I don't know how complete your briefing has been?"

"Bare bones only, Martha, my time is limited. Tell me about them."

"The shipsuit is designed for the low pressure that's standard in the crew compartment. Crewmen can wear the suit for up to eight hours under those conditions. If the ship's pressure drops, the suit will maintain pressure around the torso and limbs. Pressure loss in the crew compartment is not expected to be instantaneous, so the wearer has time to put on his helmet and lock the ring. After the ring is locked, the suit's torso inflates. Operating pressure is equivalent to 5000 feet elevation. That's lower than sea level pressure, but not so low that it requires acclimatization. The mixture of gases in the suit tanks includes enhanced oxygen and water vapor, making up for suit pressure that's slightly lower than cabin normal. Both systems supply reduced amounts of nitrogen and carbon dioxide, compared to Earth normal. Atmospheric trace gases aren't necessary. The mix reduces the likelihood of developing the bends if pressure drops rapidly.

"The third, outermost layer, is added over the shipsuit for extended operation in zero pressure. That layer is armored at the joints to reduce the chances of tearing. It's a better design than what the Apollo people had."

Chuck nodded and listened to the instructor as he continued his interrupted lesson. "Both shipsuit layers are snug, and they have to be. Think of the suit as a cross between panty hose and support stockings, or the squeeze you get if you wrap an injury in several layers of elastic bandage. The first layer is snug, but by the time you've added four or five layers, it's uncomfortably tight. The suit uses the same principle, increased pressure through addition. Neither layer is uncomfortably tight, which makes them easy to put on. Together, the shipsuit layers mean that the arms and legs do not need to be pressurized.

"Women have it easier; you men, if you aren't careful where you store your family jewels, you'll lose them. Not by forgetting where they were, but to the surgeon's knife when you finally notice what the lack of circulation has done.

"You'll wear the inner layer for the rest of the day. Tomorrow, we'll add the second layer and next week you'll put on the third layer and fit your fishbowl. They're heavy, but you won't notice the weight after you enter the pool."

Chuck followed Martha down the hall. "Is that the new fishbowl, the one with the oxygen and water canisters attached?"

"Right, it's not easy putting it on in Earth gravity because the canisters behind the helmet are awkward. If you're on the moon or in free fall, it's much easier. Just lift it up, slide underneath and pull it into position facing slightly left, twist ten degrees right to lock the interrupted threads, then secure the compression ring. It's as easy and foolproof as we could make it."

"Handy. Something else I'll have to learn, I suppose. How much longer before the older ones are phased out?"

"Probably six months. It will take that long to run all our topside employees through the school and fit their 'bowls. The old version works, it's just that the new ones are handier and the canisters are easier to change. Let's go outside and watch the construction class. They're putting one of the 'tents' together, the protective dome that will be used on the moon. Have you been up there recently?"

"No, I've been too busy. I've seen John's reports, of course. The craters are cleaned out and we've got more than a thousand fuel rods waiting for the rest of the system to be finished. He says a month, but he's assuming the habitats are ready by then.

"We're using the same companies that make the accordion-style walls that troops set up in a day. The habitats also borrow from the containerized living spaces used in Iraq and Afghanistan. Not much need to redesign them, just adapt them for low gravity and zero atmosphere. They were made to be shipped in a single container, so all we do is load the container into one of the *Giant* class ships and off it goes. The containers will stay on the moon. They'll be useful for storage. Most are airtight, which also helps. Several have been adapted to serve as bunkhouses until the habitats are livable, but later we'll set them up in a block as emergency shelters. Conversion is easy; just replace the door with an airlock, stock them with air tanks, rations, and water, and you're set. There are external racks and connectors for the air and water tanks. Solar cells charge batteries that warm the water, so it doesn't freeze after the sun goes down. The combusting toilet design isn't ready yet, but it won't take long. They're common in Alaska, we just rework the standard model. The biggest problem is the airtight seal, a kind of mini-airlock. You don't want to lose your atmosphere while you're cleaning out your toilet!"

The two walked to where instructors observed the crews, four men and a supervisor to each panel. Chuck listened as one of the instructors explained the system.

"Lock the smaller subunits into an orange-slice panel. Plug them in carefully, then close the locking clamp. If you do it wrong, you're going to ruin a very expensive piece of gear! But if you take it slow and careful, the guide pins will make sure everything lines up properly. Handling the panels is awkward down here, but it's going to be easy on Luna. Remember to go slow, don't torque the panel or you'll break a connector. We need four men on Earth, but only two will be needed on the moon. Get to know the parts, look for the index pins and sockets, and make sure the assembly numbers are the same for each section. If you do that, you won't have any problems. You assemble the orange-slice panels the same way you do the subunits. Everything fits together tightly and there are upper and lower guides that seal the joint so radiation can't leak through. If you're working dayside, you'll know when you've got it right. The PV panels on top will charge the batteries and the LED's will light."

One of the men had a question. "Will they light up here?"

"They will. Seeing the lights come on is an important training aid. The only difference is that these PV panels are dummies, the real ones are heavy and expensive, so we use battery packs for training." The man nodded.

The crew glanced curiously at Chuck and Martha; apparently, they had no idea who the visitors were.

Half an hour later, they were back in Martha's office.

"You've done a fine job, Martha. John will be glad to see the new men, he figures another ten of those domes will be needed eventually. I've got to get back to Iceland, so I'll go find Will and we'll be on our way."

"How's he doing? I saw him in the hospital and right after he was released, but..."

"He's not the old Will. I just don't know, he worries me. For now, he's still carried on convalescent leave. I think I'll take him to Australia, see if spending time with Frenchy might help. They're old friends, they've known each other since before we started the company."

"That's a good idea, Chuck. When will you do that?"

"This weekend. I thought of sending him ahead in *Lina*, but he's really nervous when she tops out in space. It's like he freezes until we reenter atmosphere. He more or less recovers before we reach the airport. I don't understand it."

"Chuck, he was badly injured. That can change anyone."

"I suppose. That piece of shrapnel in my knee sure changed me. One more thing, did that bunch of politicians head home yet?"

"Most have. They were pretty disappointed."

"I offered to haul cargoes or personnel wherever they wanted, same rates as we charge the French. But they wanted access to the impellers, and some of them hinted I should contribute campaign money! Corrupt fools, the lot of them! I'm not a defense contractor, I'm not even a government employee. If I never see them again it will be too soon.

"But they're not getting impellers, Martha. They'll fly in our ships, or not at all."

16

L ights blazed beneath the huge dome, eclipsed only by the glare of sunlight on the moon's surface. The layer of dust absorbed much of the sunlight, but men worked under the LEDs, assembling the bulldigger. Final checkout would have to wait until the machine's tank was filled, and that in turn had to wait until the diesel fuel in the storage tank melted. The fuel was more slush than liquid at the moment.

Off to the side, lifters moved emptied shipping containers to their new home under a second protective dome. The container doors had been replaced by airlocks; off-duty workers now had their own private place to sleep. The toilet problem had not yet been solved, each container had a plastic bucket for a temporary substitute, but at least the men would no longer have to bunk down in *Farside's* cargo bay. Most looked forward to having their own quarters, although some were uneasy; what if something went wrong during the night? Despite assurances from the staff, it would take time before they became accustomed to sleeping in the containers.

The habitat modules, designed to provide Moonbase's residents with permanent living quarters, would soon be ready. The blast craters had been cleared, the broken rocks moved away by busy lifters, and the surface leveled and tamped. Chuck joined John where he watched one of the men at work.

"I'm a little concerned about that stuff," John remarked, pointing. The worker was carefully spraying steam over the crushed rock base, cementing it into foundations for the habitat modules. A long insulated hose led from his wand to a boiler on the surface. The boiler superheated the water using sunlight, concentrated by a Fresnel lens molded into the boiler's transparent-metal cover. Pressure kept the water from boiling until it sprayed from the wand. It then flashed momentarily to steam, coated the rocks, and refroze almost immediately. The result was rock aggregate locked together by ice, icecrete.

Chuck took a few minutes to explain.

"Concrete won't work on the moon. It has to cure long enough for the chemical bonds to form, and you'd need to keep it warm and under pressure or the water would boil out. Cement is heavy and it has to be imported from Earth, which makes it really expensive. But rock is what we have to work with, so we need something like cement to stick the rocks together. Dolph worked with the civil engineering crew to come up with three other options. They used different names, based on what cements the rock aggregate together."

He pointed to the workman. "Icecrete is cheap, it's easy to install, goes in fast, and it will stay frozen indefinitely, especially here on the moon. There are two ways to install it, depending on how much water you've got to work with and the steam temperature when it leaves the sprayer. If you've got a plentiful supply of hot steam, you can warm the rocks enough for the water to penetrate down into the aggregate. That allows a kind of 'curing' to take place, but it takes time and you have to keep the rocks warm so the ice sets up without cracking. Letting the mix cool slowly is the key to how strong it will be. Expansion and contraction can be a problem, so you have to allow for that when you design the forms. That version of icecrete works best for foundations. A faster version uses less temperature and less steam to coat the outer rocks, meaning it sticks things together but it doesn't penetrate deep, so it's not as strong. We'll use it to stabilize tunnels, spray on a lining so you don't have to deal with falling rocks or dust." Chuck paused long enough to make sure John was absorbing what he said.

"The second idea, ceramacrete, is also fast, but it's not easy or cheap. The idea is to use a plasma torch to melt the outer layer of the aggregate. We might use that on Mars, but there are technical problems as well as costs. It works best for foundations where slump isn't a problem, and it needs an atmospheric shield to keep the plasma from blowing out.

"The third option is infusacrete, which is likely to be as strong as reinforced concrete, but it's expensive in terms of transport costs. That may change after we begin extracting metals locally," Chuck said. "The idea is that you use long metallic threads mixed in with the aggregate, and cement it together with ice or ceramic.

"As for what your guy is building now, it shouldn't be a problem. He's using three ridges of icecrete for each foundation, which leaves open spaces between the ridges. The habitat floors will be warmer than the foundation, but only a relatively small part of the foundation is in contact. Ridges and hollows expand the exposed surface area, which weakens the heating effect. As soon as he's finished, we'll cover the ridges with plastic liners, and that will help too. The moon's subsurface is below the freezing temperature of water, so it will take years before the icecrete softens. Maybe it never will."

"You may be right," commented John. "Reduced gravity also helps. The plan is to pile a meter of broken rock on top of the habitats. That's plenty for radiation protection, thermal insulation too. No icecrete needed, just loose rubble so the rocks can expand and contract. They have to; the temperature swings from 105 degrees C during daylight, that's five degrees above boiling, to minus 173 degrees at night. There's plenty of loose rock around, not all of it from the explosions. There are broken chunks wherever rocks are in direct sunlight. The outer layer heats quick, meaning it expands faster than the inside, so it cracks off. We see the same thing dirtside, exfoliation. It just happens faster up here. Anyway, we couldn't build anything like this on Earth. The insulation layer would be too heavy."

"What's next after you get the habitats in, John?"

"I'm thinking about buying a tunneling machine. Not one of the big ones, we'll just have the manufacturer scale it down until the boring head is maybe four or five meters across. Tunnels will connect the habitat zones to the garages and shops. I figure to finish the tunnels by installing a floor a meter or so up from the bottom. That way we can use the space underneath for electric cables and pipes, and it gives people a flat surface to walk on. That leaves plenty of room to walk upright. Four meters of headroom should be plenty. Then spray the tunnel walls with steam and let it freeze. I'll want to link the habitats and the garage first, then use the new tunnels for additional habitats, no top cover required. We're also going to need spaces to grow food. People in London already do that, using the shelters from World War II. Sooner or later, Moonbase will have to become independent. Everything we use comes up from Earth, but that's got to change."

"I think I can find enough in the budget to cover that. Go on," said Chuck.

"There are a few hurdles to overcome with farming plants, they're probably going to be tall and spindly, but the agronomist thinks he can fix that by adding borax to the mineral mix. The boron strengthens the cell walls."

John had found his niche. He was a born designer and builder, as his enthusiasm showed.

"We'll use two large tanks, one shallow for the plants, one deeper for the fish, and circulate the water between them. That generating system was pure genius, because Moonbase is going to need a lot of electricity. The farm tunnels will need to be heated, and the grow lights will draw current too. I'll extend the tunnels over that way." John's gloved hand pointed to the area he meant. "Plenty of room to expand the farm."

"The fish in the second tank should do fine, they adapt to reduced gravity. We may also need separate hatching tanks for the fish eggs, then transfer them to another tank until they're fingerlings. They have to be separated, otherwise the small fish will eat the eggs and bigger fish will eat the small ones. You'll need to hire a fish biologist as soon as the tanks are installed."

"Six months from now, we'll be harvesting our own fish and vegetables. We'll grind up all the leftover waste and add it to the fish tank. There will also be other nutrients, picked up from the plant farm; that's where we'll put the composted waste. The water circulates between the tanks, the tilapia eat the plant waste and algae, the plants will use the fish waste and sludge from the sewage systems. The ecosystem will need a bit of judicious tweaking, adding things like snails and so forth, but it shouldn't be a problem. Add that to your list, Chuck, you'll need an ecologist to run the farm system."

"John, I'll need professional scientists and technicians for all of it," replied Chuck. "You build it, Martha will find the people."

"If we can find water ice, we can easily electrolyze that into hydrogen and oxygen. Chuck, you give me a year or two and Moonbase will be a complete, self-sustaining colony."

John paused and sipped from the water tube by his jaw.

"Question for you, Chuck: plants and fish aren't a problem, but what are you going to do about human changes? I've been reading the medical reports; there will be bone loss, and that's just the start. Hearts, lungs, for that matter the overall circulatory system will get weaker. That's just what they know about, there will almost certainly be other problems. What I'm saying is the base can be self-supporting except for people, but they can't stay here forever. You might need shifts, maybe replace the staff as often as every two or three weeks."

"That's my problem, John. Your problem is to get it built and functioning. What about you?"

"I don't know. I'll probably do what Dolph suggested, spend a week or two on a ship now and then. The rest of the time, I'll try to exercise more. That might slow down the bone loss, and for sure it will keep the circulatory system healthier. But it has to be vigorous exercise, something that gets the heart rate up. I'll have to think about that. The usual kinds of exercise probably won't work. The elastic undersuits will help, I think."

"Work on it, John. I don't want my people getting sick."

"I like the way I feel right now, Chuck. The fake legs don't bother me at all, what with the low gravity. They clip on outside the suit legs, of course, but all I had to do was modify the legs to cover my stumps, then add boot clips. It's almost like that explosion never happened. Anyway, you promised I could get my pilot's certificate if I built Moonbase, and that might be even better than living permanently on Luna."

"Something to look forward to," the workman chimed in. He had been listening to the conversation.

"The icecrete is set, so all I need to do is put the plastic jacket over it. Feel like giving me a hand, boss?"

* * *

CHUCK FLEW in again three days later. John was taking a break when *Lina* landed, so Chuck radioed him and asked if he could join them in the crew cabin.

"Not much room in here, is there?"

"I don't need much, John. Do you know Frodo?"

"Seen him around. Howdy." John extended his hand. "Good to see you up and around, Will."

Will nodded, but remained silent. Chuck glanced at him worriedly. Would he do better in Brisbane with Frenchy? Chuck shook his head, a tiny movement; if that didn't work, he had no idea what to do next. Could they afford to keep Will on as a director if he was too nervous to fly? Would he be willing to sell his interest in the company? For that matter, could they afford to pay the billions that Will's share was now worth? Frenchy was still chairman of the board; he would decide. Hopefully.

"Do you want to look around outside? The bulldigger is almost finished with the last section of trenches, and the first loop is already providing power. There's nothing to see behind where the bulldigger is working, just moon rubble and dust over the fuel rods. I can show you the pump house if you'd like. The pumps are running off the first pair of Stirling-cycle generators. We'll have the remaining generators going by next week."

"Will, want to come with us?" Will just shook his head, still not speaking. Chuck followed John out the airlock and motioned for him to shut off his suit radio. Placing his helmet in contact with John's, he spoke, letting the vibrations pass from helmet to helmet.

"I'm worried, John. Did you ever see anything like this when you were in the Army? I don't know what's going on with Will, it might be some kind of PTSD."

John shook his head. "I can't say, Chuck. I saw guys with the thousand-meter stare, you knew they had gone about as far as they could go, but this is different. Will was a pilot, but now he's afraid to fly?"

"It's more than that. He doesn't get nervous until we leave the atmosphere. It's like the stars are making him afraid."

"I never heard of anything like this, but maybe pilots knew of it. What are you going to do?"

"I'm going to leave him in Brisbane for a few days. The new house is big enough, there are extra rooms. Frenchy outdid himself; there's a live-in staff and they won't have a problem taking care of one more. I can only get there on weekends anyway, so that's the only time the staff will have four adults in the house. I hope Frenchy can bring him around, because I'm at the end of my wits."

"It might be good for Frenchy, too. He spends a lot of time, maybe too much time, with the kids, according to what you told me."

"Yeah. Well, let's go look at your project. Turn your radio back on, please."

They soon arrived at the garage. Four of the lifters were parked there, each connected to the battery charger, still drawing power from *Farside*. Chuck looked at the meters and selected a lifter with sixty-five percent charge.

"Should be enough. Want to drive?"

"No, you take it. I'll hang on to the back seat. We won't be out long, you can see where the bulldigger is. Just follow the dust cloud!" John chuckled.

Less than a minute later, Chuck brought the lifter to a hover and watched the machine. "How can you tell it's operating? I see the boom moving, but there's no sound, no diesel smoke...

"Look at the treads. See how the dust is vibrating? We can't hear it, but you're seeing the vibrations from the diesel, spreading through the tracks. As long as you can see those, the engine is running."

"Hard to believe, a diesel engine running on the moon."

"I know. The engineer that thought this up was either a genius or batshit crazy. For the moment, I'm going with genius, but it wouldn't take much to change my mind!"

* * *

CHUCK ASKED Will if he wanted to fly copilot on the trip back to Earth, but he refused. He spent most of the trip looking down at his hands, clenched together in his lap. He finally glanced around after reentry, when they were on the final leg of the trip. The *Lina* was descending through 80,000 feet and the Queensland coast was in sight before his hands relaxed. Chuck watched him glance out the side, then look up at the display panel.

"You've flown one of these, Will, a larger one. You still don't remember?"

"No, I... there's something, but it just won't come. I remember a man hitting me, but nothing after that. Other things are cloudy, so I can't tell if they're dreams or real. Some have to be dreams, but how can I tell? They all seem real."

"Just relax then, we'll be on the ground in a few minutes. Frenchy is meeting us. He won't drive, neither will my wife, not yet, so they're using Bert as a driver. I stay home with Lina and the babies most of the time. Frenchy has been spending a lot of time out of the country. He says it's something to do with finance, but whatever it is, he's keeping it close to his vest."

"I don't follow business news as much as I once did; I used to read the Wall Street Journal, newspapers, The Economist every week, but that stopped after I got involved with the company. I just didn't have the time. I keep getting the papers and magazines because I never bothered to cancel the subscriptions. Did you ever meet Sol Goldman, the CEO of that company Frenchy had his money in? Before New Frontiers, I mean?"

"Not that I recall. Frenchy began pulling his money out to finance New Frontiers, and I don't recall that he ever mentioned Goldman after that. No, I'm sure I never met the man. I wouldn't mind, because I'd dearly love to punch him in the mouth. Frenchy is convinced he was behind a lot of what went wrong while we were starting the company."

"You can forget that idea. He's dead, suicide, according to the paper."

"Really? What caused him to do that, I wonder?"

"Depression, according to the doctors. They gave him something to calm him down and he overdosed. Some think it was accidental, others say it was deliberate. Even the people he exercised with...he had a regular date at a gym to play squash, and he golfed...began avoiding him. The paper didn't say why, just that he became withdrawn. Anyway, he's gone. I wonder if Frenchy knows?"

Chuck considered the news while monitoring their descent. If Goldman *had* been the one behind Lina's rape and the arson attempt, good riddance. But soon calls began coming in over the radio, providing landing instructions and telling him where to meet customs agents, so the thought slipped his mind. A short time later, *Lina* locked in the hangar, he met Frenchy and the three set off for home.

17

A month went by before Chuck returned to the moon. Moonbase was livable; food and water still had to be brought up from Earth, but the power system was working and the first five habitats were in place around the central crater. A protective dome covered the crater; it would be sealed to the surface and pressurized later on, but for now, only the habitats held air. A second dome protected people working on the surface, and the third covered the shipping-container living area.

Chuck parked *Lina* near *Farside* and shut down the impellers. The older ship's tanks had been refilled; she now served as Moonbase's emergency vehicle should something go catastrophically wrong. The power cable was still in place, but now it drew power from the fuel-rod plant to keep *Farside's* batteries charged and the fuel cells warmed, meaning they could be brought on line in less than a minute.

He attempted to radio John as he left *Lina's* cabin, but got no answer. Puzzled, Chuck checked his suit radio, but everything seemed normal. He listened to messages as the workers talked back and forth, so finally he radioed one of the foremen to meet him near the big tent where the bulldigger was parked.

Chuck spoke to the foreman as he approached.

"I tried to call John, but he didn't answer. Is he sleeping?"

"No, this is his duty shift. I think he's doing his mandatory exercise."

"Exercise? That sounds excellent."

"I think it was your idea, or maybe it was just something you said. Anyway, people change in low gravity, so John's got us doing an hour of exercise every morning and another hour at the end of each shift."

Movement caught Chuck's attention, but it was only there for a second. He tried to turn his head, but the helmet's limitations forced him to turn to look where he'd seen the motion. Strange...it almost looked like...

"Is that a *dog*? Dammit, did someone bring a pet up here? I'll have someone's ass if he did!"

The man kept a straight face as he replied, "No dogs, no pets of any kind. Besides, where would we find a suit for a dog?"

"Then what the hell was that thing I saw? It was short, four legged, and moving like a bat out of hell! Something's going on here, and I want an answer now!"

"I'll let John explain it. He's behind you, someone must have told him you were here."

Chuck turned around, carefully stepping in place; he wasn't accustomed to wearing the third layer of the suit. He was struck dumb when he saw John.

"John, what in the world...what happened to your legs?"

"Nothing, I just took them off. The suit covers my stumps, so taking the legs off was no problem, they just snap on over the suit. I took my old legs, the ones I got from the VA, and modified them. They wouldn't work up here anyway, the gravity is too light. The springs in the feet are designed for Earth-normal gravity, so I couldn't compress them enough to get any spring in my step. No pun intended. Anyway, I took them to the shop and a couple of the guys gave me a hand, enlarging the stump socket until it would fit comfortably over the suit legs, adding snaps so they would use the same system everyone else does. It's how they lock moon boots to the suit legs. I took the leg extension off the left leg, then cut off everything on the right leg except two inches. The right leg was shorter after the surgery, so the extra length compensates. They're technically feet instead of legs now, but they work great. Like them?"

"I don't know. Why would you do all that?"

"Well, after I replaced the Earth-normal springs with springs that were only a sixth as strong, I decided to go whole hog. I put pads on my gloves, with an extra layer where the hands meet the wrists. I flex my hands back now when I'm exercising, so the pad protects the heel of my hand. I'll have you know I hold every speed record on the moon. Want to race?"

"How the hell can you race in those ridiculous things?"

"What say we take a little run? You've got your three-layer suit, I've got my modified version. How about we race to the end of the plumbing line, you can see the rock cairns that show where the fuel rods are buried. Just stay to the right of those, run to the end of the line, and come back. Tell you what, I'll even give you a head start."

"You're serious?"

"Serious enough to bet you a bash at the best hotel in Reykjavik next time we're dirtside. Anyone else want to run with us?" By this time, the entire shift had come up to watch.

"I like the idea of exercise, but I don't know…"

"You can afford the bet. There's the course, take off."

Chuck nodded, then decided to pace himself. He walked halfway, then began trotting, the usual long gliding steps of someone with experience in reduced gravity.

He had gone less than a hundred yards when John raced past him, bounding gorilla-like. The pads on his gloves made contact, then the short legs swung up between his arms and pushed off strongly.

The bounding gait was faster than Chuck would have believed had he not seen it himself.

"You win. That was you I saw before, wasn't it? What about the other men? Can they do something like this?"

"Sure, the light gravity really makes a difference. I made extensions that fit over their forearms so that the front 'legs' are long enough to swing their natural legs up under their body. They can keep up with me on the straightaways, but they can't turn as fast. It's my low center of gravity, I expect. Anyway, it's fun, and the exercise is keeping us healthy."

"What about radiation?"

"We only pick up a fraction of a rad, thanks to the new suits. Later on, after the tunnels are completed, we can run in those and not pick up any radiation at all."

"You've got your blowout, next time you're dirtside. Bring your crew if you want."

"I'll definitely take you up on that!"

* * *

CHUCK'S RETURN was timed to reenter atmosphere just as Australia came into view. Dropping down, he swung around as Brisbane passed beneath him, then touched down in front of the leased hangar. This time, there was no one to meet him; Chuck had finally gotten his Queensland driver's license and bought a car, which remained in the hangar while he was away. Other than the right-hand controls, it was similar to the Volvo he'd owned in the US.

Brisbane traffic was heavy, so getting home to Burpengary took longer than expected. Finally he pulled into the brick driveway, locked the car, and went in. He greeted Frenchy and Will, who were busy keeping the twins happy.

"Where's Lina?"

"She expected you half an hour ago," Frenchy said. "You're taking her out to dinner."

"I am? Well, I'm glad someone told me. Do I have time to get cleaned up?"

"Of course, although I wouldn't take longer than necessary. Women don't mind keeping men waiting, but they don't like it when it's the other way around."

"I don't feel like driving, especially if I sample the booze. Have you got Mac's number?"

"Sure, you hold Robbie and I'll see if he's available."

"Thanks. Come here, squirt." He took the squirming child, who promptly decided she didn't like the new arrangement. She cried lustily until Chuck put her down on the mat. She hiccupped for a moment, then quieted down. Will put Bobby down and the twins crept toward each other.

Chuck was watching them when Frenchy returned. "He'll be here in half an hour, if that's acceptable. Should I call him back?"

"No, half an hour's fine. I'll go up and grab a quick shower. A shave wouldn't hurt either. If Lina comes down before I do, tell here where I am."

"Will do," answered Frenchy.

Chuck had watched Will as he played with Bobby. The child was progressing well; other than a slight favoring of his left leg, he moved almost as well as Robby. Will also appeared to be progressing, smiling as he played with the babies. Maybe he would recover completely? Chuck hoped so.

Lina was waiting when he came down from his shower. Chuck wore typical lightweight Australian clothing, trousers, loose shirt, and loafers. Lina was dressed for a night out in Brisbane, a slinky black dress and heels, with the pearl necklace and earrings that Chuck had given her two years before. She frowned momentarily at Chuck's casual dress, then kissed him and took his arm.

"Don't wait up, dad. Ask Mildred to put the babies to bed in half an hour, please."

Chuck asked, "Mildred? Is she new?"

"Right, she's the new nanny during the week. She's very good."

"And the lady we had before?"

"She prefers to work weekends, so she can spend more time with her family. She found Mildred for us."

"That's a good recommendation. Where are we going?"

It's an area called Fortitude Valley. Lots of restaurants, live music, bars, pretty much everything we could want. You're taking me to dinner, then dancing."

"I should have dressed up more, shouldn't I?"

"You're probably okay. Australians are pretty laid back."

"That's good. Any special reason? I didn't forget our anniversary or your birthday, so is there a special occasion?"

"Other than that you haven't taken me out for more than a month? No, no special occasion at all."

Chuck was apologetic. "Honey, I'm usually exhausted at the end of the week. You know that."

"I do, and I also know you're working way too hard. You've got gray patches at your temples, did you know that?"

"Well, it's not as if I could turn the job over to someone else. I'm finally getting a handle on it, so maybe I'll have more time for us now."

* * *

EIGHT MEN SAT around a table in Baku, Azerbaijan. Four of them had met before; the new arrivals were much more senior. In addition to the current head of Roscosmos, there were senior bureaucrats from other members of the Grand Alliance. For the moment, the alliance operated without public scrutiny. The American representative was Pinchot Forberger, now deputy chief of staff to the president of the USA. He opened the discussion.

"So far, nothing noteworthy has happened. That's got to change. You Russians are even more desperate than the rest of us. Your space program is facing collapse and it's not just the money, you've lost some of your best people. The brain drain has accelerated, now that your economy is headed into the tank. I question whether you can do your part. If you can't get yourselves in gear, we'll go ahead without you.

"I'm authorized to tell you that the US is going ahead with a plan that has several possible avenues to success. We will soon have a research program that's similar to the Manhattan Project of the Second World War years. The tentative name is Project Los Angeles, and if you want to share in our discoveries, you'll be expected to provide commensurate amounts of money. As for China, we expect your contribution will be to provide Project Los Angeles with money and the necessary rare earth elements. We expect that the project will need magnets that are unlike anything currently in existence. As for Europe, you need to make up for your failure to grab that crashed ship. Did you ever get anything from the two hijackers you captured?"

"No. Unfortunately, they died in prison. It is regrettable. There was a fight between prison gangs, I'm told."

"So. Another failure. I question whether this alliance needs four members. We may decide to go it alone, but this time we'll do it without your spies." He pointedly looked at the Russians. "If we do succeed, we will expect considerably more than what you've done so far."

"We also have excellent scientists," grated the Chinese representative. "Perhaps we should also pursue an independent venture."

"You have scientists, and they put out a lot of new papers every year, but how many are ever cited by other researchers? If other researchers don't cite your discoveries, then how important are they? As for you Russians, you do have one asset we expect to need. Your rocket motors are still useful, although you haven't improved the design in years. You also haven't even attempted to launch unmanned probes, much less try for a landing on the moon. At least China has plans to do that. Do you have a timetable?"

"One year. If our vehicle is not ready, we have approval to purchase transport from New Frontiers. I would rather not do so, but if it is a question of using that company or not getting to the moon at all, we will pay their price. They're very busy, your former countrymen. How many others are they carrying into space?"

"I can't answer that. They've worked with several nations, I know that much, and I know the Saudis approached them but were turned away. There were a few face-saving reasons given, but the CIA believes NFI simply didn't want to take the Saudis to space. Whether they refused other requests we just don't know. As for Saudi Arabia, we think it has to do with the terrorism issue, but we can't be certain. NFI won't discuss it."

"That seems somewhat high-handed of them. Pardon the pun; I did not mean to make a joke."

"We will meet again, this time in Washington, in one month. Have someone at the meeting who has the authority to decide.

"Our people are getting impatient. I've told you our intentions, some of them, but there are other plans. Convince us that we should share our discoveries with you. So far, you've done nothing to convince me that your participation is worthwhile."

Forberger stood up and walked out of the room.

18

M ark Triffin, the president's chief of staff had grown blasé. The short, balding former mayor and company executive had long been accustomed to meeting rich and powerful people. Now he controlled access to the most powerful man in the world.

This morning's meeting was between the two of them, just the president and himself, in the Oval Office. There had been many such.

Laying the laptop on the desk, he greeted his boss. "Good morning, Mister President. I've got the information you asked for. I didn't want to put it on paper."

"Probably a good idea, Mark, this place leaks like a sieve. Wipe the information after we're done, okay? You found it once, you can find it again. Tell me about this NFI outfit."

"It's a private company, closely held. The original corporate filings were in Delaware, but the company moved their headquarters to Switzerland about three years ago. There were a number of investors in the beginning but they sold out to a man named Fuqua, who's been running the company until a short time ago. We don't have access to all the records, the Swiss are secretive as you know, but it appears that most of the stock is held by Fuqua, his daughter Felina, and her husband Charles Sneyd. Sneyd is the grandson of the man who invented the impeller. He worked on it too, so there's more to him than just family connections. The fourth largest block of stock is held by Will Crane, the sole remaining investor from the original company. A few other shares are in the hands of employees, given as performance bonuses we believe, but Fuqua's extended family holds more than half of the shares. They control NFI, in other words."

"Go on. I'm having coffee, want some?"

"Thank you, sir. Yes, please."

Mark waited while the president poured him a cup, then continued.

"There's been a quiet shakeup, according to what we get from the Swiss. Fuqua is still chairman of the board, but Charles Sneyd now runs the company. He prefers to be called Chuck, Fuqua is known as Frenchy, and the daughter is Lina. They've renounced their American citizenship, that happened three months ago. Crane is still an American citizen, but it's possible he'll go that route too. We're not certain, but it looks like Crane may have been pushed aside. He was on the books as executive vice president for operations, but at this time he's on leave of absence. Sneyd was a minor player until a few months ago, but suddenly he's chief executive, Fuqua has been pushed upstairs, and Crane is on leave of absence. The CIA thinks Sneyd may have engineered a coup."

"So the company is headquartered in Switzerland and the people running it are no longer American. More tax evasion?"

"No sir, not this time. There was an accident, a death, and NFI refused to provide answers. There may have been other regulatory issues. There were court filings, but NFI shut down their factory and none of their senior people could be subpoenaed because they were out of the country. For all practical purposes, NFI shut down American operations except for a small contract with DARPA. They subse-

---

quently reorganized as an offshore company with a nominal headquarters in Switzerland, but with operations in a lot of countries."

The president nodded while his chief of staff scrolled down the report and pointed to the screen.

"They had a factory in New Mexico to make the devices, that's where the accident happened, but it's closed now and listed for sale. It's located on a ranch that belongs to Fuqua, and he wants to sell that too according to the real estate agent who lists it. A part of the ranch has already been sold. Fuqua built a generating system on the property, primarily to supply power to his factory but it was also tied into the grid. He was strapped for cash at the time, so he raised money by selling power through a New Mexico company. The eastern portion of the ranch, along with the power plant, was sold after the factory was shut down. The CIA thinks Fuqua used the money and the income he got from government contracts to expand offshore. It's a remarkable achievement; NFI may be the largest company in the world, based on net worth, but if not, it's only a matter of time."

The president held up his hand and Mark paused while he thought about it. "So NFI is big, but are they important? Walmart is big, but in the end they're only stores, importers and resellers. If they went out of business, other companies would move in."

"NFI's different, Mister President. They're not only diversified, but they hold a monopoly. As long as they're the only ones with a functional space drive, they control space."

"Continue with your briefing, Mark." The president poured himself another cup of coffee.

"Fuqua wants to sell the factory and the ranch as a package. So far, no one is interested. It's too bad, because the factory was essentially self-contained. It even has its own airstrip."

"So why did they shut it down?"

"As I mentioned, there was an accident and one of their employees was killed. The Department of Transportation got an injunction which would have forced them to cease operations temporarily, pending resolution of certain questions. The FAA was involved too. Instead, NFI shut the plant down and moved a part of their manufacturing operation to Mexico. They had a contract with the Defense Advanced Projects Agency, and they used the Mexican company to build the devices DARPA was interested in, at least some of the components. The Mexican company had nothing to do with the propulsion system, NFI did that themselves. It appears we, the government that is, helped finance the company's development. But not anymore, they're rolling in cash now. They're working for a number of countries, launching satellites and so forth, but their primary business is hauling spent fuel rods to space. Several of our own companies would like to employ them, but the Nuclear Regulatory Commission balked. Congress won't authorize it either. NFI's ships have never undergone certification, they simply ignore any requests, and since they're not an American company, there's nothing we can do."

"They're putting that stuff in orbit? What does the UN say?"

"No sir. They're sending it off to the sun, so the UN isn't involved."

"Tell me about this accident. Shutting down their whole operation...that seems extreme. One accident? Those things happen all the time. I'm surprised I didn't hear about it."

"You were campaigning for governor at the time. Anyway, the man was flying one of their machines when he was killed, which is why Transportation and Aviation acted as they did. But because NFI shut down so fast, the existing records are spotty. NFI was there one day, the next day the company employees were gone. A month later, even their security people left. They simply locked up and left.

"The building is empty now. The regulators wanted information, you can probably guess why, but the only people they ever managed to talk to were low-level security guards. Now, no one at DOT or the FAA is willing to talk about what happened. It's possible there may be more to the story."

"Put someone on that. This doesn't sound right, there's got to be more. What else did they do? Was he the only casualty? Find out. There's *got* to be more information somewhere; look at tax records, see what their neighbors have to say. This is skimpy, too skimpy. There will be records somewhere, put enough people on it to find them. Put the FBI on it."

The president refilled his cup, then took a swallow.

"I'm not blaming you, Mark, but you don't build a spaceship overnight. Someone, a lot of someones, knows something. Find them. I really wish they hadn't shut down. We could have worked through the regulatory issues. There are waivers, we do it all the time. Imagine how much business we'd be doing, what it would mean to our balance of payments, how much tax money that would bring in! And that's just the tip of it, we're being shut out of space. One lousy private company! We've spent more than a trillion dollars putting people in space, sent men to the moon, and now we're no better off than Costa Rica! Worse! Neither of us has a space presence, but at least they didn't spend a lot of money trying! What about the Russians?"

"They're no better off than we are. Not that *they* didn't try; there was an incident, the FBI investigated it. They outed a couple of Russian agents who were in the country illegally, and eventually we swapped them for four of ours that the Russians were holding. NFI has reason not to love the Russians. They tried to steal the device. Devices, now."

The president studied the items on the laptop. "NASA is pissed too. We were launching satellites for a number of countries, but NFI has undercut NASA's costs. A half-ton satellite at ten thousand dollars a pound adds up. NFI charges half what we do, half of what the Russians or the French can do. Goddammit, we're becoming a second-rate country! Do you know what that will mean next election?

The opposition will crucify me, they'll call me the president that sat on his ass and watched while the USA was left in the dust. One superpower, a bunch of other powerful nations, and one--lousy--company sits up there and thumbs its nose at us. I won't have it! You do whatever it takes, find me an angle. Set up a meeting with the directors of the CIA and the FBI, I'll light a fire under their butts! Tell them I'm concerned about NFI, so they'll know what to bring. Better bring in the chairman of the joint chiefs and the director of the NSA too.

"There's something else. I've got a bunch of scientific people pulling my chain. They want to set up another Manhattan Project. They're calling it Project Los Angeles, probably a good idea, but I have no idea whether Congress will fund it. I've had a bunch of people from the Congress talk to me, but only two of them seemed to be for the idea. Their reaction was strange...maybe they've got something personal against the company. I'll take care of the Congress, you get me the rest of what I need."

"Mister President, there's a low-level group that meets from time to time, they're also interested in NFI. Are you interested in talking to them?"

"Not now. How much more time do we have?"

"You've got a meeting in two minutes, Mister President. It's a trade delegation from..."

"John, do you have legs that can handle Earth gravity? We usually run the ships at one gee to protect the crew, so you'll need another set if you intend to leave Luna."

"It won't be a problem. The sockets on my other legs can be changed out; I've got a set that fits over the shipsuit and one that fits the stumps, as well as one I'm using that fits over the outer layer. The springs are easily changed, I've got a couple of sets of those. For that matter, I could reuse the ones I took off my VA legs. I'd only need one of the lower leg extensions, to replace the one I cut up."

"That's good. I always wondered how good the legs were, the ones the VA supplied. I met guys who were unhappy with theirs while I was in and out of the hospital."

"Yeah. I don't know, Chuck; did they treat me different because I lost both legs, or because I was an officer? I don't know, but some of my troops were really bitter. Maybe I got better treatment because I was at Walter Reed. It's in Washington, close enough that a lot of politicians cruise through looking for a photo op so they can claim they care about the troops."

"You sound bitter too, John."

"You could say that. Given a choice, I'd reinstate the draft. Too many poor kids carrying rifles, vanishingly few rich kids or politicians' kids. I don't want to talk about it, okay? There's nothing either of us can do."

"Okay. You know why we run the ships at one gee, right?"

"Bone loss, heart and circulatory system damage, loss of lung function if I remember correctly," replied John.

"That's close enough. Plus we need the impellers to generate the plasma field, so we might as well run at a full gee. It solves a lot of problems, not to mention it gets us there fast!" Chuck said.

"Come on, I'll show you what we've done since the last time you were here." John led the way to the edge of the crater, now stabilized. *More icecrete?* wondered Chuck. *Or maybe that's the infused product, the one that uses metals.*

John jumped over the edge, landing softly in front of the habitats ten feet below. "Come on down, you can do it. It's not that much of a jump."

"If you say so. What if you fall?"

"I have, several times. The helmets can take it, so can your legs."

Sighing, Chuck stepped off the edge and fell slowly. John reached out a hand and steadied him as he landed, knees slightly bent. "That's the way. Nothing to it, once you get used to the gravity. We can't enter the habitats; only the residents have permission. It's their space, I try not to violate it."

"Good policy. I've seen what the insides look like, before they were collapsed and packed to ship up here. You're putting six people in each one?"

"Six men; it's cramped, but better than the shipping containers. One habitat has two women. As we get others we'll put them in there too, then I suppose we'll need another habitat."

"Makes sense. They're plain, but they look okay. Did they fix the toilet problem?"

"Yes, there's now a sealed dehydration chamber. It's separated from the toilet by an airlock, and there's a mechanical lockout that keeps both doors from being open at the same time. Flushing uses a liter of water, but that's captured and recycled. Everything works fine, so far."

"Good to know. Okay, I just wanted to check in. I need to head back, I've got a meeting with a Chinese delegation before I can go home."

"How are the kids doing?"

"Growing like weeds. Bobby's not keeping up with Robbie, not that it bothers him. He just works a little harder. They're pulling themselves up on a railing Frenchy installed around their play area. He swears they'll be walking any day now. They're both saying things like Mama and Papa, but Papa is Frenchy, not me. I suppose I'll have to work on that, if I ever get a few days free. But the crises don't come around once a week, not even once a day. It's more like once an hour," Chuck sighed.

"Well, you knew the job was dangerous when you took it. My guys used to tell me that one when I bitched about something."

"Yeah, that's one. The other one was 'if you can't take a joke...'"

"I heard that one too."

* * *

THE CHINESE WERE WAITING when Chuck arrived, lined up around a large circular table. Chuck nodded, thought of bowing and decided that was too Japanese, so he took his place in the remaining chair.

"Gentlemen." Chuck waited for the translator to catch up. "As you know, my company is interested in purchasing certain commodities that China produces in abundance. I hope we can come to an agreement."

One of the Chinese replied, and this time Chuck's translator took longer to catch up. "We believe you can also be of help to our ventures. We wish to land a scientific party to evaluate a region of the moon, and we wondered if your ships might assist. It may be that we will place a party there for a somewhat longer period of time. Are you interested in a deal, Mister Sneyd?"

The haggling started. "How many people, where, and for how long? You are Mister Zhang Wei, I believe?"

"I am. Let us discuss the cost of each trip, the turnaround time for your craft, and the amount of cargo you can transport in a single shipment."

"I can provide that information, not today but certainly in less than a week. Are you intending to pay in renminbi or dollars? I can make you a better deal if you're willing to bypass the currency and go directly to trading rare earth elements for flight time. As you know, currency can be exchanged, but it is best used in the nation that issued it. Exchange rates can vary, China has recently devalued her currency, and I would regret accepting payment in RMB only to find it had been devalued again. You understand, I'm sure."

He glanced around the table. Two of the Chinese were smiling, the other faces were expressionless. Not surprising; many Chinese love playing poker.

"Does your device use rare earth elements? We would pay well for one."

"I cannot discuss our propulsion system. As you know, I'm a business-man, not a scientist. I doubt I have the information you want. But," Chuck shrugged and spread his hands, "at some time we may choose to sell ships. Friends would, of course, be considered favorably when such comes to pass."

"But not now?"

"No. I can discuss your transportation needs, I'm willing to accept the rare earth elements we need for batteries and magnets, but if that's not on the table..." Chuck looked around the table.

"No, no, we are willing to barter. But I do hope you will remember us when the device goes on the market."

"Count on it. We do not forget friends." Unspoken was the corollary; NFI did not forget enemies either.

"Can you transport a party of scientists to a location on the far side of the moon? Say, ten persons with supplies for one month?"

"A month? That's quite a long time. Shipping isn't a problem, but you are aware of the radiation hazard, are you not? We can also provide your party with a protective dome our company has developed. It protects from radiation, and also shields anyone working beneath it from observation. If, of course, that has anything to do with your decision to put your party on the other side of the moon."

"I... see. Yes, we would be interested in such a shield. Assuming we can come to an agreement, of course. And follow up trips, to bring supplies and perhaps replace some of our scientists? For a longer period even, perhaps six months or a year? Could you do that, and are you willing to do so?"

"Of course. It's not a problem. Most of our ships are contracted for, they're transporting certain materials to space, but we have others. *Giant*, for example, can carry ten people easily, complete with enough supplies for an extended stay. If you provide us with a location, I'll have the radiation shield in place before your people arrive. I may also be able to help with supplies, advice if nothing else. I would not want your people to be endangered. We do have experience in space, you know. What did you intend to supply your people with? We repurpose shipping containers to house our people, you could do the same. Of course, we would expect compensation. The shipping containers require modification, and we can sell you the kits to make them livable."

Half an hour later, meeting ended, Chuck headed back to *Lina*. Behind him, the Chinese group split into smaller groups. One of the Chinese left with a man who'd attended the meeting but who had not spoken at all.

"What did you think, Comrade Kim?"

"I think you should know that elements of the government do not want to do business with this NFI company. The costs are likely to be high. Are you certain of your support?"

"I believe so. The Chairman's wife's sister has extensive interests in mining. She will be happy to provide the materials this Chuck person desires. She also intends that her family be represented among the group on the moon. Family is very important in China, you know."

"I know, in my country also."

19

Mark spoke to the secretary, then knocked and entered the Oval Office.

"Good morning, Mister President."

"Morning, Mark. What have you got for me?"

"I have your itinerary for the day. You're scheduled to meet with the security council later; will you want me there?"

"I don't think so, Mark. I glanced at this morning's briefing paper, so things appear to be in control. Have you found more information about that other matter we discussed, the NFI company?"

"I think so. Some of my conclusions were wrong, as it turns out. Sneyd didn't take over the company, it was an amicable transfer of power. There are health issues involved."

"But the facts are essentially the same?"

"Yes, sir."

"Skip it for now. When am I meeting with the security council?"

"The meeting is to start at 3:20 and last an hour. If necessary, the time can be extended for another hour. I can shift a meeting with your political strategists to tomorrow."

"Sounds good. Did you hear back from the FBI?"

"Yes, sir. They picked up a rumor...I'd rather wait until I'm sure. It's not confirmed, so I don't want to raise false hopes, but we may have an opening."

"Sounds interesting." The president was distracted. "What about the rest of the week?"

"The Nigerian President is visiting Friday. You'll give a speech in the Rose Garden, there'll be photos, the usual drill."

"What are we meeting about?"

"Nigeria wants more trade, you accepted because you need to bolster your civil rights credentials among black voters. I'll have a detailed briefing for you before he arrives. The Secretary of State's meeting him at the airport."

"That's right, I do. Too many minority voters went for the opposition, we'll need to do better. Am I scheduled to visit this Project Los Angeles? We don't want to call attention to it, do we?"

"No, sir. I can set up a briefing, possibly a quiet visit. No publicity, I mean."

"Go with the briefing, I'll let you know if I want a visit. Who's on the agenda next?"

"There's a delegation from Taiwan..."

* * *

CHUCK, in *Lina*, followed *Giant* to a landing between the photovoltaic plant and the dozen domes the Chinese had bought from NFI.

Seen from space, the Chinese base appeared several times larger than NFI's own installation. Chuck thought about it, then realized that Moonbase's power plant was hidden, as were the habitats. Even the dome that had covered the original blast crater was gone, sold to the Chinese. The crater, roofed over, was pressurized, as were the access tunnels; the only visible sign that humans had ever been there was the two-meter armored glass dome over the emergency exit.

Two of the huge protective domes remained, one covering an outdoor workshop, the other shielding the emergency housing village. Wolfgang wanted to sell the modified shipping containers to the Chinese, but Chuck had resisted. Having a place to put people, should something happen to the underground base, was cheap insurance. It meant that *Farside* was now free to make regular supply runs.

Small, unobtrusive, blisters on *Giant's* dorsal held that ship's own insurance policy. Each contained a heavy machine gun, old but serviceable. Chuck locked *Lina's* hatch, then looked at the two blisters. A small red light between the two positions blinked in acknowledgment. No one would approach either hatch. The Chinese had assembled two-person vehicles, electrically powered and similar in appearance to the original Lunar Rover. The machine guns ensured that the vehicles kept their distance.

There had been considerable debate, first about arming the big ships, then regarding what to use and where to position it. Should the guns cover the impellers, or only the hatch? Finally someone pointed out that even if someone managed to steal an impeller, he would have no place to take it. The Chinese base depended on NFI ships to maintain their lifeline. So the blisters covered the hatch, and when Chuck brought his ship to a landing near *Giant*, *Lina* was also protected.

Chuck joined the crew, helping unload supplies. If the Chinese knew who he was, no one let on. He took a break half an hour later and looked around.

An astonishing number of Chinese had appeared from beneath the domes, picked up containers, and were now carrying them under the protective shield. Was this where they broke down the cargoes? Their transport system was simplicity itself; metal poles were inserted through rings at each corner of the containers. Twelve workers, three at each corner, laid hands on the extended bars, picked up a container, and walked away with it.

Where had all the people come from? Chuck suddenly understood; some of the containers they'd just unloaded might carry people. He shook his head ruefully.

The Chinese government was testing long-range rockets now, but could they keep the base supplied? All those people, they'd need food, water, oxygen, equipment. Perhaps the Chinese could keep it going, now that most of the work was done. Clever...the Chinese had used NFI to bootstrap their way onto the moon!

Giant was finally unloaded, and the captain walked to meet his counterpart. Presenting an electronic register, he held it while the Chinese scanned the list, then nodded. He pressed the buttons in a sequence known only to the Chinese, accepting the delivery. The captain nodded, then both turned away. Chuck boarded *Lina* and brought her to a hover, waiting. He fell in behind *Giant* and trailed the big ship, splitting away after they reentered atmosphere. He landed half an hour later in Brisbane and was soon home, playing with the toddlers.

An hour later, the children off to bed in the care of the nanny, Chuck joined Lina on the veranda.

"Where did Frenchy disappear to? Come to think of it, I haven't seen Will either."

"They're having a boys night out." She clicked her tongue, disapprovingly. "It's a celebration. Will's doing a lot better, although he still hates to fly. But that may change too, it's just too soon to tell.

"So it's just you and me tonight?" Chuck waggled his eyebrows expressively. Lina glanced at him, surprised, then understood. "One more glass of wine and maybe we'll see, big guy." The two smiled at each other.

* * *

PETE WAS WAITING when Chuck reached his Reykjavik office. "Come on in, maybe Adelheid can scare us up a cup of coffee. I thought you were in Rovaniemi."

"I was. I've spent the last six weeks there. Before that, I was in India for a few days, South Korea, then Brazil, South Africa...there were days I didn't know whether I was coming or going."

"Really, all those places? Why don't you tell me about it?" Chuck hung his coat in the closet and sat down. Adelheid brought cups, a carafe of coffee, and a platter of pastries, then vanished silently through the door. Pete's visit had upset her itinerary.

"It's the new impellers. The South Africans make the coils and the Koreans machine the rotors. We get frames from Brazil, other parts from India... Bangladesh too, I almost forgot that.

"Anyway, we get parts and subassemblies from all over and I wanted to make sure of the quality before building the new units. Final assembly will be done here or in Rovaniemi.

"I thought of doing it in the cave, but decided to leave that alone. It was a good bolthole when we needed it, and who knows? We might need it again.

"There are people at the ranch just in case, but no one's staying in the cavern. There's not a lot to see down there anyway."

Chuck nodded. "Good thinking. I can't see us needing it, but I won't sell the old place. Are they keeping the brush cleared from the cemetery?"

"They are. There's a guy that rents out goats, he brings his flock over every month and they keep the area around the ranch house clear."

"Goats?"

"Goats. They'll eat anything."

"Well, whatever works. About the impellers?" Chuck glanced at his watch.

"I told Adelheid to clear your appointments for today, that's why she's pissed. We're going to Japan."

"We are? Why?"

"*I'm* going to make sure the spec book they sent was accurate, *you're* going to beam appreciatively and bow a lot. The first shipment of reactors is ready. The Finns worked up a modification based on the specs, it's mostly a variation on the *Giant* class but with a SMR instead of fuel cells. Different wings too, they had to be strengthened so we could mount the larger impellers on the ends. The tanks are still in the wings, but they all contain oxygen now. The *Cigar* class, that's what we're calling them in-house, can make it to any of the inner planets. The extra oxygen will come in handy. Anyway, as soon as I confirm that the SMRs are what they say they are, the Finns will start work. Six weeks to two months, they say."

"That fast?"

"They say they can do it, and I'm not going to argue. It's amazing how fast things happen when you tell people to spend what they need to. They subcontract a lot of stuff, just do final assembly in Finland."

"We're probably overpaying them. Lots of new millionaires in Rovaniemi."

"Reykjavik too." The two grinned at each other.

"What about you, Pete?"

"Tell you the truth, Chuck, I quit working for the money a long time ago. Now I do it for the fun of it. I've got bank accounts, investments, so have my engineers. Even the mechanics are doing well. It's good business, because they're loyal to NFI."

"I'm glad to hear that. I've certainly got more than I'll ever need, so I understand about not working for the money. I think Frenchy kept doing it because he knew people needed to get off Earth. I'm doing it because a million people depend on me."

Chuck sipped at his coffee and thought. "I could hire an experienced manager. They leave one company, end up managing another one. Some succeed, some fail. I could offer enough money now to hire one of the successful ones away from whoever they're working for. Some are probably good people, but there's no way to be sure. Could I turn the company over to them and still sleep nights? People like that work for themselves, not for their employees. I thought military people were different, and maybe the junior officers are. But by the time they put stars on, they're managers and politicians, not soldiers. Maybe not all of them, but too many are. That million people I mentioned, they may not know me and I don't know them, but I'm still responsible because NFI indirectly pays their wages."

"Chuck, you're going to kill yourself if you're not careful. And then who will take over?"

"I'll watch it. You ready to go?"

"Sure. Next stop, Japan." Pete put down the half-empty cup and the two left for the hangar.

* * *

THE PRESIDENT WAS NOT HAPPY.

"Who the hell picked those people? Congress? Project Los Angeles, my ass. Project *lost*, more like it. Bunch of...goddammit, they don't even have a plan! How do they expect to come up with that impeller thing?"

"They're the best we've got, Mister President. Can I get you a scotch?"

"Make it a double. I don't know, the people who designed the bomb were probably just as feckless. But if that asshat in charge doesn't produce damned quick, he's hosed. I'll fire his ass, it's not as if there was a shortage of generals." The president drank some of his scotch and sat down. "Thanks, I needed that."

"Mister President, I mentioned a group some time back. I've also heard a rumor, something to do with an intercept. NSA noticed something. Do you remember me mentioning it?"

"Yeah, I figured you'd tell me when you found out something more."

"The group is working on their own plan. I hired a man named Forberger to represent us and he seems to have gotten their attention. We're talking senior ministers now, cabinet-level people on their part."

"So who do they represent?"

"China, the European Union, and Russia are the main players. The EU...I can't say I'm impressed, but I think the Russians and Chinese are serious."

"Are they? And minister level, Mark? You're sure of that?"

"Forberger is sure, and I trust his judgment. He tells me he's pushing them hard."

"Set up a meeting, next week. I want to talk to this Forberger."

Mark took out a notebook and made a note.

"There was also a rumor, I mentioned that before. I don't have confirmation, but I think it's worth looking into. I may need operatives."

"Delta force, you think?"

"SEALs, Mister President. NFI bought a ship, it was before they built their factory. The ship was appraised before they bought it, the original owners intended to scrap it. It was old, rusty, so I wondered why someone would want the thing unless it was the scrap metal value. But if NFI disposed of it, I never found a record. There are records listing the transfer of money, but after that, nothing."

"Why would they buy a ship? You're talking about a seagoing ship, right?"

"Yes, sir."

"You said they were short of money back then. Why spend it on a ship? What can you do with a ship? You know what this reminds me of? Drug cartels. They buy an old ship and load it with drugs. If they get one trip out of the thing, they're in the black. I wonder if that's what Fuqua did? Could he have been smuggling dope?"

"I don't know, Mister President. It's just that the name popped up and NSA's computers made the connection. I think it's worth looking into."

"Do what you need to do, Mark. Can I put off whoever I'm supposed to meet with next?"

"Yes, Mister President."

"I thought maybe this project thing might work. It's just another waste of money. Congress pats themselves on the back, picks out a nice piece of pork, but nothing's happening and nothing's going to happen." The president was depressed, and it showed.

"It's not about that company, it's about the future of this country. Study your history. We became a great country because we had great people and natural resources to work with, land, water, coal, oil, metals, timber. But all that existed before we got here, and nothing was done with it. It was people that made the difference, people with vision! But that was then. Our people...well, you know what they're like now. We have entrepreneurs, sure, but there's no Henry Ford, no J. P. Morgan."

The president sipped moodily.

"Sure they got rich, Morgan and Ford. But they cared about the nation too. Now? It reminds me of Rome toward the end, the country hasn't yet fallen but not we're not growing either. No vitality, Mark. The natural resources are gone, the ones that were easy to get. Our problem is finding the best way to use what's left, and since it's cheaper to buy from Chile or Argentina, we import everything. The country's been poisoned, even the land is not what it was. Farmers have to use *more* poison just to make a damned crop, people don't want to work hard on a farm...hell, they don't want to work at much of anything! Sit around an office, shuffling paper." The president sloshed more scotch into his glass. His hand shook.

"Farmland's salty now. It comes from too much irrigation. We even import *food* nowadays. This country fed the world, Mark, now we can't even feed ourselves. Our influence...we don't have any. We can't get rid of the aircraft carriers, we just keep paying more for every new airplane, and we can't stop, we can't even slow down. I understand Churchill a lot better now than when I read about him in college, trying to hold off Hitler on the one hand and hang on to the empire on the other.

"I refuse to let it happen. I'll be goddamned if I let history view *my* administration as the one that let America down. Space, that's where the future is, and Sneyd is standing in our way. I'll do whatever it takes, Mark." The president smashed his hand on the desk.

"I feel like getting drunk! How about you, Mark, want to join me?"

"I'll see about rearranging your schedule, Mister President. Perhaps later. If you'll excuse me?"

"Yeah, go ahead." The president finished the glass and poured himself another.

Mark paused by the secretary's desk on his way out. "No visitors. The boss is indisposed. Better alert the Secret Service guys."

"Again?"

20

S ven Nelsen was content.

NFI had been good to him; the former first mate had satisfied the requirements for a master's license, then worked a year under Captain Sperry. Sperry had moved on to command a spacecraft and Sven had become *Tesla's* second captain. Now, Master at the age of 54, he had few ambitions unrealized. If there was any shade of disappointment, it was because he found the task easier than anticipated. It was also vaguely unsatisfying. Sven considered briefly what being master of a ship with sails had entailed, the numbers of men needed, storage of salted or pickled food, barrels of fresh water, the constant need for maintenance...

But Sven had his own maintenance concerns. Four impellers hummed contentedly along, as functional now as the day they'd been installed. But only four; small leaks in the outer container allowed humid sea air to enter, and parts had rusted or corroded. The first impeller had failed after six months of use. Jim Sperry, at that time master of *Tesla*, had ordered a replacement and swapped out the defective unit, replacing it with the ship's only spare. A return message had promised that a new unit would be forthcoming within a month, but that hadn't happened. Two months later, Jim tried tele-phoning directly. But Morty had died and Frenchy and Will were out of contact. A month later, he tried contacting the company again, only to find the telephone disconnected.

Left with no option, unwilling to see the ship fail, with no resources, Jim had resigned. He sent a report, which was acknowledged. No human saw it; the reply came from an automated server. Sven took command, reported this fact, and received his own acknowledge-ment. With no orders to the contrary, with shipments already contracted, Sven took *Tesla* to sea. He had no spare impeller, but he still had eight that still worked, the same number they'd had at the beginning.

And so the routine was set. A radio report continued to be submitted twice each day, once at noon, the other at midnight. The date and time were entered, as were the ship's coordinates. The date and time of the response from NFI was also logged. Routine requests for replacement impellers were no longer being sent; a single response, a month after Sven became the captain, carried the message 'No longer available'.

But *Tesla's* impellers still worked, the diesel generators thundered their reliable song, and Sven loved being in command.

Eventually, other impellers failed. Vibration opened tiny holes and corrosion set in. In each case, Sven ordered the defective impeller placed in storage where it joined others that had failed. After the third failure, he'd ordered the casings opened to see if he might salvage parts and make one good impeller from three defective ones. But by then the corrosion was advanced; sea air is unforgiving. And anyway, no one on board knew how the impellers worked, so the idea of perhaps making new parts to substitute for ruined ones never got beyond a fleeting thought.

A fourth failure joined the others.

But the remaining four impellers worked as they always had, and there was no sign of failure. *Tesla* no longer had the reserve of power her designers had intended, but even so, the old ship was faster than most tramp freighters. Sven, lacking other instructions, carried on, hauling cargo, hiring new workers, purchasing diesel fuel, oil and replacement parts for the generators when needed. These events were duly reported and receipt of the messages acknowledged.

The last failure had occurred more than a year ago. Four large marine-version impellers, designed for *Tesla* but also for other ships that had never been purchased, drove the ship at a cruising speed of eight knots, with a maximum of fourteen knots. Best fuel consumption dictated the slower speed, but at least he still had something in reserve.

Sven had his command, he was at sea doing what he loved, so he was content.

* * *

PAK SUSILO ENTERED the bridge and stood politely, waiting while Sven finished updating the ship's log. The radio operator would copy the information into his own log and transmit it at noon.

"Pak." The honorific pleased his Indonesian sailors, and Sven was happy to oblige. He'd never quite understood their naming customs; some had only one name, some several, and if there was a system Sven had never found it.

"Adi."

"Is there a problem, Pak Susilo?"

"It may be so, adi. Can the adi come now?"

"Certainly. Let me call Pak Iskandar to the bridge."

Ten minutes later, Susilo leading, Sven found himself examining plates on the ship's starboard midships side. The plates were moist.

"What am I looking at, Pak Susilo? Is this a problem?"

"I have inspected the bilge, adi. It must now be pumped twice daily."

"Unusual. Do you suspect a leak, sprung plates?"

"The plates are not sprung, adi. They weep."

"Is it condensation, Pak? The air is humid, warm, but the sea is cooler."

"Only a few plates weep in this way, adi. They are thin. There is rust."

"You're saying we need a drydock, Pak? The plates need to be replaced?"

"There are frames too, adi. There is corrosion between the frame members and the plates. My crewmen cannot get to it."

"How many plates, Pak?"

"Perhaps twelve, adi. This is one of the worst."

Sven looked at the water. A drop formed as the moisture collected, then flowed slowly down the curve of the old ship's side. It didn't look dangerous. But if enough was accumulating in the bilge to require twice-daily pumping...

"Keep an eye on it, Pak Susilo. If it gets worse, we'll head for Puerto Rico. I'd prefer to finish the voyage if possible, then look for a dry-dock."

"I have seen it before, adi. Other ships. This one is old, a very grandfather of ships. She tires, adi."

"Can we make it to the United States, Pak Susilo? Or should I divert to Freeport in the Bahamas? They have dry docks there."

"I think the United States is possible, adi. But within one year, there must be repairs."

"One year it is. I'll notify the company. We'll discharge our cargo and head for Boston or Philadelphia in ballast. I'll let the company decide which location they prefer."

"What of the crew, adi? Repairs will take months."

"The crewmen will have jobs, Pak Susilo. I will see to it. The company does not lay off workers."

"I will tell the men, adi."

Sven rubbed his forehead. Repair? How much longer would his impellers last?

There was really only one thing to do. He opened the log and began typing. This message would be longer; there was a lot of information to enter. The usual short signal, compressed into a one-second burst, would not suffice.

Receipt of the message was acknowledged. It was not routine, so the server kicked it out. A clerk looked at it, decided this did not concern him, and forwarded it on. Eventually it made its way to Martha's desk. The message made no sense. Finally, she forwarded it to Wolfgang, Director of Flight Ops. He had never heard of a ship named *Tesla*. He reviewed the classes, operational and projected: *Farside, Insect, Giant, Cigar*. This name didn't fit anywhere. Was it a hoax? Maybe Chuck should know. Wolfgang forwarded the message and soon forgot about it. The Finns were experiencing delays in shipments of the complicated cable wiring systems...

Martha had independently arrived at the same conclusion, a possible hoax. Both messages landed in the same file on Chuck's desk, routine matters that he would deal with when he had time.

Tesla's report was detected in another location. This one recorded the message but didn't acknowledge receipt. It never did. The NSA intercepted thousands of messages every minute, and most were never seen by human eyes. Eventually, Sven's report found its way into a digest that reached the desk of a new, and eager, employee. She wondered what it meant, and decided to flag the message.

* * *

CHUCK LEANED BACK, massaging his temples. The headache was back. The chime from his intercom didn't help.

"Yes, Adelheid?"

"Pete and Wolfgang are here, Chuck. Shall I show them in?"

"No, we're leaving. I'll be gone until after lunch, so move my appointments. If it's important, add them to the end of the list and I'll see them before I go home. Otherwise, make room later in the week."

"Yes, Chuck." Chuck grinned; he was certain she sighed, again, but this time she'd cut the connection before he heard. Sometimes she held the button down. Chuck made a mental note to send flowers. Good people were rare, it was worth a gesture of thanks to let them know they were appreciated.

"Let's go, guys. You can brief me in *Lina*. Rovaniemi first, right?"

"Right. I'm flying right seat today, Chuck?"

"You are. Time to get you out from behind that desk."

"I'm happy for the chance, that's not a secret. Sometimes I wonder..."

The three boarded *Lina* and began the checklist.

"So what's up, Pete?"

"Lot of work, Chuck. Martha's smashing the champagne today, then we're visiting the design studio. We've got mockups, two versions, and scale drawings. See what you think."

"I don't know what I think, Pete. For the first time, we'll have ships I'm not qualified to fly. *Cigar*...the pilot's course is being designed, so it's not set in stone, but Martha's people think the transition course will be at least four months long, maybe six."

"Jim Sperry didn't take that long."

"No, but he got special treatment. He was one of the company's first employees, been around since we started. He had individual instruction from day one, reactor classes in the morning with his copilot and operating engineers, simulator time in the afternoon. No days off for any of them."

"Jim's a good man, really motivated. In a way, I'm glad he's getting *Cigar*. First captain of *Mantis*, that was the first upgrade to the *Insect* class, now first captain of *Cigar*."

"He's had a good career, but Jim says two more years. He wants to retire and do a lot of fishing. He only stayed around this long so he could command a nuclear ship. You remember, that was what Morty intended all along. He had to settle for fuel cell power because the small nuclear reactors weren't available."

"Jim deserves it. We're starting to lose people to retirement, Wolfgang. We need a ceremony, something nice, I'll be there if I'm available, you handle it if I'm not. Maybe Frenchy, if he's willing. Let our people know we appreciate what they did for the company. Something nice, more than just a watch and a handshake. Schedule a retirement ceremony once a month, okay? Make it happen."

"I'll do that, Chuck. It's good motivation for our new employees."

Takeoff was routine. Chuck and Wolfgang paid casual attention to the board, letting the computer fly the ship. They topped out above the stratosphere, then began descending toward the boreal forest far below. Off in the distance was Rovaniemi and north of that city, their leased field. Suddenly a red light flashed in the upper center of the display, accompanied by a musical voice. "Radar contact."

Chuck looked at the display, confused. "There's nothing showing on the radar, Wolfgang. What's going on?"

"It's that new long-range radar south of Murmansk. The Russians lopped off the top of a mountain and stuck it up there about a month ago. It paints us every time we take off or land."

"Search radar?"

"We think so. There's no indication it's a tracking radar, part of an air defense missile site. It's got more power and longer range, but as far as we can tell, it's just a radar. Maybe they're going to put in an airport."

"Notify me if it changes. Wolfgang, it's your call. If the Russians are watching Rovaniemi, that could be a problem. We could move the base if we had to. We'd still be flying out of Rovaniemi when new ships are delivered, but everything else could be shifted farther to the west. Sweden, maybe, or Norway. Greenland could work too. I'd prefer to keep the base in the north or south, a cross-polar course is the shortest way to reach Asia."

"I'll keep that in mind. Starting descent now."

"Time to check my messages." Chuck opened his laptop and scrolled down. "This is interesting. Sven Nelsen...I remember that name, but it's tagged routine so I'll look at it later."

* * *

MARK WALKED into the briefing room and looked around approvingly. Most of his time was spent upstairs; this time, a small collection of military officers and a civilian deputy assistant secretary waited.

"Thank you for coming. The president has approved a tasking. The Air Force is tasked to provide intelligence, so plan satellite coverage accordingly. Your packet contains the operations order. If there are questions, see me later. I'll just summarize briefly to let all of you know what your part in the operation is. Area of interest, southern Caribbean, item of interest, a ship. The mission statement is Appendix One of your briefing packet. Ship registry, Liberia. Crew, mixed nationality. Cargo, unknown. Identity of master, unknown. Location, unknown, suspected to be northbound from eastern South America."

"Drug smuggler?" The speaker was a burly commander wearing the uniform of the US Navy.

"Possibly." Mark's answer was immediate, smooth, and meaningless. He'd gained a lot of experience during his political career; appear to answer a question while always leaving escape room.

"Tasking, US Navy and Special Operations Command. The packet contains your warning order. Two destroyers, two RHIBs and crews, SEAL qualified."

"Two boats and crews? One should be enough." The speaker was a stocky Navy Senior Chief Petty Officer. Conspicuous on his uniform, he wore the SEAL trident, commonly known as the 'Budweiser'. Not all SEALS like the name, especially when a non-SEAL uses it.

"Two," Mark confirmed. "It's that important. Mission, board and search. Depending on what you find, take the ship into custody and escort it to the nearest US Navy base, Guantanamo excluded."

"Why the Navy? Drug interdiction is a Coast Guard mission. They've got specialized equipment and experience."

"But the Navy has more experience with SEAL operations. This has to go off fast and quiet, we don't want reporters involved. First priority after boarding, shut down communications, then search the ship. Do it quietly. If you find what I expect, take the ship into custody. Use of force authorization, as appropriate. The mission is capture, not sink. Any questions at this point?"

There were none, so Mark continued.

"Appendix two, equipment and personnel. Appendix Three..."

* * *

THE SUN DROPPED toward the horizon as Chuck shook hands with the visitors. The small, private ceremony was almost over. *Cigar*, the first of her class, resembled the *Giant* series but was powered by a single

SMR. A number of other changes had been made, some visible. The four wings were now thick stubs, the eight impellers on the wingtips huge. The wings were, in essence, specially-shaped containers for high-pressure oxygen. Cigar was expected to fly among the inner planets; the extra oxygen would be needed.

Martha stood on the service gantry's platform and swung the champagne bottle, suspended by a line attached to an overhead support. It smashed satisfyingly against the prow; the bottle had been pre-scored to ensure it didn't bounce off, unbroken. Her speech was short and practiced: "I christen thee *Cigar*. May you voyage safely among the planets."

For a moment, it seemed that the gantry was moving away from the ship. Martha grabbed the rail, then realized that *Cigar* was sliding away. Balanced by the four smaller impellers in the nose, she drifted just high enough not to drag the wingtip skids, located between the impellers. Clear of the observers, she accelerated vertically, on her way to the moon. The cargo, two small modular reactors, had been loaded the evening before. *Cigar* would land them on the moon, then return to pick up two more.

Far above, a brilliant blue flare signaled transition through the Van Allen belts. The glow faded, but never died out entirely. A tiny blue comet curved away, now on course to intersect the moon's orbit.

Chuck walked away, depressed. She was going where he could not go. He remained tied to his offices by responsibility, not so visible as chains but no less real.

Wolfgang and Pete found him there half an hour later.

"You all right, Chuck?"

"Yeah, I'm fine. Just a little let down. I wish Morty could have been here."

"I know what you mean. What did you think of the mockups?"

"I think the toy-top shape has advantages over the thin saucer. Pete?"

"I agree. It's not aerodynamic, but it's got enough power to land on Earth if it had to. You know the story, given enough power..."

"Even a brick will fly!" chorused Chuck and Wolfgang. Chuck smiled for the first time since *Cigar* launched.

"The Finns like that shape better. Not as easy to build, maybe, but in any case, the final assembly will be done on Luna. I'll fax them the go-ahead. *Cigar* is...well, it's a brute, that's what it is. I don't know what to say about *Frisbee*. I guess I'll just wait until it launches."

"How long, Pete?" Chuck asked.

"Six months to a year. She's a big bastard, no getting around it. Even on Luna we'll need special handling gear. As for an assembly building, you're going to need the biggest one ever built. Storing the SMR's on the moon makes sense, but we're still a long way from building *Frisbee*. I'll be hiring another crew. Architects, I think, plus engineers. Where do we find people who can design a building for the moon? It has to hold pressure and be stressed to support weight in a sixth of a gee. I wonder...you mentioned a Chinese base, I wonder what they've been doing?"

"Good question. It's time I paid them a visit, this time officially. I'll see if *Giant's* free, maybe one of the other ships with guns. Or install guns on *Farside*. There's no room on *Lina*, she's cramped as it is."

Pete nodded slowly, then said, "Suppose we armed all the ships? Everything except *Lina*."

"Why?" asked Chuck.

"That Russian radar bothers me, the one that lit us up as we were coming in to Rovaniemi. Radars are expensive, they need crews. Why put a radar out in the back of beyond? The Russians already know what we're doing, so why a new, very powerful radar?"

"You think they'd try to shoot us down?"

"I think I'd rather be prepared if they try. But if they launch an air-defense missile, I don't think there's a lot we can do. But antipersonnel guns, to keep hijackers at bay, that shouldn't be a problem."

"Approved. How much weight are we talking about?"

"I'll let you know when I find out. Not the Alpha pods, they're too heavy and I don't think we'll need them. Something lighter, but effective."

"Just keep me informed. No reason to announce this, see if you can fair over the installation. Make it a nasty surprise that we keep in our pocket until we need it."

21

C huck decided the best way to deal with the puzzling message was with a phone call. Text or fax might work, but voice allowed greater flexibility. Sven answered after the second ring.

"I'm Charles Sneyd, NFI. I'm not sure I understand your report."

"You're Chuck, Morty's grandson?"

"Yes. Do I know you? Your name sounds familiar."

"We met once, I think. I spoke to your grandfather, but you were there. I was sorry to hear he'd passed on."

"Thanks. I miss him, a lot. You still work for the company, right?"

"I'm the captain of *Tesla* now, I took over after Jim resigned. Anyway, I think it's time to scrap the ship. I hate to do it, but I don't think she's worth repairing. Even the frame members and hull plates are showing wear, they'll need to be replaced."

"Scrap a spaceship? We've barely got enough for our current needs! And why would frames and plates need replacing?"

"You don't remember, do you? *Tesla's* ocean-going. It was your grand-father's idea, but Frenchy and Will were there at her maiden voyage. With the new propulsion, I mean."

"Now that you mention it, I do remember something. I was supposed to go with Will and Frenchy, but I was hospitalized for a few days. I took Frenchy's job; did you know that?"

"No, I'm pretty much out of the loop. I haven't been able to contact anyone who knows anything. I send reports, but all I get is 'Message received.' Well, and a message saying the impeller models on *Tesla* have been discontinued."

"I'm not surprised. Most of our models are new. *Tesla* would have versions that are at least five years old now, maybe six. How are they working out?"

"Five aren't. Four are as good as the day we sailed. The others failed because sea air got to them, the bearings seized up. They were rusty, corroded, and some of the bearings just fell apart. The other four work fine, but I think it's time to salvage what we can. The hull can bring in a few dollars as scrap."

"You think it's that serious, this business with hull plates?"

"I do. So does my chief engineer. He's my below-decks supervisor, and I trust his judgment."

"With no propellers, there'll be questions raised. I see only one option at this point, salvage the propulsion system, then tow the hulk to the shipbreakers." Chuck avoided mentioning 'impeller'.

"I see what you mean. Storing them in a warehouse wouldn't guar-antee their security." Sven was also being cautious. "There are a couple of secure locations I can think of, since you mentioned a spaceship."

"Yes. I thought of that too."

"So we go ahead and salvage her. What about the crew?"

"We've got jobs for the men if they want them. They might prefer to find another ship, but if they're willing to retrain, we don't lay good people off, not without giving them a choice. As for you, there's a school you might be interested in. We're always looking for candidates with proven judgment. You qualify. You could be captain of a different kind of ship."

Sven hesitated, thinking.

"Good to know. That was one of my questions. Pak Susilo thinks we're okay for perhaps a year, so I think it's okay to finish the current trip. I agree with his call, but the longer we wait the more dangerous it becomes. We're controlling the leaks for now, but I wouldn't want to risk *Tesla* in a storm. I've only got two more stops to make, consignments to deliver, but I won't take on more cargo. I figure two weeks to Boston after we offload the last of the cargo. Can you have the arrangements made by then? I could put in at Charleston before that if you think that's best. A crew could pull the...ah, propellers...in a day or two and strip out everything important in a week. Could you have a crew available in, say, a week to ten days? I can't give you a specific time, because I may not be able to offload immediately. Harbor masters decide who gets dock space."

"I'm sure we can. I'll get back to you by next Monday. By the way, I really appreciate the job you and your men have done. It was important work."

"Good to know. I won't keep you, Chuck. Thanks for calling."

"Take care, Sven." Chuck broke the connection and laid the phone down. Maybe this was one of the times when he should consult Frenchy. Today was Wednesday, and he'd be in Brisbane by Friday afternoon.

* * *

THE FIVE MEMBERS of the National Security Council were waiting when the president arrived. They stood politely until he had taken his seat and waved them into their chairs. He took a sip of water from the waiting glass, and began.

"It's time I brought you in on something I became aware of last month. There have been feelers from Russia, China, and the European Union; the contacts have been low level up to now and nothing substantive has been agreed on, but this may be an opportunity."

The president glanced around the table. The vice president looked bored, the rest attentive. Well, the vice president wouldn't be involved. If she became part of this, the president, wouldn't care anyway. The term 'over my dead body' came to mind.

"You should know that Project Los Angeles is likely to be a bust. Congress supports it so I won't make a fight of it, but I think it's more pork than possibility. That leaves us with a problem, what to do about space."

The secretary of defense was making notes or doodling on his pad. It was hard to tell from the president's seat. A quick thought flashed through his mind: *Was it time to replace the SecDef?*

"NASA can't do much, considering what the funding cuts did to their budget. That leaves us at an impasse, with NFI blocking our way into space. Rockets have limits, and we've just about reached that point with ours. Rocket ships can take us to the moon, they already have, but they can't take astronauts to Mars and bring them back. The costs are simply astronomical."

The others smiled and the president grinned.

"My scientific adviser tells me that our budget won't support building a base on the moon. Not just NASA's budget, but the entire national budget. We could get the astronauts there, but we couldn't support them. We've been paying the Russians to carry our astronauts to the ISS, and some think we should pay NFI instead. He also says that there's a consensus among the scientific community that NFI already has a base, but short of sending a rocket to orbit the moon we can't be sure. If they have one, it's on the far side. The Chinese may also have something up there. They hired NFI to do something, but the Chinese won't say what it was."

The president paused to let that sink in, and sipped at his water.

"This is where we stand. NFI has us over a barrel and I don't like it worth a bucket of warm spit. I think we ought to do something about it. That's where the contacts I mentioned come in. Our representative, a man named Pinchot Forberger, thinks this grand alliance is the way to go. Instead of trying to make NFI see reason individually, he thinks that collectively we can do what we here in Washington can't. That's why I called this meeting; I'll want your thoughts in memo form. If this leaks, expect to look for another job. And that's the least that will happen to you. Don't piss me off on this, I won't have it."

The president glanced at each member in turn. Even the vice president was now looking at him. Some of the faces showed traces of alarm.

"I need to know what you're thinking, so make sure it's in the memo. Should we get involved, or stay out and chart our own course? If we decide to join the other nations I mentioned, when should I involve Congress? Should we shoot for a loose association, or a treaty? Keep it low level, which is to say deniable, or should we involve heads of state? I can't give you much time. I've got that nomination to the court of appeals to push through. So I want those memos within ten days. Do you have any questions?"

There were none, which didn't surprise the president. Questions would be asked of staff members when the boss wasn't looking over their shoulder.

"Thank you for attending, gentlemen." The president stood, the others stood, and waited while he left the room. Two secret service agents waited outside and swung in behind the president as he headed upstairs.

* * *

MILTON SMART WAS TIRED. The second trip to space had taken longer than usual. He'd hovered *Bee* just long enough to set the beacon, then release the clamp holding the first fuel rod. He'd then drifted past the berm separating the two locations and released the second rod. For whatever reason, the third rod refused to release. It was far too hot radioactively to be approached, even wearing a three-layer suit. Finally, he'd taken it into space and managed to launch it toward the sun. The clamps had worked fine in zero gravity, after stubbornly refusing to function in the moon's sixth of a gee. NFI wouldn't be happy, they wanted every fuel rod they could get, but they'd just have to live without that last one. Delaying his return even more, he'd had to refuel at Station Eleven. But this worst-ever trip was finally coming to an end.

The green forest below opened and the cleared space in front of NFI's hangars became visible. Milton called up the checklist and read off the first item, only to be interrupted by a flash and loud chime.

"Radar alert. Radar alert. Radar..." Milton shut off the sound and glanced at the blinking light. This time it was flanked by two other lights, both glowing a sullen red.

"What the hell, Porky?"

"We've got company, Milt, direction three five degrees, toward Murmansk. Range, two fiver fiver kilometers. Two contacts, they're flying low, but they're damned fast. They're still in Russian airspace, but coming our way. Range is down to one niner fiver kilometers."

"Shit. Fuel state, eighty six percent. Good thing we topped off on our way down. Recommendations, but make it quick."

"Get the hell out of Dodge. If you try to outrun them on the deck, it might work, but you'd have to head due west. They can't carry enough fuel to do much, not at that speed. The other option, go high. I think they're fighters, so max altitude is probably angels 100."

"I'm going high," Milton decided. "Tighten your belt, autoprogram canceled, I'll be pulling gees. I can't outmaneuver a fighter, but maybe I can make him run out of gas. Call in a report, I'm busy." Milton dialed impeller power to 100% and eased back on the stick. The computer translated his entry and *Bee* curved left and headed up at three point four gees, all the computer would allow."

"Shoot or no shoot, Porky?"

"I don't think this is covered in our orders. If they shoot at us, return fire. We may not be able to use the Sidewinders, I don't know if we can get them to track."

"I'll try to aim the cameras their way. What are they doing?"

"Looks like they're also heading upstairs. Converging course, I think they're trying for an intercept. Milt, they'll catch us before we can get to orbit. We're already within long missile range, but they haven't fired. Maybe they don't intend to; they might be intending to force us to divert to Russia. We're accelerating, but they've got the advantage."

"So they do, Porky. But unless they fire one of their missiles, that speed will work against them. Stand by, keep feeding me range..."

Milton dialed the impellers back, then reversed them, gently. *Bee's* acceleration dropped to zero gee, leaving them held by the harnesses, then reversed. Two bright specks flashed through the sky, above where *Bee* would have been without the radical maneuver.

"Now we head for the deck. Maybe we can lose them, maybe we can even land. They can't get in position to do anything before we're on the ground."

Milton changed course, diving for the ground far below. Dialing power back, he brought Bee down in a shallow curve until they were flying just above the treetops. There was no sign of the Russian fighters.

"Any sign of that Russian radar?"

"Nothing on the scope. Want me to update that last report?"

"No, not yet. Let's keep the radio off, I'm switching off the radar too. Let them find us using the mark one eyeball...if they can."

Half an hour later, Milton resumed radio contact. The hangar door was open, waiting, when he eased Bee onto the apron.

CHUCK WAS ALERTED IMMEDIATELY. He listened silently to the replay, then called Adelheid.

"Bonuses for Milt and Porky, prepare a recommendation for my signature. Conference call, Frenchy, Milt, and me. Do we have any former fighter pilots flying for us? Find out. Then find out what the Finns are saying, the Russians overflew their territory. Suggest they make a diplomatic protest, if nothing else. Let Pete know what happened, see if he has a recommendation about upgrading armaments on our ships. I want a meeting with the Finns, the factory managers. If they came at us once, they can do it again. Meeting with the Iceland ministers, purpose, possibly upgrade our base in Reykjavik. Meeting with Wolfgang, find out what our pilots think. They deserve to be heard, some might not want to fly for us if enemy fighters are involved. Got all that?"

Adelheid scribbled furiously.

"I have it, Chuck. Will there be anything else?"

"Not right now. I'll be available when you get the conference call set up."

"I'll call you, Chuck."

Adelheid left silently, leaving Chuck staring out the window.

* * *

"MISTER TRIFFIN, DO YOU HAVE A MOMENT?" The speaker wore the uniform of an Air Force Colonel.

"Go ahead, colonel."

"I have some of the information you asked for. We think we've located the ship you described. She's currently proceeding north, speed eight knots. Nearest land at the moment, Grenada. Presumed last port of call, Caracas, Venezuela."

"Venezuela? Are you sure?"

"No, sir. We extrapolated backward, based on her course, and that was the nearest city. If she hugged the northeastern coast of South America, she could have come from anywhere."

"So what's her destination?"

"Best guess, Puerto Rico. She won't get there today, though, not at that speed. She's just an old tramp; I'm surprised she's moving as fast as she is. We got a high altitude photo from an ObSat, the name isn't clear but it seems to start with a 'T'."

"Can you get a closer look?"

"Not with a satellite, sir. We can dispatch a recon plane, if you're willing to authorize the flight."

"Do it. How long?"

"I'll let you know, sir. Flying out of Florida..."

22

C huck concentrated on his driving. He was tired, so watching the traffic took more attention than usual. The trip home took almost an hour, but finally he parked in front of the garage, behind the main house. He left the car outside; one of the employees would wash it and move it inside the garage.

Frenchy was on the veranda, looking off to Mount Coot-tha, blue in the distance. *He's looking old*, thought Chuck. *When did that happen?* Frenchy, hearing him step through the entrance, turned and held up a cup in salute. "Welcome home, Chuck."

"Thanks, Frenchy. How are things going?"

"About the same as usual. The twins wear me out, I need a cup of tea to recover!"

"Where's Lina?"

"In the nursery, getting them bedded down. You'll have to wait until later if you want a playtime."

Chuck shook his head. "I'm exhausted. It just never ends, does it?"

"Not really. Swat one bug, a hundred others take its place. What is it this time?"

"Two things, one of them critical. Got a few minutes to talk?"

"Sure, I'm not going anywhere. What's on your mind?"

"Start with the easy one. What do you know about a ship named *Tesla*?"

"We bought it years ago, before we left the US. It was one step ahead of the ship-breakers then, but we needed a test bed for the impellers. We gave up on that idea. To be honest, Morty thought it was worth trying, so I went along with him. It was junked as soon as we closed down the New Mexico factory."

"It didn't get junked, Frenchy. It's still going, but now it's falling apart. Some of the impellers have failed, the hull is going too. Sven Nelsen's the captain now. He wanted approval to junk her, and I agreed. We'll pull the impellers and sell the hull for scrap."

"The impellers failed? Did he say why?"

"Corrosion, salt air got inside the shells. Four are still operating, the rest are stored in one of the ship's compartments."

"So that doesn't impact space ops. I worried, for a moment. But it sounds like the right thing to do. When will this happen?"

"Two weeks or so. I'll have a crew meet him in Charleston to salvage what they can. I promised him a slot in Martha's school."

"Makes sense. I remember Sven, he's a good man. Good people, especially managers, are hard to find. But I can't see Sven behind a desk."

"I'll keep an eye on his progress. I told him we'd find work for his crew if they wanted to stay with us."

"Yeah, that's a good policy, never lay off employees. They can always leave, but they stay loyal. Treat people good, they'll treat the company good. You mentioned another problem?" Frenchy sipped his tea, then grimaced. He set the cup on its saucer and massaged his left forearm.

"Something wrong, Frenchy?"

"Little numbness. I think I need more exercise. But about that problem?"

"I need advice, Frenchy. *Bee* had a close call. Two Russian fighters crossed the Finnish border and headed for them on an intercept course. The crew thinks they only meant to harass *Bee*, maybe try to force them to divert to Russia, otherwise they'd have fired a missile. We got tentative identification on the Russian planes, it's that new Sukhoi fighter. It supercruises at Mach 2 and has longer range than the MIGs. For armament, there's a 25mm autocannon in an internal bay plus two long-range air to air missiles under-wing. It's bad news."

Frenchy gave off rubbing his arm. "You know more about our ships than I do, but none of them can pull heavy gees in a turn. We've got an advantage in altitude and top speed, but if they manage to surprise one of our birds, we'll lose people. You're fairly close to the Russian border up there; I think the Russians just told you to find another base."

"You're right. It's a shame, the Finns have done amazing work. Maybe we could keep the base to launch our new ships. Maybe if we stopped bringing ships in for maintenance and refueling, that would quiet the Russians down. I don't know...I don't see how we can expand the Reykjavik base. We could afford to buy more land, but I doubt the locals would sell. The Icelanders are okay with us being there but they won't be happy if we try to expand."

"Probably not," agreed Frenchy. "But we need at least one more base, maybe several. We've been lucky so far, but we have too many eggs in too few bases. Have you thought of basing ships here in Australia? I don't know what the current government would think, but there's plenty of room. There's a big desert in the interior and the outback is sparsely settled. It's ranch country for the most part, not all that different from New Mexico."

"I don't have time to massage the politicians down here. How about you doing that?"

Frenchy paused for a long moment, then sipped more tea.

"Chuck, I don't want to. You might as well know, I've got heart problems. Too many years of too much pressure, too little exercise, maybe too much alcohol. It's more than burnout. If I take on a new job, it won't be good for me."

He put down the cup. "I enjoy playing with the kids and I think it's helpful, having a man in their lives full time. Lina needs me too. What would you think of Will being our contact with the Australians?"

"Will? You think he's up to that? I talked to him a week ago and he's still adamant that he doesn't want to fly, at least not in our ships."

"I understand, but that seems to be his only phobia. I think he could do it."

Frenchy paused, thinking.

"I'll talk to him if you want. I might have better luck convincing him to take the job. We've been friends a long time."

"Would you? I really don't want to get involved in business this weekend. I need time with Lina and the twins."

"Enjoy yourself. I'll speak to Will when he gets back. He found a poker game in town and couldn't resist."

* * *

THE VOICES WERE QUIET. There was no reason, but somehow it seemed appropriate. Perhaps that was the usual practice among SEALS before a mission.

"I'll go over the plan one last time. We're on a parallel course, four zero kilometers forward of the target's last reported position. Your course is 330 degrees, distance to intercept approximately sixteen kilometers. We expect to approach from amidships, but if she made better time than expected we'll turn and overtake. Weather is a factor, plan for it. Winds are decreasing, waves expected to moderate in height, but probably not before you approach the objective."

The speaker, a master chief petty officer, paused while he consulted a tablet.

"Boat One approaches from starboard, board according to SOP. Minimum noise. Secure the comm shack, the bridge, then take the rest of the crew into custody. Signal the boats. Cox, you'll radio the squadron, who will then come up and escort us while we search the ship. Boat Two intercepts from the port side, same drill. Be careful after you board. Sixteen men, tight space, we don't want blue on blue. Deadly force is authorized only if fired upon, make sure you're not the one being shot at. Say checklist status." This was directed at the boats' coxswains.

"Checklist complete" was followed by another quiet voice, repeating the same message.

"Launch in one minute."

A short time later, deck now empty, the teams waited. A low hum announced their departure. Disturbed water showed white briefly, illuminated by the full moon. The water calmed briefly before the waves resumed, and only the soft noises of the destroyer disturbed the night as it plowed ahead through two-meter waves.

* * *

"ADI, YOU MUST COME QUICK!"

Sven shook his head muzzily. "What...who...Pak Rafi, is that you? Who is on watch?"

"I have called the crew, adi. There are pirates."

"Pirates? There are no... where did they come from, Pak Rafi?"

"They come from behind us, Adi. There are ships."

"You mean fishing boats. Pirates don't use ships."

"Pak Iskandar has said ships, Adi. They are close, and there are boats."

"I'll come. Radio a report, then ask Pak Susilo to join me on the bridge."

"Yes, Adi." Rafi hurried away.

Why would they want an old freighter, wondered Sven? *The cargo is worth only a fraction of what bigger ships carry. Do they intend to take the crew hostage, demand ransom for their release?* And what was his duty?

Experienced eyes took in the weather situation. Wind from due aft, seas...

Susilo entered the bridge. "Adi?"

"Get the men into the boats, Pak Susilo. Make for Puerto Rico, it's northeast. Notify the authorities as soon as you arrive."

"Yes, Adi. What of you?"

"It's my ship. I'm damned if they'll take her, not without a fight! You get the men off as fast as you can and I'll see whether this old girl still has a finishing kick. With luck, I'll get to Ponce about the same time as you.

"But I want you out of danger, so take the men and go."

"As you command, Adi." Susilo vanished as silently as he appeared. Sven looked at the radar screen. Yes, there was an image, fuzzy. That was probably what Iskandar saw, or maybe the two ships he mentioned had now merged into one image. But not fishing boats;

Iskandar had known what the scope image meant. Pirates with ships? Strange.

Two lifeboats pulled away to starboard, angling forward. Smart; *Tesla* would keep them from being seen, even considering the moonlight. Sven clicked the switch, disengaging the autopilot. He now exercised direct control of the ship.

The diesel generators thundered as Sven advanced the impeller thumbwheel. He gently moved the control stick, directing a course change toward the Puerto Rico landmass. Thinking for a moment, he moved another control, this one located to the right of the stick. The two forward impellers responded, lifting the ship's bow slightly. It was all the old ship could do, now that she had only half her impellers. Would it be enough?

* * *

"Shit, course change. Target is increasing speed. They've seen us."

"Understood, break radio silence and report to Home Base. Advise Boat One."

"Break radio silence, chief?"

"That's what I said, knucklehead. *They* already know we're here!"

"Aye, aye, master chief."

The wind had been from aft before; now, as the boat increased speed, it changed, coming from the port quarter. The boat porpoised, taking the waves at an angle.

"Who would have thought that old ship had this much speed! What's her knot reading, cox?"

"We've got the legs on her, master chief. She's probably doing twelve knots right now, maybe a little faster. We'll be up to her in about half an hour, if you want to join your men."

"Tired of my questions, cox?"

"No, master chief. I can run this boat with one hand tied behind me."

"I've heard that said about you, cox. That you drive like you were using your other hand for something more interesting."

The master chief chuckled. The coxswain did not. Some exchanges you just weren't going to win.

Sven glanced at the radar screen. There were now two distinct returns, so Iskandar had been right. Two other shadows appeared and vanished among the wave return. Could those be the pirate boats? If so, they were damned close! Sven checked, but the impeller controls were against the stop. Apparently, his attempt to lift the bow hadn't worked. Maybe he could get more speed by returning the gimbals to their previous setting. He carefully twisted the control, then looked out the bridge windows. Were the boats in sight?

Tesla's bow eased down. Ahead, a rogue wave, slightly higher than its fellows, pitched up in front of the bow. *Tesla* slammed into it, shuddering, water cascading over the bow. Sven staggered, then gripped the armrests of his chair. *Tesla* eased upward, seawater flooding into the scuppers. For a moment, all was as before.

A faint vibration shook the deck. Bridge windows rattled. Sven had time for a brief concern.

* * *

"Shit, master chief! Look at the objective!"

"What the hell...?"

The chief hadn't intended it to be a question, but the coxswain replied. "She broke in two, master chief. That's the aft portion, the bow is gone. She's going..."

The open hold gaped amidships, the sea poured in. The old ship swayed to port, then rolled to starboard. For a moment it appeared she could survive even this indignity. Then, tiredly, *Tesla* gave up the fight. The remnant sank by the stern, the open middle rising for a moment, escaping air bubbling as the wreckage sank.

"Radio Home Base. Look for survivors."

"Aye, aye, master chief. You won't find any. She went down too fast."

"We have to look, cox. Work out a search pattern with Boat One. I'll tell my guys to keep a sharp lookout."

But the boats found no survivors, not even bodies. Whatever had been there, the sea had taken. Sven's body was never found. In the best traditions of the sea, he had gone down with his ship.

Twelve kilometers away, two lifeboats chugged on, unknowing.

23

Frenchy found Chuck having breakfast with Lina the following morning.

"I spoke to Will. He's willing to contact Australian officials, but he pointed out that he's not really a company official. He was, but let's be honest, he can't handle space operations, because he's not willing to go into space. We talked it over. I've decided to retire, effective immediately. I've named Will chairman of the board."

Chuck glanced at Lina, surprised. "Did you know of this?"

"No, but I'm not surprised." She hesitated. "Dad, you've spent a lot of time with us. You're no longer making those trips to the mainland. It's not like you, giving up."

"I didn't exactly give up, Lina. I did something I needed to do."

Chuck had watched the exchange. He asked, "Frenchy, did those trips have anything to do with Sol?"

"You're pretty shrewd, Chuck. I had nothing to do with his suicide. Yeah, I outmaneuvered him. I bought up enough stock to force him out, then sold out. Whatever remaining stock he held dropped in value, almost overnight. He used finance against me, I just repaid him."

Frenchy sipped his coffee, looking out over the manicured grounds. "I don't really have a goal, now. That's one reason I'm willing to step back. Will's a minority stockholder, we hold a clear majority of the shares, but by holding the CoB title the Australians will respect him. It will make things a lot easier when he talks business."

"I thought you might have had something to do with Sol's getting the boot. I can't say I'm sorry. Accidental overdose or not, he did it to himself. Anyway, where did you have in mind for a base, assuming the Australians go for the idea?"

"We had that Russian problem because they were close enough to put pressure on Rovaniemi Base. They're still there, so we may have to move the assembly operation too; the Russians crossed the border once, they can do it again. We might want to move a substantial amount of our heavy manufacturing to South Korea. Think about it, and if you think it's worth looking into, have someone take a hard look at the problem. We should be ready, not be forced to react. As for Australia, the largest cities are around the coast. I think there's only one city of any size in the interior, which makes matters easier. There's a desert in the middle, not much commercial activity at all, and the outback is mostly grazing. A large base located somewhere around the area where Western Australia, the Northern Territories, and South Australia meet would take care of our needs. It's not set in stone, won't be until we work out the details, but it appears like there's plenty of suitable land. And we can afford it."

Chuck nodded. "We can. I'll talk to Will. He can point out how well Finland and Iceland have done financially, Japan too. They were worried when we first started working together, but not now. Roughly two thirds of their spent fuel rods have been removed, and their balance of payments is healthy. The Koreans might like to get in on that."

* * *

CHUCK HAD BARELY RETURNED to his Iceland office when Martha telephoned. After the customary greetings, she told him the reason for her call.

"We've lost contact with *Tesla*, Chuck. We got a short message, not clear. As best we can figure, she was attacked by pirates. I know, it sounds ridiculous, pirates in that part of the ocean, but that word was clear. I asked the Swiss representatives to help, but we're not really a Swiss corporation and it didn't happen here. They're sympathetic, but not interested."

"I'm not surprised. We don't really have a presence in that part of the world, do we? Where was she the last time she reported in?"

"The report didn't include coordinates, none that we could hear. She was in the Caribbean at noon, heading north, and extrapolating from her last position using her reported speed, she would have been off the eastern side of Puerto Rico."

"And nothing since. Tell you what, have someone take that extrapolated position. Then input her speed and time from then to now, use that as the radius, and draw a circle. The area can be searched from the air, and I've got just the thing to do it. Even if pirates captured her, we might be able to do something. We just have to find her."

"I understand. I'll get back to you in half an hour, Chuck." Martha broke the connection. Chuck pushed the intercom. He could have used Adelheid here...maybe she would be willing to transfer? But all the secretaries were efficient, just different.

"Contact my pilot and tell him to call me. Have *Lina* prepared for flight as soon as possible. Three crew, pilot, copilot, observer. I'll have coordinates by the time they're ready. They're to search for a ship."

"Yes, Chuck."

The search turned up nothing. The weather had cleared, the seas were moderate, but there was no sign of *Tesla*. Chuck fretted, then went back to work. There was nothing he could do.

* * *

Mark knocked and waited. The president didn't answer, so he continued to wait. Finally, there was a response; the president opened the door to the oval office and told Mark to come in.

"I was in the washroom. You've got the material I asked for?"

"Yes, sir."

"On paper this time? Okay, help yourself to coffee while I take a look at it."

Mark drank a cup of coffee and waited. The president didn't acknowledge his existence as he skimmed the thick stack of documents. Mark used the presidential washroom, then poured another cup of coffee. Finally, the president looked up and rubbed his eyes.

"That's a lot of material, but it's not complete. Did you look at this?"

"Yes, Mister President."

"Why does it say 'estimated'? With all the high-powered accountants working for us, surely they can do better."

"I asked, Mister President. I was concerned the report might not be what you wanted, but...can I give you a verbal briefing? You have half an hour open, if you're willing to use it for this."

"Go ahead. I'm not happy about this. You tell them after you leave here. I expect results, not goddamned guesses!"

"Yes, Mister President. We've been over the organization of the company and in general terms, it hasn't changed. One thing that may, or may not, be significant. Fuqua has retired. He's still a consultant, but takes no part in the day to day operation of the company. Sneyd is still in charge. Crane took Fuqua's place as chairman of the board, but his ownership percentage has not increased. Sneyd and his wife hold the power."

"Go on."

"NFI's net worth can only be estimated. They have business relation-ships with a number of nations. Some of those we know about, but probably not all. They may be paid in cash, but they also have a habit of bartering."

The president interrupted. "Bartering? Explain this."

"The Chinese pay them in yuan, but also in commodities. NFI trans-ports their goods and people to space. We believe they have a base on the moon now, apparently a large one. NASA launched a reconnais-sance flight that circled the moon a number of times. It took detailed images, so we know there's a large base and a tiny one. One of NFI's ships was parked by the small one, so we conclude they haven't both-ered to put substantial assets up there. NASA doesn't find that surprising, considering the difficulties. The Chinese, however, have wanted this for a long time, so we think they took the opportunity to have NFI set up their base instead of doing it themselves."

Mark paused and flipped through the stack of paper, looking for the page he wanted.

"China is testing a new heavy-lift rocket. Our best guess is that they'll use it to supply their base, now that it's built. NFI apparently doesn't need one. There are three large dome-shaped covers, but the satellite got a partial look at what's underneath. One appears to be empty, the other is storage for shipping containers. We think they're using the containers to haul cargo for the Chinese base. We couldn't see what was beneath the third one, the view was blocked by the other two."

"The Chinese have a base on the moon, and we don't." The president's voice was soft. Mark looked at him in alarm; often he took this tone when he became enraged. But there were no other signs, so Mark continued.

"That's one example of bartering. They needed rare earth elements, we do too, but the Chinese claim they can't provide what we want. We conclude that NFI is getting all of China's production that's surplus to their domestic needs."

The president nodded, so Mark continued.

"NFI has an ongoing contract with Japan. Some of it has to do with currency flow, balance of payments stuff, but NFI is also buying small modular reactors. They're using the same model we are, but *they* get a discounted price. Some of that is because they discount Japanese flights, the rest is because they're part owner of the company that produces the SMRs."

"Mark, you're saying that when we buy those reactors we're paying *NFI*?"

"Yes Mister President. The sum is considerable, so even after Japan collects their share, NFI benefits. The payment is in dollars, which creates a different problem."

"I'll be goddamned! They're strangling us, and we're *paying them to do it!* Mark, give me the bottom line. How much is NFI worth?"

"Upwards of a trillion dollars, Mister President. That's the low estimate."

"A trillion? How the hell...what's the middle estimate?"

"Seven and a half trillion, Mister President. Some think they're worth twelve trillion."

"Unbelievable. That's almost equal to our own gross national product! Mark, have we tried to work with them?"

"Not from the executive branch, Mister President. A Congressional delegation spoke to them, but it appears they got nowhere. The last official contact we had was before they shut down their North American operation. The Defense Department was interested in buying some of their products, but nothing came of it. NFI refused to sell. There have been no further contacts."

"Maybe it's time I got involved. Directly, I mean. Congress...they have their own aims, and a man like Sneyd wouldn't be impressed. Suppose I called Sneyd directly. He was in the Army, wasn't he? Would he listen to me?"

"Marines, Mister President. I don't know. Our last contact was through Fuqua, but that isn't likely to be of much help now."

"There's only one way to find out. Set it up, Mark. I'll talk to Sneyd when the comm center gets him on the line."

The president laid the papers down. "You mentioned something the last time we talked about NFI. You said there was a rumor we might be able to use? Have you followed up on that?"

"I have, Mister President. Nothing came of it."

"Unfortunate. Okay, let the comm center know. You stand by, I might need you."

"Yes, Mister President." Mark walked out, carefully closing the door.

The secretary looked up, expectantly; sometimes Mark had information she found useful. But not this time; "Get me a line to the comm center. The boss wants to make a phone call."

The secretary took the information. Mark sat down and waited as she discussed the call with the officer on duty. Mark's attention wandered; he caught snippets of the conversation, 'headquarters' and 'private secretaries', then 'Australia'. That caught his attention, but finally a call went out to Zurich. Mark and the secretary looked at each other; it had taken too long, and the president often showed his displeasure when that happened. Other calls were made. If anyone knew where Chuck Sneyd was, they weren't willing to say, not even to the White House communications officer. Finally the secretary's phone rang. She listened to the call for a moment, wide eyed. She then wrote a short message on a memo pad, tore off the sheet, and handed it to Mark.

"You tell him. I'm not going to. He's not gonna be happy!"

Mark shrugged and picked up the paper. "He's not happy a lot, lately." Sighing, he knocked on the door and waited to be summoned.

"I have an answer, Mister President."

"Well, go ahead. Is Sneyd on the line?"

"No, sir. We were unable to get through to Sneyd. We did talk to someone at their headquarters, a Martha Simms. She's an executive vice president of the company."

"And she couldn't tell you where Sneyd is? That's ridiculous!"

"She...ah, called his private secretary. One of them, he has several. She told the on-duty communications officer that they were all quite busy just now, Sneyd included."

"Did they tell him the president of the United States was calling?"

"Yes, sir."

"And what did he say?"

"Mister President..." Mark hesitated, then decided there was no use waiting. "He said he was busy, and that you should try calling him later."

"Thank you, Mark. And thank the comm center crew, please."

Mark nodded, and left. He almost made it out the door before he heard something smash against the wall.

24

The Puerto Rican officials had been suspicious. Pirates, off their coast? *Tesla's* crew had been held for twenty four hours while their story was checked. Eventually, lacking evidence of any crime other than their irregular entry, the men were released. Most had little money, so even arranging an international call to NFI had taken time. Even after the call went through, Susilo had a difficult time with the company's bureaucracy. His thick accent didn't help matters. Insistence that they worked for the company as sailors on a ship named *Tesla* worked its way up the chain, eventually reaching Martha. She notified Chuck and arranged for the crew to be fed and housed until transport could be arranged. The mention of NFI worked magic. By the end of the second day, no longer broke, the crew booked tickets to Zurich. They also visited a department store and bought new clothes, hoping to avoid attention during the flight.

That turned out to be a dismal failure. Clothing suitable for a summer day in Puerto Rico, while colorful and comfortable, attracted stares from people waiting in the airport. Asians in the styles favored by Hispanics were viewed askance, and with a certain amount of suspicion. This continued when they deplaned; none had a passport.

But a representative of NFI was there to explain their plight, and finally they met Martha. Chuck was also there virtually, thanks to a videoconference call. Later, after the men had been taken to a hotel where they would stay while their future was sorted out, Chuck conferred with Martha.

"I don't like it. We have no idea what happened, and by now anyone could have the impellers."

Martha nodded, then said, "Maybe, but there's been no ransom demand. Could Sven have managed to get away?"

"I don't see how. It was an old ship, on her way to be junked, and only half the impellers worked."

Martha leaned back and picked up a pen, toying with it. "Two ships, two boats. That doesn't sound like pirates, at least not the kind of simple pirates we've seen before. They can't afford that level of investment, not when they're trying to capture one small ship. How much could *Tesla* bring them? An old ship, on its last legs...Chuck, something's fishy."

"You think someone found out she had impellers on board?"

"That's the only way this makes sense. We searched the area off Puerto Rico, but suppose the ships came from Venezuela? *Tesla* was there, discharging cargo. She also picked up a load of...let me see, crockery. There was a shipment of pitchers and vases, things like that, made by local people. Apparently, it sells better up north than it does in Venezuela. Could someone have realized that *Tesla* was different?"

Chuck was silent, thinking about what she'd said. "Keep talking, Martha."

"Venezuela doesn't have a huge navy, but they've got patrol craft. Those might have been what the crew spotted. As for small boats, there's no shortage of them in that part of the world."

"Recommendation, Martha?"

"Search the area again. Start with that presumed location, but this time search due south, spreading out in a cone covering the northern coast of South America. I don't see that we have anything to lose."

"Good idea. Okay, I'll see to it. What about the sailors?"

"I'll see if they're interested in going to school. If they are, we'll find a place for them."

"Thanks, Martha. I'll get back to you."

* * *

CHUCK DISPATCHED *Lina* for a second search, then went back to work. Subassemblies for the new ships, some made in India or South Korea, others in Indonesia and the Philippines, had begun to fill NFI's pipeline. *Giant* picked up shipments as soon as they were ready, then hauled them to the moon. Rotating assembly crews worked ten day shifts at Moonbase, then went home. A second crew moved in, and ten days later a third crew took their place. The men loved it; ten days in space, then ten days at home with money to spend, followed by ten days learning new skills...

The information spread around the world. Good jobs, good pay, plenty of time off; NFI's Swiss office now had a waiting list of applicants. Few were accepted; NFI could afford to be selective, and was.

New reactors, all following the small modular design developed by Japanese scientists, were also available. Each month, *Giant* or *Goliath* picked up a reactor and took it to Moonbase for temporary storage. Pete's staff now worked on a different kind of design; *Giant*-class ships would be taken out of service on the moon, power rooms stripped out, and new, stronger frame members installed. Their fuel cells would be stored as spares for the older *Farside*-class ships. They were simply too small, too old, to justify being converted to nuclear power. Chuck wondered what to do about them, but put off the decision. There would be time later.

Frodo showed up later that afternoon and asked to speak to Chuck. Adelheid, transferred from Rovaniemi now that the base faced closure, had taken over the Iceland office. She notified Chuck and Frodo was shown in a few minutes later.

"Good to see you back so soon. Did you find *Tesla*?"

"No, but I found something else. I went ahead and completed the search just to be sure, but I came back north and took a second look. There's a US Coast Guard cutter and a commercial ship of some kind there. I didn't get a good look, but I got camera footage. They're not anchored, but they're staying in position. Between the time I first saw them and when I came back after searching south, they hadn't moved."

"Not anchored?"

"Not there. According to the chart, there's no anchorage. There are a couple of ridges near that extend into the area, but the rest is really deep, around six kilometers. The Muertos Trough is even deeper."

"Are you thinking the same thing I am, Frodo?"

"If you're thinking that's a task force looking for *Tesla*, I am."

Chuck shook his head. "It only makes sense if the ships *Tesla's* crew spotted came from the US, not Venezuela. But how would they know?"

Frodo hitched his chair closer. "You got a message from *Tesla*, right?" Chuck nodded. "Was it encrypted?"

"I don't know, probably. But it would have used an older version, something that's at least five years old, maybe ten."

"You know there are ears everywhere. Satellites, big antennas...wouldn't the US have a way of monitoring conversations? Puerto Rico is a US possession, after all."

"Let me summarize, then. You tell me where I'm wrong." Frodo nodded, waiting.

"Sven radios a report. This one was longer and contained more information that the routine position reports he usually sent. It also came from an area that the US has an interest in."

"Right, they have security concerns, and Cuba is pretty close. There's still a lot of unrest in that part of the world. The US...what's that agency? The one that snoops on conversations?"

"Most likely the National Security Agency. Go on."

"Somehow, they picked up the radio message. Decoding something that old, piece of cake. *Tesla* was originally bought in the US and rebuilt there. There were almost certainly records, and if someone looked deep enough, they would have tied it to NFI."

"You're making sense. I don't like it, but I think you're right," said Chuck.

"So they send someone to take a look. Something went wrong. The crew takes to the boats. The only one missing now is Sven, right?"

"Right."

"Sven does something, or the ships sink *Tesla*. They know where she went down, and now they're looking for her. It only makes sense if they believe that she carried impellers."

"Those sons of bitches!" Chuck was angry, and it showed. "They're as bad as the fucking Russians!"

Frodo looked at him, alarmed. This wasn't like Chuck, who rarely allowed his voice to rise. Maybe going home had something to do with that.

"Take it easy, Chuck. We're only guessing. We don't know anything, not for sure."

Chuck leaned back in his chair and closed his eyes. He was still in that position when he spoke.

"How likely are they to find *Tesla*?"

"It's going to be a stone bitch, I think. Searching those seamounts and canyons, it's like trying to find an airplane somewhere in the Rockies. Even if they know exactly where she sank, ships don't just go straight down. They tend to drift around, especially assuming she sank through six kilometers of water. There are currents, thermoclines. They might not be within a kilometer, maybe ten kilometers, of *Tesla*. If she really sank, I mean."

"But they'll find her eventually."

"If they're willing to spend the time and money, Chuck. They found that Russian sub in the 1970s. Deep free-diving subs are a lot better now than they were back then. So yes, if they want her bad enough, they'll find her."

"Thanks, Frodo. You're not flying now, are you?"

"No, I'm done for the day. It's been a long day, and I'm tired."

"How about a drink?"

"I could use one."

"Well, let's see." Chuck opened the cabinet. "Pretty good selection. You name it, we've got it."

"Scotch?"

"Single malt, Laphroaig, Macallan, Lagavulin..."

"I'll have that last one, Lagavulin. Neat."

Chuck nodded and poured two fingers into each glass, then handed one to Frodo.

"Cheers. You did a good job. Speaking of that, are you happy being my personal pilot?"

"Absolutely. Fly that little sportster of a ship, or one of the space trucks? I'll stay where I am."

* * *

THE PRESIDENT WAS STILL ANGRY.

He'd been furious, at first; how *dare* that man refuse a phone call from the President of the United States of America! Who the hell did he think he was? Not even the premier of China would do that, Russia either. Still angry, he'd eventually gone to bed, but couldn't sleep. A pill helped, but a midnight call to deal with the aftermath of flooding in Florida had left him groggy.

Three cups of coffee later, he was grouchy when Mark brought him the morning briefing papers. He opened the folder, glanced at the summary, then closed it.

"Mark, you mentioned contacts with China and Russia. Who else is on that list?"

"The European Union is aware of it, Mister President. I don't know how committed they are."

"It's time to find out. See how long it will take to set up a meeting. Heads of government, maybe one or two aides at most. Maybe that jumped-up asshole will listen if we stick a sharp stick in his eye!"

"Yes, Mister President. They'll want an agenda."

"Work it out, Mark. Let me know when you've got something, but here's my thinking. NFI's holding onto space, but we've got the planet. They need stuff, food and water, air, a lot of other stuff. If we work together, we can shut them off. Not so much as a drink, not a pound of hamburger, not a single breath of air. When they come crawling, the shoe will be on the other foot. Let *him* beg me to talk to *me*!"

Mark nodded and left, cell phone already in hand. Moments later, Pinchot Forberger answered. Mark arranged for the two to have dinner that evening. Over cocktails, he brought up the president's idea.

"Shoot down spaceships? The Russians had a go at one, missed him. On the other hand, they didn't try to shoot him down, just scare him. Okay, I'll start working on this. Got a time frame?"

"Soon. The boss is seriously tweaked. He wants Sneyd's guts for garters."

"I'll see what I can do."

Messages were dispatched, but there was no immediate reply. Heads of government don't drop everything; they want to discuss issues, look at them carefully. Mistakes can be devastating.

The EU had internal problems. The northern nations were restive; in their view, the EU was costing more than it was worth. SA similar attitude prevailed along the Mediterranean, but for a different reason. Nations there faced the brutal prospect of economic collapse. France and Germany felt that holding the uneasy alliance together was essential; one had only to remember the bad old days, when bloody war was followed by catastrophic famine and decades of rebuilding.

Russia had commodities, oil, gas, timber, even diamonds. More, in fact, than the nation could use, but the excess could only be sold at deeply-discounted prices. The national leadership felt the pressure, not only from citizens but also from the oligarchs. They missed the old days, when wealth flowed in instead of dribbling slowly away. If the western nations were really in trouble, might there not be opportunity? After all, England had once been the seat of empire. Would it be worthwhile to join the western nations now, or would it be better to wait and pick up the pieces when they collapsed?

China had come to the same conclusion. Unlike Russia, China mow had a growing industry building rockets, ships that were almost ready to make supply runs to the moon, and for that matter a base on the moon itself. But NFI held the whip hand. Could something be done to weaken them? They made regular runs to Japan, and China now had missiles in place along the coastal areas. There were also missiles on the artificial islands in the South China Sea. Radars were also there.

The following day, a meeting took place. Senior Chinese officers listened and a plan was put forth. Two days later, reflecting the urgency felt by the leadership, the plan was approved.

25

Several months had passed and much had happened.

Chuck, depressed, canceled his morning appointments. A newspaper interview in the United States had come to his attention. The interview, conducted by a newspaper in Florida, quoted a sailor who claimed that a 'drug ship' had broken up and gone down with all hands. He'd also inadvertently revealed that it had happened during a pursuit by US Navy ships.

What to do? What *could* he do? He'd called Frenchy as soon as he saw the article, but Frenchy had been no help. A sailor's boast wasn't proof, of course, but when considered in the light of a possible salvage operation...the ships were still there, doing something...the story took on plausibility.

A private company with no diplomatic standing, NFI couldn't even file a diplomatic protest. As for a lawsuit, there was no proof, and in any case, it wouldn't bring Sven back.

Depression faded; anger took its place, but there was no outlet.

Chuck headed for the hangar. NFI would have to do without him for a day; he was going home to visit Lina and their four-year-old twins.

Will had good news; the Australian government had declined to permit a foreign-owned corporation from building a base in the outback, but had pointed out that a citizen of Australia could purchase land and engage in business so long as regulatory requirements were met and taxes paid.

Frenchy, Lina, and Will had immediately applied for Australian citizenship. Lina, the mother of two babies born in Australia, received approval first, but the others soon followed. The ink was barely dry before a subsidiary corporation, New Frontiers Australia, was set up. Lina was listed as company CEO and Will dealt with business matters. As for the future citizenship of Robbie and Bobby, they could sort that out for themselves when they came of age. Agents and a small army of lawyers headed for the outback, looking for a suitable location to build a base.

The new company's reputation was enhanced by association with NFI. There would be good jobs and prosperity; hadn't that happened to every nation that allied with NFI? A few politicians had been uneasy, but had remained silent. Jobs and money were a combination that no politician could ignore.

Spirits bolstered by good news, Chuck flew back to Iceland the following morning. Perhaps the Greenland government would also act soon; the Reykjavik base was crowded, and as new ships completed their acceptance voyage, it would only get worse. At least the new ships required no refueling; the SMR power units would not need replacing for at least five years, and in any case, servicing would be done in Japan.

A decision coalesced in Chuck's mind as he flew north.

He radioed Adelheid and asked her to set up a meeting with representatives of Japan, Indonesia, and India. The US government either had or soon would have access to impellers, even though broken and soaked with seawater. They could be reverse-engineered. The process might take a year, but it would happen. What then? Should the nation that had dealt so harshly with NFI, that had caused the sinking of *Tesla* and the death of Sven, become the second entity with impeller-driven ships? And what about filing a patent? Could NFI ignore the possibility that the US government would patent whatever they discovered during the examination of *Tesla's* impellers? A second phone call went to the legal staff. What should be patented? The modified Tesla coil that was the heart of the impeller system, a single primary and multiple revolving secondaries, was the heart of the system. Could a patent application be designed that would cover the coil, but not tie it to the impeller?

Questions, followed by more questions. *That's why they pay me the big bucks*, Chuck thought.

The underlying anger remained, but was gradually supplanted by other concerns. Good news arrived that afternoon. Chuck was soon on his way to the moon.

"She's magnificent!" Chuck looked at NFI's latest acquisition. She sparkled, not only from the new skin, but from the charged particles striking her plasma field.

Frisbee had been completed ahead of the type-class ship, *Saucer*. Something had gone wrong during *Saucer's* assembly, and as a result construction had paused. Work had gone on, some of the assembly workers being sent to *Frisbee* and *Disco* while engineers tried work-around after work-around. Eventually, the ship's interior had been gutted; the wiring harnesses, exposed, would soon be replaced, but meantime the projected launch day had been set back by about two weeks. The harnesses had been manufactured in Indonesia; whether the defect was due to inadequate quality control or sabotage had not yet been determined, but no future deliveries would be accepted until the question was answered to NFI's satisfaction. Meanwhile, a South Korean firm, using the original specifications, had taken up the slack. Their plant was turning out new harnesses, including a replacement for *Saucer's* defective one.

Instead of being the first, it appeared that *Saucer* might be the third ship in her class to launch.

Frisbee floated above Luna's surface, held aloft by impellers barely above idle. Fully stocked and crewed, the first true interplanetary ship would soon depart for Mars. Smaller craft now hauled cargo to Mars, but they were cramped and needed to make landfall every ten days to replenish supplies. *Frisbee* carried enough to support her crew for six months.

Cigar and *Stogie* would escort *Frisbee* during her maiden voyage. Each had already made independent trips to the red planet, surveying the surface and selecting sites for bases. The moon was a stepping stone; Mars, lacking only an atmosphere, would be humanity's second home. *Frisbee* would provide temporary quarters while workers built the first four bases on Mars. Equipment had been ordered, fuel rods stockpiled; lessons had been learned. Marsbases One through Four would be much easier to build.

"They're waiting, Chuck." Reminded, Chuck contacted *Frisbee's* captain. The order given, *Frisbee* accelerated straight up, increased sparkles showing the impeller field had strengthened. Someday he might visit Mars, but not now. There was a desk waiting, papers to examine, people to see. The adventure would continue, but Chuck would be more observer than participant.

Chuck sighed. He had one more stop to make, then he would head for Reykjavik.

Lina arrived at the Chinese base a short time later. Today's nominal pilot was Alex Reutnor, taking over for Frodo, but Chuck decided he needed more stick time and kept control during the approach. He relinquished control to Alex as the hatch opened, then sprang directly from the hatch and landed, taking two steps to arrest his momentum. John followed, but walking or jumping on the moon was now second nature. Behind them, the hatch closed and *Lina* drifted up, hovering twenty meters above the surface. A small delegation of Chinese left the dome and headed their way.

Chuck and John went with the Chinese to a large domed structure and entered the airlock. Moments later, they found themselves inside. Their hosts removed their helmets, so John and Chuck did likewise. Chuck had come prepared; he opened a flap on his suit and took out a small translator.

"That will not be necessary, Mister Sneyd. My name is Chang Jiang. I received my doctorate from the Massachusetts Institute of Technology."

Chuck blinked, and smiled. "You know who I am?"

"Yes, Mister Sneyd. Occidentals, contrary to rumors, do not all look alike." The man didn't crack a smile, but his eyes twinkled.

John carried much of the remaining discussion. Chuck asked to examine the domes the Chinese used for living quarters. Impressed, he returned to the original dome and joined the conversation.

"I like what I saw. You've done good work. Are you interested in selling domes? Or if we provide the materials, could you build them to our specifications? Americans prefer more living space, so one of your domes would house no more than two of our people."

"We would prefer to build new ones. Selling these units would not be wise. They are the property of China, you see."

"Are you implying I should not mention this to the Chinese government? Our current contract will expire shortly, so I'm not sure whether we will even have future dealings with China. What of you? Can China provide you with the supplies you need?"

"They believe so. If that effort fails, our government may decide to abandon this place. We have made regular reports, and as soon as our people return to China physicians examine them. The first of our people who came to the moon have been returned to Earth; those you see have been here less than a month. So you see, our scientists have learned a great deal about what reduced gravity does to the human body. In that sense, we have accomplished what we were sent to do. China may now decide that the wisest course is to wait until space science matures. One day, men will walk among the planets, but perhaps not yet. I have not been told of China's future plans. This leaves me with questions, because I have responsibilities not only to my country but to my people. In exchange for building your modules, I would like assurances that you will assist if I need your help."

"That's easy enough to do. Are you sure there's nothing else we can do for you?"

"Perhaps later, Mister Sneyd. An assurance of safety, should we need it, is valuable in its own right. It is insurance, and insurance must be paid for, not so?"

"Of course. If you'll get John a list of what you need, I'll see that it's brought.

The conversation continued for a time, then the Chinese escorted them back to where they'd landed. *Lina* drifted gently to a stop and the hatch swung open.

"One day, I would like to ride such a ship," said Chang Jiang, wistfully.

"She's much like the one that brought you here," Chuck replied.

"I saw nothing of the ship. I was brought, with others, in a different way."

"In a shipping container, you mean."

"You know of that?" Chang Jiang was surprised.

"It was obvious, as soon as I realized there were more people than flew up as passengers." Chuck laughed, and a moment later the two Chinese joined in.

"I am happy to be of assistance to you, Mister Sneyd. To have our own factory...my associates will be very pleased. We long to have businesses of our own, you know. It is possible, but not easy, to start with nothing in China and grow to become successful."

"I'll keep that in mind. If I find other products that you could provide...?"

"We are happy for the opportunity to work with you. Farewell, Mister Sneyd."

John opened the conversation as soon as *Lina* lifted off. "I thought it was simple corruption at first, what they refer to as having their own rice bowl. I think it's something else, though."

"I agree. I think Chang Jiang is worried that China may abandon them. Would China do that?"

"Your guess is as good as mine. China has changed, gotten...I don't know, different in how they deal with their citizens. There are two Chinas, maybe three. People in the interior, they're Old China. The ones living in the big coastal cities, they're New China. Hong Kong is China with a dash of England. As for the government, they're similar to any other government. The people at the top are plutocrats, even if they pretend otherwise. The Chinese people are different too, more outspoken than they used to be. Maybe that's why their government treats them different. But any nation will sacrifice people for what they consider the greater good, so I just don't know what they'll do.

"As for our dealings with China as a nation, they haven't dealt fairly with us. We offered them a price for passengers, another price for cargo space, primarily because passengers need air, water, food, comfortable seating, and so forth. We can haul four cargo containers in the same amount of square footage as twenty passengers. We stack the containers, but we can't stack people."

"What, you're trying to ruin the air travel industry?"

*　*　*

THE THREE SHIPS returned from Mars five days later. *Frisbee* orbited Earth under minimum staffing levels while the rest of her crew caught rides to the surface in *Cigar* and *Stogie*. They had family to see, last minute purchases to make, and some wanted a final blowout before leaving Earth. They would visit the home planet from time to time, but there were simply too few ships available for passenger flights.

Frisbee remained in orbit and the two *Cigar*-class ships continued to shuttle cargoes to the moon. When the new bulldiggers were ready, they would be loaded aboard the *Cigars*. By then, it was hoped that the first domed shelters would also be ready.

China launched two of her new long-range rockets with supplies for the moon. John messaged Chuck; perhaps Chang Jiang's worries had been for nothing.

A week later, a rover left the Chinese base. The vehicle traveled slowly across the surface, towing a trailer containing a shelter, air tanks, food, and water. The two men on the rover reached Moonbase after an epic journey; there had been accidents and breakdowns on the way. John radioed Chuck, and a relief shipment was soon on its way. The men explained that the only radios that still worked were the ones in the suits. The replacement batteries for the two high-powered radios, delivered as part of the second shipment, had worked fine at first, then failed catastrophically, destroying both radios.

Of the two men who'd made the journey, one died almost immediately. The other lingered for two weeks before dying from radiation sickness.

26

The telephone's burr woke Chuck. He sat up and glanced at the lighted numbers on the bedroom clock, then carried the phone into the dining room before answering.

"They did *what,* John? Wait a minute, are you sure?"

"They were already sick by the time they got here, Chuck. Chang's people are almost out of water and oxygen. They're down to less than four days' supply. I sent off an emergency shipment using two lifters with the canopies installed. The solar cells will stretch their range, they can run full speed for four hours or so. After that, the pilots will have to set down long enough to recharge the batteries, but they'll need rest anyway. Good thing it's daylight phase. They'll be there in another ten hours or so."

"I'll replace your supplies...let me see, Monday. It will take that long to get everything together. If you're short, I can send *Frisbee* as soon as I can round up her crew."

"We're okay for two weeks, but sending Frisbee isn't a bad idea. Put her in lunar orbit; we may need to evacuate the Chinese. What the hell were they thinking?"

"I don't know. I think we need to talk to Chang. By Monday, I can have two cargoes ready in Reykjavik, oxygen, water, emergency rations. I'll need to retask one of the *Cigars* and that will take a day or so. The first load goes directly to Chang, the other will replace what you sent off and increase your emergency stocks in case this happens again. It's a bit of a shuffle, but we can do it."

"Good idea. Sorry to disturb your weekend, Chuck."

"Sometimes you don't have a choice, John."

Lina rolled over when Chuck sat down on the bed and sleepily asked if anything was wrong.

"Nothing to do with our people, but the Chinese on Luna have problems. Beijing may have decided to cut her losses, just abandon them."

"Chuck, that's horrible! What are you going to do?"

"John sent an emergency shipment and we'll talk to Chang on Monday. Interesting guy, he went to MIT."

"Are you coming back to bed?"

"I don't think so. I doubt I'd be able to sleep."

"I'll get up too," Lina decided.

Chuck brushed his teeth and dressed, then went to the dining room. Lina had set coffee to brewing and had put out rolls, butter, and jam, then gone back to the bedroom to make her own preparations for the day. Chuck was drinking his second cup when she rejoined him.

"Did I tell you how much being with you does for me?"

"Not often enough," Lina dimpled. "But it's mutual. I don't know...maybe it's the absences between, but weekends are wonderful."

"You're the only thing keeping me sane. The kids too...they're growing so fast! I wish I could be here more often."

"I know. Bobby misses you, maybe not so much now. What possessed you to buy the dogs?"

"I didn't intend to buy two. I figured a small dog, maybe a dachshund, would work best. They're shorthaired and affectionate, and it's time the kids learned responsibility. Feeding a dog doesn't take much time. But then I looked at the Bassett, and he had that sad, hound look..."

"You're just a softie!"

"I admit it. Anyway, the dogs also love each other, and the kids will be going to school next year."

"I know. Time passes so fast..." Lina looked down at the cup, then topped it off.

"It will get better. As soon as the new base is finished, I'll transfer most of our operations here. I can get home almost every night. For that matter, we could build a second home out there. We could still visit here whenever you wanted."

"I don't know, Chuck. What about schools? It's the Outback. Stations are miles apart, there's almost nothing to do. You've got your work, but I can't see raising kids like that."

"Well, there's time. We can think about it. A visit to the base during the week, that's easy enough to arrange."

"Maybe. I'm going to check on the kids, want to come?"

"Sure."

Lina gently opened the door. Buddy stirred, then looked up sleepily before closing his eyes. Bassetts do not suffer from insomnia.

Poppy never stirred. She was in her favorite space, between the two children, sharing their bed and cover. She had simply taken it as her due and moved in, willing to share her new bed with her adored friends, but as for sleeping alone...

Lina had tried. The poor thing had cried for hours and the children had joined in. Finally, Lina relented. It was what it was.

Robbie was barely visible, only the top of her head showing above the light coverlet. Bobby was on his back, left hand extended beneath the cover toward Robbie. Robbie's hand was there, in contact; the children had never spent a night apart since being released from the hospital. Perhaps things would change, now that they had the dogs as objects for their affection. Quietly Lina backed out, and Chuck closed the door behind them.

"What does the doctor say? Is the cane going to be enough for Bobby, or will he need a wheelchair?"

"He thinks the cane is enough for now, and maybe Bobby won't even need that. We'll see. It doesn't seem to slow him down."

"I noticed that. He keeps Frenchy hopping!"

"Grandpa's the man, that's for sure! But he loves every minute of it. He's looking better too. I was worried for a while."

"Me too. I haven't seen much of Will."

"He stops in every few days. He's spending most of his time in Sydney or Canberra."

"Politics?"

"That, and a lot of business interests. The new base is expensive."

"We've got the money," said Chuck dismissively. "It's a necessary expense. I just wish the Russians would leave us alone! We're not doing anything to them!"

"No," replied Lina thoughtfully. "But maybe they don't see it that way. The US government either. Have you heard any more from them?"

"No. The ships are gone now. I don't know if they found *Tesla*, or just gave up."

* * *

"THAT'S IT? It doesn't look like much."

"That's an impeller, Mister President. It's been soaked with sea water, so there's a considerable amount of corrosion, but that's it. This one is almost intact, except for the exterior shroud. Two others have been partially disassembled. Would you like to see those?"

Regina Jones held a number of degrees, including two doctorates. She was also a hard-driving administrator. The president was more than happy to have her directing the reverse-engineering project. Unlike the floundering Project Los Angeles, this one showed real promise.

"This is interesting, but it's not ground-breaking. It's an electric motor, frequency-controlled. That means they can increase or decrease how fast it revolves based on the input frequency. NFI made a few tweaks, but it's still only an electric motor and it's nothing we can't understand. Maybe we can even improve it. This other device, however, it's not like anything I've seen before. It's obviously meant to rotate, but what does it do? Over here," she walked to a third table, "is the one we've disassembled completely. As you see, there are windings here which also resemble an electric motor. To be honest, none of us have the faintest idea of what it does. The frame is quite robust, meaning the designer expected considerable stress."

She turned and faced the president. "We don't understand it, but we're going to build one and see what happens."

"Thank you, Doctor Jones. Please keep me advised." The president nodded at Regina and walked away. He waited until they'd left the building, then asked, "What's next, Mark?"

"You've got a meeting tomorrow with a deputy from the European Union. He's coming in tonight."

"What does he want?"

"I've got a full briefing laid on for you this afternoon. I expect it has something to do with the Grand Alliance."

"Not much of an alliance, so far. All right, who do I need at the meeting?"

"I've alerted representatives from Defense and Commerce. The deputy is in charge, but he's bringing two aides, a French general and the director of a consortium of German industrialists. They wield considerable clout in the EU."

"Add one more to my team, Mark. Someone with a financial background."

"Yes, Mister President."

* * *

CHUCK LANDED LONG ENOUGH for John to board, then *Lina* lifted off for the Chinese base. *Giant* had already offloaded her cargo of consumables, then returned to Earth for a second shipment, this one to Moonbase. After discharging her cargo, she would return to her normal schedule.

Only a few of the Japanese fuel rods remained, and even the French stockpile was less than half its former size. Some of the rods, too depleted to be used, had been launched toward the sun; others powered Luna's generation system, the remainder had been parked in orbit around Mars. Tagged with simple transponders, they would be ferried to the surface when the trenches and plumbing systems were ready.

Chang Jiang met them as soon as they landed. "I am very glad to see you. We owe you thanks. John, the oxygen was urgently needed. Your act saved many lives."

"Chang Jiang, we are in this together. You help us, we will help you. *Giant's* shipment should keep you going for another two weeks at least. By then, we'll have another cargo for you. I don't know if you've found it yet, but Chuck included a replacement radio in the shipment, and this one's not encrypted. It's powerful enough to reach our relay, and from there it goes to the satellite system. You can call China or anyone else directly."

Chang Jiang hesitated. "I will not do that, John. Chuck, I have a printout to show you. Will you come with me, please?"

A silent Chinese brought tea and small cakes as soon as they were seated in the domed 'office'.

"This is a record of a message that was sent three weeks ago."

"I'm sorry, neither of us reads Chinese. What does it say?"

"You are welcome to take it with you and have one of your people translate it. It orders me to attack your base. I did not know what to do, so I spoke with my people. We are in agreement. There will be no attack."

Chuck, astonished, glanced at John, who had turned to see how Chuck would react.

"Attack Moonbase? Why?"

"The sender did not explain."

"How were you to do this? Do you have weapons up here?"

"A few. Five automatic rifles and a pistol were sent with the first rocket shipment. They are for my use. Our people may need encouragement. Leaders are often armed."

"So how did they intend for you to take Moonbase? And why?"

"Sabotage. On the moon, this is easy; remaining alive is much harder. I was ordered to place explosive charges against your habitats. Your people would die from decompression. We were to do this, then capture a ship. The message said this was the only way for us to return to our mother country."

"So that's why they sabotaged your radios. They thought you might tell us what they intended."

"Yes, Mister Sneyd. So I surmise."

"You know that your two men, the ones you sent?" Chang Jiang nodded. "They're very sick. One may have died by now. The other is unlikely to recover."

Chang Jiang nodded. "They knew they would not return. I intended to go, but my people convinced me that I was needed here. Death comes to all. It matters only when, and how a man faces the end. Even today, we hope our remains are returned to our families. Wang Chen and Sun Li accepted even that, the knowledge that their families will not know how they passed. No man can face death with a better spirit. We say, 'their face shines forth greatness.'"

"I understand. But what do we do now? Our base is too small to take your people."

"There is another option, if you are willing. We have your domed shelters ready, so...

* * *

CHUCK DROPPED John off at Moonbase before going on to Reykjavik. He composed a message on the way. Frenchy might have advice to offer. Should he ally with the Lunar Chinese, or not? The Chinese wanted their own location on Mars and were prepared to work for NFI as long as necessary to achieve that goal. What would the Chinese government say if they learned of this? What were the long-term effects of planting a colony that had its own aims? Would those aims support, or act against, NFI's interests? Deciding he'd written enough, he sent the message through the company's satellite system. Frenchy would receive it within a short time and might well be on the phone by the time Chuck arrived at his office.

He had barely stepped to the ground when one of the mechanics ran up. "Chuck, they need you at the office. I'm supposed to tell you it's an emergency."

Chuck frowned. This couldn't be about the message he'd sent.

"What's wrong?"

"*Giant's* been attacked. She was damaged, there's also a lot of collateral damage. There's been a radiation spill too. It may mean war."

"Slow down. Who attacked? Where did this happen?"

"Chinese fighters from the mainland. They were definitely after *Giant*, the first missile hit the portside wing. The second missed and blew up when it hit the ground. There are Japanese casualties, I don't know how many. *Giant's* crew is safe, at least for now. They're going to try to reach orbit with the dorsal and ventral impellers. They'll need oxygen, that wing hit took out a lot of their reserve. If they can resupply from one of the orbiting fuel stations, they may try for the moon."

The mechanic caught his breath, then continued. "The Japanese launched fighters from Chitose and Misawa, but the raid was over before they got airborne. The Chinese came from somewhere near Wuhan; they refueled over the East China Sea, then went north. South Korean radars picked them up when they passed Gwangju and Busan, but they thought it was a routine training flight and didn't think to notify the Japanese. Anyway, they turned east about forty kilometers south of Niigata and caught *Giant* while she was loading. One of the Japanese missile batteries got off a shot, we don't know which one. It didn't hit anything, but it may have spooked the Chinese. They broke off the raid and headed southeast. One of our foremen is former navy, he says they're probably meeting tankers over the Pacific. After that, who knows?"

"Damn. Okay, thanks, let the office know that I'm on my way."

27

The office was crowded. One was an administrator, the others were involved with operations.

"Contact the Japanese consortium, the one that handles the shipments," said Chuck. "See if there's anything we can do." The administrator nodded and left.

"What do we know?" asked Chuck.

"As you can guess, things are pretty chaotic," said Arnbjorn, the foreman in charge of preparing ships for flight. "At least one missile hit the ground and blew up. There were a number of fuel rods waiting there in temporary storage, separated from each other by berms but with no overhead cover. At least one was damaged by the explosion. There have been reports of radiation leaks, how bad we don't know. *Giant's* cargo bay caught some of it, so before the wing can be repaired she'll have to be decontaminated. The crew is safe; the cargo bay's shields are between the contaminated part and the cabin."

"Where's *Giant* now?" asked Chuck.

"In orbit. It was touch and go, but she made it. Eventually she'll go to the moon to have the damaged wing replaced, but not until we know how severe the contamination is. The crew will be taken off as soon as we can get a ship up there."

"Getting the crew off is the thing to do, but keep me informed." He sighed and stood up, walking over to the window. Iceland was calm, people went about their business. Half a world away, confusion and terror reigned.

"What about the strike force?"

"Japan's Self Defense Forces have patrols out, but so far they haven't found anything. The UN has been informed, but no one's saying anything yet."

"They're not noted for fast action," agreed Chuck. "Regardless of what the Japanese do, we've got our own problems. China is targeting NFI. They ordered their people on Luna to hit Moonbase, and now this. Recommendations?"

No one replied. Most looked around to see who would go first. Finally Arnbjorn spoke. "We cannot allow this to continue. I know the captains and copilots of the ships, I talk to them when they land. They are not trained to fight. Our ships are not designed for war. They are freight haulers that sometimes carry passengers. Even the machine guns are stored, except when I am told they might be needed. The men who do this work are not part of my crew." He looked around, but no one wanted to interrupt. "We are not safe here. We are an island nation, but so is Japan. It did not help them."

"Keep going," said Chuck.

"I see to it that ships are refueled, that the cabins are cleaned and oxygen and water tanks are filled. If there are gripes from the pilots, I inform the mechanics and they fix the problem. In any case, all systems are inspected carefully before each flight. We know how to do this, but we have no one trained to operate or repair the weapons. There are also two men who inspect the missiles on the wings.

"We are not a military nation. Even during the world war, when danger was greatest, we asked the British and the Americans for help. Now I must ask: by permitting your spacecraft to land in our country, are we putting our people in danger?"

"I don't have an answer, Arnbjorn. As you said, our ships haul freight. We are not a military threat to anyone."

"But you are the only ones with space-going ships, real spaceships. You are also very wealthy. Men and nations will envy you. They will envy us too, because we work with you. Our country benefits from this. There are jobs that pay well. But is this enough, considering the danger?"

"You're a long way from China, Arnbjorn."

"Russia is not so far. They have a military base on the Gulf of Finland. It is almost due east of us, only about two thousand five hundred kilometers. Russian submarines have been detected. Russian airplanes, the Bear bombers, have been seen. We have seen the reports from Finland. Russians have forced you to close your base. We know these things. Months ago, Russia. Today, China. Will Russia hesitate because we are not their enemy? I do not think so. You are. I think they will come if you are here."

"So you think Iceland's government will act?"

"Yes. Your presence places us in danger."

"Thanks for being honest, Arnbjorn."

"I liked my job. It was exciting, knowing that the ship I worked on would go into space. I will be sorry to lose my job, but there are other jobs. I had work before you came, I will have work when you are gone. I have saved my wages, so perhaps I will buy a fishing boat."

Chuck nodded. "Anyone else?"

"Your men have talked, Chuck. You have other places you can go.

Perhaps you will no longer carry the radioactive things to space. Your company is wealthy, you do not need to do this dangerous work."

"We don't, and yet we do. Someone must. You are fortunate, because you have geothermal and hydropower. Your population is also small, so your situation won't change. But nations that lack your resources used nuclear power to make up for the shortages. Now, they have pools of water holding used fuel rods. The rods contain poison as well as radioactivity. What will happen if the dangerous materials are *not* removed? Sooner or later, the water will leak. The danger will spread, not only on the land but into the ocean. It has already happened in France. What then of your fishing boat, Arnbjorn?"

Arnbjorn shrugged and shook his head, but said nothing.

"Thanks for your input. Well, I've got work to do, and I imagine you do too." Chuck waited as the others filed out, then sat down behind his desk. It was time to call Frenchy and Will. If Iceland's government closed the Reykjavik base, the new Base Australia would have to take up the load.

NFI was running out of options.

* * *

"Mister President, next week's conference has been canceled. The German envoy and the French minister offer their apologies. They claim to have urgent matters at home. The secretary of state is here now. She's received a note, and wants to discuss it with you."

"Who's the note from?"

"It's signed by the president of the European Commission. Of the various presidents of this or that, he is probably the most influential."

The president sighed. "I wonder what's got him upset? Send her in."

Mark nodded and opened the door. "Lucinda, the president will see you now."

"So what have you got for me, Lucy?"

Lucinda Morris hated being called 'Lucy', as the president well knew. Appointed as a political favor, the two had never gotten along well. "The note is from the president of the European Commission. The diplomatic message is essentially doubletalk, but there is also a private letter. It came via the diplomatic pouch, and I was asked to hand-deliver it. Apparently, it contains sensitive information."

"I see. Give me a minute then, I may want to send a reply. Help yourself to coffee or something stronger." The president sliced open the sealed 8" by 10" envelope and removed stapled-together typewritten sheets. Scanning rapidly, he absorbed the gist. "No reply. Convey my thanks verbally, please. Was there anything else?"

Lucinda fumed as she left the office. *Male--damned--chauvinist! I'm a cabinet officer, not a delivery person!*

"Mister President, you really shouldn't bait her like that."

"Tend to your knitting, Mark. I don't want her getting uppity. This note," he waved the pages, "makes the other stuff understandable. Marko is facing a revolt of sorts. That grand union thing, the EU is pulling out of it. They've got serious political problems. The northern nations are unhappy, the Mediterranean nations are threatening to withdraw, again, and this time even the French and Germans are going their own way. That's what this amounts to, though that's not how he put it. They're all afraid of what the Russians and the Chinese are doing. The EU has only held together as long as it has because Germany wanted it and France went along. But both had disastrous wars last century, so if they are seen to be involving themselves in another one both their governments will fall. I can understand his problem. The EU is too loose to be a real nation, but at the same time it won't ever become one unless they act together. As for the grand coalition, it's not. The Russians are doing whatever they want, so are the Chinese. Maybe we should too.

"Maybe I should send a note of my own. No, I've got a better idea.

Two of NFI's owners, that Fuqua guy and the other one, Crane, are both in Australia. Maybe I can talk sense to one of them. Get in touch with our ambassador. Explain that I'm under a lot of pressure and I don't want this situation to get out of control. Make me sound sympathetic, okay? But emphasize that I want to talk to them. That Sneyd guy too, he's an ass, but sometimes you have to deal with asses. It comes with the job," said the president.

"Yes, Mister President. You have a tour scheduled, a chamber of commerce from Minnesota. You're supposed to go with them while they tour the White House."

"Find someone else, Mark, one of the secretaries. Maybe the vice president if he's in town. I'm going across town, Regina Jones has something to show me."

"Yes, sir. Do you want me along?"

"Yeah. Alert the secret service, we'll go by convoy."

"Yes, sir."

Arranging everything took time. For presidents, even a short trip crosstown was a logistic effort that called on a number of agencies. Each needed to be told their role in the undertaking, vehicles and personnel assigned, and police escorts arranged. As a result, a number of residents were late getting home. The afternoon commute was snarled, traffic was worse and a number of accidents happened. The police had seen it before, so they were philosophical. Drivers were not. But the president knew none of this, nor would he have cared. He wanted to go crosstown, so that ended the matter.

Doctor Jones met them at the entry and escorted them to a large room. This was not the same room where they'd viewed the recovered impeller devices. It was smaller, for one thing, and contained a single table. A small item sat on the table, more model than space drive. Heavy cables from the device led to a pair of connections mounted to the table.

"That's it? Explain why you couldn't bring that thing to the White House." The president's tone was cold.

"Because it's connected to a large power supply and control unit. Those are in the room next to this one."

The president was mollified, barely. "Does it work?"

"It does. We scaled down the units you saw before. Size isn't important, except that larger units have greater potential. This one looks small, but even so, it has enough power to push a golf cart. We still don't understand how it works, but it does. Six of these could power a hovercraft as soon as we shrink the control system. Something else, this one is relatively crude. I'd call it a first generation device. It generates an electromagnetic field, we know that, but it does it mechanically. I think we can do the same thing electrically. The only thing holding us back at this point is the control system."

"Really? How would you do that?"

"Mister President, I mean no offense, but how much do you know about physics? About fields and how to propagate them, about electronics, about math...and that's only the beginning."

"You wouldn't be trying to baffle me with bullshit, would you, Doctor Jones?" the president asked sourly.

"No. I've got the best team I could hire away from industry. Suppose you let us get on with the job."

Mark listened, wide eyed. No one talked to the president that way! He waited for the explosion, but was astonished to hear a chuckle.

"I'll do that, Doctor Jones. You said this one works. Are we going to see a demonstration?"

"Yes, Mister President. If you'll follow me...?"

Thirty minutes later, heading for the White House, the president finally broke the silence. "By golly, she's touchy! But she did it. That other bunch, the Project Los Angeles people, they're a waste of space."

"Maybe not, Mister President." Mark was cautious. "I checked, because they're asking for a supplemental appropriation. They've gone a different way. If they're right, they're on the verge of building an antigravity device."

"Goddamnit, as soon as I think I understand one thing, they come up with something even more outlandish! I'd fire the lot of them, if it wasn't for the Russians and the Chinese. If our people don't invent something, their people will. It's like toothpaste, once it's out you can't put it back in the tube. I tried that once, Mark. I was a kid, and I heard that one. I figured if I could stretch the tube out, while the toothpaste was covering the opening, it would be sucked back in."

"And did it work, Mister President?"

"No," the president said ruefully. "I pulled the end too hard. The tube split open and squirted toothpaste all over me. My pop wanted to use his belt at first, then he said that a kid that had to try things for himself would manage to kill himself or grow up to be president."

28

Chuck sat on the couch, arm around Lina. The twins were in bed, Frenchy had gone with Will to inspect the new base. A week, two more, and it should be ready. Lina had turned on the television, where a reporter was describing the aftermath of the strike that damaged *Giant*.

"This video was taken by a Japanese worker during the attack." Giant managed to leave the ground, but wavered alarmingly before lifting far enough to rotate into lift position. "As you can see, a spacecraft belonging to the company New Frontiers was damaged. There was some question whether the ship could fly at all, but according to reports, it is now in orbit." The scene switched to a view of workers in white coats wielding shovels. They wore caps and paper breathing masks. "The men you see are all volunteers. Scientists say the masks they're wearing are virtually useless. They're cheap and commonly available, but were never intended to protect the wearer from hazardous materials." The scene switched again, this time to a man wearing a white shirt and tie. "Doctor Abrams, you've seen the video. What can you tell my audience about what they've just seen?"

"Two things, Graham. They're all older men. As you saw, they're using shovels to scrape away the topsoil and put it into ordinary trash receptacles. I'm told the men volunteered, which is just as well."

"What do you mean, Doctor?"

"Just this, Graham. They're removing the residue from two fuel rods that were shattered during the attack. The lab coats and masks suggest to me that they know what they're doing. There are no young people, no women doing this. That tells me something else; these men expect to die."

"This is a suicide mission, Doctor Abrams?"

"I would say so, yes. They know what happened during the Fukushima meltdown. There was nothing they could do about that, it was simply too large and the radiation leak too extensive. This time, they believe they have a chance to contain the radiation."

"What will they do with the containers, Doctor?"

"I don't know, Graham. They may bury them, or maybe they will ask New Frontiers to remove them, but I don't think that will work. It's my understanding that New Frontiers' ships are designed to transport undamaged rods. There are supports built into their ships for that purpose. There's no way they can lift plastic dustbins."

Lina watched, fascinated. Chuck left the room and sat down on the veranda, reaching for his cell phone.

"Pete, I've got a job for your guys. I'll be there in a few hours, so you'll need to work fast. Here's what I want you to do."

Ending the call, Chuck went back inside. A new announcer was reporting.

"Japan has asked the UN to convene an emergency session. At this time, we have no confirmation that the UN will do so. Our Beijing reporter attempted to contact someone authorized to speak for the government, but no one has returned our calls. One man, speaking anonymously because he had no authorization from the government, denied that Chinese aircraft participated in the alleged attack on Japan. When we showed him copies of a video taken during the attack, he pointed out that there were no visible markings on the aircraft. He said that a number of nations have similar aircraft, some sold by China, some by Russia, or possibly resold by a previous buyer. He also suggested that the planes might belong to NFI, but when our reporter pointed out that NFI is not known to use jet engines, he ended the conversation. Back to you, Graham."

Chuck cleared his throat. "I'm needed at the office, honey. I'll get back as soon as I can."

"What's the matter, Chuck?"

"They need someone to authorize repairs, some modifications too. You know Giant was damaged, there's also decontamination that needs to be done..."

Lina looked at him suspiciously, but Chuck's expression was bland.

"If you have to go, I guess there's nothing to be said. Bobby will miss you; he needs to see more of his father."

"Just as soon as Base Australia is finished, baby."

* * *

THE SECRETARY-GENERAL FACED A DILEMMA.

Japan had demanded an emergency session, and a quiet canvassing of members from south Asia and Africa showed that they supported Japan. But Russia, China, and the United States in rare agreement threatened to veto any attempt to hold China responsible. The Secretary-general waffled, unable to decide. Should he allow the empty gesture to go forward, meaning that once again the UN would be revealed in all its toothless futility? And at the same time anger the big three, who provided most of the UN's operating funds?

While he dithered, other nations acted, quietly. An unanswered attack of this magnitude was a clear threat; if the UN would not even consider the matter, other solutions must be found. Conversations ensued, envoy to envoy. Chuck would have been gratified had he known; the consensus was that while NFI had profited, smaller nations around the globe had also benefited. China, on the other hand, had aggressively pressed their own interests to the detriment of their smaller neighbors.

The European Union's ambassador listened, but said little. Like the others, he had no doubt regarding which country had attacked Japan. He remained neutral, while noting how many other representatives reached quiet agreement. If the UN would not or could not act, they would refuse to lend support to the big three. Should it come to that, the small nations would ally to protect themselves. India and Indonesia separately reached the same conclusion; if China was bold enough to attack Japan, would she hesitate to do the same to them?

The US president knew none of this. If China or Russia heard the rumblings, they ignored them.

Japan quietly made overtures to a number of nations. Israel agreed to sell fighter planes and tanks, as well as export versions of their Iron Dome anti-rocket system. Israel also decided to beef up her own forces; money from the sales would pay for that.

* * *

CHUCK DEPLANED from *Lina* and walked to where Pete waited.

"How's it going?"

"Another hour, maybe two. The guys have worked their asses off."

"Tell them thanks, Pete. I need a cup of coffee. How about you?"

"I could use one. You're really going to do this?"

"Yeah. I can't ask anyone else."

"You might be surprised, Chuck. Just be careful."

"I intend to." The two men drank their coffee in silence. Half an hour later, there was a knock on the door. "Pete, can I talk to you?" Pete set down the cup. A few minutes later the two left. Chuck finished his second coffee, then stood. Three framed pictures stood on a small table. He looked at them for a moment, then gently turned the pictures face down.

He found Pete outside the hangar. "*Colossus* ready?"

"As ready as she'll ever be. Last chance, Chuck."

Chuck nodded, but said nothing. The hangar seemed cold, but he wouldn't be here long. Climbing the steps, he pressed the button by the hatch. It closed behind him as he walked into the crew cabin.

"What are you doing here? I said no copilot."

"You can fire me when we get back," replied Frodo. "Let's go."

Chuck shook his head and sat down in the pilot's seat. Frodo was already wearing his shipsuit; Chuck hadn't removed his after the flight from Brisbane. A glance at the telltales was sufficient; the lights glowed a reassuring green. "You're dialed in, Chuck. Let's go."

"Anybody would think you wanted to be a commander, the way you're giving orders."

"Maybe I will be, if we come back."

"When we come back, Frodo. Think positive."

"I'm positive this is the dumbest thing I've ever done."

The big ship lifted on autopilot, then cleared the hangar door. Moments later it transitioned for altitude and headed for the sky.

"I guess it's time to give them a call. I'll do it." Frodo nodded as Chuck pressed the transmit button.

Colossus began descending soon after crossing the north pole. "How are you going to do this?"

"Piece of cake. All we have to do is hover, then see if Pete's fix works."

"I was busy. What did he do?"

"Installed two sets of grapples in the cargo bay. They came off a pair of trash trucks. The hard part was adapting them to *Colossus'* hydraulic system, the one that operates the clamps. There's a false floor too, so we can double-stack the trash cans. You guide the grapples using the bay camera and pick up the trash bins. Just push them onto the floor, let the new ones push the older ones back. As soon as we're loaded, we head for space and launch the cans toward the sun. It's probably the weirdest thing we've done, but who cares? I just hope the shielding is good enough."

"It hasn't failed before."

"This is probably the biggest load we've ever hauled. More radiation, too, but I think we've got a chance."

"Yeah."

Two hours later, *Colossus* loaded, they headed for space. Frodo glanced at the dosimeter, but said nothing. There was really nothing to say.

Behind them, ambulances began arriving. Two of the Japanese workers had collapsed. There would be others.

* * *

THE PICKUP WAS TELEVISED LIVE, and the broadcast was transmitted around the world. Lina watched as *Colossus* moved from container to container, sinking until a plastic bin was hidden, then lifting to repeat the process for the next one. From the outside, nothing could be seen; the grapple forks were hidden by the ship's sides. It seemed almost magical.

In Tokyo, pedestrians stopped to stare at the huge screens that usually showed advertising. The crowd grew, choking off the streets. The police did nothing; they had joined the watching throngs. In time, the screens resumed their usual programming. People slowly drifted away.

Colossus launched her unlikely cargo as soon as she cleared the satellite belt. The collection of plastic containers sailed on; already past escape velocity, they would eventually be absorbed in the photosphere. *Colossus* turned back and moved into a high orbit near the drifting *Giant*.

"Now what, Chuck?"

"Now we wait. You didn't know NFI had a junkyard, did you?"

"I can't say I did. We probably ought to get checked out when we get back. You do have a way for us to get home, don't you? We picked up some radiation, but I don't know if it's enough to make us sick. Depending on how much we've already picked up during earlier flights, I mean."

"Good idea. I like you and all that, but I don't intend to spend a few weeks up here with you, twiddling my thumbs."

"So how are we going to get home?"

"This is the hairy part. I've been meaning to try this, but we just never got the chance."

"Try what?"

"Take a look out the port window."

"Is that *Farside*?"

"Yep. Ever done a spacewalk?"

"No. You?"

"I never had the time."

"No safety rope?"

"Not unless there's one in the cabinets behind us. I'm not going back into the cargo bay to look."

"Can't say I blame you. So we just suit up and go?"

"Except that when we go, we go careful. Farside's what, about five kilometers away?"

"Close enough. Just take it slow when you push off. She'll pick us up if we drift off course."

"Momma told me there would be days like this."

As it happened, *Farside* remained in place. A lifter picked up Frodo, then Chuck, transferring them to the ship. Chuck glanced out the portside window to where *Colossus* floated a short distance behind *Giant*.

"Chuck, can either one of those be salvaged?"

"I honestly don't know. Time will help; the short half-life elements will decay pretty quick. The others aren't as dangerous."

"That's a lot of money. How much did they cost?"

"Two of them? Together, at least a quarter billion dollars. Probably more."

"Wow."

"Easy come, easy go," said Chuck.

* * *

Farside's pilot turned and grinned at them. "I've got my orders, Chuck. You two are going to a hospital for a checkup."

"Orders from who, Wolfgang?" asked Chuck.

"Frenchy and Lina. Will got in on it too."

"I'm outnumbered, then. Where are we going?"

"Tokyo. They probably know as much about radiation sickness as anyone."

"Probably," agreed Chuck. He buckled in and leaned back against the seat back. Conversation lagged.

Two ambulances waited at the airport. A gowned and masked attendant scanned them carefully. Satisfied, he wordlessly indicated that Chuck was to enter one of the ambulances, Frodo the other. Chuck was soon lying on a gurney, belted into place. The gurney was short; his heels hung over the end. The rising and falling sound of the warning siren accompanied them on their way, dying away as the ambulance turned into the hospital. Attendants surrounded the gurney, soft Japanese instructions directed the unloading. Moments later it rolled through the entrance. Chuck glanced to the side. A few people stood, then bowed deeply. Moments later, they turned and faced away. Curious, he thought. But it didn't seem important. He closed his eyes and let the attendants take him where they would.

29

Chuck remained hospitalized for almost a month.

He was too miserable during the first two weeks to want visitors. Frenchy stopped by during the third week, and there had been another visitor before that, a mysterious deliverer of gifts.

Frenchy explained why Lina hadn't come. "You're going to be a father again, Chuck. Lina's three months along. She wasn't certain when you left, but she is now. There was nothing she could do at this point, so we decided she should stay home and I would visit. She sends her love. I've been handling things as your replacement, and it's been routine up to now."

"No more attacks?"

"Not a hint. It's all been quiet, but I authorized the move to Australia. We're keeping the bases in Rovaniemi and Reykjavik as emergency landing fields, they're already under lease, but everything else is being done now from Base Australia. By the way, there's a petition being circulated to name it Chuck Sneyd Base."

"Absolutely not. Maybe Frodo Baggett field. I could go along with that."

"No more nausea?"

"Not for the past week. Have you seen Frodo?"

"He's doing well, and he'll probably be released before you are. He's younger, so the treatment worked better."

"Do you understand what they did? I was pretty out of it for a while. I think I puked up last year's dinners."

Frenchy chuckled. "They did a number of things. There were several transfusions, a protein to stimulate your marrow cells to replace the damaged cells, and maybe some other things I didn't hear about. Whatever they did, it worked. You look a lot better now."

"I feel better too. Make sure Frodo is taken care of, Frenchy. I never intended to use a copilot, I figured the autopilot would hold the ship steady while I operated the grapples."

"It was a brilliant idea, I'll say that. Was it your idea or Pete's?"

"Both of us. The hydraulics were already there, we just unbolted the lockdowns that clamp the rods in place. Pete's guys welded in a mount and attached the trash-truck forks."

"You saved a lot of lives. Getting that stuff to space, it makes the rest of the cleanup much easier."

"What happened to the men who shoveled up the dirt."

"They died, Chuck. Some right away, a couple lasted about three weeks. They're all gone."

"Damn. You know, I saw them doing that. I couldn't stand by."

"I understand. Hold that thought, Chuck. You're scheduled for a press conference."

"The hell you say!"

"I say. We need the good publicity. Who brought the fancy gown and the swords?"

"I don't know. I asked, but nobody will say. One of the nurses had her son look up the kimono. He said it was very old, more than a century. Frodo got one too. I'm not sure about the swords, but they're traditional."

"Are they old too?"

"No. I'm told they're modern, but made in the traditional way, by hand. Each one is made by a master team, led by a swordsmith, but there's a guy who designs the hilt, the tsuba is made by a different master, another does the polishing. They're beautiful."

"So who do you think brought them?"

"They won't say, but the doctors and nurses bow toward them when they come to the room."

"You think it was the emperor? Or maybe one of his people?"

"It wouldn't have been the emperor himself. He's pretty reclusive. But he's done things like this before, given people special gifts."

"Special indeed. Do you want me to take them with me? I could have them delivered to Brisbane."

"No. I think the hospital staff wants them here, in my room. It means something to them. Not the samurai stuff, but their code of bushido. Maybe later."

Chuck looked at the twin stands, one holding the kimono, the other resting on a table. Two sheathed swords rested in wooden mounts, the laquered wood gleaming.

"So we're going to have a baby! Frenchy, it's just as well. The doctor tells me...well, there's a chance that I can't father children now. Even if I could, I probably shouldn't. He won't say no, but he feels there's a chance that Frodo and I caught some genetic damage."

Chuck's expression brightened. "Anyway, when is this press conference? The hospital hasn't told me they're releasing me."

"It will happen here. I'll stick around if you want."

"Absolutely. I wouldn't have it any other way. They should see that we're not all crazy!"

Chuck was dressed in a robe that apparently held some significance. Not the kimono, that was still there in its place of honor, but a padded robe that hid the signs of radiation. Chuck had lost nearly forty pounds, and it showed. His face was thin, almost emaciated. Most noticeable of all, he was totally bald. The staff raised the upper part of the bed until he was almost upright, then backed away. A disapproving doctor entered, looked around, then barked something in Japanese. Chuck had begun picking up a word here and there, but he understood none of this, at first. Moments later, attendants brought the two swords and laid them carefully along the edges of the bed. Moments later, the newsmen entered and waited by the door. A photographer took several shots, bowed, and left.

The doctor spoke clear, if accented English. "Fifteen minutes. No more."

Two of the newsmen, Japanese, bowed assent. The other was probably American, maybe Australian. He nodded, a gesture that was almost a bow in itself.

"Thank you for seeing us, Mister Sneyd."

"You're welcome, but you should probably speak to Mister Baggett. I only flew the ship, he was the one that picked up the bins and stored them."

"We interviewed him two days ago. He told us you were in charge. You are really the director of New Frontiers, Incorporated?"

"Well, it's actually chief executive officer. But yes, you could say I'm the director."

"You knew the risk was considerable?"

"I expected we would survive. This was not a suicide mission. The real heroes are the men who cleaned up the worst part of the spill. We couldn't have done anything if it hadn't been for them."

"They have not been forgotten, Mister Sneyd. You may be sure of that. But they are Japanese, their families are here. You are a very rich man, some think the richest in the world. Your company may also be the largest in the world. Why would you risk your life?"

"Well, I didn't really risk my life," Chuck shrugged uncomfortably. "I knew there was danger, but I had a lot of faith in my people. It was the old men that did it; I knew they were killing themselves. I couldn't just let it go for nothing. Anyway, it was a team effort. Another ship picked us up in space and brought us here. The hospital people have been great too. I'm grateful to them."

"We will not forget, Mister Sneyd. The medical staff reflects the will of our people. You left your ship in space?"

"Well, yes. There was no other place to leave it, and we needed to get away as soon as possible. The cargo bay is contaminated."

"This was one of your larger ships, is that true?" The questioner this time was the westerner.

"Yes," agreed Chuck. "There are two of them in orbit now. I don't know if they can be decontaminated. I hope so. They're expensive."

"How expensive, Mister Sneyd?"

"Well, between the two of them...maybe you should ask Mister Fuqua. He's the man who built the company."

"Mister Fuqua?"

"Between the two of them, right at three quarters of a billion US dollars."

The doctor stepped in at that point. "The interview is finished. Leave now."

The interview was finished, but not the fallout. People around the world watched it. A follow-up interview was conducted, this time with Frenchy.

"Mister Fuqua, I understand your company refuses to allow others to buy the space drive?"

"That is correct."

"Certainly you have enough money; you can't spend what you already have. Why would you not share the discovery with other nations?"

"We will, eventually. That's no secret. But we...I speak for my son-in-law and my daughter...don't want to see the same things in space that we see on Earth. The constant jockeying for profit, the envy, the hatred..."

"But your company has made huge profits!"

"We hope to make even more. But we provide a service that nations desperately need, and they often repay us in a similar fashion. We have exchanged space flights for manufactured goods, occasionally for commodities, other times for basing rights. We've done business with China as well as with Japan, so I don't understand why that nation would turn on us and attack our ship."

"The Chinese ambassador denies this, Mister Fuqua. He claims that China is a friend to NFI."

"No. We have had independent confirmation."

"Can you share this evidence with us, Mister Fuqua?"

"No. That's enough, gentlemen. I have work to do."

* * *

THE PRESIDENT WAS LIVID.

"Goddammit, Mark! I'm facing reelection and suddenly I'm looking like a cheap villain. How the hell did this happen? Our own people suddenly see NFI not as the greedy bastards they are, but as heroes! I've got to turn this around quick or the White House door will hit me in the ass next January. I'll need to meet with my campaign staff, not here, someplace neutral. You can't be there either. Set it up, but tell them to keep it quiet. See what kind of a spin I can put on it. There must be something. Sneyd is in Japan, nothing I can do there. They're pissed already."

"Mister President, they have formally asked the United States to live up to the terms of their treaty. I have it on good authority that since they never got a reply, they're rearming as fast as they can. They've got money now, a lot of it. They're buying arms, the Iron Dome system and tanks from Israel, fighters from France...that Eurofighter is supposed to be a good plane...even planes from us."

"I know it. I tried to stop it, but Congress forced my hand."

"They don't want to upset the Japanese any more than they have to. They need those small reactors. The states that already have them know they'll need servicing and replacement, the ones that don't have them yet want them. It's that, or go back to burning coal and gas."

"Yeah, yeah. Bastards. We could build our own, you know."

"We could, but we'd start way behind. It's cheaper to buy from the Japanese."

"Yeah, it just gets better and better. What's this about the Koreans?"

"The Japanese haven't said anything, but our sources in South Korea say they've initiated contacts with South Korea. They want an alliance of small Asian nations. The Japanese expect they'll have to go it alone. The UN won't help, we stopped that, and you ordered that we not reply to the request for assistance."

"The Koreans won't go along with that, Mark. They hate the Japanese."

"They might. They fear the Chinese more. Plus there's that lunatic in North Korea, he's rattling his saber again. That new missile...there's really no place in the world that's safe now. They claim they have a hydrogen bomb too, and this time they may not be bluffing."

"It just gets better and better. What about the Chinese and the Russians? They try to hit NFI and blow it, now there's not a peep from them. I've got to do something, something decisive. See if their ambassadors will meet with me. Maybe it's time we struck back before NFI hands us our heads on a platter. You know, Mark, if I'm out of here next year, so are you. You like having your own private executive jet, meeting with admirals and generals. Come up with something, Mark."

Mark understood the need. He searched, asking questions, often late in the evening. One of the people he talked to worked for Project Los Angeles.

"Mister President, I've got something. It may not be important."

"Keep talking."

"The lab in Nevada, the one you thought would never produce anything worthwhile? It looks like they might have. If my contact is right, that is. He claims they've discovered antigravity."

"Goddamn, Mark! Antigravity? Is he sure? How soon can we expect a working space drive?"

"Not in time to help your election, Mister President," said Mark dryly. The device is huge, and it only produces a small field. At least a year, more likely it will take them ten years. Depending on funding, of course."

"Of course. Well, it's Congress' baby, so why don't you leak this to a few of them? The Speaker, the majority and minority leaders, committee heads, people like that. Maybe a lobbyist or two, get them to light a fire under Congress. Call in some favors."

The president paused for a moment.

"Mark, if NFI refuses to share their drive, maybe all we need to do is slow them down. We're in position to catch up, maybe even leave them in the dust. Our new impellers will be better than anything they've got, and when you couple that with the antigravity generator, all we need is time. Get with the Russians and the Chinese. I want to issue a joint announcement. No more raids, not now. Maybe later on, so tell them to be ready. I want to send NFI a message. Make sure the public knows I'm doing it, the Russians and the Chinese are following my lead. I need to be the leader here."

The president stood up and began to pace. Mark waited, then asked, "What should the announcement say, Mister President. The Chinese and the Russians will want to know." His tone reflected none of the sarcasm he wanted to use.

"We're going to declare war on NFI, Mark. If they won't share space with us, and make sure you include as many nations as possible in this, we'll shut the bastards off from Earth. No water, no food, no air, nothing. We'll starve them out. If any of their ships land on Earth, it's fair game. Fighters, missiles, we'll shoot them down on sight."

30

The president was grumpy. He had not slept well, and it showed. He scowled at Mark and said, "So what did the Russians say?"

Mark was careful, but there was really no way to sugarcoat this. "They said no, Mister President. The Chinese too. Wars are between nations, not between national alliances and private companies. I asked if there was a partial solution, and they agreed tentatively to statements of disapproval about NFI not sharing the drive system. They've learned that we salvaged *Tesla*, and they want access to what we found. I told them we got nothing important, just wreckage. I don't think they bought it. If we don't give them something, they won't even go for the statements of disapproval."

The president drank his cooling coffee and poured another cup. "I won't turn anything over to them. We found it, we'll keep it. I'm going to have to take some risks, Mark. Have you looked at the national debt, the balance of payments, our gross national product? The economy has gone downhill, and don't thing the opposition hasn't noticed. My record stinks, and if I can't turn this around, I'll be another one-and-done president. I won't have it!"

"It's not that bad, Mister President," Mark demurred. "There have been reverses, but you can always release the information about having impellers of our own. Antigravity, too."

"Yeah, once. And maybe then the Russians and Chinese will declare war on *us*. But not now, the election is too far ahead. In the meantime, I've even got the treehuggers on my back. Make no mistake, Mark, people are listening to them. We need more levees, higher ones, new pumps too, and we don't have the money. The sea is rising. Drive along the Atlantic coast, the Gulf too, and you'll notice something. Dead trees, Mark. Salt water killed them. It doesn't have to happen every day, it only has to happen often enough to kill the trees and wipe out lawns and gardens. Billions won't fix it, I need trillions, and Congress won't authorize squat! I need to distract people, give them something else to focus on. I can't even start a war! The only issue I've got is NFI, and they fucking ignore me!" The president's expression alternated between gloom and anger as his voice rose.

Mark could think of nothing to say.

"Get out, Mark. Find me some good news. Get with my speechwriters and come up with a statement. Set up a press conference in the Rose Garden. On your way out, have someone send another pot of coffee."

Mark nodded and left. "He wants more coffee, and look out. He's not in a good mood."

* * *

CHUCK SPENT his first week catching up. Much had happened while he was in the hospital. Frenchy and Will joined forces to brief him on developments.

"Base Australia works. We've still got construction going on, primarily hangars and shops to take care of the new ships that are coming on line, but flights are happening. The major difference now is that we launch over Antarctica instead of the North Pole, but the distances are roughly the same. The last of the Japanese fuel rods are gone, transported to space. I approved purchase of four bulldiggers for Mars. They'll be finished in about a month. Meantime, the one on Luna isn't being used, just odds and ends jobs when the lifters are being used somewhere else, so I approved sending it to Mars. The Chinese are using it now, the ones we rescued from the moon, and their old base is abandoned.

"We've laid out the sites for four Mars bases for ourselves, and as soon as we have places to house them, I'll send work crews up. Moonbase is down to less than half strength, most of our people are down here on Base Australia or working on one of the new ships."

Chuck nodded. "What about the new ships? The Rovaniemi site is closed, right?"

"It's dormant, but there's a caretaker staff. We may need it for an emergency field, and anyway the lease runs for another ten years. There are a few flights in and out of Reykjavik, but everything else is flying out of Australia."

"That sounds like what I would have done. What about the *Saucers*?"

"Progress, but *Frisbee* is still the only one that's operational. *Disco* and *Saucer* are taking more time than expected. Some good news, though; *Giant* and *Colossus* have been salvaged. The external decontamination turned out to be easier than we expected, thanks to Dolph. We sprayed the hulls with water, then scraped off the ice. That cleaned the hulls, and unbolting the cargo bay liners took care of the rest. The ice was put into the bay liners, and we used Goliath to launch everything on an escape trajectory. The sun won't mind."

"Pretty smart. What else has Dolph been up to?"

"Writing up patent applications. We haven't filed yet, but they're ready."

Chuck nodded. "Let's hold on to them for now. As soon as someone else has an impeller, file everything. It probably won't stop them, but it may slow them down. What about the space stations? Are we still servicing those?"

"Right, the Indian station is doing well, so is the Indonesian one. Japan wants one, bigger than either of the others. They also intend to put observation satellites in orbit, so I agreed. As soon as they're ready, we'll launch them. Meanwhile, they're rebuilding *Giant* and *Colossus*."

"Busy, busy. Okay, I've been thinking. I had a lot of time in the hospital, between puking my guts out. I think it's time to lease impeller ships to the Japanese, the Indians, and the Indonesians."

"Just them? Not the US?"

"Just them. They've done well by us. They also don't have the capabilities that the US, Russia, and China have, which means they're less likely to try building their own ships. I intend to explain that even if they try duplicating our impellers, it will take time. Add in the costs and time to develop a ship to use them and it's cheaper to just use ours. It won't happen immediately; they've got to send pilots and support people through the school in Zurich. Contact Martha Simms and let her know to expect them. I'll do the meeting if you want. The pilots will have to be experienced and fluent in English. The mechanics and other crew will need to understand English, but not to the same degree as the pilots."

"You do it, Chuck. We've had a follow-up request from the Saudis. Same answer?"

"Same answer, it's still no. There's a strain of fanaticism there, I won't be the one to take them into space. If they want a station, they can contract with the Russians or the Americans."

"I'll let them know. They may not be able to afford it, now that oil is so cheap. That's really all they had going for them, and the money is bleeding away."

"Tough. It's not our problem."

"I'll contact the Japanese and the other two. Which ships?"

"Six of the *Farside* class, two for each of them. As soon as they have the people to operate them and keep them going, I mean."

"You know this is going to piss off the big three, don't you?"

"That's not my problem either," said Chuck.

* * *

LIFE RETURNED TO ROUTINE. An uneasy, undeclared truce held between Japan and China. Meanwhile, China added land to the artificial islands in the South China Sea. The small airfield was being used occasionally, mostly by light aircraft. Vietnamese fishermen claimed to have seen fighters coming and going from there, doing touch and go landings. Whether any remained was not known. Commercial flights now avoided the area, and several military flights reported that their radar sensors had alerted, indicating the presence of air-defense radars. The talks between Japan and South Korea were ongoing, and had expanded; they now included a number of other south or southeast Asian nations. Australia had been approached, but was keeping her distance for the time being.

Lina no longer suffered from morning sickness. She often visited Base Australia now, suggesting improvements from time to time and spending the evenings with Chuck. The twins had visited on two occasions; the entourage had included not only Lina and the children, but two nannies, chauffeurs, and Bert, the silent security man. He appeared to enjoy the trip least; he had allergies, severe ones, and they flared up in the Outback. He used an inhaler whenever it happened, but insisted on making the trip. It was his job, he explained.

No public announcement was made, but locals in Zurich noticed the increase in Asian students at NFI's academy. Pilots, being pilots, met some of the locals. The Indonesians avoided alcohol for the most part, but not the Indians and the Japanese. Russian, Chinese, and American intelligence agents connected the dots until a picture emerged.

"They don't work for NFI. So why is NFI training these guys?"

"I can think of one reason. They've been tight with those NFI people, so I'm thinking they're going to sell them spaceships. Probably the old ones."

"You think?"

"What else?"

"Okay, add it to tomorrow morning's intelligence summary."

THE PRESIDENT SAW it and summoned Mark. As a result of the meeting, Mark met with representatives of China and Russia. Aides were directed to prepare a joint announcement, to be released in each country. While they worked, Mark chatted with the other officials.

"What's this about the Saudis cozying up to you Americans?"

"They have concerns. They're in the same boat we are, shut out of space. They don't like it; they see themselves as leaders of the Islamic World and I suppose they are, part of it anyway. But the Indonesians are Islamic too for the most part, just more moderate than the Wahabi faction in Saudi Arabia, and *they've* got a station in orbit. The Iranians don't recognize the Saudis as leaders either. Anyway, they've got money and we need the alliance. It's just that simple. What about you Chinese? I hear the North Koreans are back in your pocket."

"An amusing turn of phrase. They are a client state, but no more than that. They serve a useful purpose as a buffer between our people and the South Koreans."

The officials smiled at each other. Mark noticed that the smiles never reached their eyes. He suspected much the same could have been said of his own expression.

* * *

FRENCHY TRAVELED to Luna to observe the launch of *Saucer*. Will refused to fly in space and Chuck accepted his doctor's opinion that he should avoid further radiation exposure. The three met when Frenchy returned.

"*Saucer's* on her way to Mars. She'll remain in orbit there for the next month. *Frisbee's* there already. They'll be habitat ships until people can move into the bases."

"Shouldn't take long. Look how far along the Chinese are. They've got a virtual town now, domes for living, a fuel-rod power plant operating, and a big supply dump. They've found water underground too. Their last shipment was soil, plain old dirt. We bought the topsoil from Argentina and they're spreading it out, mixing it with dirt from Mars. They figure they'll have full-scale farms in ten years or so. They're harvesting dry ice from the south polar cap, so that gives them plenty of carbon dioxide to work with too. The power plant provides the energy, and they're already getting a small amount of greenhouse effect from the carbon dioxide in the domes. The plants photosynthesize the carbon dioxide and release the oxygen. They figure that within ten years they'll be collecting oxygen from the domes. It's something for us to try too. There's no shortage of carbon dioxide, not really. The ice cap is about eight meters thick on the south pole, only about a meter thick over the northern pole, but even so that's a lot of carbon dioxide. More than we'll need for the foreseeable future."

"Dolph claims we can pick up all we want from Venus."

"Really?"

"He says just float in the upper atmosphere, suck in carbon dioxide and compress it, chill it, and we've got all the dry ice we'll ever need. He thinks we should terraform Venus."

"And how does he propose to do that?"

"Well, he's a physicist primarily, so he's not absolutely sure. But he thinks biologists might be able to cross single-celled plants with seaweed, the kind with air pods?"

"I think that's what they call giant kelp. Go on."

"Anyway, he thinks the solution is simple plants with air pods, maybe with their own supply of water in a bladder. He thinks it could be done. The idea is to seed these in the upper atmosphere to float around and reproduce. They'll start converting at least some of the carbon dioxide to oxygen."

"How long does he think this will take?" Will's sarcastic tone showed his doubts.

"Maybe a thousand years. Maybe even longer, although he pointed out that biologics can multiply like crazy when they get started."

"He doesn't think small, does he?" remarked Frenchy. "But there's something more important to consider. What about that press conference? Did you hear it?"

"I did. Can't say I liked it," said Chuck.

"I'm worried. Do you think they can actually prevent us from landing on Earth? The spokesman said it was only fair, we were keeping them out of space, they were entitled to keep us from Earth."

"They can't do it, Frenchy." Chuck's tone was positive. "We choose where we land. Japan, Australia, Indonesia, India, South Korea...those are all friendly countries. The northern Europeans too. They can't patrol the entire world, they don't have that many planes."

"What if they *do* manage to shoot a ship down? Say one of the *Giants* or *Cigars*? They're reactor powered now, all of them. It's more than just losing impellers, a crash could spread radiation."

"Like I said, they can't do it, but they can try. I'm getting tired of this. They can't build their own ships, so they intend to steal ours. We're not stopping them for going to space, they've been there before. Our ships are just better. Piss on the lot of them. If they *do* manage to hit one of our ships, I'll respond. They're not nearly as powerful as they think they are."

31

The president was in a pensive mood. Whatever had troubled him yesterday appeared to be in the past.

"So what am I doing wrong, Mark? I've tried everything I can think of. Nothing has worked, not really. Oh, we'll get our own impellers, maybe even better ones. We'll get our own antigravity too, but it won't happen during my presidency. I'll be the guy who couldn't get things done. So what do I do now?"

Mark hesitated. "Mister President, I don't know if you want to hear this."

"Go on," the president was impatient.

"I'm reminded of what a politician said, a long time ago. 'Change sides.'"

"What? Change what sides?"

"Maybe yours, but definitely pull back from the Chinese and the Russians. They have their own agenda, and bluntly, it's not at all what you intend. You see NFI's space operations as a strategic advantage, and maybe it is. But any advantage that's built on technology spawns an arms race, and sooner or later the other side catches up. You gain a temporary step, but it comes with a cost. The Chinese...they hit that NFI spaceship, but that wasn't the real target. They wanted to knock the Japanese back on their heels. Japan got rid of something dangerous, and they got rich by allying with New Frontiers. NFI hauled some of *our* spent fuel rods too, but only because we paid France to be the middle man. The French made money too, count on it. Anyway, the Chinese wanted to cut Japan off from support, that's why they were willing to go along with you, and meantime they're pushing ahead to claim the entire South China Sea as sovereign territory. That's what's *really* going on. They want those artificial islands as a stepping stone, Japan was suddenly getting rich, their economy was booming...those reactors they're selling us? Europe is buying them too. Not everywhere, but most places. Even Germany...they still had coal fired plants, as well as wind and solar power, so after they shut down the big fission generating plants, switching to a distributed system using the small reactors allowed them to get rid of the last coal-fired generators. So Japan is getting rich, China has economic problems, it's a no-brainer. I don't think they figured on those old men moving in so quick to clean up the contamination, they certainly had no idea NFI would help, but even so, the raid was a partial success."

The president looked at Mark, open mouthed. "Why am I not hearing this from the CIA? Shit, even the State Department...if you knew this, why wasn't I told?"

"Mister President, you never asked."

"So what about the Russians? What are they after?"

"Best guess, Europe. They want to revive the old USSR. The only real obstacle is us, the USA. They have a commodities economy that's getting weaker, so getting a leg into space will allow them to keep their economy going. Iron, copper, iridium, a whole bunch of metals are out there, just waiting for someone to claim them. They don't really have a choice; their manufacturing sector turns out cheap weapons, but as for an auto industry, heavy machinery, exports...Europe has better manufacturing, so does Asia. The Russians can't compete, and they know it. So they bust their butts, trying to steal NFI's space drive. If they can get it, they automatically get a giant leap forward over the rockets they're using now. Even those, they're antiquated. The Russians are also losing their best brains. Put it all together, they're facing regime collapse and they're desperate. You've played into their hands. Oh, you didn't start this Grand Alliance, but you didn't stop it either."

Mark paused while he marshaled his thoughts.

"We had NFI, but we shut them down. It happened during your predecessor's term, but it really doesn't matter who did it. We blew that one, big time. The way I see it, the only way to get back on track is to make peace with NFI. Whatever it takes, get them back on our side. Did you know their CEO was once a Marine and the guy who invented that space drive was a soldier? We should have done everything possible to encourage them, tax breaks, federal security instead of shutting them down, whatever. Now you're thinking of declaring war on the biggest, richest, corporation in the world. You're going up against a hero, a guy that people can't forget lost his hair while he was trying to help people when he had no need to. A man who's richer than anyone in history, but who's got a conscience and a sense of noblesse oblige."

He took a deep breath. "I should have realized this, but I didn't. I went along, and I made things worse. Oh, we got wrecked impellers out of it, but if anything I probably made things worse in the long run."

Mark looked up. "Mister President, I'll have my resignation on your desk within the hour. You need someone better in the job. I'm sorry."

The door closing made the only sound. The president had been paralyzed by surprise. Mark was quitting? Surprise gave way to fury. Was this the first rat, leaving the sinking ship?

He got up and paced; anger wouldn't help. He needed a plan.

How much did his secretary know? Had Mark told her he was quitting? The president looked closely at the woman, but could see no outward sign. Was she squinting a bit, maybe trying not to smile?

"Get me the Secretary of State. Not a phone call, I need her to come here."

* * *

"Gentlemen." Chuck glanced around the room, but the watching group were indeed all men. "Congratulations to all of you. Please hold the applause until everyone has been called. When your name is read, come up to the stage and receive your certificate."

Chuck paused while the shuffling of feet died down. As soon as it was quiet, he resumed, "Your country needs you. At the conclusion of this ceremony, you'll board the appropriate ships. The honor graduate from each nation will fly as copilot; your commander is employed by NFI, and until we release the ships to your nations, they're still company property, so be patient. By this time tomorrow, some of you will command spaceships that wear your country's colors. Others will be copilots, and in time I expect you'll get your own commands. Each nation will want to honor her first astronaut-commanders and pilots, so we'll keep this one as brief as possible. Martha?"

Half an hour later it was done. The newly-fledged astronauts, all pilots who had gained additional certifications to operate *Farside*-class spacecraft, were on their way. Newly-designed wings graced their dress uniforms as they marched out the door. Chuck watched, and sighed. They were going where he could no longer go. The risk was not great, but then, he had a family to think of. Lina and the twins needed him.

Chuck was still depressed when he arrived back at Base Australia.

"Glad you're back, Chuck." Will had been waiting when *Lina* landed. "I've met with a delegation from the Commonwealth government.

Short story, they want their own space station. I'm inclined to help them. Frenchy knows about it, and he thinks it's the smart thing to do. This is our only operational base dirtside, so we need their federal government as much as they need us."

Chuck thought it over. "Are there any drawbacks? Any downside? Tell them I'll have a decision by tomorrow. Work out the logistics, and if you don't see problems, you can make the announcement. Alert Martha, tell her to get ready for the next class. Put the Aussies in with our people when the next class starts."

"Neither of us thinks there's a problem. You've already handed over impeller-powered ships. Handing over a couple more of them...well, it's like pregnancy, you can't get more pregnant. Speaking of which, Lina wants to know when you're coming home."

* * *

THE AMBASSADOR LISTENED to the conversation, told the Secretary of State that he'd do his best, then broke the connection. What he was supposed to do, that was clear, and the former general, now retired, knew an order when he heard one. But how? He couldn't just go up and knock on their door! Well, that was where a staff came in; the thing to do was see what they thought. There wasn't a lot of time; he was due at a cocktail party in less than an hour.

"Use a couple of local hires, general." The ambassador preferred his aides use that title for any except formal occasions. He had been a general for a long time, an ambassador for less than three years, thanks to a talent for fundraising. The president had been grateful, and when asked, the general had decided that being Ambassador to Australia suited him just fine. Why, he might even learn to surf and water-ski!

"Why local hires?" asked the general.

"Shouldn't we see how it goes before we commit the embassy, sir? If we send one of our accredited people, there'll be no hiding it from the Aussies. Our local people are discreet, they know to keep things to themselves. Give them a note, a business card, ask them to deliver it. Nothing elaborate, just a simple note asking Fuqua or Crane to call us. I don't think Sneyd stays there, there might have been some sort of rift. Maybe it's just business keeping him away. Still, he's got a villa at their desert base now."

"How will our people recognize them? I doubt they know Fuqua, for that matter any of them. I've never met them, they don't attend diplomatic functions. This would be a lot simpler if they did."

"I'm sure we have photos. I know what Sneyd looks like, that poster is in half the houses around the world. Every teenager has one. I think Fuqua was in some of the pictures too. Crane, he's been here in Australia for a while, so I'm sure some of our Australian contacts have pictures. Collect as many pictures as we can, make them into a kind of flash card set, then give each of our people one."

"You think that would work?" asked the general.

"We can always try using someone from the diplomatic staff later. For that matter, as soon as we know for sure who's there, you could go yourself."

"That's what the secretary suggested, but I don't like being used as an errand boy. Go ahead, draft a note for my signature and see about having those photo cards made up. Two should do it, I think. There's no need for a twenty-four hour watch, if they report to Fuqua's house at nine o'clock, they can stay until five. With two of them, they can take separate breaks for lunch or bathroom calls."

"I'll see to it, general."

* * *

CHUCK SIGHED, laid the last report down, and rubbed tired eyes. Finally there was good news. The first contingent of settlers had moved onto the Martian surface. The steady flow of *Giant* and *Cigar* class ships had built huge open-air stockpiles of supplies. Great domes protected them from the distant sun, heavily staked to prevent the domes from flying away during the occasional Martian sandstorm. The Chinese-made habitats had been dug in until only the upper portion of the dome projected above the ground. The entrance was igloo-like, in that it was protected from the gusts when they came. It only remained to be seen if the soil remained fertile after it was thawed out. Still, as John had pointed out, bacteria survived for thousands of years in the permafrost, ready to resume life after the ice melted. If necessary, earthworms could always be shipped up. How long would it take before the Martian dirt became host to the soil microorganisms?

If there was a disappointment in the report, it was *Disco*. One glitch after another plagued the ship. Would she ever join the others? In any case, she would be the last *Saucer*-class ship to be built on Luna. There would be others, but they would be true Mars ships, Mars-built, and used by the brand-new citizens of Mars. *Frisbee* would remain in orbit for now; *Saucer* and *Stogie* were on their way out. They would stop long enough to examine the Trojan Asteroids that orbited eccentrically between Mars and Jupiter. Would they prove useful? Mars could certainly use a cheap supply of raw materials.

After radioing the results of the survey, the two ships would go on. The Asteroid Belt itself was a relatively short distance, and some of the larger asteroids were minor planets in all but name. Ceres might serve as a distant base, even if the drills brought up no usable material. Eventually, supplies used up and her cargo bay empty, *Stogie* would attempt to capture ice blocks from Jupiter's thin rings, perhaps even go on to Saturn. Would the Jovian or Saturnian moons be usable? The two ships were provisioned to remain away for as long as six months.

Humanity was in space, and this time they would stay.

32

Major Katsuro Genda picked up his helmet and took the ground shuttle to the flight line. The planes glistened in the dim light of dawn. Katsuro felt the same small thrill the sight always gave him. On the fuselage gleamed Japan's bold red circle. Men, some of them Katsuro's ancestors, had looked on that same insignia before climbing into the cockpit. For some, it had been the symbol of willing sacrifice.

Airplanes had come a long way since warriors guided their Type O Mitsubishi fighters down the decks of proud aircraft carriers. But while planes now were new and different, they were still flown by warriors. Even on a day like this, when the mission wasn't combat but a routine patrol over the South China Sea, he resolved to remain alert. Major Genda glanced at the other fighters that would accompany him today. Crews helped pilots settle into cockpits, then waited for the signal to start the twin jet engines. Major Genda nodded satisfaction, then signaled readiness to his own ground crew. Fumes, then a burst of smoke signaled that engines were starting. Katsuro ran his finger down his own checklist, dutifully insuring that each step was completed before moving to the next. Moments later, the big fighter shook as the twin engines rumbled to life. Crews completed the arming process and pulled the chocks from the wheels.

Major Genda smiled, satisfied. It was time to fly.

* * *

THE BIG SHIP HOVERED, then eased onto the skids. *Hornet* had brought Dolph and his research team to Base Australia, along with the results of their latest experiment. Chuck welcomed a smiling Dolph, while his team supervised unloading a large wooden box.

"So what's so urgent that you had to bring these guys to Australia? Were you getting tired of winter?"

"I'm loving the warmth, that's no secret, but I've got a recommendation and something you should see. It will take time to set up, so maybe we can talk about my recommendation first?"

"Sure, come on in." The two were shortly occupying chairs in Chuck's office, coffee in hand and snacks on the low table between them.

"I'll get right to it. You told me to ready the patent applications and I've done that. I don't know if it will keep anyone from using impellers, but if nothing else we can demand royalties. I think it's time to go ahead and file the applications."

Dolph chased a bite of doughnut with a swallow of coffee, then continued. "I've got two reasons for suggesting this. The first is that if the secret is not out by now, it soon will be. The US government salvaged at least one impeller from *Tesla*, maybe more, and they've got a very competent team working to reverse-engineer it. I know, because I was offered a job. The guy...he's a friend, by the way...didn't say doing what, not exactly, but I picked up enough to know what they're up to. He told me who I'd be working with, that got my attention, then he mentioned space and told me it was only a matter of time before they had working ships. That means impellers, so telling me what they wanted me to do clinched the idea. They found *Tesla*."

Dolph finished his doughnut and reached for another, this one an old-fashioned cake doughnut. He took a bite, then continued.

"You've also turned ships over to three tech-savvy nations; I'll give odds they know what's inside those impeller housings by now, so the secret isn't, and it's time to protect NFI's investment."

"Point taken, Dolph. You said there were two reasons?"

"The impellers will be useful, but not for spaceships. We've developed a *better* impulse system. It's all electronic, so it's more dependable than impellers, plus the big unit will use less power than the array of impellers in the *Saucer* class ships. We don't have a name for it yet, but it interfaces directly with space-time's electromagnetic and gravitational fields. Maybe we should call it the matrix drive, but whatever you call it, we've got a working model. Expanding it until it's big enough to power an interstellar ship is not going to be easy; the field generator doesn't naturally sync with any other generator. It not only syncs with space time, it changes the relationship, at least locally. So we either find a way to work around that or use one huge driver to propel the ship. One of those small modular reactors puts out enough power to run this drive unit, but maybe not the interstellar version. It may not be a problem; we think we're close to sustained nuclear fusion."

"People have been close to that for nearly a century now," said Chuck dryly. "What makes you so sure yours will work?"

"It's not really mine," Dolph admitted. "One of the Indian engineers found a way to stabilize hydrogen, pure H-one. The process strips the oxygen atom from pure water...it has to be pure, that's the only real drawback; if the feed is contaminated, it either shuts down the reaction or the power plant kicks out high-speed protons. Anyway, we can inject the stabilized hydrogen directly into the center of the magnetic containment field. Once initiation takes place, our unit bleeds off enough energy to keep the field going. From that point on, the rest of what it produces is essentially free energy, and unlike the laser and pellet reactors, this one runs continuously."

"How long, Dolph?" asked Chuck, eyes glazing over.

"How long to perfect this, or how long did the reaction last?"

"How long before it shut down?"

"Well, only a few milliseconds. But it was working. I'm sure the next one will work even better."

"What happened to the first one, Dolph?"

"Ah...we had containment failure. It kind of wrecked the device," Dolph admitted.

"I don't like the sound of this. How big is the device you intend to build?"

"All up? We could probably fit it into a trailer. You know, one of the eighteen wheel kind?"

"I don't want to melt Sydney into a puddle, so don't put it in a trailer. Build it into a ship, or at least into one of the modular bays. Use one of the converted *Insect* class birds, they should be big enough, and we can spare one. Before you try it again, though, take the ship into space. You may blow yourselves up, but at least you won't take a chunk of Australia with you."

Chuck grinned as Dolph looked down, crestfallen. "You can still run your tests, but let's err on the side of caution, okay?"

"Well, you're the boss." Dolph sounded disgruntled. "But that's not what I want to show you. How much power do you have available?"

"We're using two teakettles to power the base right now; that's what the guys call the small modular reactors. We'll need a third one after the next expansion. I could have one taken offline, but I've got to have at least one to run the base. We've got maintenance crews working on ships, I can't shut that down."

"One reactor should be enough; this is only a model, after all, and anyway we'll only need the reactor for an hour or so. The model is small, but even so it's big enough to propel that little ship of yours. Too bad you only have fuel cells; they just don't have the necessary juice."

"The *Lina*?"

"That's the one."

"And it works?"

"Sure does. I've brought a video. The directed impulse is a function of how much volume is contained within the space-time field, so it decays as an inverse-cube..."

"Spare me, Dolph. Let's take a look at this gadget, then you can show me the video."

* * *

A THOUGHTFUL CHUCK flew home that afternoon. He changed into shorts and a tee-shirt, then went to the children's wing to see what Lina was doing. Frenchy was mock-wrestling with the twins, their high-pitched squeals of excitement revealing how much they enjoyed the play. Lina sat in an armchair, watching; this was obviously not a new development. Chuck bent over, and she raised her face for a kiss.

"I think he's holding his own, wouldn't you say?"

"You mean dad? Yes, for now. But they're growing."

"Bobby is right in the thick of it."

"He always is. Walking still gives him trouble, but he adapts. He's also very bright. He's taught himself to read, Chuck."

"Really? I knew he was interested in books, but..."

"I started out reading to him, to both of them. Now he reads to Robbie."

"Are you sure? He could be repeating what he heard you say."

"No, he's using different books. He's reading."

"I need to spend more time with them. It's just that there's so much to do, it's one crisis after another, and there's never enough time. Frenchy looks like he's getting tired," Chuck mentioned.

"You're right, time to end it. Okay, you two, let grandpa up! Bobby, show daddy how you read to Robbie."

Frenchy drew a glass of water from the tap before joining them. Robbie sat down and Bobby reached for one of the books scattered around the play area. The book showed evidence of much use; clearly, it was a favorite. *They look for familiar things*, Chuck thought. *They know they're going to love the way it ends. It's a shame that life isn't like that.*

"Whew. That was fun!" Frenchy sat down and took a sip.

"I could tell. How's everything going?"

"Personally, I'm doing well, and the kids are too. Lina, she complains a lot..." Lina shot him a look. "Well, you do, sweetie."

"I've got reason! I look like a cow! I don't walk, I waddle!"

"Less than eight weeks to go," Chuck soothed. "Walking is good for you."

"That's easy for you to say!" Lina glowered.

"What's Will up to, Frenchy?"

"Trying to keep the Australians calm. Have you been watching what's going on, up north I mean?"

"Not really. I've had my hands full. We're filing the patents on the impeller system, so the secret won't be secret much longer. Dolph also has a couple of new toys to play with, if he doesn't blow himself up first. *Disco* is still not finished. I don't know what to do about that, maybe replace the construction manager, but as far as I can tell it's just bad luck, not mismanagement.

"*Stogie* and *Frisbee* left yesterday; we're finally surveying the area around Mars. Most will live aboard *Frisbee*, including the science people. *Stogie* requires a crew of three, two pilots and a flight engineer for the teakettle, and they'll be drawn on a rotating basis from the qualified people on *Frisbee*. *Stogie* is insurance in case something goes wrong and support for the main effort. She's better able to get close to an asteroid because she's smaller.

"They'll start with the Trojan asteroids, then go on to the main belt between Mars and Jupiter. With luck, there's something we can use. *Stogie* is carrying plenty of supplies, so they could be away for six Terrestrial months. Anyway, that's what I've been doing, trying not to let the house burn down. What's happening north of here?"

"Maybe a war. I read a lot of newspapers, and it doesn't look good."

"Sure, you follow market reports, I knew that. But war... Frenchy, are you sure?"

"No. But what I'm seeing is polarization, and it involves us, NFI I mean. It's not something we want, but it's there; if you're not with us, you're against us. Diplomatic pressure, a couple of military moves, that's all it took. The smaller nations are afraid the same thing will happen to them that happened in Japan. Powerful nations have used the smaller nations as battlegrounds in the past, and the damage took years to rebuild. Japan is rearming, and I think that's a red flag. They're not trying to develop their own nukes, but they've got the knowledge, so I wouldn't be surprised if they did. The Chinese are pushing ahead into areas claimed by several nations. They're openly flying fighters off the artificial islands they built in the South China Sea. There have already been minor clashes between Chinese ships and Vietnamese boats. Vietnam says they were innocent fishermen, but they were probably spies. They don't trust China. We don't hear a lot about that, but it's real."

Frenchy sipped his water, then watched Bobby pensively. "North Koreans are flying fighters off those islands too, and that may even be worse. Maybe this is Beijing's way to rein Kim in, but I can't see it working. North Korean artillery has fired at least a dozen shells at a small island near the Demilitarized Zone. It's too small to have a name as far as I can tell. The South Koreans are worried and the US hasn't responded, which makes the Koreans really jumpy. If they start mixing it up, China may find herself dragged into a war. They might just be trying to pick up mineral and fishing rights in the South China Sea, but mix in the North Koreans and all bets are off."

Frenchy paused long enough to sip more water.

"The Indians?" Frenchy shrugged. "There have been border clashes between them and the Chinese. The disputed area is close enough to Pakistan to pull *them* in if a war flares up, and all three have nukes. Saudi Arabia and Iran are bristling at each other, waiting to see which one will blink first. Australia doesn't want to take sides, but she'll probably go with Indonesia and India if she has to. Oz is buying fighters, modern tanks too. Infantry, artillery, they've got those, but their air forces and navy need upgrading. To be honest, they really don't have much of a navy, but they've asked Will if they could use our ships if war breaks out. He hasn't agreed yet, but this is now our only functioning groundside base, so we could end up in this whether we want to or not."

"Damn. You think it's that serious?"

"It's serious. How serious?" Frenchy shrugged again. "I doubt anyone knows for sure. It wouldn't take much. One act of stupidity, that's all it would take. The smaller nations are afraid, with reason, so they're picking sides. So maybe world war three."

"Damn. Will it spill into space, Frenchy?"

"That's the question, isn't it? We've got better ships, but not many, and some are off in space, hauling supplies to Mars. The Russians and Chinese have a lot of missiles, nuke warheads, too. *Giant* was damaged by a conventional bomb; if they start shooting nukes, we'll lose ships. Maybe all of them." Frenchy looked out the window, lost in thought for a moment.

"The North Koreans have a new long-range rocket, that's confirmed, and they're claiming they have a hydrogen warhead. Again."

"What do the Europeans and Americans say? They should know. Have the North Koreans really set off a hydrogen bomb?"

"It's not conclusive, that's what the papers say. The Europeans say they detected a seismic event and the Americans confirmed that much, but they haven't said anything else. The Americans have been pretty quiet, actually. Maybe it's the election; as usual, they've got their knickers in a knot."

* * *

CHUCK REMAINED thoughtful during the rest of the weekend. Could people really be crazy enough to trigger a world war? And did NFI really have anything to do with what was happening? He asked Frenchy about it, late Sunday afternoon.

"I don't think we're the *cause*, but we might be the trigger. Look at the situation before we started flying spaceships. There was an uneasy balance, Russia on one side, the European Union doing business with them but not happy about the Crimea. But they needed Russian natural gas, so they couldn't afford to put up much of a complaint. Down south, there was Georgia and South Ossetia. Then Putin moved north, pressuring the Ukraine. He's also trying to be the power broker in the Middle East. Then *we* enter the picture, providing a needed service, but at the same time using the profits to really move into space. We did that, jumped past Russia, China, and the USA, but look at what's happened since we began investing in the smaller nations. Japan was facing a declining population and a mountain of debt until they partnered with us. They got rid of all those dangerous fuel rods, then made a ton of money off the SMRs. Now they've got a space station and they're servicing it with their own ships. They've added more technology too, new stuff and different. Robots, self-driving electrical cars, some biologic discoveries too. Their people are having kids again, the prosperity effect. But from China's point of view, there's a dangerous new rival in the neighborhood, and we definitely had something to do with that. They hated each other even before World War Two. China's trying to follow the old Japanese plan to create a co-prosperity sphere, but this time dominated by China. A newly-prosperous and resurgent Japan is not in China's interests."

Frenchy paused to gather his thoughts, then continued.

"France, too. They were brokers as well as customers, and they made money by shipping cargoes in our ships. Some of the fuel rods were theirs, but some came from Germany and the US. Just like Iceland and Finland, they got prosperous fast. The Finns made enough to build up their air force, I knew that much, but maybe they invested in their ground forces too. But they didn't keep all the money we paid them, they bought subassemblies from south of the Baltic. Latvia, Estonia, Lithuania, and Poland all profited. We had money, we spent it, the money got spread around, so a lot of different economies boomed. As for the countries around the Baltic, they're a lot more confident now, no longer quite so fearful that Russia will try to do what she did in Ukraine.

"There's also an American brigade in that area, so the tripwire is back in place. It's assigned to NATO as a cover, but it's American and everyone knows it. There are NATO air defense units too. So yes, I think we had a part in this. We never intended any of this to happen, but when the US booted us out I had no choice. I had to find people we could work with, then the money rolled in, we spent it..." Frenchy looked away. "That earlier balance was based on fear and weak economies, so when that changed, suddenly governments were no longer afraid. They were still cautious, so they improved their financial and military positions. While that was happening, Russia's economy imploded when the price of crude oil dropped. China had a housing crisis that left *her* economy barely treading water. We were the Robin Hoods that took money from the big nations and spent it in the smaller ones. The dynamite was already there, but I think we lit the fuse."

Chuck's voice was soft. "Is there anything we can do? Anything we should do?"

"No. With luck, they'll jockey around and find a new balance."

The conversation was interrupted by a knock on the doorjamb.

"Yes, Bert?" The man was normally a silent presence, there, but almost invisible unless Lina or the children needed to go somewhere. A combination driver and bodyguard, he was awesomely competent.

"You need to turn on the idiot box, Frenchy. There's trouble brewin', ay."

Frenchy found the remote and turned the television to a news station. The speaker was Asian, Japanese according to a note at the bottom.

"...was attacked this morning. According to sources, the flight was intended to demonstrate the principle of freedom of navigation. The ministry will only confirm that our missiles were fired defensively. Four JM-56 fighters have returned to base. Others may have diverted to coastal airfields because of damage, but the ministry refuses to comment at this time. Back to you, Colin."

The Australian announcer was slow to resume the broadcast. "As you just heard, a Japanese flight reported being attacked early this morning in the South China Sea. The exact location has not been released. A fishing boat in the vicinity reported smoke trails, but whether they came from missiles or shot-down aircraft has not been determined. Chinese sources have not responded to requests for information, but the Chinese Ambassador has been called to the Japanese foreign ministry. A source close to the ministry says that a protest will be filed. Others speculate that Japan may even break off diplomatic relations with China.

"In local news, a storm is bearing down on the south Tasmanian coast..."

Chuck looked at Frenchy. "It's started, then?"

"Maybe. It depends on what happens now. I wonder *when* this happened?"

"He didn't say. Wait, there's more." The announcer reappeared; a banner scrolling below his face announced Breaking News in large red letters.

"Sources in South Korea confirm an earlier announcement that North Korean military forces have again shelled a small island north-west of the city of Incheon. South Korean officials have announced only that a small observation outpost has not reported in since the shelling. Forces along the Demilitarized Zone remain on high alert, and military officials report movement of armored vehicles north of the DMZ."

Chuck glanced at Frenchy. Shoulders slumped, facial wrinkles suddenly pronounced, Frenchy said, "The Chinese might have been willing to back off. The North Koreans may believe this is their chance. They're far behind the South Koreans economically, they can't even feed their people. The south has a strong economy, and this time they've got well trained and well-armed ground troops. The only real thing the north has is the bomb. I'm afraid they might use it.

33

No further reports came in during the night. Nations around the world held their collective breath, waiting. Chuck kissed Lina and the twins, then headed for his office. He began making calls as soon as *Lina* took off.

Wolfgang had rounded up as many pilots as possible. Some were off duty, others were flying. Some of these were in deep space, between Luna and Mars. The others were waiting in the employees' lounge when Chuck walked in.

"Thanks for coming. I hope you've been following events to our north. NFI's situation has changed, and some of you may choose not to continue as you have been."

He paused long enough for his audience to consider his statement.

"We've got enemies. They've tried to force our ships to land, tried to hijack one, and on two occasions military aircraft have behaved aggressively. During one such attempt, a missile struck *Giant*, severely damaging her. This attack also resulted in contaminating *Giant* with radioactive particles. One of our people has been killed, another severely injured. It may get worse before it gets better."

The pilots were absolutely silent, their eyes intent on Chuck.

"I can offer you three options at this point. One, you continue to fly for NFI, without specific limitations. I expect there will be an added bonus for those who choose this course. A second option is limited flying, in which you will fly shuttle routes between Luna and Mars. Those who take this option will not be exposed to enemy attack. Space is always dangerous, but your salaries already address that."

Chuck looked around the room. Almost all the pilots met his gaze, which he interpreted as a hopeful sign.

"The third option is resignation. If you aren't prepared to continue flying with NFI, I understand. You hired on to haul cargo, not get shot at. The terms of your employment have changed, not by my choice but because unforeseen events have happened. If you chose this third option, no hard feelings. Good luck to you in whatever the future holds.

"There are going to be changes. Up to now, NFI has attempted to avoid conflict. We closed down our first factory, we've stopped using our bases in Iceland and Finland, but that has encouraged our enemies to become even bolder. Starting as soon as our ground crews can make the arrangements, I intend to arm our ships. I do not intend to develop purely military spaceships, not at this time, but I recognize that it may come to that. The armament will be defensive in nature. I also intend to defend Moonbase, again passively. But I'm no longer prepared to be cast as the victim. NFI will have teeth."

The room was dead silent now.

"You're dismissed for today. Some of you have schedules to meet. Should you choose to not make those flights, that's your option. For now, I think it's safe enough. I would have no qualms about flying any of the flights myself. You are probably aware of why I no longer fly beyond the upper atmosphere." Chuck rubbed his bald head, resulting in a few chuckles. "But the choice is yours. If you choose resignation, please report to personnel as soon as possible to begin the process. Wolfgang, you can shift people around as you see fit or cancel flights if you don't have enough pilots. Those who are currently training in Switzerland will be offered the same choices as I gave you. Should they choose resignation, that will happen immediately. Depending on your choice, some jobs may not be available. We're going to need people who are prepared to accept the possibility of attack. I'll reconvene this meeting tomorrow at 9am for those who choose the unlimited option, who indicate their willingness to fly armed spacecraft. If you choose the outer space limited option, see Wolfgang. Wolfgang, I'd like you to remain behind, please. Gentlemen, the rest of you are free to go about your business."

The men filed out, some already involved in low discussions. How many would choose the more dangerous option? Soon, only Wolfgang remained.

"Let's go up to my office. I've got a couple of ideas and some questions."

"Sure. Do you have any idea how many of my pilots will leave?"

"No, but I decided they're not military and they're not mercenaries either. I don't want someone who'll get cold feet later. We can find people; it might hamper us in the short run, but the people flying out of Luna or Mars don't have to choose immediately. The ones I'm most concerned about now are the pilots flying out of here, from Earth. I'll be meeting with Pete and Dolph later on today to talk about ship weapons and the best way to protect Moonbase, but I should have time to get back with you. How about 4pm?"

"I can make that. By then I'll have a good idea of how many guys want to look for other jobs. What about training?"

"To use the new arms, you mean?" Wolfgang nodded. "We'll need something different, maybe a range here in the Outback. Australia wants our help, so I don't see why they wouldn't help us. Defensive arms only, so we're not talking about a bombing range, just a place pilots can practice using guns or missiles."

"Sounds good. I'll be in my office if you need me." Wolfgang left the room.

* * *

"I NEED a way of protecting our ships and a way of protecting Moonbase." Dolph looked at Chuck. Pete had begun sketching on the pad in front of him.

"What did you have in mind? Keep in mind that none of our ships are military, so in essence you're doing what groundside nations have done throughout history. They stuck guns on their ships and hoped that would be enough. Sometimes it was, when the ships had to contend with pirates, but when merchant ships faced warships, they lost. How are you going to stop air-to-air missiles? A fighter can pull high-gee maneuvers, our ships can't do that. You may be asking the impossible," said Dolph.

"Maybe not," said Pete. "You mentioned protecting Moonbase, and that gave me an idea. But first, why Moonbase? Do we really need it?"

"It's not that we need it so much, but that I can't allow the opposition to have it. As long as we can hold the moon, they can't use it to attack our ships in deep space. It's like the idea of territorial limits, you protect your own assets by keeping the other guy away."

"Good enough. I can do it. It will take time, so I hope the war doesn't start before we're ready."

"You sound pretty sure, Pete. We don't have many weapons, just a couple of auto-cannons, some rockets in pods, and half a dozen elderly Sidewinders. Keep in mind that there may not be weapons to buy. It's a seller's market; everybody is going to be lined up at their door, and I have no idea how much inventory they have."

"We don't need them. We'll make our own."

Chuck looked at Pete skeptically. "Make what? Using what?"

"Using what is the easy part. Rocks."

"You're not joking, are you?"

"Nope. What do we have a lot of? Rocks. Actually, I'm thinking more of cobbles, rocks fist sized or maybe just a little smaller. We'll need a lot of those. Think of icecrete, rocks held together by frozen steam."

"I remember that. But will they stay frozen...okay, they will, especially at high altitudes. But we don't plan on using our ships down on the deck, they'll *be* at high altitude! How do you plan to maneuver your icecrete bombs or guide them? How do you know they'll hit the enemy ship?"

"First, I don't intend to guide them, so they don't need to be maneuvered. Ever shoot a shotgun?"

Dolph had listened the exchange, befuddled. "I've done that! I'm a pretty good skeet shooter!"

"Good for you," said Pete dryly. "You aim where the target is going to be. The pellets spread out, so you don't need pinpoint accuracy. As for lethality, the fighter provides that. Running into a fist-sized rock at high speed is guaranteed to bend the bird. Since they're cheap and not all that heavy compared with metal, you can carry four or so pods that hold twenty rocket-propelled icecrete warheads. All you need is a simple bursting charge in the middle, timed to go off maybe a hundred meters ahead of the ship. It works for missiles as well as ships. Fire a few rockets, pop their bursting charge with a cheap proximity fuse, that gives our ship time to turn and get the hell out of there. As for Moonbase, the same idea works, just make it space mines. Again, all you need is a simple proximity fuse with a lockout for friendly ships. Use something like an IFF, identification friend or foe transmitter. Shouldn't be too difficult. Best of all, it's cheap as rocks, so we can put thousands of the things in orbit over Moonbase."

"I didn't expect this! But I like it, so go ahead. Pete, see if you can buy more snakes; they're also cheap, and a homing missile is going to get the attention of a fighter pilot. I don't necessarily want to kill them, chasing them away works fine. Having more than one option is better, I think."

"I'll see what I can find, Chuck. Unless there's something else, I need to get going."

"Yeah, you guys have fun. Maybe think about hanging a snake or two on *Lina*. I'll be doing my own flying from now on."

* * *

TWO MEN SAT IN A CAR, watching. The house was imposing, with huge columns that supported a small portico, desirable in Brisbane's occasionally-rainy climate. The driver watched, his passenger thumbed through a deck of photos mounted on card stock.

"Just these four? What's all the excitement about?"

"The ambassador didn't say. He said go watch, so we're watching. If we see any of the blokes, we try to talk to him. We hand him the note and say thank you. What he does is up to him, not us. We go back and let the staff find other jobs. It pays well enough," admitted the speaker, "and it's not like we were working for some of those crazies. I'd rather go back on the fishing boats than work for the Arabs."

"Too right, mate. What about the Sheila?"

"Hand her the note, maybe she'll give it to one of the others. Mostly I think they gave us her picture to let us know if the others are home. They don't mix much."

"Ay, you know it. What are all those trucks on about?"

"Digging behind the house, I shouldn't wonder. Maybe they're putting in a pool or something."

"Not a bad job, driving one of those things. Maybe we can ask one of the drivers."

Rod, the passenger, got his opportunity a short time later.

"Say, mate, what's happening in that big house? Some of the neighbors are wondering."

"Nothing to do with you. They've got kids, the lady wants a place for them to play. There's a wading pool too. Can't do much today, though. Rain predicted, so as soon as it starts we'll shut down. Probably have to wait until things dry out, ay." The truck driver sounded gloomy.

"Thanks for the info, mate. Good luck gettin' on with the job." The two nodded to each other, then Rod returned to the car to inform his partner.

* * *

"IT'S A MESS OUT THERE!" said Lina. "I can't even walk around the grounds! I'm going crazy, cooped up in here!"

"There's no help for it, luv. Can I make you a nice cup of tea?"

"No. I'm going for a short walk, so maybe when I get back. It looks like rain."

"Don't get caught out in it, luv. Those cobbles, not easy to walk on when they're wet. I'll just have a word with your man. You can't be going out alone, Chuck gave orders."

"Bert's not feeling well. He thinks it's allergies, but I think it may be asthma. I'm going to insist he see the doctor. I'll be all right, I'm only going around the block. It's not as if I were going shopping or something!"

"Still, luv, you know what Chuck would say, your da too. You should listen to them. They've got your interests in mind."

"I'll only be half an hour. I'll have that tea when I get back."

Lina shrugged into a light raincoat as she left the house. A soft mist had begun, not yet rain, but likely the rain was on its way. Still, it wasn't stormy, not something to worry about. And she really did want to get out for at least a little while.

Closing the door behind her, Lina looked at the sky. At a guess, she had at least enough time for a short walk, even as swollen as her belly was! She closed the gate, then turned left.

Rod had been half asleep, expecting that his mate would see anything he missed. Spotting movement, he looked idly at the house, expecting to see the trucks pull away, job interrupted by the rain. Indeed, distant motors revved behind the house, indicating that the workers were on their way out.

"That's her, innit? The one in the piccy?"

"Let me look at it...I think you're right. But this one is preggers, nothing in the pic about that. Did anyone mention it?"

"Not a peep. What do we do now?"

"I don't know. You'd think if one of the blokes was home, he'd be walking with her. Wouldn't catch me letting my missus out in the rain, not that far along I mean."

"Well, this may be our best chance. She can always say no."

"I guess it's worth a try. Keep the note covered, wouldn't do to have it soaked through."

"You want to talk to her?"

"You too. The ambassador gave us both the job, mate."

The two men stepped out of the car and closed the door. Rod held the note inside his raincoat as they walked toward Lina.

She had been enjoying the walk, paying almost no attention to her surroundings until she heard the car doors close. Glancing up, she saw two men heading toward her. The one on the right had his hand inside his coat. Suddenly the fears came flooding back. *They're going to kill me!* her mind screamed. But the house was close, all she had to do was go back...and the construction truck was almost at the gate...

Lina turned, too quick. Pregnancy, the lack of balance, slippery cobbles at the entrance...

Her right foot slipped. Awkwardly, Lina tried to catch her balance, then realized she was falling. *My baby!* She had time for only a thought, then her leg was going, she tried to twist to protect her swollen stomach, and banged her head against the cobbles. Horrified, Rod and his driver stopped, frozen.

"What do we do now? They're going to blame us for this!"

Rod turned suddenly decisive. "We call for help, that's what we do. Get on the phone, we need an ambulance. She's not moving. I'll see if I can help, but you call this in, understand?"

"I'll do it. You sure you know what you're doing?"

"I was a digger before I took this job. I know enough not to move her, okay?"

The truck had stopped, blocking the vehicle gate. The driver swung down from the cab and ran toward Lina. The two men got there at the same time, the construction worker swearing as his foot slipped.

"What happened?"

"She fell. Careful, my mate's called for the wagon."

"She lives there, in the big house. You watch her, keep the rain off, like, and I'll see if anyone's home."

Far off, a faint wail announced that an ambulance was on the way. Moments later, people began streaming out from the house.

"Don't touch her, okay? She's breathing, I think she hit her head when she slipped."

Moments later, the siren abruptly stopped as the ambulance arrived.

Two men, carrying emergency cases, ran up to the crowd. "Step back, give us room, there's a mate."

The men muttered quietly to themselves as they rapidly completed their examination. A police car arrived moments later. Rod backed away and signaled the driver. The two men got into the vehicle and pulled away. Two policemen questioned the construction truck driver, who saw the other car backing up, preparing to leave. He reached for a pen and wrote down the license number.

The police officer watched, then asked, "Something I should know about?"

"Maybe. That car was parked and two men got out. They were walking toward the lady when I saw 'em."

"Did they do anything to her?"

"No, not that I saw. Twenty meters away they were, ay. But she turned and fell, like them two scared her. Here's the car number."

"Thanks. Probably doesn't mean anything, but I'll add it to my report. She fell, you say?"

"Just started to rain, it had. Slippery, like, and down she went. Pregnant, you know, shouldn't 'a been out in the rain anyway."

34

"What the hell happened?" Chuck was furious.

"Apparently she fell. She insisted on going for a walk, the grounds were torn up and muddy because of the construction, it hadn't started raining but there was just enough mist to make the walkway slick..."

"Where was Bert while this was going on? Dammit, he's supposed to keep her safe!"

"Bert's sick. Lina thought it was allergies at first, but she left instructions for him to see a doctor. She thinks it might be asthma."

"So who called the ambulance?"

"We've got a name, but it doesn't mean anything. One of the construction workers saw her fall, so he got there right after it happened. Another man had just arrived, apparently a former soldier. He said he was a 'digger' and had had medical training. The two kept the rain off until the ambulance arrived. There was a policeman too, he interviewed the construction worker."

"But not the bystander?"

"It doesn't say in the police report. I asked the officer to let us know if anything else turns up."

"You say she's awake now?"

"She's awake, and mad. Her doctor wants her to stay in bed until the baby is born."

"I suppose that's a good sign. The baby wasn't harmed?"

"No. The witness said it looked like she tried to protect her abdomen. That's why she hit her head. If you're ready, we can go in. Be ready, though; I told you she was mad."

Frenchy smiled at Chuck, and the two walked into the room. Lina's expression showed her fury. Chuck almost smiled; a large area on the side of Lina's head had been shaved and a sticking plaster applied.

"How are you feeling, love?"

"I'm fine. The baby is too, he kicks me every two minutes! Do you know what it's like to be kicked in your kidneys from the inside? I have to pee every time, and the nurses won't let me get up! I'll be an invalid by the time they let me out!"

"Just take it easy for a day or two. You took a knock, so maybe they'll let you use the bathroom after they're sure your balance is okay. What possessed you to go out in the rain?"

"It wasn't raining when I went out," Lina said defensively. "Anyway, I was doing fine until I saw those men. Chuck, I think one of them had a gun!"

"He had a gun? You're sure?"

"Well, I didn't see it, but he had his right hand inside his coat. The other one didn't, his arms were swinging normally. Both were walking toward me, I could tell that much, but I noticed right away that the other man was different. His hand was tucked in, so he walked crab-like. Not much, but I saw it."

Chuck's expression was bitter. "It's happening again. I'm calling the police. I've had enough of this crap!" He reached for the cell phone, but it rang before he could dial.

"Chuck," his reply was followed by a silence lasting almost a minute.

"What about our people?" was followed by another silence.

"You're sure it came from there?"

Frenchy tried to watch Lina and Chuck. Lina had stopped in mid-tirade; something serious had happened. Chuck's face was pale.

"I'll get to the base as soon as I can. Ask Wolfgang to stand by, and see how many pilots are willing to fly a mission. Point out that there's some risk involved. Bonuses will be authorized. If necessary, I'll fly the mission myself. I've got a problem here to sort out first." The room was silent; only the soft crackling of the phone as someone continued the call. Finally, Chuck sighed and ended the connection.

"It's bad, Frenchy. Lina's here, I need you to make sure the twins are okay. I've got to go. It's Moonbase. The North Koreans launched a missile, one of the new ones they announced two months ago. No question about who fired it, but the tracking radars dirtside lost it. They thought it failed, or maybe went into orbit. It looks as if the breakup they thought they'd spotted was a planned separation of the second stage; the first stage had already dropped away. Anyway, they lost it. The third stage fired an hour later, heading for the moon. The trackers lost it again when it passed behind the moon's edge. This time, the North Koreans weren't bluffing. They had a hydrogen warhead, and it blew up over Moonbase. The crew that was working on *Disco* is gone. *Panatela* was inbound from Mars and spotted the flash, so she diverted and took a look at Moonbase, or what's left of it. Apparently, the rocket missed, but it was close enough. The crater is less than a kilometer away, but the surface has been scoured clean. Moonbase is gone, so is Axel and his assembly crew. Twenty six men, just wiped out."

The phone burred again. Chuck frowned and tapped the screen, accepting the call.

"What now?" The faint scratching noises began again. "Where?"

"Okay, tell them not to approach it. Passive scans only. Photos, anything you can get. Abort the survey until we decide what to do. Put a lid on it..." The scratchy noise went on."

"Lovely, just lovely. I guess it doesn't matter, it was going to leak anyway. This is too important. I wonder what the dirtside nations are going to do?" The faint noise continued.

"Tell the crew well done. As for blabbermouth, let him know quietly that I'm not happy. But just that, no punishment, okay?"

Chuck ended that call too, but this time the anger had gone.

"Frenchy, I'll talk to you in a minute. Frisbee found something, just off the edge of the Jupiter Trojan asteroids. I need to call the police. See if you can hire someone to stand watch here, private security. Maybe the police will send someone."

Frenchy nodded as Chuck punched the screen again. Moments later, he had a police representative on the line. "I need to speak to the officer in charge, please."

Apparently, Chuck didn't get the answer he wanted. "I don't give a damn what he wants. You get his ass on the fucking phone *now*, or I'll call the damned minister in charge. If your man is too busy to talk to me, I'll keep going until I find someone who *isn't*. Or I'll put my own armed fucking guards outside my wife's room, you got that?" The voice on the other end sounded alarmed at this; the noises got louder.

"So fucking sue me! Get that asshole on the fucking phone *now*!"

Another voice took the place of the first. "This is Chuck Sneyd. My wife reported that she was approached by a man with a gun! I'll have my own security as soon as I can hire some, but I need a police officer at the hospital as soon as possible. Maybe two of them. Armed."

This time the silence lasted more than a minute while Chuck absorbed what the voice told him.

"No guns? Just a piece of paper? You're sure?" The quiet scratching noise resumed.

"I'll still feel better if a police officer can watch the room until I can get my own people. Okay, no guns. But I'll be having a word with that ambassador!"

Chuck ended the connection.

"The two men were employed by the American Embassy. They had a photo deck with pictures of all three of us, Will too. The men don't have criminal records and they didn't have guns. They had a note on embassy stationery asking one of us to speak with the ambassador. The man you saw, Lina," Chuck looked to where Lina listened to this, openmouthed, "was trying to keep the note from getting wet. Give the American Ambassador a call, Frenchy; I'm going to be busy for a while. Oh, and that other call? *Frisbee's* crew spotted something. It appeared to be blinking, so they decided to take a closer look. They don't know what it is, but it's not natural. It didn't come from Earth, either. It's just a big ball that reflects light. It looked like it was blinking because it's spinning, a complete rotation in about two minutes."

"Strange. It's just a spinning ball? Like a big Christmas ornament?"

"That's the first impression, yes. The other part...I would have had to release the information anyway, but one of the crew was on the radio to *Stogie* at the time. They chatted about it, and the guy on *Stogie* transmitted it back to Mars. It wasn't even encrypted, so as soon as someone on Earth picks up the radio spill, they'll know. I told our guys not to get close."

"Sounds good, Chuck. You've got your hands full."

"Yeah, you take care of Lina and the twins. I'll get back as soon as I can. You talk to the American ambassador, I'm not interested in diplomatic speak at this point." Chuck turned and left the room.

"He didn't even stop to kiss me goodbye," Lina said wonderingly. "Dad, what is he going to do?"

* * *

"WOLFGANG, how many of our pilots signed on for the near-space runs?"

"All but two, Chuck. They're older men with families. The others," he shrugged. "They understand that they'll be drawn in anyway. Countries will need pilots, these guys are the best we could find. They can fly for us or be drafted to fly for someone else. They like flying our birds, and the money doesn't hurt either."

"So be it. It's time to offer them another choice. How soon can you collect everyone who's not already on a run?"

"They're in the lounge, Chuck. I think they understood something was up."

"Let's go, then."

The two men walked down the corridor. The low buzz of conversation stopped as they walked in. Chuck picked up a cup and drew coffee, then turned and faced the pilots. All conversation had stopped.

"Our birds will eventually be armed, but it won't happen overnight. The armament will be defensive, but as for protecting Moonbase, I waited too long. By now you've heard. Axel's crew was working on *Disco* when that North Korean missile hit. They're dead." Chuck paused to let the bald statement soak in.

"It's time for the bullshit to stop. My people are not targets. From this point on, if anyone attacks NFI, we will strike back. No exceptions.

You may be tasked to strike your home country. Think about it carefully before you decide. The best defense is an offense that can't be stopped, one that I'm willing to use. I need four volunteers for a hazardous mission. If none of you volunteer, I'll fly it myself. But it *will* be flown, and if necessary, flown more than once."

Wolfgang interrupted Chuck. "You won't fly a mission unless you fire me first. That's my job. I'll have volunteers, or *I'll* fly the bird. Axel was a friend. I'm going to have to see his wife...did you know he has two little girls?"

"No, I knew he had a family, but I never got to meet them. As for who flies, let's see who volunteers. Any of you can leave now, no questions asked, no recriminations. But this is the last time. From now on, you'll take missions as assigned or submit your resignations. No exceptions." Chuck waited to see who would leave. None of the pilots moved. Finally, one drawled, "We all knew Axel, the guys on his crew too. They worked on our ships before they started building *Disco*. I want some North Korean ass. If you don't need all of us, we'll draw straws."

Chuck turned away long enough to get his feelings under control. Finally, he turned back.

"Thanks. I won't forget. Here's what we're going to do..."

Chuck went back to his office to let Wolfgang decide who would fly the missions. A blinking light announced a video-mail, source *Frisbee*. Chuck tapped the screen, calling up the message.

"Mister Sneyd, I'm Commander Victor Smith. I am the pilot for the Green Shift crew. Blue crew found the object, but my crew collected the data. The screen insert shows what we've been able to find out."

Chuck paused the message and looked at the inset. The object floated against the black of space, most of it hidden. Slowly a glow began, grew stronger, then faded. Above where he'd seen the first image, another glow began. It took him almost a minute before he decided he knew all that a visual image would tell him. Different areas of the object were illuminated at different times. He was able to pick out a triangular depression as the glow began, then another as it faded.

Pressing the screen, Chuck resumed the message. "As ordered, we recorded the image and backed away. The image you're seeing was taken more than a hundred kilometers from the object. We measured it on radar, and found that our radar image was blinking at the same rate as the visible light image. We processed what you're watching through our on-board spectroscope; the radar return does this automatically. It's how we know whether a contact is approaching or receding. We approached the object side-on; we didn't realize it was moving at first. The object's image shows the equator. We did not maneuver above or below it, so we don't know what the axial poles look like.

"We saw no sign of an engine. It may be possible for the object to move under its own power, or it may have been placed here. We don't know. The exterior is smooth and transparent, we got that much from reflected light coming from Jupiter. We also analyzed light from the sun and compared the spectral signatures with what we got from the object. We found no discernible difference. We therefore conclude that the blinking is reflected light, and that the object is not moving in relation to nearby spatial objects.

"The view into the interior is not clear and we were unable to improve on the definition you see in the insert. One of our men thinks the objects are essentially corner reflectors, intended to bounce energy back to a source. Radars use such a device for calibration, and as I mentioned, some of the reflectors are sized to reflect millimeter-wave radiation. Some reflect visible light, and they are color-specific, within limits. Some reflect in the infrared band, others red-yellow, while slightly smaller ones reflect in the green-blue band. We observed some which were even smaller, but we had no means to check. We think they reflect in the ultraviolet and X-ray bands. Some may respond to gamma rays, but again, we had no test equipment so we couldn't be sure.

"The object is unlike anything we know of. We conclude it is extraterrestrial in origin. We believe it to be passive, hence harmless, or at least neutral. Since the reflected radiation matches the radiation of nearby sources, we were unable to determine the object's composition.

"Best guess, and we have two, is that it's a lighthouse in space or a warning beacon, something like what's used to mark channels so ships aren't endangered. Both are similar in intent. If it's meant as a warning, there may be others. I recommend searching the other Trojan group and the asteroid belt itself. If the object is a kind of lighthouse that responds to any electromagnetic frequency, then there should be others to warn travelers of the hazard zone. If it's meant to mark a safe passage for spaceships to use, there may be others, but perhaps in a line. Which means they could be anywhere, or there may be no others. At any rate, we believe further investigation is warranted.

"*Frisbee*, proceeding as ordered. Captain Smith, reporting. Message ends."

Chuck cleared the screen and leaned back, thinking. Wolfgang found him there half an hour later. "We only had two ships available, both converted *Insect* Class. They're big enough and both have undergone recent maintenance, so I don't expect problems there. I picked four volunteers, none of them Asian. No reason to borrow possible trouble. Would you bring up a world map, please?"

Chuck nodded and looked at the screen as the image formed. "The target is almost due north, so the time there is the same as it is here. The two ships will travel to the Terrestrial Trojans, astronomers found the big object, but we had to issue astrogation warnings to our people so they would know to avoid that area. Anyway, they'll select two as close to what the mission calls for as they can find. As soon as both are loaded, they'll rendezvous at the edge of the leading L4 zone and head for Earth in company. Planned reentry point is just north of Okinawa. Descent will take some time and positioning must be exact, so their course allows time to make whatever adjustments are necessary. By the time they pass through the upper atmosphere, rotation will have brought the target into view. Planned separation point is here, north of Chuju-do. We estimate a flight time of twenty-eight minutes forty-three seconds. The upper atmosphere winds are expected to have negligible effect, and weather in the vicinity of the target is clear. The pilots have had their briefing, and they should be taking off just about now. The only thing we're not sure of is how long it will take them to find suitable objects. Too small won't have enough of an effect, too large will create more collateral damage than needed. If they can't find what we need, we'll abort this mission and reschedule, using lunar resources."

"Good plan, Wolfgang. Are you satisfied with it?"

"I am. I would fly the mission, but it's not my place any more than it is yours. As for the pilots...one of them mentioned he'd read about the guy who flew the Enola Gay, Paul Tibbets. He wondered back then how Tibbets felt. He said that he no longer needs to wonder.

35

Frenchy called Chuck. The break was welcome; Chuck fretted. Somehow, waiting for something to happen was worse than taking part. Had it been the same, waiting with his fellow marines for an attack to commence? Frenchy got right to the point.

"The police have given me a copy of the note. They've questioned the two men who were walking toward Lina and they're satisfied with their story. No criminal background, no weapons, they never actually got close enough to touch Lina or even speak directly to her. She reacted, understandable considering her history, but that wasn't the fault of these two. They had no way of knowing. Get this, one of them has an application pending with us! He wants a job with NFI!"

"Can you handle it? If you want to hire him, go ahead. But if there's any doubt, the answer is no."

"I agree. What do you want to do about the note? It's signed by the US Ambassador."

"Scan it and send me a copy. I'll decide what to do after I read it."

Chuck punched in the phone number listed in the note. The call did not go well.

"No, I won't speak to his administrative assistant. Put the ambassador on the phone immediately or I'm disconnecting. Tell him it's Chuck Sneyd calling, and he's got one minute to get on the line. He wants to talk to me, I couldn't care less if I talk to him. Understand?"

The ambassador was on the phone ten seconds later. Chuck's temper had not improved.

"What the hell do you want?"

"Mister Sneyd...this is Mister Sneyd, is it not?"

"It is."

"First, allow me to apologize for the unfortunate accident your wife suffered. I just received an update; she's doing fine, as is her unborn child, but is fretting at being kept in the hospital."

"Apology accepted. Now why are you so anxious to talk to me?"

"I'm just the messenger, Mister Sneyd. Can I call you Chuck?"

"No. If you're the messenger, then this is another call from your president."

"It is, Mister Sneyd. He's tried repeatedly to establish contact, either with you or someone in your company."

"Got a number?"

"Yes, Mister Sneyd." The ambassador waited politely for a moment. "Go ahead. The conversation is being recorded, I'll get the number from the record."

The ambassador dutifully read off the number of the White House switchboard, and as soon as he finished, Chuck ended the call. The ambassador looked at the phone and sighed. All those weekends, raising money for the president's first campaign, and now this? Maybe it was time to go back to being a simple businessman.

Chuck punched in the number sequence and got a recorded message. Angrily he pressed zero, which got a response.

"White House. This call may be recorded in the interests of security. May I help you?"

"This is Chuck Sneyd. You have one minute to get the president on the phone. No assistant, no secretary. One chance only; if he wants to talk to me, this is the only opportunity I'll give him."

"Yes, sir. One moment please."

Chuck drummed his fingers on the desk, waiting. A canned announcement indicated he was on hold, which didn't improve his mood. A few minutes later the announcement stopped.

"Mister Sneyd, you're a hard man to talk to."

"I have nothing to say to you, as far as I know. I hold you responsible for the death of one of my people. Sven Nelsen is presumed lost, killed when *Tesla* sank. He behaved a lot more honorably than your people have."

"Mister Sneyd, I had no direct knowledge of this. If the US Government bears responsibility for this, let me sincerely apologize for it now. I'll look into the matter and when I find out what happened, I'll get back to you. I was told your ship sank accidentally."

"That's not what my sailors said. *Tesla* was being pursued by boats while two of your warships shadowed her. That's not an accident. *Tesla* was in international waters at the time."

"Well, let me look into the matter. I'll see what I can find out. If we're in the wrong, I'll also speak to Congress about reparations."

"Reparations, you son of a bitch? Captain Larsen is dead and you think reparations will get you off the hook?" Chuck was working his way into a full rage. His secretary opened the door when she heard the shouting, then softly closed it, deciding this was a good time to get a soda.

"See here, Mister Sneyd! There's no call for that!"

"*I'll* decide whether my language is called for or not! What the fuck do you want?"

"I want to make peace. Is that reason enough to call you?" The president's voice had risen. Two strong-willed men found themselves in conflict.

"Make peace *how*? I've never done anything to harm you, or for that matter the USA. Now you want to press the reset button and sing folk songs together, all buddies again?"

"Back off. Right now. If you can't do that, then I've wasted my time. A lot of people are likely to get killed if you're not willing to listen. Some of them will be people you're responsible for. Is that clear enough, or shall we end this?"

"I'll listen. No guarantees. As for who might get killed, you should remember something. I know where you live, is that clear enough?"

"Is that a threat, Sneyd?"

"You're goddamned right it is. Are you aware that the North Koreans fired a missile at our base on the moon? They killed some good men, *my* men!"

"I didn't know that. You're sure?"

"I know about my dead employees, and I know who fired the missile. By the way, last I heard, your people weren't admitting that the North Koreans had a hydrogen bomb. They did, at least one. That's what they hit Moonbase with."

"Mister Sneyd, I knew nothing of this. I didn't know they had that kind of weapon, and when they tested their long range missile, it broke apart in the stratosphere."

"It didn't break up. It worked almost perfectly; the warhead blew up less than a mile from Moonbase."

"That's worrisome, Mister Sneyd. Kim is unstable. Our contacts within the Chinese government consider him a loose cannon. They have some influence over him, but that's not the same as control. I'm not sure how much help we can give you."

"I don't need your help." The president filed that bald statement away; he would think about it later. "But since you're on the phone, there's something else. If you really want peace between NFI and the USA, leave word with your comm center. When I call, they forward the call immediately. No stalling, I don't have time for that."

"Agreed. I'll see to it. What else?"

"We have something in common after all. Do you know about the object we found?"

"The one in space? I've had only a sketchy report, more rumor than anything. You don't know anything about it, not really, is what the report said."

"Close. We've got some guesses, no hard knowledge. I'm going to send an expedition to see what we can find out. Are you interested in providing some of the scientific staff? Full sharing of all findings?"

This time, the answer was delayed, only a few seconds but it was noticeable. "I'll agree in principle. We'll need to work out the details. Can I appoint someone to work with you or your chief of mission?"

"Do that. You understand, this puts everything else on the back burner? It didn't come from Earth. I have no idea yet what it means, a great opportunity or a great danger, but you can figure the people who put it there are more technically advanced than we are. It's been there for some time but we're only now able to find it."

"I see what you mean. I won't hide anything from you. Is that acceptable?"

"It is. Get your team together, limit the number to ten. More than that you don't need, fewer might not be enough to make a breakthrough. If one is even possible."

"I'll see to it. Mister Sneyd, can I call you back? I've got an urgent message that's just coming in."

"Take your message. Sure, call my secretary and we can arrange a time. We're both too busy to answer unexpected calls."

"I'll see to it."

The call ended and the president leaned back in his chair. For once, looking at the furnishings didn't help. History, tradition...and maybe none of it meant anything. Sneyd, rude bastard that he was, had hit the nail on the head. There was another civilization out there somewhere, and they were more advanced than anything on Earth.

Pressing the button, he answered the call. Moments later, he sat bolt upright. "Yes, send them in. Is it the full National Security Council?"

The door opened and a small delegation entered. "Mister President, there have been developments. We recommend you increase our readiness status immediately. War is not imminent, but significant events are occurring."

"Keep talking."

"Mister President, Pyongyang has been heavily damaged by what appears to be an air strike. Kim Jong Un has not been heard from, although I must caution that there are no reports of his death at this time. Fighting has broken out along the Demilitarized Zone. Both sides have issued statements blaming the other."

"Predictable. I don't suppose it matters. Let historians sort it out. Anything else?"

"There have been incidents in Russia and China. They appear to be domestic in origin, and may or may not be significant. It's too soon to tell."

"That's all the CIA has to report? Okay, keep me informed. Local, we can deal with the aftermath. Rebellion, revolution, that's more serious. Have someone look into it. What else?"

"Russia and China have issued a joint declaration. They've declared their airspace closed except for their own aircraft. They threaten to shoot down any intruder, and they specifically included NFI's ships in this. Do we have a response at this time, maybe close our own air space?"

"Not closed, but maybe a limited response? We don't want any fighting to spill over into our zone. Exclude the Russians, the Chinese, and their close allies from US airspace. Our allies should be informed that their airplanes will be inspected, but not considered hostile solely by virtue of national origin. Gin up an announcement, cross every I and dot every T."

"Should we also exclude NFI's ships, Mister President?"

"No. NFI's ships are to be considered friendly as of now." There were looks of surprise, even astonishment, around the circle.

"Yes, Mister President."

"So we've got a war breaking out in Korea, and someone bombed Pyongyang. Do we know who?"

"Mister President, we believe the strike was conducted by NFI's ships."

The president felt a chill; the hairs on the back of his neck stirred. Suddenly Sneyd's comment made perfect sense. But a strike that destroyed part of a city...

None of this found its way into his tone. "We'll want to be sure, won't we? Schedule a meeting with the full council tomorrow, say nine o'clock? I'll want position papers, whatever the CIA can find out, recommendations. This is not our war, not so far. Tell me more about this strike; nuclear weapons? You said Pyongyang was heavily damaged?"

"Yes, Mister President. The strike destroyed several of the residences Kim is known to use, but not all of them. There were casualties, we don't yet have an estimate. The area around Kim's palaces is exclusive; the only homes in that area are used by senior officials in his government. A number of them are almost certainly dead."

The president thought for a moment. "General, the North Korean Army is directed from the top down. What will the loss of the command structure do?"

"We can't say at this time, Mister President. Satellite coverage is partially blocked by smoke and dust. We infer the locations where the fireballs hit for the time being, and we should have a precise location after the air clears. We know the fireballs...meteors, most likely...came from space, which suggests NFI is responsible. No missiles, no nuclear weapons. But North Korea has an arsenal of nukes, and if the South Koreans begin rolling their army up, they may use them."

"Do we respond, General? Your recommendation?"

"It's a political decision, Mister President. We may want to send a message, don't use nukes. But if we do, China may decide to come in. China and Russia have huge stockpiles, and they share a border. If one goes nuke, the other may also jump in. If the nuclear cat gets out of the bag, India, Pakistan, maybe Israel will feel encouraged to use theirs. Mister President, no offense intended, but this is why they pay you the big bucks. The decision is above my pay grade."

The president looked at each member of the National Security Council in turn. The decision pressed in on him. What to do, what *not* to do?

He realized suddenly that many of his predecessors had faced similar crises, where a single wrong step could lead to America's destruction. Nuclear winter...he suddenly smiled. Maybe *that* would reverse global warming!

But what of the extraterrestrials? What if they arrived and found humanity convulsed, war threatening to destroy all of humanity? What would they do?

What would they do?

The series continues in Book Three, NEO: Near Earth Objects.

WHEN YOU'RE ready to continue, read on; I've included an excerpt of NEO: Near Earth Objects.

NEO PART ONE: EARTH

NEO, CHAPTER ONE

Chuck kissed Lina goodbye, hugged the twins, and nuzzled the baby's tummy. The happy gurgle and toothless smile grabbed at his heart. Another day, he might have been tempted to take a day off, even a weekend, but not now.

Lina collected the children and boarded Chuck's personal ship for the trip to their home in Brisbane. Chuck watched the takeoff, then left the villa. The rising sun cast long shadows across the Australian Outback as he walked the short distance to his office.

Adelheid, his starchy Finnish executive secretary, was already waiting when Chuck walked in and poured coffee, his third cup of the day.

"Morning, Adelheid. Who's first on my agenda today?"

"I am, Chuck. Would you like something with that coffee before we begin?"

"No, I had breakfast at the villa. Lina and I have too little time together as it is. You need a meeting? Is something wrong?"

"Yes. You're working too hard and you're not getting enough exercise. You need to delegate more, and I've got a few suggestions."

"Suggestions?" Chuck stalled and sipped at the coffee. "What kind of suggestions?"

Adelheid began obliquely. "Does the prime minister meet with everyone who wants a bit of his time?"

"No," said Chuck slowly. "But he's heading up a country. Same with any other head of state."

"Just so. He doesn't have time, and you don't either. You need someone else, two someones actually. And we want you to take more breaks and exercise more."

"We? Who's we? Lina put you up to this, didn't she?"

"We talked." Adelheid's tone was noncommittal. "She's really more concerned about you getting more exercise, but it's also obvious that you need more help."

"I'll schedule exercise times. I've actually been thinking about doing just that. Make a note; I want an instructor."

"Certainly. What kind of instructor?"

"I was thinking about those swords, the Japanese ones. They make a fetish out of being able to use them, so I wondered how hard it would be to learn how it's done. Maybe I'll need two instructors, one in kinjutsu and the other in kendo."

Adelheid made notes. "I'll see what I can find. I'm not sure the two subjects are taught in Australia, but if they are I'll see what can be done."

"I'll also need equipment. Have someone find out what I'll need and order it, billed to my personal account. Get me another pair of swords too, good quality. The others are masterpieces and I don't want to damage them by using them to practice with."

"I'll see to it."

"Thank you. Now what was it about more assistants? I've got you to keep me on the straight and narrow and Wolfgang to run flight ops. Will's working with the Australian government--by the way, ask him to stop in when he has time--and I've got people heading up other offices."

"You need a real chief of staff, someone I can report to. I'm managing the office staff, but you need a full-time assistant who has no other responsibilities. You also need an assistant to handle negotiations with foreign officials, and if you're going to continue being involved in military matters you need someone to take charge of that too."

"You're talking about a cabinet, the kind the US president has."

"I am. You also need someone to head up the company education system. You won't need as many people, because the Australian government and the states and territories deal with most of the matters that concern the US cabinet."

"Maybe I do," said Chuck. "I hadn't thought in those terms, but that's part of what I want to talk to Will about."

"So we're agreed? I can begin my search for suitable assistants?"

"Sure. There's something else. Buy a large safe for the villa, one for the Brisbane house too. Bill them to my personal account."

"Very well. How large is large? Did you have something specific in mind?"

"I do. Lina doesn't want me to leave my swords out where the kids can cut themselves, but I don't want to give them up. I earned those things." Chuck rubbed his nearly-bald head, the result of a radiation overdose while he and Frodo loaded waste canisters of contaminated dirt. Some of the hair had begun to regrow, but it appeared patchy so he shaved it off. Maybe, at some point...but that was for later, and it might never happen.

The contamination had been caused by a Chinese air strike that broke open fuel rods waiting to be loaded on NFI's *Giant.* Japanese men, all elderly, had chosen to clean up the spilled fuel rod contents and put the dirt in plastic containers. Chuck and Frodo, inspired by the old men, had flown the containers to space and launched them toward the sun. None of the volunteers who cleaned up the spill had survived, and Chuck and Frodo had been exposed to enough radiation to make them very sick.

"I understand. I'll see to ordering the safes. She's right, you know."

"I know that, but part of me wants the swords around for protection. I've got enemies, and I don't even own a pistol now. As for the arms owned by the company, you know how tight the regulations are, and the Australian states are loath to grant us an exemption. Although that may change, now that I'm giving them spaceships. We're also providing space on our satellite fields for Australian military planes. I'll tell Will to work on that too when I see him."

"Yes, Chuck. Will there be anything else?"

"I don't think so, not right now. I need a couple of hours to finalize notes, then I'll begin meeting with people. Who's first?"

"The Japanese ambassador would like to see you at your convenience."

"Move him to the top of the list. Who else?"

"The US ambassador requests a meeting, and the South Korean ambassador as well. See why you need someone to handle foreign relations?"

"Things were easier when I was a customer meeting with sales reps," Chuck grumbled. "You meet with the US ambassador. If I want anything from them, I'll call their damned president. Give me half an hour between meetings and schedule the Korean after the Japanese. What's the status on the Korean Demilitarized Zone?"

"Latest reports say that the buildup continues on both side of the line, but for the moment all they're doing is yelling at each other and occasionally firing an artillery shell."

"Better than open warfare. Although it may yet come to that, depending on who assumes power in the north. Still no sign of Kim's body?"

"No, Chuck. We have very little information, but it appears their army is still cleaning up after the meteor strike."

"If he's alive, he'll turn up, and this time I'll make sure. I want the message to be clear; if you attack NFI, kill our people, then expect us to go after the one who ordered the attack. If we miss him once, we'll keep trying until he's dead."

"I'll keep that in mind," said Adelheid. "If there's nothing else..."

"Not at this time, thank you." Adelheid nodded and left. Chuck topped off his coffee and woke his computer. He needed to make notes, as he'd told Adelheid, and after that a number of overnight reports were waiting for his attention.

* * *

Wolfgang Albrecht finally overcame Adelheid's resistance, half an hour before Chuck planned to quit for the day. She showed him in after admonishing him not to keep Chuck past his planned quitting time.

"I thought you might have a few minutes for me," said Wolfgang.

"For you, certainly. What's up?" asked Chuck.

"If you've got half an hour, I've got a briefing for you."

"About space?"

"That, and the progress we're making converting the *Giant*-class ships. Do we have delivery dates for the first ten fighter ships?"

"Not yet. I hoped the Asians would play nice together, but they're not willing to forget past issues and that's slowing things up. The Japanese don't really want to apologize to the South Koreans, the Koreans don't trust the Japanese, the Indonesians and the Australians are wrangling over who should block the flood of would-be Asian immigrants. As for the Israelis, they're part of the bloc, although not yet ready to fully ally themselves with the Asians. The rest of the group is willing to deal with them, but they understand that if they get too cozy they're inviting terrorism from the whack jobs in the Middle East. Including the Saudis, who are pissed off at us and the world in general these days." Chuck's voice was weary; he'd been dealing with the disputes for weeks.

"So is one of the countries refusing to work with the others? The fighters...Chuck, we need those. If one country won't help, it's time to find another source."

"That's not it. They'll work with *us* even though we're not Asian, but they don't want to work together. As for the Israelis, the Japanese and the Koreans have bought Iron Dome systems for several of their bigger cities but they consider that 'just business'. It's frustrating." Chuck walked to the window and stared outside. "We need them working together, but they can't see beyond their own prejudices. Anyway, what else did you want to talk about?"

"I thought you might want a progress report on what's happening on Mars."

"Yeah, sure. I'm going to have a cup of coffee. Want one?"

"I guess so. Anyway, I've got updates. The Mars Chinese have a problem, but we can deal with it."

"I thought they were doing well. They started farming, didn't they?" Chuck poured the coffee and handed Wolfgang a cup.

"That's part of the problem. They had a dome on the surface and tried planting stuff underneath it. It's no longer transparent now, it's more translucent. They get *some* sunlight, just not as much as they'd hoped. The sun is weaker on Mars. The surface farm is producing, but they're not getting enough photosynthesis to renew their atmosphere. They're putting in underground hydroponic farms, but they're not operational yet. The plan is to swap labor for oxygen until the farms take over."

"You need to explain that. I'm tired."

"Too tired to think? Chuck, you really need to back off."

"I will, I will. I've already got Lina and Adelheid on my case, I don't need you too. I'm going to start exercising as soon as she finds an instructor."

"That's a cop-out. You could just go for a walk, maybe a jog."

"Jogging is out. The knee is better, but it's still stiff, always will be. Scar tissue buildup. I suppose I could walk."

"Suppose I show up at lunch and we start going for walks? How about I have one of the crews scrape out a dirt track around the perimeter? We could walk on that, and the dirt would be soft enough to be easy on your knee."

"Let's do it. But about the Chinese, what happened to their dome?"

"It got sandblasted. They're south of the equator, so it's Martian summer down there right now. The south polar cap is sublimating. The carbon dioxide freezes in the winter, the dry ice then sublimes as soon as the temperature rises. It's not warm, but it's warm enough, and all that carbon dioxide creates a kind of polar high. The winds start blowing and they can reach 400 kilometers an hour. They pick up dust along the way, and the dust has pocked the armored glass panels in their dome."

"I think I understand. Less efficient photosynthesis, the plants grow slower, and they can't convert enough of the carbon dioxide. So the

Chinese have to buy oxygen instead of harvesting it from under the dome."

"That's it. They intended to set up fans between the underground farm and the habitat clusters, which will help as soon as the plants grow big enough. I think they'll probably wind up doing what we're doing, put *everything* underground. Grow lights are more efficient than sunlight anyway, at least they are when you're that far out."

"Yeah. They work just fine for marijuana cultivation, and I've never heard any of the growers complain that they're not efficient! What else?"

"The tunneling operation is doing well. Mars will soon have a highway, only one way for at least another year, but they can already send vehicles from our settlement to the Chinese village. They can also come to us if they need to; there are pullovers every five kilometers. Six months from now they'll have two tunnels, but it will take time to build the second road."

"How deep are the tunnels?"

"We settled on 100 meters. It's going okay. The tunneling machines don't break down as much, now that we've got the bugs out."

"Same kind of diesel engine we used on the moon?"

"Right. The oxygen feed to the engine was the problem, we weren't filtering it enough. The injectors got plugged, and in some cases the tiny grit was enough to erode them. They had to be replaced."

"Expensive," commented Chuck.

"That wasn't the big problem. The machine just stopped, right in the middle of the tunnel. The boring head was right up against the forward wall. The crews had to dig out the rock on the sides just so they would have room to work on the engine. The escape ramps helped, the ones that go from the road-tunnel to the surface. Getting through the airlocks also took time, and that's the real problem, time.

The boring machines were down for a standard day, sometimes more. We couldn't even use more workers, there was no room for them to work."

"What about running the tunnels in parallel, one machine working only a few centimeters from the other? People could cross from one to the other in case of a breakdown."

"Can't. We could order enough machines and hire more crew, but then the block-setting machines wouldn't work."

"You're talking about the tunnel-lining machine."

"That's the one. It sets the blocks in position, squirts cement in the joints to make them airtight, then the shaker collapses the dirt on top of the arched top. We don't pressurize it right away, of course. We have to install the airlocks first. Otherwise, we stand a chance of losing too much air if the lining *does* spring a leak. It shouldn't be a problem, though. There's a hundred meters of Martian dirt and rock overhead, that's enough to keep the pressure in the tunnels. Even considering how many square centimeters of lining the tunnels have."

"Lots of kilograms of air pressure per square centimeter, and huge numbers of square centimeters. And don't forget that in Martian gravity, the stone blocks and the overburden doesn't weigh as much as it would on Earth."

"We've accounted for that, Chuck."

"I know--I knew it all along. I'm just tired." Chuck rubbed his face, then refilled his cup. "Better wind this down, the coffee will only keep me going so long. I need time off. It all starts again tomorrow."

"John's people have also started moving one of the asteroids, a small one. It's mostly nickel-iron, but there are some low-density metals too."

"Not like the ones we recover on Earth?"

"Not quite. Most of the lighter elements burn off in the atmosphere, so only the dense stuff makes it to the surface. But everything else is going well, the Saucer-class ships are a major help. Morty had that figured too."

"Grandpa was brilliant, no question. I miss him. Anyway, *Disco II* is working out?"

"No problems at all. The North Koreans did us a favor, in a sense. They blew up *Disco*, and for all we know we'd *still* be trying to get that collection of problems sorted out."

"Yeah. If only they hadn't blown away our crew, maybe I could see it that way."

"I know. I didn't mean it like that, Chuck."

"If that's all, I need to head for home. The building maintenance crew is waiting to clean the office."

"That's it. We can talk more tomorrow."

"Tomorrow? Oh, right. We're walking at noon."

"You've got it. See you tomorrow, boss."

NEO, CHAPTER TWO

The day dawned hot and humid, usual in the tropical South China Sea.

The first destroyer of a three-ship screen, the advance element of a squadron, plowed through low waves, heading north. The new CVN *John F. Kennedy*, screened by cruisers to port and starboard, followed the destroyers. Unseen, a pair of attack submarines trailed the surface group. They were skippered by nervous captains; no submariner likes operating in shallow water, and shoals occasionally shift position in response to storms and currents. Behind the ships was the new US base in Cam Ranh Bay, and Spratly Island lay 15 nautical miles to starboard.

"Think they'll be back, Skipper?" The speaker was the executive officer of the destroyer *Edward Byers Jr.*, DDG 1004.

"You a betting man?" asked Farragut Childs. "I'll give odds they'll buzz the *Johnny* between, say, 8:00 and 10:00 a.m."

"Not on sure things, I'm not," replied his exec, Ennis Schwartz. "Our radar feed is being passed back to the *Kennedy*. They acknowledged receiving the stream."

"Good enough. The *Johnny* has her combat air patrols up by now. According to the last briefing, they intended to launch the Hornets as soon as they cleared the bay."

"Just a question, Skip. What happens if the Chinese buzz the carrier again?"

"Admirals and carrier captains don't discuss their plans with lowly destroyer skippers, X.O. They give orders, and ours are to patrol ahead, keep our eyes open and our mouths shut." The two chuckled.

Behind them, officers on the *John F Kennedy* were also discussing the situation.

"What have you got for me, CAG?"

"The CAP is on station and I've got two standby birds ready. No change in orders?"

"None. Proceed as directed."

"Aye, aye, sir. I'll be in Pri-fly." The commander-air group headed for his duty station. The flight crews already had their orders; no further action was necessary unless someone in the chain of command amended what had been briefed.

A pair of F/A 18 fighters cruised high above the squadron. The flight lead was known by his call sign, Cowboy; he kept a picture of his barrel-racer girlfriend in his tiny stateroom, and his squadron mates had tagged him with the nickname. His wingman was known as Menace, not for his fighting prowess but because he'd experienced an unfortunate hard landing during an early flight. Parts of a wheel assembly broke free and scattered across the flight deck.

In the lead jet, the pilot and backseater were tense, waiting; neither had spoken in the past ten minutes.

"Talk to me, wizzo."

"Four launched from Hainan. They were at radar max range, and I had them for a second, then lost two when they went down on the deck. The other two are still heading for the ship. It's possible the ones I'm not seeing are hidden behind that pair. I'm guessing they know we're up here."

"Don't seem to give a shit, do they?"

"Nope. I guess they think we're afraid to push the button."

"What about that guy upstairs?"

"I make it one of NFI's bigger ships, probably *Giant* class. He's just hanging out up there, a big-assed light in the sky. I hear the light has to do with that secret drive system they use. He's just about over the *Johnny*."

"I wish I knew what he thought he was doing," fretted the pilot. "I'm more concerned about those Chinese J-10s. I hope you're right, that the other two are down there too. I guess we're about to find out. Hang on to your hat." The pilot pushed the stick gently forward, watching the Mach number climb on his HUD.

"Copy. You should have good position when you pull out. Distance from *Johnny*, two zero klicks." The WSO peered at his scope. "Menace is conforming, he'll be on your port when you pull out. Still no target separation...I've still got two images on the scope. That NFI ship is still hanging up there, no change in position."

"With luck, he won't pee in our soup bowl." The pilot grunted as he leveled the plane and the gees built up. Ahead in the distance, the *John F Kennedy* serenely sailed on. "Any sign of those other two?"

"Not a peep. Range to bogeys, designating them bandits at this time, seven klicks. I'm watching our six, nothing back there."

"Range, bandits to *Johnny*?"

"Five klicks."

"Time to see how serious they are." Moments later, one of the Chinese fighters appeared to jump left on the radar screen as it took evasive action, breaking off the course that would have led it over the carrier.

"I don't think he liked it when I lit off the tracking radar! Aw...I'll bet it was a lot more fun when they thought this was just a fun flight."

The weapons systems officer's voice was tense. "Watch yourself. I'm picking up a track from that Chinese island. I've got two bogies, inbound. Maybe they were sitting on that airfield, waiting."

"Maybe. Okay, let's go back upstairs. I've still got a few reserve knots to play with, so I should have legs on that bird. More J-10s, you think?"

"Probably the two I lost earlier," agreed the WSO. "Shit...I'm picking up a transmission from the ship. That second bird didn't change course, he clipped the island and crashed. *Johnny* got the rescue helo off, but no reports yet. Watch your fuel state. Johnny is advising that we may have to recover at Cam Ranh Bay. Pri-fly is out, the automatic carrier landing system is down, and they're checking the flight deck for damage. If we do manage to recover on the ship, it will be manually with the landing signals officer."

"Well, we've got fuel for the moment. The extra fuel tanks always give me a warm fuzzy feeling. No chance of launching a tanker, I suppose."

"Not until the deck is cleared."

"Casualty reports?" asked the pilot.

"Not so far."

"What about the other J-10, the one that got nervous when I lit him up?"

"He joined up with the other two and they're headed back for that island. Want to take a look? Maybe buzz their base? I'm really pissed at them."

"No. We'll be professional and hope that the investigation board won't decide I waited too late to light those two bandits up."

"You think they might blame that crash on us?"

"They'll be looking for someone to blame. You and me, or the admiral. What do you think?"

"I think I'm glad that Delta is hiring."

"Drive a flying truck? I never expected you to say that."

"It's flying. And I would get a lot more stick time than I'm getting now. Waste of time getting my wings if I can't fly. Wait one...okay, the deck is clear. You want to go home or divert to land?"

"Might as well see whether we're grounded. I'm heading for *Johnny*."

Chuck was studying the latest delivery estimate for the first of the fighters he'd ordered. There was finally movement among the various nations who were producing the component parts. The first airframes had been delivered to Japan and most of the remaining parts were on the way. The Japanese consortium projected that installing the avionics package would take at least a month, while adding in necessary pilot support and control equipment such as ejection-equipped seats, fly-by-wire controls, oxygen systems, and displays would take an additional month. Testing might take as much as two months; the modules that made up the avionics, easy to install and maintain by design, might reveal problems when they began working together in a real airframe. There might be no way to speed up the process, but on the other hand there might; money can solve a lot of problems. Chuck began making notes.

Adelheid's interruption couldn't have come at a worse time. He sighed and accepted the call. "Is this important?"

"The Japanese ambassador is here with the Korean ambassador. They insist it's urgent."

"Give me a minute to put the reports away. I need to talk to them anyway, so maybe it's for the best."

Chuck put the documents back into folders and locked them in the office safe. He had barely finished when Adelheid showed the two men in. Chuck offered them a choice of beverages; the Asians chose scotch, while Chuck contented himself with coffee. After greetings were exchanged, he steered the conversation to business.

"I need to talk to you, but before we get to that I'm curious about what's bothering you."

"If I may?" Ambassador Mori glanced at Ambassador Kim for permission, then continued. "We are concerned about events in the South China Sea."

"I've been rather busy. Perhaps it would be best if you brought me up to date," said Chuck.

"Of course. As you know, American ships and aircraft patrol in the vicinity of the Chinese base in the Spratly Islands." He waited for Chuck's nod. "Chinese ships routinely follow the ships and Chinese aircraft fly very close to the Americans."

"I've heard about that. Risky business," acknowledged Chuck.

"There was an accident three days ago. A pair of Chinese fighters were headed toward the new supercarrier, the *John F. Kennedy*. No one knows exactly what happened, but a pilot misjudged the distance and crashed into the superstructure. I'm told you call it 'the island'?"

"I've heard that term. Go on," said Chuck.

"There were deaths. The Chinese fighter plane was their new two-place variant and both crewmen were killed. Twenty-three Americans were killed outright and more were wounded, some critically so. The Americans blame China, the Chinese say it was the fault of the Americans for being in waters China claims."

"No surprise there. There might have been fault on both sides. Go ahead."

"So we surmise, Chuck," said Ambassador Kim. "But there have been developments."

"What developments? I can't believe I missed all this!" Chuck's gaze switched between the two men.

Ambassador Mori replaced his glass after taking a health slug of the scotch. "We are aware of developments that have not yet been made public. Such incidents might be worked out over time, and in most cases, they are. But China has recalled her ambassador to the United States, and the US has retaliated by recalling their ambassador. This signifies a break in diplomatic relations. A Chinese diplomatic note was delivered to the United Nations suggesting that the incident might lead to the gravest consequences. Among diplomatic circles, this is often a preliminary to a declaration of war."

"Are you sure? War makes no sense. The US, last I heard, is the largest market for Chinese goods."

"It still is, or was," said Ambassador Kim. "But politics being what they are, market forces have undergone a shift and Americans now buy more domestically-produced products. Trade agreements, not all, but some, have been suspended. International trade in general has suffered, not only China's balance of trade but that of Japan and my own country. We believe that China intended to replace the losses in the American market by moving into Africa. They've been quite successful there, but it hasn't been enough to offset what they've lost in western sales. This latest suspension will only make matters worse."

"I knew about most of that, but the report I saw said that they were buying more commodities, metals, petroleum, things like that. The net exchange value is supposed to be causing more drain on the Chinese economy."

"Exports are approaching parity with imports at this point. We believe that China hoped that moving into the South China Sea would regain the trade surplus she needs to prevent shrinkage of her economy. She now faces a recession unless something is done. It is believed that there may be major petroleum reserves near the disputed islands. Fishing is important too; whichever nation controls the seas also controls the fishing rights. If China can force her claim, she will need to import less in foodstuffs and also less petroleum. As a result, the economic advantage to be realized by control of the South China Sea is fourfold.

"China's economy is also important to controlling her population. As exports dwindled, jobs were lost, factories closed, and domestic unrest became more common. The government cracked down, of course, but the pressure is still there beneath the surface. China must reduce the unhappiness of her people, and we believe this means she must now act aggressively. A diplomatic note and the recall of her ambassador may not quiet the unrest."

"Whew. A war between the two superpowers...haven't we seen enough bloodshed? How many millions died in World War Two? And the Korean War, the Vietnamese war, the wars in the Middle East..."

"There have been others," Ambassador Kim's tone was gentle. "My country's war has never ended. Artillery shells fall on our northern border almost every day. My government has been patient, understanding the chaos north of the Demilitarized Zone. But our patience is not unlimited."

"I understand your concerns. But that doesn't explain why you've come to me."

"I would like your word that this conversation goes no further." Ambassador Mori's tone matched the grim look on his face. Chuck had never seen such deep lines around the ambassador's mouth.

"You have it. I may have to share aspects of it with trusted members of my company, but I won't release it to any media outlet and I won't pass the word to any government without your express permission. Will that do?"

The two ambassadors looked at each other. Chuck saw no sign of a signal, but they looked back at him and nodded. Ambassador Kim resumed. "We have been approached by representatives of other nations. We have begun taking steps to form an alliance. Much remains to be worked out, of course, but I believe we must continue."

"You're talking about a military alliance."

"That, and possibly more. Past history has been...unfortunate. Our disagreements have weakened all of us. We cannot compete with China or Russia while we remain divided. For the sake of all, we must change."

"It won't be easy. You're going to have to apologize for some of the things that happened, probably do even more than that. Japan's behavior toward other nations during the war was unconscionable."

Ambassador Mori bowed his head. "Yes. To abase oneself in shame is not easy for my people. We would rather die; such is the traditional way to expiate shame. It is much to be preferred as an individual solution, but this time it will not cleanse the damaged reputation of our families, or our nation. Too much has happened, too much time has passed. But the danger is such that we must accept even this most bitter pill."

"I understand. You should recall that I grew up American, although I am Australian now as well as American. My family is here. For that matter, I hoped to become a citizen in space, perhaps a citizen of Mars as soon as we have a government. But that may not be possible.

You'll understand that I may be unable to go into space again. I've had too much radiation exposure as it is."

Both ambassadors bowed deeply and held the pose for long seconds.

"We do. We honor you for your sacrifice on behalf of my country, and also for what you've done to support our economy. That goes for both of us. China's economy suffers, but thanks to our relationship with NFI our balance of trade remains healthy."

"It's mutually beneficial. I'm glad to know you're working to end old disputes. By the way, I was looking at projected fighter deliveries. Is there any way for you to speed those up? If war is about to break out, having fighters on hand is critical."

"Whatever can be done will be done. We have another offer for you personally. Your secretary has made it known that you wish to train in traditional Japanese martial arts?"

"Yes, although I had no idea it would come to your attention. Now that I have swords, it seems appropriate to know how to use them."

"We have spoken to a sensei who lives in Canberra. He referred us to another who teaches in Sydney. He has agreed to accept you as his student."

"Canberra? You have a real network, don't you?"

"Japanese expatriates maintain a certain sense of community. It is not easy to abandon all ties of family and culture. Such ties are especially strong among those who practice a particular discipline."

"Well, I hate to disappoint you, but there's no way I could break away to train in Sydney."

"It will not be necessary. He will conduct the preliminary classes here, if that is acceptable. When your training has progressed to a suitable point, a master will come to you from Japan."

"Really? That's wonderful! But I may not be able to progress fast enough to suit the sensei. I have a stiff knee, and exercise doesn't seem to help."

"It will be dealt with. It is not a problem. There is one final request, however."

"Well, you've definitely got me in a good mood! So why don't you go ahead and ask me?"

"We came to you because you are the head of NFI. We believe your company should be part of our alliance, the Asian Confederation."

NEO, CHAPTER THREE

Sleeping on the offer hadn't helped. Chuck still had not decided whether joining the Asian Confederation was something NFI should do. Was he getting in over his head? The other members of the fledgling alliance were full nations with long histories, established political systems, and citizens who supported their leaders. NFI, for all that it had accomplished, was still only a privately-held corporation.

He arrived at the office early. The formidable Adelheid hadn't managed to beat him in, for once. Chuck set up the coffeepot and called up a browser while he waited for the coffee to brew.

Hmmm...it appeared that a family of private bankers, the Rothschilds, had once held a similar dominant position. Bankers and business people for the most part, they had become advisors and financiers to kings and had exerted enormous political as well as economic influence. Had they ever been equal partners in a multinational alliance? The evidence, like most having to do with the secretive family, was equivocal. Perhaps they had not; they'd found it more profitable on occasion to back both sides in the many wars fought between nations, particularly in Europe. He poured coffee into his favorite Iittala mug, gift from a friend in Rovaniemi, as Adelheid knocked on his office door.

"Good morning, Chuck. I've scheduled a meeting with a candidate for your foreign relations advisor. He'll be here in an hour."

"Excellent. I've got his first task waiting, assuming I like the way the interview turns out. I'll call up his resumé and familiarize myself before I see him. What's next after that?"

"You're scheduled to walk for an hour with Wolfgang at noon. I've talked to your new sensei; he'll start next Monday. I've scheduled the *Lina* to transport him here and return him to Sydney. That will be standard procedure while he works with you. By providing fast transportation, he'll be able to come here each Monday, Wednesday, and Friday."

"If I need *Lina*, you can use one of the other ships. Something will be available."

"Yes, Chuck. The safes you ordered will be delivered and installed later this week. Lina and I discussed placement, so that's solved. She'll show you where she decided to put them when she returns. Your new swords and the other equipment will be delivered on Friday. I ordered them from Japan and delivery is being expedited."

"Good. What else?"

"I consulted with your physician, and based on his recommendation I've ordered a knee brace. He mentioned that it may become necessary at some point to operate on the knee. There have been new developments since you were wounded, and he feels that a surgeon can probably go in using a tiny incision and remove most of the scarring. Recovery time will be short."

"It wasn't short before! I hope it doesn't hurt as much as that earlier surgery did!"

"They've come a long way since then, Chuck. And of course, you'll have the best surgeon available. I'm told that makes a difference."

"I hope so," grumped Chuck. "I'll look at that resumé. Give me a heads-up when he arrives."

"Yes, Chuck." Adelheid's voice left no doubt that the instruction was unnecessary. She left the office and Chuck clicked on the file. Hmmm...the photo wasn't great, but the man's record was. University, degrees, JD and PhD in international relations...

As for his record of previous employment...

Chuck looked out the window and thought about it. On paper, the man appeared ideal. But what about his loyalty? Would he be able to transfer that to NFI? The chime interrupted his musing.

"Chuck, he's here. When should I show him in?"

"Now. No interruptions, please."

"Yes, Chuck."

The man was shorter than his photo revealed. No matter; Chuck was interested in his mind and whether he had the necessary judgment to do the job. A parallel consideration was whether the two of them could work together. Chuck walked over and shook Mark's hand.

"Adelheid will have told you what I'm looking for. What do you think of the job?"

"It's not what I've been doing, but I think I can help you."

"I hope so. I have two questions before we continue. Why did you resign?"

Mark met Chuck's eyes. There was no hint of evasiveness. "I made a mistake, a serious one. I was the president's closest advisor and confidant. I let him down, so I felt I had no choice but to resign. I still believe that was the correct choice."

"I thought it might be something like that, although I wondered whether the president might have asked for your resignation. How do you get along with him these days?"

"We're not exactly friends, but then we never were. It was more of a business relationship, but with a kind of warmth between us. It's difficult to explain."

"And the president also feels that way?"

"I believe he does."

Chuck nodded. "That was question one. The other is more serious, but since you gave the president honest service I'll expect an honest answer from you. If I accept you as my foreign policy adviser, where will your loyalty lie?"

"You're really asking if I might be unable to provide dispassionate advice where the president or the US is concerned. I wouldn't want to reveal any confidences from my previous job, but I see no reason why I can't give you loyalty. I hope you understand, I won't betray my nation, and if you're hiring me as a way of scoring points with the president then I don't want the job. With those caveats, I believe I won't have a conflict of interest working for NFI."

"Are you willing to tell me if that changes?"

"Yes." Mark's answer was unequivocal.

"You're hired. Adelheid will take care of the paperwork, you'll make more than you made before, although based on your resumé that probably isn't a consideration."

"No. Money isn't a problem."

"Good. Your first job is to advise me regarding an offer. Right off the top, what do you know of the relationships between the smaller South Asian nations?"

"Quite a bit. I did my dissertation on the history of relationships in what was once Indo-China. I've kept up with events since that time."

"Excellent. Are you aware that there's a movement underway to form closer ties?"

"I hadn't heard that," Mark said. "But I'm not surprised, considering what's going on with China."

"So what do you think of it? Take a seat, grab a coffee if you want--I run on that stuff!"

"I'm worried. China pulling her ambassador is serious. It was one thing to harass American ships, but that went wrong in a way I doubt anyone saw coming. What she'll do now depends on domestic considerations. The Chinese people are restive, and it's worth remembering that previous governments changed through revolution. The Central Committee certainly won't have forgotten! They may choose the cautious course, but there's also the chance that a hothead will take the initiative. If that happens, there will be war. It will almost certainly go nuclear, given the disparity in numbers between the Chinese military forces and what the US has available. That budget sequester really hurt American preparedness. The US military has only begun to recover and the Navy finally has new ships, but they're untried. Some of the senior officers are experienced, but the crews have never heard a shot fired in anger."

"Will the smaller nations stand with the US?"

"They might. Is Vietnam one of them?" Chuck nodded.

"The Vietnamese are currently working with the US. They're buying American weapons and trading basing rights to pay for them. Their economy is improving, but they don't have the capital to build or support a modern force. They need the Americans and the Americans need them, as a counter to China's expansion south. It's worth remembering that the Vietnamese fought a long, hard war not so long ago. I think they'll do it again rather than be dominated by China."

"So you believe that if China and the US go to war, Vietnam will intervene on the side of the US?"

"A lot will depend on what China does. If China pushes the attempt to control the South China Sea, I think Vietnam will respond. Whether that means there will be an alliance between them and the US, I'm not prepared to say."

"What about the other nations who have claims to those islands?"

"I think they might follow Vietnam's lead. Indonesia probably will, and as for the Philippines and others, it depends on their perception of the threat to their own interests."

"Now the big question: should NFI join with the US, the Vietnamese, or both?"

"Depends. Have you been invited to join, or do you expect to be invited?"

"Yes." Chuck did not elaborate.

"Then you have two choices, possibly three. Join, wait and join later after you see whether Australia also joins this alliance, or say no. If the answer is no, you may be endangering your business relationship with those nations. They stand to gain, so I doubt they'll force a break; you've demonstrated that you have military capability by striking North Korea, and they need that. You're now based in Australia, so that also has to be considered. You can't really afford to be part of an alliance that your host country refuses to join.

"The question is whether you gain from this, and how much. I don't know enough about your business arrangements yet to advise you."

"You've done quite well. I'll bring this up to the Australians and see what they intend doing. I can act a lot faster than a government can.

Somehow, I can't see them joining Japan and... ah, the other possible partners"

"They may not," agreed Mark. "But Indonesia might, and if Australia's neighbors join, she may be forced to by circumstances. If she refuses, China might decide Australia is the perfect base to press her claims to that part of the Pacific."

"That won't happen." Chuck's tone left no room for interpretation.

"I'll need work space and staff if I'm to do the job effectively."

"See Adelheid. One last thing; I'm looking for a military advisor who can also act as minister for military affairs. Know anyone who might fit that bill?"

"Off the top of my head, I can think of several. You're space-based, but you also operate in the atmosphere. The closest analogue to what you need is a navy admiral or an air force general. I know of a few American officers, but they may not be able to answer the questions you asked me earlier to your satisfaction. There's an Israeli Air Force general who might suit your needs."

"Get settled in, make me a list, include a thumbnail bio. See Adelheid if you need housing until you can find a place of your own. I've got an appointment to go walking."

* * *

Chuck grabbed an apple from the lunchroom and headed for the newly-graded track. Wolfgang was already there.

"I'll eat this while we walk. How's it going?"

"Pretty good. Dolph's arriving later this afternoon, but I can tell you most of what he's here about. The new matrix drive is working well, the latest version of the small nuclear reactors we're getting from Japan are smaller and lighter than the previous models, and they put out almost the same wattage figures. The main thing is that he wants to recruit another scientist."

"Feeling overworked, is he?" Warmed up after their first lap around the kilometer-long track, the two lengthened their strides.

"Maybe, but he thinks she's underused and underappreciated where she is," said Wolfgang.

"Really? So that's why he wants NFI to hire her?"

"That's what I hear. And I've got pretty good sources in Dolph's department."

"You do?"

"It pays to know what's happening. I depend on Dolph's people. I run the ships, but they provide the propulsion and electrical power systems."

"Makes sense. I need to slow down, the knee is stiffening up. Any news yet about that fusion power system?" Chuck asked.

"Still not working. But at least they haven't blown anything up or melted down one of my ships. Wonder who that is?" Wolfgang nodded to a man who was approaching them.

"I guess we're about to find out." Chuck stopped, glad of the excuse to rest.

"Mark sent me. He said you'd want to know."

"Know what? Catch your breath; we can wait." The messenger nodded and paused.

"It's the Indonesians. They sent a message and the commo department sent it to Adelheid. She sent it on to Mark."

"I understand. What message?"

"They've lost one of those ships you transferred to them." The messenger was still catching his breath.

"One of the *Farsides*? It crashed?"

"No. It's been hijacked. The Indonesians don't know who the hijackers were, but Mark said to tell you he thinks they were probably working for the Chinese or the Russians. He'll meet with you as soon as he has more information."

"Thanks. You take a few minutes off and catch your breath before you head back. Wolfgang, I've got to get back to the office. I imagine you'll also have work to do. It's time to upgrade your IFF systems; whoever got the ship will copy the drive, so if there are other ships that look like ours, we need to be able to tell the difference. Use your information channels to let Dolph know. We also need to finish converting our ships to nuclear power and matrix drive. If the Russians or the Chinese have the hijacked bird, they've got the tech base and manufacturing resources to copy it."

"I'll take care of it, Chuck. Will you have time for me later?"

"Let's shoot for four o'clock, and I'll tell Mark to join us. You need to meet him anyway. I'll pass along information...no, I'll have him pass the information directly to you. He's my new foreign policy advisor, but there's no need for me to decide what you need to know. If you have questions you can't resolve with Mark, bring them to me."

Wolfgang nodded, then set off for his office, almost running.

Chuck was slower. His left knee was hurting. He'd probably overdone the exercise and stressed the leg more than he should have, and this was not the first time it had happened. Maybe, when things settled down, maybe he should see about that surgery? Meanwhile, he would start wearing the brace, at least while exercising. He hobbled across the campus toward his office.

Moments later, a small electric runabout pulled up beside him.

"Could you use a lift, Chuck?"

Chuck nodded and climbed in, carefully working his leg in and straightening it out.

"Did someone send you?"

"Not exactly, sir. We saw you walking and the foreman noticed that you were limping. He sent me, but to tell you the truth any of us would have been happy to pick you up. We try to keep an eye on you when you're out of your office."

"You do, do you? Would it by chance be a way of letting your foreman know when the boss was on his way?"

The driver grinned, but didn't reply. The rest of the trip was made in silence.

When you're ready to continue, NEO is available from Amazon in ebook and audio versions. A print version will be available in September, 2018.

ABOUT THE AUTHOR

Jack Knapp grew up in Louisiana and joined the Army after graduating from high school. He served three tours in Germany and traveled throughout western Europe before retiring. His current circle of friends and acquaintances, many of them fellow members of Mensa, live on every continent except Antarctica. Jack graduated from the University of Texas at El Paso before beginning his second career, teaching science.

Always an avid reader, he took naturally to writing. He's experimented with ESP (The Wizards Series) and woodcraft/survivalism. The deep woods of Louisiana were his playground, the setting for his Darwin's World Series. He's a knight of the Society for Creative Anachronism, so combat scenes involving swords, spears, and bows and arrows are reality based.

Recent novels examine the challenges humanity will face when we begin to spread out into space. Beginning with a startup company building the first practical spacecraft (The Ship), to growing a business in space while overcoming Earth-based obstacles (NFI: New Frontiers, Inc), to humanity's first contact with a non-human species (NEO: Near Earth Objects and BEMs: Bug Eyed Monsters) the novels are largely based on current events. A fifth novel in the New Frontiers Series, MARS: the Martian Autonomous Republic of Sol, is due out early in 2017.

Jack's boundless imagination is evident in all his books.

How imaginative? You'll have to read his novels to find out!

Made in the USA
Monee, IL
25 June 2020